BLOOD
REPUBLIC

JAMES R DUNCAN

Primal Light Press
A Purveyor of Fine Fictions

www.primallightpress.com

Primal Light Press
www.Primallightpress.com

Library of Congress Cataloging-in-Publication Data

ISBN number 978-0-9976302-0-6

Book design by www.damonza.com

Printed in the United States of America

This book is dedicated to my mother, Donna, who was always there, no matter what. And my black lab, Jake, the greatest dog the world has ever known... good boy.

"The only true wisdom is in knowing you know nothing."

—Socrates

BLOOD REPUBLIC

Somewhere Near the Missouri Border

It wouldn't be much of a crawl through the muddy field. Harmony wanted the silver necklace, needed it. But, there was the matter of the dog.

Boom. Boom. In the distance mortars thudded earth, the ground trembled. *Boom.*

Smoke rolled like ghosts passing between the dead horse Harmony now hid behind and where that squat dog chewed ten yards away. The necklace was on the corpse the squat dog ate.

Once the battle had moved on, Harmony slinked from the brambles to hunch behind the bloated horse, a thick raised cross branded into its flank. She had always wanted a horse, so when she first saw its stiff tongue and bloody eyes she almost cried, but then did not. She told herself she wouldn't cry again until she could reach him, the pale man who had started the war, and end this death and destruction once and for all.

Harmony clenched her jaw in determination, white breaths puffing from trembling lips. She pressed bleeding palms to the horse's ribcage and shifted her weight so one bare foot could scratch the other. Her sharp brown eyes scanned the devastated pasture. On the horizon, the dead and dying of the battlefield looked like dark anthills in the red glow of dusk. Feral packs of dogs moved swift and lean between the dying soldiers as moans from those chewed twisted through dank air. A huge red and white flag tattered from buckshot lay in the field, *Make America Great Again* embroidered on it. Blackbirds cawed in an ash sky, and chilled rain limped down to mix blood with dirt. Dangers, for a seventeen-year-old girl, were everywhere.

With her father's Asian eyes and the blonde hair of her mother, Harmony was a striking beauty, but now also bone-thin, scratched and dirty. Her sodden yellow hair tangled over sun-scorched collarbones. The purple-flowered dress she'd once dreamt of dancing in at prom was so worn it hung like spider webbing at her knees. She had a tiny red rabbit tattoo her mother didn't know about at the base of her neck. Mud was splattered on one cheek.

A year back when the troubles started, Harmony had briefly given in to fear and despair. She'd cried as the skin sloughed off people's faces from the dirty bombs popping in Denver, and sobbed when the hollow-eyed Birmingham kids were herded into concentration camps. By the time those so-called holy crusaders had thundered down Wall Street Harmony might have wailed forever, except the doctor had slapped her, hard.

Two choices, he had screamed. *Only ever two—never fear!*

So she would get the necklace, she would at least have that. A talisman to glint normalcy through the baking days, a charm to whisper during the freezing nights of the way things used to be. The necklace would be a symbol of her mother's love; Harmony would at least have that.

Boom.

Flies buzzed from the gaping wound in the horse's belly, the stench thick and acrid. Harmony covered her nose, and the blood-matted beagle's eyes darted to her. Its metal tags jangled with each chomp and lunge at the corpse. Pieces of red meat and sinew stretched, then tore, out of the soldier's blue coat with each of the dog's tiny backward thrusts, its teeth snapping frantically. The dog's nervous growl wobbled while the meat lumped down its throat, but its eyes never unlatched from the girl.

Poor, poor puppy, Harmony thought. *Someone's pet before the war.*

She threw a rock.

The dog yelped, its back legs scurrying for the bushes, front paws tangling over each other to tumble beneath the collapsed Exit 41 sign. It crouched there, whimpering, as Harmony inched forward around the dead horse. *Poor puppy*, Harmony thought again, with horrible memories of those interstate thugs roasting that little white dog outside the abandoned gas station, the National Anthem scratching out over an old AM radio. *How had it come to this?*

Harmony paused. No immediate threat seen. She lifted her worn dress over scarred knees.

She dropped into the blood-curdled mud and crawled fast toward the dead man. She crawled through entrails and limbs, charred flesh, and awful things catching between her fingers and toes. Harmony's breath came in quick pants, taking in deeper gulps of the diseased air than she wanted, but she couldn't risk hesitating, not in the open.

She lunged to the blue-uniformed corpse, her mud-stained fingers fumbling over the dead soldier's neck. She snapped the silver chain.

Harmony gazed down on the charm in her bleeding palm, nails broken and ragged, and felt an almost-forgotten strain to the sides of her mouth. Even as the icy rain trickled down her neck and rancid mud sucked to her skin, she smiled without conscious decision for the first time in months. A little laugh bubbled from her stomach like a spring of cool water, and a tear of joy plunked onto her hand.

Donald Duck.

Donald Duck was her favorite. His quacking voice had always made her laugh when little, and looking at the charm she remembered her mother promising to take her to Disneyland as soon as the election was over. Except, the election had never ended.

"Side," a voice growled from behind. "Declare."

Harmony's heart kicked and she pushed one hand against the body, twisting her head back to see a man with a handlebar mustache aiming a six-shooter at her face. How had it come to this? "I'm..," she stammered. "I'm independent. I—"

"Fuck that, no independents no more." He was older, gangly, with a bloodstained Nike *Just Do It* T-shirt and little soul left in red-veined eyes. "Lawton says two choices now, hypocrite or freak." The man's black baseball cap was turned backward and he did not wear a signifying red or blue sash around his arm like many civilians who had joined as the fighting had engulfed the country. He spat on the ground and gripped the pistol tighter. "I said, declare."

Harmony's heart thrashed and her breath quickened. If she claimed the wrong side he would surely shoot her, but that was the way fear worked; she could not, would not, give in to it. So she breathed deep, clutched her one hand tight, and stood, glaring up into the brute's eyes. She was, after all, her mother's daughter. "I'm Harmony Daniels."

The man's eyes widened. His gun and jaw sank.

"And I said," Harmony raised the grenade she had just slipped off the dead soldier's belt, fingers from her other hand moving to the pin. "I'm independent, you stupid son of a bitch."

In death, the albino who had started America's second civil war once hissed to her, *truth.*

Catastrophes *happen*, Democratic vice presidential candidate Annie Daniels thought, *when fear chokes intelligence.* Senator Daniels ignored the pleas of her chasing staff as her sleek legs churned beneath a charcoal skirt many thought an inch too short. Under her azure blouse, a red and black skeleton tattoo everyone had already seen etched down her shapely back like she was being hugged by the dead. The clack of her black heels on pink marble bounced into limestone walls and echoed down the corridors of San Francisco's City Hall. *I'm America's last hope. Me.*

"Senator, stop," the mayor called, throwing a hand to his felt fedora. "Please?"

Senator Daniels did not. She was accustomed to people chasing her.

Annie was thirty-six, had obtained a doctorate in evolutionary biology from Harvard, and had a sharp tongue and bleeding heart as famous as her liberal intellect and Nordic beauty. She had flawless cream skin, long flaxen hair spilling over her gray wool blazer, and brutal blue eyes as vibrant as her blouse. She looked like an innocent debutante, yet had a personal history that could make a sailor proud. And right now she marched toward either a final victory, or the absolute ruin, of her life's ambition.

"But Senator," the mayor panted, "the riots." Mayor Sam Buckhall, six aides, three advisors, and one Secret Service Agent all spun like frantic stars around Annie's departing sun. The fedora-wearing mayor was Samoan and wheezed trying to keep up with the younger woman's pace. "The terrorist threats, and the Texas rancher standoff. Please don't change your speech, Senator."

The Democratic ticket consisted of current Vice President Marcus Freeman and Senator Annie Daniels, a self-declared socialist from California, as the vice president's running mate. Three weeks ago that Democratic ticket had received only 101,461 more popular votes than the Republicans across the entire nation, making it the closest popular vote win in the history of the United States. Like every election since the founding of America however, Monday's Electoral College vote, in three days, was what actually decided who won the presidency, not the popular vote. And since last night's news from Ohio broke, the electoral vote was now suddenly projected to tie.

An hour ago Annie had also learned that her only child, Harmony's, prognosis had turned to death within four months. So moments earlier Senator Daniels had secretly gulped a handful of bright pink pills in the City Hall bathroom to kill the first panic attack of her life, then announced to her staff a change to the morning's speech. She was now going to demand Republican Governor Hampton Stone concede his candidacy for president and call him out as a goddamn fraud on top of it, try to end this election right here and now, before Monday's vote. None of her advisors thought that was a good idea.

"But Ferguson and Detroit, Senator, the rioting. Why not just call for a fair—"

"Fair?" Annie's eyes sliced back at Mayor Buckhall. "Last chance to win a goddamn presidential election, Sam, not running a preschool."

You're the devil's spawn. A voice sounding much like her dead father growled through that jittery jumble of chemicals now saturating brain. It was a bad morning for Annie to be off her game. Although her words sounded confident, as she marched everything inside Senator Daniels felt like it was unspooling from the inside. The effects of those recently recalled Zentanels she had just swallowed in the bathroom seemed erratic, their chemically induced calm crashing against Annie's consciousness in unpredictable waves. One minute she felt calm, sharp and certain as ever, the next her peace drowning into frenetic black doom as her mind whirled with images of Harmony's grave, dirt hitting the coffin. *What's the line you won't cross, you evil slut?*

"*Cyber-Care* can't die," Annie said. "I won't let it."

"But Dayton," the mayor continued, his little steps scampering behind her long strides. "Windows were smashed, ma'am. Shouldn't you play it safe?"

Since the popular vote just three weeks ago the country had already endured four racial riots, a renewal of Occupy Wall Street protests, two school shootings, a massive banking hack, and an ongoing armed rancher standoff in Texas that began over Second Amendment gun rights. Worst of all, there had been another thwarted terrorist attack from radicalized Islamic extremists on American soil, and the liberal Chief Justice of the Supreme Court had unexpectedly died this summer. After two months of the Republican-led congress blocking any new Supreme Court appointment, whichever side now won the presidency would not only control the White House, but also be able to influence the highest court's interpretation of America's laws for a generation. Annie knew winning this election wasn't just for bragging rights, it was for America's very soul.

"Unless you're a rich, Christian, white guy, Mayor, letting Stone steal the election isn't safe." She put shaky fingers to the pulse throbbing in her sleek neck. "We won the popular vote, not the fundamentalists. Send Dayton some fucking windows if it makes you feel better." Annie tried to breathe deep, sound calm, as she strode toward the stairs leading down to the main rotunda, but her lungs cinched tight. "It can't fucking tie."

Nine swing states still argued over run-off elections and overnight news had broke from Ohio that its Secretary of State, a Republican, had suddenly halted that state's ongoing recount. That halt reversed Ohio's twenty electoral votes to the Republican ticket, meaning the Electoral College would now officially tie at 269 to 269 on Monday. If the Electoral College did tie for only the third time in American history, the first time in two hundred years, it meant the next president and vice president would actually be chosen in the House of Representatives, regardless of the popular vote. No one thought that was a good idea, even some of the Republicans who held a twenty-three-seat majority in it.

Too much? Annie wondered as she crested the marble stairs, glimpsing a speck of blood on her pale finger from her dying daughter coughing in the limo before dawn. *Maybe all too much.* While in her early twenties Annie had spent years volunteering in the Peace Corps and at homeless shelters trying to raise public awareness for various non-profits, but nothing ever truly changed for the better. Old white guys always advanced, everyone else got chewed up in the unlevel capitalistic gears. So she had gotten into politics to fight for real fairness and logic in this patriarchal world of violence and greed. *Unruly. Shrill.* That was what they had first called her. As she had won more elections to climb further up the rungs of power those characterizations had only gotten more intense. *Bitch. Evil.* But whatever the slur, it always meant the same thing—*get back in your place, little girl.*

She fought down a smolder of tears and curled her fingers into a fist before anyone could notice the crimson droplet, her hand reflexively touching the pill bottle hidden in her blazer pocket as she descended the steps. *Snakes.* Her brain buzzed like an electric charge and her heart thumped with panicked power, the cadre swirling down the steps after her like a school of nervous fish. *Goddamn snakes everywhere.* One foot stumbled and she shot a hand out to the stone railing for glorious support. *Don't lose it.* Her father's voice cackled in her sizzling brain. *Just don't lose it, whore.*

"But, Senator," Eli Boze, her young aide, called. He raced down behind her in a powder-blue suit, checking two phones, his tall Afro bobbing. "Vice President Freeman wonders, respectfully, if maybe your daughter's prognosis isn't clouding your judgment, ma'am? …Respectfully."

"And maybe Marcus needs to grow some balls." Annie wiped at Harmony's bloodstain again. "Respectfully." Her heels clacked off the bottom step and onto the last long stretch of glistening marble to the outside doors, sweat clinging to her blouse. "Now's the shot, Eli." She could not let the Electoral College tie, could not let the bad guys steal this election by the decision going to the Republican-held House. "Religious Liberty Amendment, my ass," she growled. "Bunch of misogynist cavemen using Bible bullshit to justify their hate." Annie nervously raked one hand's red nails through her hair. "We're the good guys, fuck the Republicans."

Once you pull the trigger, her father had long ago snarled in rare, lucid advice, *ya better hit your mark.* Of course, he'd been holding the gun to his own temple.

The big oak doors to the outside were visible now, and Annie took a deep breath to keep her emotions in balance, calm the voices in her head as her steps quickened. *Should I do this?* A bank of television cameras and two thousand Democratic supporters waited outside on City Hall's sweeping stone steps beneath the cold December sky. They chanted Senator Daniels' name and waved blue signs for the liberal lion they hoped would become the first female vice president in history and usher in a new era of logic, fairness, and peace. *I've got to do this.* She threw a hand back to the recalled pill bottle hidden in her pocket for reassurance, smoothly cinching her gray blazer to cover her shallowing breaths. Muffled chants bled through the nearing doors, the cheers and claps rising from icy depths. *For Harmony, for Cyber-Care, for progress.*

"Senator Daniels." A black woman with glasses and a notepad raced up alongside her. "Postpone your speech, madam. The tensions are too high, half the country—"

"Postpone? If the process plays out— who the hell are you?"

Eli glanced up from his phone, worried, as Annie glared at the woman trying to keep pace with her.

"Beatrice Howe, madam, the new—"

"Never mind." Annie's throat knotted dry, her sharp blue

eyes flashing back to the fight ahead. "Stop talking." She pulled her blue-clad shoulders back those last two steps. "Just stop talking."

Annie's small pale palms slammed into the heavy doors and they burst outward to reveal a basking, blinding winter light, then an ocean of blue shirts and signs waving Senator Daniels' name. Thunderous applause swept, churned, drowned down over Annie Daniels while she, and she alone, went to save the world; recalled pharmaceuticals sizzling through her blood and nearly half the country calling her antichrist.

Rapturous cheers, confident waves, big smile.

Better hit your mark, her father's voice sneered again. *You evil bitch.*

Senator Daniels Speaks — 72 Hours
Until the Electoral Vote

(Chaguitillo, Nicaragua: Friday, 9:09 a.m. PST / 12:09 p.m. EST)

Everything, Amos' dying father had once lovingly told him, *is connected, son.* Amos was Annie Daniels' thirty-two-year-old brother, uncle of Harmony, and he had slightly different memories of their father, Amos' hero, than his older sister did. *What you believe matters, Amos, make us proud.*

Major Amos Daniels knew in his heart of hearts that if you had the courage to believe in God, God would believe in you. Amos hated politics and all the half-truths and false promises that went with it. Love God, love your country, and do the right thing. Simple.

Four a.m. local, Amos and three other Green Berets of ODA 311 had fast-roped down from MH-6 Little Birds into dense tropical flora five clicks south of Chaguitillo, Nicaragua. They had quick humped their way over the ridge with seventy pounds of gear on their backs, through three hours of sharp leaves, flapping bugs, and eighty-five degrees before sun up to start over-watch of the target hacienda below. The Nicaraguan operation was supposed to be cake. Via video briefing, the new four-star in charge of the United States Special Operations

Command (SOCOM), General Harper, had told Amos their sole objective was to destroy a single laptop of a government official, then get out without anyone knowing they were there. What was on the laptop was classified to even the major and his men, but whatever was needed in the never-ending battle to protect America, Amos proudly did.

After cresting the ridge with pink-yellow dawn bruising the sky, Amos put eyes on the Nicaraguan official's dilapidated estate in the valley five hundred yards down. Major Amos Daniels was tall and had brown eyes so sincere they almost looked wet. He had a clean-cut jaw you could bust rocks on with the same pale skin tone as his older sister, but his buzz-cut hair was the color of rawhide. If it wasn't for a severe burn he'd gotten in Afghanistan curdling like dried lava up the right side of his neck to mar his ear and hairline, Major Daniels could have been the model for an action hero. Amos' courage and honesty had made him a legend in Special Forces, with more people ready to die for him than most people had Facebook friends.

The team had hunkered in a grove of banana-like trees to start the twelve-hour stand-to for dusk when they would once again have the visual advantage. Eight hours in though they started to get bored and loopy. Numb with heat and blisters, sweat stinging their eyes, the update on Senator Daniels' unexpected speech started streaming across the team's laptop and got Stork jabbering. They were far enough up the hillside that no one could hear them.

"Your sister's a nut," Stork now whispered to Amos' camo-clad back.

Amos stood watching the target even though nothing had moved within the house for over an hour. The three lower ranked men sat in a circle on downed logs behind the strong-shouldered major, all hidden within the speckled shadows of the grove.

"It causes all," Stork continued, "both small and great, both rich and poor, both free and slave, to be marked on the right hand or the forehead—that's the Bible." Engineering Specialist Ty Stoughton was known as Stork because of a certain avian-like ugly to his lanky arms and face. "That *Cyber-Care* chip is bad news, boss. Glad a moral patriot like Governor Stone got your vote, instead of the likes of her and the pansy. She could really be the antichrist."

"Didn't vote," Amos answered without turning around. Tree trunks in the grove were smooth and cylindrical, their big fronds drooping wide and heavy, everything smelling so thick and alive it was like breathing through a damp rag. Amos flicked a spider from his M4 barrel, then dropped the weapon on its sling to pull binoculars back up to his eyes. "Never do."

"Whoa. Whoa. Whoa," Stork rasped, his head jolting up from digging through his combat kit, sweat dripping off that beak he insisted was a nose. "You kidding?" Stork glanced in shock at the other two. "Didn't vote?"

"Would have voted for Stone, I guess." Amos shrugged his wide shoulders with a glance at the team. "Just to get some morality back maybe, but what am I going to do, backstab family?" Two fingers of the hand not holding the binoculars absently brushed a chained crucifix with tiny pink stones hanging from his neck. He turned back to visually devour every nook and cranny of the big Spanish-style home on the valley floor below. "Doesn't matter anyway, politicians are all the same."

The Nicaraguan official in the hacienda with the laptop was a Deputy Lupe. On the video briefing, General Harper had only said Lupe was suspected of 'anti-American activity' and they had to handle it lightly. Deputy Lupe was supposedly the equivalent of a senator in the US, but in Nicaragua that apparently meant he had all the perks of being a dogcatcher by the looks of his dying estate. A quiet and mostly barren yellowed farm stretched out around the main house, nothing else for miles. Even though in disrepair now it was obviously expansive, and they calculated the Spanish Colonial had the typical layout of a first and second floor of rooms in a square around an open courtyard. Supposed to be a cake job, straight sneak and smash in the dark of night, with no hard contact expected and no chance of anyone getting hurt. Amos had no idea how bad things were about to go with this though, and everything else, over the next three days.

"Nobody's vote counts," Warrant Officer Jacari Jones countered Stork. "Voting for president don't matter unless you're in a swing state." Jacari Jones was a bald, ripped black guy with a raised pale scar across his ebony forehead. He'd nearly made the Seattle Seahawks before enlisting, and he was Muslim when he wasn't succumbing to the wiles of Jenny Waltman or bacon. He sat chewing gum on a log that had a long line of big red fire ants marching in and out of it he couldn't care less about. "Rock the vote, my ass. American elections are a scam, Stork."

"Vote not count?" Stork was inspecting his green military duct tape with boney fingers, squinting as he twisted and turned the roll. "You guys home-schooled or something?"

"Please," Jacari sighed. "I got more civic knowledge in my shot-up toe than you got in that whole chicken brain of yours." Jacari spit his gum out into the fronds, then unwrapped a fresh purple square and popped it in. "You probably don't even know, birdman, but you ain't voting for president when you cast it, you're actually voting for a bunch of no-name electors nobody knows diddly-squat about. They the ones pick the president, not you. Statistically, a president could get elected with only twenty-two percent of the popular vote, and winning just eleven states. That democracy? Will of the people?"

Amos had left eight of his team back at MacDill, and as the daylight hours ticked on with nothing occurring but ridiculous political conversations he was starting to get the feeling even four of them was overkill. Absently, his right hand drifted to his damaged ear, touching where the lobe had melted into the crust of browned neck skin, right where he could always still feel that sting of things which had happened in Afghanistan, the things he'd been forced to do.

About an hour ago, Amos had seen a frail Hispanic guy with a potbelly show up at the hacienda. The potbellied guy had been in a van with a busted window and carried a crocodile briefcase as he disappeared through the rotting front doors of the house. Besides for that, the biggest excitement thus far had been a cat, apparently blind, trying to pounce on some sort of bug between the van and the big, lopsided front doors.

"Well, Specialist Jones," Stork responded behind Amos' back as he dug down into his kit again, "didn't really want your ilk voting anyway."

"What's that, racist shit?"

"Hell no, black's not your problem, being a moron is." Stork and Jacari grinned at each other. They could say anything to each other, and often did, because they each knew they would lay their life down for the other.

Jacari flipped Stork off with a smirk. "Just leave Major alone, birdman. You know Famous Amos and Annie ain't tight no more since *the incident*. Leave it."

"Voting is a civic duty, all I'm saying."

"Mother of God," the fourth Green Beret finally grumbled

at Stork. "Your mouth just don't stop, do it?" Weapons Specialist Gary Bills, aka Thump, sat on a rusty barrel. His shaggy black hair and thick beard resembled a wooly mammoth. He was methodically licking two grimy fingers and, once moist, shoving them down into a box of dried lemon Jell-O powder and coffee grounds. Once he covered them in the grainy mixture, he brought the thick fingers up to slowly lick them clean—again and again, with the methodical urgency of a grandfather clock. As he had been eating, his bloodshot eyes glared unblinking at Stork like a caveman meanly watching dirt.

"At least even someone of your limited intellect has the common sense to vote Republican, correct?" Stork answered Thump. "Please tell these gentlemen—"

"Democrat," Thump grumbled, slow-chewing gobs of the Jell-O powder and coffee grounds. "Voted Democrat."

Stork's mouth dropped open. "Son of a bitch."

"Weed," Thump mumbled. "The weed…" he belched, "I like it."

Jacari held his stomach to keep from laughing.

Amos glanced over his shoulder with a grin at the flustered Stork. "Seems like people on both sides could care a little less about politics if you ask me, Stork." Amos tugged at his body armor from the creeping heat, swiping buzzing gnats from his damaged ear. "We just do our job and protect America." Amos tapped a single forefinger to the silver crucifix around his neck. "I've got faith the Lord will put the right person in office, and point our guns at the bad guys."

But that was when Amos caught a glimpse of movement in the front drive from the corner of his eye and spun back, jerking his binoculars back to his face. The potbellied guy with the crocodile briefcase had emerged from the big front doors.

The guy set the briefcase down, then produced a cigarette and lighter. He kicked at the poor cat with his boot, lit the cigarette, and took a puff. Thick curls of smoke wafted around his head as he stared up at the baking blue sky. The guy had spindly arms and no apparent weapons. He walked down the drive to the van and opened the back door with a faint rumble.

He yanked out a young, tear-streaked girl, her hands and mouth duct taped. Dark hair, brown skin, mud-splattered dress and sobbing, the Nicaraguan girl couldn't have been more than sixteen, about Amos' niece Harmony's age. The man pulled her along by her wrists toward the front doors of the house as she sucked for breath through the tape, tears spilling. It was obvious to Amos she would soon have things happen to her that should not, and nothing in Amos' character could allow that to happen. With his eyes still riveted below, the major snapped his fingers back toward the guys—they quieted.

"Talk to me, Chief," Jacari whispered, slinking to his weapon. "Op For?" Stork and Thump immediately reacted to Amos' body language as well. They crept to the edge of the perimeter and hunkered down, weapons in hand. Years of training and months in the bush meant Amos' team responded to each other with no words necessary. Down below, the house swallowed the girl and man, the big doors shutting behind them.

Amos lowered, turned to his men. "Civilian girl," he whispered. "Bad way."

"Busting her out?" Thump chambered his M16, his bearded countenance all seriousness and determination.

"Amos," Stork's lean face cautioned. "Cent Com's not authorizing hard contact."

"We're not calling it in." Amos started stripping off his vest and the extraneous gear he wouldn't need, trimming down for the quickest assault possible. "We're going now."

"But the laptop," Stork warned.

"Wherever Famous Amos goes," Jacari whispered with a grin, "I follow." He ripped out his Glock 17, checked the mag, then re-holstered it with a snap.

"What if the objective gets botched, Major?" Stork growled. "The laptop—"

"There's a girl in trouble." Amos glared at Stork with his eyes determined as a starved animal. "We serve the GOOD, Lieutenant, not red tape." Despite their orders, despite the obvious danger of it being daylight, and despite the fact they would have to forgo the actual mission, they were going to breach the hacienda to rescue that poor girl before any harm could come to her. "Faith, Stork, not fear." Amos tapped his crucifix with the small pink stones again. "Faith."

And the men would follow him, because he was Major Amos Daniels.

***

Cha—Boom! A shotgun blast echoed down the valley, birds flapping from trees and Thump whacking to the gravel drive with a grunt. Moments earlier, Amos had ducked the rusty chain, Thump staying back to cover the front portico of the house and the shadowed balcony overhanging the front doors. The plan was for Amos to get to the van, then once he was in position to cover, signal for burly Thump to move to him. Stork and Jacari had paired off to enter the big hacienda from the rear.

Amos had made it to the back of the van and had been peeking out with his M4 raised at the rotting front doors of the house when Thump's boots prematurely crunched the gravel behind him. That was when the unseen shotgun exploded from above. A white flash came from that second floor balcony and metal pellets ripped the van's side, buckshot peppering the gravel drive. Amos threw himself backward to the ground as buckshot whipped over him.

Between the van and the gate, about twenty yards behind Amos, Thump rolled with a groan, the big man clutching his neck. The sound of metal clacking on metal said another round was being chambered. In moments of heat and action, Amos Daniels was one of the people who grew calmer, more focused and centered. He pushed to his feet, preparing to dive out over his injured friend to protect him from the next blast of buckshot then drag Thump back to the safety of the van, but before he could move Thump lurched back up with a growl and started lumbering forward.

Cha—Boom! The shotgun thundered from the balcony and more pellets ripped Thump's shin before he made the cover, the second wave of buckshot rattling the front of the van again, windows cracking, metal pinging. Thump hopped, tumbled in behind the van, seething, one palm gripping his neck with blood trickling beneath it. Thump had a fuck you glare fixed on the house in front of them.

"Call that covering, sir?" Thump snorted.

Amos grabbed Thump's wrist and pulled it down. The wound wasn't bad—scratches—but it probably stung like a son of a bitch. "Call that running, tubby?" Amos slapped a palm to Thump's shoulder with a grin.

Moments later, the old doors to the hacienda splintered opened as Amos and Thump crashed through the huge entryway to the rotting mansion. Inside, there was no opposing force, but instead of a typical Spanish interior, things were bizarrely more like an Islamic Mosque than something typically found in Central America. Massive, intricate walls with a stone floor and high arched ceilings stretched down either side of the hall, all covered in Muslim geometric patterns of azure blues and vibrant yellows. No images of people or animals on the walls, only vast mosaics of block-like, swirling geometric patterns allowed in Islamic design from floor to ceiling.

Amos angled himself and Thump down the strange corridor with guns tight and level, crouching low. They checked for opposing force, pivoting around corners of numerous arched open doorways on the sides. Checking, searching, moving forward. Amos had to find the girl, had to save her. They moved in the direction of a wide, open archway at the far end of the hallway, broken shafts of sunlight pouring through it to indicate a path to the interior of the massive house.

Once inside the center courtyard they found it an open area with no roof, only the clouding blue sky above. The sun cast lazy shafts of light down around the red Spanish roof tiles of the surrounding second floor. The soft rays partially lit an otherwise shaded circular fountain in the center of the courtyard. The fountain was white stone with a winged Christian angel carved at the top, but its head had been knocked off, a calligraphy version of the word *Allah* that Amos recognized from his ISIS training painted in black on its chest. Cool water gurgled from the decapitated angel's hands into the basin at its bottom. The basin was covered in the same radiant blue and yellow ceramic tiles as the interior, and there were two massive shattered flowerpots beside it.

The broken sunlight caught tiny random splashes of fountain water from the shadows in quick snaps of illumination as if fireflies were bursting into existence for millisecond lives. Amos stepped quickly across the dirty tile toward the fountain, through the swirling curtains of light and shadows, with gun and eyes shifting and boots clacking, as all become gloriously centered for him. *Find the girl. Protect the girl.* It was as if all of his senses crackled alive while Amos moved, catching every atom of the breeze's churn, all rustles of life or movement in any direction. He could almost smell the water, almost feel the microscopic changes from warm to cold as they stepped through the alternating shadows and sunlight. Amos could nearly taste the colors of the tiles and hear the plants' vibrations, almost see what would happen before it occurred. Within him there was no doubt, no thought needed, and his actions flowed reflexively, efficiently, ruthlessly forward in burning truth toward saving an innocent girl's soul. God was with him.

Pop. Pop. Gunshots came from somewhere on the other end of the house, from the top of the wrought-iron stairs leading to the second floor, past the fountain and on the other side of the courtyard. *Pop.* A girl shrieked.

I'm coming, Harmony. I'm coming.

Every muscle in Amos' body sprang forward in singular, coordinated purpose. He sprinted for the stairs, taking them two at a time, his lungs churning. The sound of Thump's boots cracked the steps right behind him. Angry male Spanish shouts came from a hallway on the second floor.

At the top of the stairs Amos ran with abandon, racing past open doorways like he knew through every fiber of his being exactly where the poor girl was. He could not let her die; he would not let her die. At the end of a rickety hall, the floor sagging with rotted wood, Amos flew toward a large door of chipped, peeling blue paint, the reinforced heel of one boot raised. There was a splintering of wood and locks as the door crashed inward.

In the room haphazard furniture was everywhere, and for a moment Amos reeled with plaster and dust swirling in his eyes, the dust thick as smoke. The potbellied Nicaraguan official was behind the girl, pulling her into a corner. Amos rasped, blinked stinging eyes, his weapon flying upward, muzzle at the man. The official wore long pants and a belt but no shirt. His hairy upper body was half-hidden behind the terrified girl. The official grimaced and twitched, the brown girl looking ready to wail, plump tears silently rolling down her cheeks.

"Easy now," Amos whispered to the Nicaraguan official. "Easy."

The official had jammed the gun barrel into the girl's chin so hard her head pushed back. His forearm yoked tighter around her neck as she panted for breath. Her green dress was torn and hanging off one caramel-colored shoulder. There was no clear shot on the man, only a portion of his skull poking out from behind her. The risk of killing the girl was too great to shoot, but Amos kept the barrel of his M4 tight on the exposed sliver of the man's head. A laptop fitting the description of the mission target lay on the end of the rumpled bed.

Thump leapt into the room beside Amos, his weapon also raised, and Amos heard the sound of additional boots stamping down the hallway toward them.

"Liars," the official growled in heavily accented English, his face full of anger and confusion as if he had somehow been betrayed. "American liars!" The man's small eyes twitched back and forth between Amos and Thump— fevered, questioning, bewildered—then to the door and the nearing footfalls. The slightest spasm of his finger would blast the girl's skull apart. "Why?"

"The girl," Amos whispered. "Just let her go." Amos glanced into Thump's eyes, motioned at the laptop.

"I tell no one 1776," the man begged. "Why?"

Thump snatched up the laptop, but the official did not seem to care. The thunder of boots in the hallway was growing louder, and the official's eyes widened further. Amos had no idea if the footfalls were Stork and Jacari or opposing force coming to kill them. The official squeezed the girl even tighter. "I no care about your election, I tell no one 1776! Why?"

"Easy." Amos raised the palm of one hand while lowering his own gun, trying to draw the man's eyes into his own, into his calm. "We just came for the girl." The boots in the hallway grew louder, the offcial's face twitched feverishly toward the door. "Let the girl go," Amos whispered again as the entire floor, all the ancient wood, started to vibrate with the nearing footfalls. "Please let her go."

"I kept my word," the man sneered, jamming the gun harder into her jaw, glancing quicker and quicker to the door. "I told no one 1776."

The footfalls were almost there.

"Easy. We don't know anything about 1776," Amos whispered. "We just want you to let the girl go."

And Amos swore with more time the man might have let her go, that the man's arm and eyes were about to soften and that she might have lived, but there was the blur of a body at the broken door, and those shots cracking the air.

Bam, bam, bam! In an instant, three dead. *Bam.*

Everything is connected, Amos' hero father had once lovingly told him. *Beliefs matter, son.*

"It is impossible to reason without
arriving at a Supreme Being."
—*George Washington*

(Raleigh, North Carolina: Friday, Friday, 9:17 a.m. PST /
12:17 p.m. EST)

"Only three days to go, and there's still this goddamn menace." Former Pastor Governor Hampton Stone sighed at his running mate as he watched Senator Annie Daniels speak from the podium on his television, people they didn't know dying in Nicaragua. "That two-bit hussy can't make America great again."

Hampton Stone was old but vibrant, spray-tanned nearly orange with a wispy mop of blonde hair many thought was a toupee crowning his jowly face. He was rich and powerful, and had a body type his wife affectionately referred to as "morbidly obese." The Republican candidate for president was currently wedged into his plaid armchair sipping imported chamomile tea and wearing a rumpled charcoal silk suit with blood-red tie. It was softly snowing outside, yet beautifully sunny, and Hampton wished he were out on the porch watching his black lab snort in the snow drifts rather than enduring Senator Daniels' speech in the attic office of his North Carolina Governor's

Mansion. Annie was at least pleasant to look at, but anger was already beginning to percolate in the famously passionate man.

"*What we have,*" Annie bellowed from California through the blustery air in a paraphrase of Thomas Paine, her long golden hair dancing in the dawn December light, "*right here, right now...*"

Three days. Now that he'd tipped Ohio in his favor, Stone only needed to make it three more days with nothing upsetting the electoral tie and the Republican-led House of Representatives would give him the presidency. But there was her, a firebrand and a leftist ideologue who would never give up. And even as Stone roiled warm with frustration, parts of him registered an uncontrollable physical attraction toward the woman thirty years his junior. She was amazing. Nuts, amoral and a deviant, but amazing.

"*Is a chance to birth this great nation anew,*" Senator Daniels continued from the steps of San Francisco's City Hall, a blonde strand whipping over her pillowy lips. Annie had just used the word hypocrite for the sixth time in her passionate diatribe against the conservative right, in general, and the former evangelical pastor Stone, in particular. "*In the next three days Americans still have a rare chance to reform this country in logic and fairness we trust, instead of regressing into hate, and fear, and superstition!*"

"So, decent, normal people of faith shouldn't be protected too?" Stone grumbled to Texas Congressman Buddy Dukes. "Only the perverts and the lazy and the illegals?" Governor Stone's words, despite their bitterness, had a Southern twang slow as a babbling brook. He'd been accused of being a bigot, misogynist, womanizer, and ruthlessly greedy ever since he had catapulted the modest nest egg of his father's dry cleaning

rules, there had been several high-dollar lobbyists, political action committee reps, and even the most powerful individual lobbyist in Washington, Yanic Goran. They were all looking to give Stone money, if Stone agreed to influence legislation and regulations that would help them make more once he was elected. That recording, Stone was sure, was what would be up on Senator Daniels' website within the next forty-eight hours.

"Dang, we need a counterattack, Hampton," a panicked Buddy Dukes exclaimed. "What if we bring up that porn stuff she did in college?"

"Everyone knows about that, Buddy, and half of this depraved country doesn't care." Stone glared at his running mate. "I thought somebody told me you were smart. Weren't you supposed to be smart?" Stone rubbed a tiny orange hand across his always dripping nose. "Surrounded by heathens and idiots and... fucktards." Hampton made a reflexive sign of the cross over his chest which morphed into a quick scratch of his crotch. "Should have stayed in dry cleaning."

"*All that you and your so-called religious right stands for, Pastor Stone, is a lie!*"

"Then what?" Buddy asked. "What's the counterattack?"

"Shush. You need to listen more, Buddy, speak less."

"But if there's evidence you've violated campaign finance laws, Hampton, there could be an FEC investigation. What if people pressure their House representatives to turn against—"

"Sometimes, Buddy," the governor turned, his old eyes holding something dangerous that chilled the younger man quiet, "you just need to let your enemies..."

"*Pastor Stone, I call on you to not only quit, but to admit,*" Annie shouted in a fevered, impassioned end, her eyes taking on a glimmer of pill-drenched wild, "*that GOD IS A LIE!*"

And hearing her words, a deep exhale escaped from Hampton Stone's chest, a faint smile curling over the former pastor's thin lips. "…hang themselves."

* * *

"God a lie," a conservative newscaster shouted into the camera within seconds of Annie's speech ending. "Reckless, repugnant, irresponsible, and rude. We finally see Atheist Annie's true nature!"

Over thirty million American households got the bulk of their daily news, their sole facts about the country and world, from that conservative newscaster's daily three-hour conservative broadcast. They trusted the words coming from the newscaster's mouth as fact, but what hardly any of those millions of Americans knew about that middle-aged woman with the beehive hairdo and American flag pin on her lapel was that she didn't really care about the election; she was an actor. An actor who got paid more money the more she got people emotionally worked up.

"Annie Daniels can claim a moral patriot like Governor Stone is enflaming tensions, but it is clearly she and her socialist, godless, cronies who are trying to skirt the constitutional process!" She leaned forward and scowled a glossy lip, making sure to twist a bit so the American flag pin was clearly facing the camera. "I say it is time for Annie Daniels and Marcus Freeman to concede. God bless America!"

* * *

"Courageous." A liberal newscaster, skinny, white and male with horn-rimmed glasses glowed into the camera on the other major news station immediately after Annie's speech ended. "God a lie? How can I find the words to adequately express the admiration I once again feel for the progressive Senator Annie Daniels?" His voice was high-pitched, and he seemed like a man trying to exude a graceful femininity. "*Cyber-Care* is nothing to be afraid of. It has the potential to truly solve gun control, health care, and erase hate speech from the country once and for all. *Cyber-Care* will help America leave the errors of corrupt free market capitalism in the past, vaulting us into a future of true reason and equality. Someone has needed to finally speak the truth about religion, which is causing most of the strife in this world and stopping the progress of Cyber-Care, and I say Annie Daniels is a hero for doing it."

Over thirty million American households got the bulk of their daily news, their sole facts about the country and the world, from that young liberal broadcaster. They trusted the words coming from his mouth as fact. What they didn't know was that he really didn't give a shit and the majority of his political opinions were only derived from what he thought would make beautiful, liberal women like him enough to get a date in New York City.

*"There was never a democracy that
didn't commit suicide."*
—John Adams

(San Francisco, CA: Friday, 10:01 a.m. PST / 1:01 p.m. EST)

N*o God,* Annie thought, fighting images of her muddy, booze-stenched father leering over her teenage bed. *Only logic and science can save us.*

As soon as she'd finished her speech, Senator Daniels spun from the podium to march back through the City Hall doors, doubts screaming through her sleep-deprived, medicated mind, and nausea bubbling like acid in her throat. She began ripping at the perfectly manicured red-painted thumbnail of her left hand thinking it was Harmony's blood that she could not remove. She was exhausted.

Her speech had been a bluff. The video she had of Stone at the Barkley Fundraiser was too garbled to be used as actual evidence that Stone had done anything illegal. Annie needed Stone to quit, plain and simple. That was her most probable path to still pulling out a victory and keeping the country from patriarchal fundamentalists and saving her dying daughter's life through the cutting edge technology of *Cyber-Care.* A hardball roll of the dice, sure, but she hadn't made the rules, men had. She was just determined to beat them. Pain shot up her arm from where she dug at the nail, but it felt good.

"Do you want me to reach out to the Governor Stone's camp directly, ma'am?" Eli Boze raced to keep up. Castor, Senator Daniels' Secret Service agent, followed behind, everyone else left glad-handing the crowd outside. "See if Stone wants to negotiate regarding the tape, Senator?"

"Hell no. I don't want to actually talk to that sun burnt, wig-wearing, manatee. I'd puke." Annie wrapped her arms around herself in the chilly hall, breathing in deeper as they escaped all the judging eyes. "I just want him to fucking quit."

Earlier in the limo, Harmony's thinning arms had painfully clutched her own rib cage, hacking and coughing as tears rolled down both mother and daughter's cheeks, blood flecks splattering Annie's fingers as she tried to hold her dying daughter's long blonde hair back. It was bad enough for any parent to witness their own child's mortality, but Annie was racked with guilt that she had yet to get *Cyber-Care* passed, that she was now in a position where she might actually lose this election and America's soul, to the likes of Hampton Stone. *Cyber-Care* was so much more than just healthcare reform. It would be the backbone of America's evolution from good ol' boy greed-dominated white capitalism into a more loving, enlightened society of fair solutions and everyone finally truly becoming equal. Free healthcare, free college, much higher minimum wages, and hate speech monitored in all communication. In addition to the economic and social benefits of *Cyber-Care's* chip system, Annie had already gotten millions earmarked to the bill for immediately funding the stem cell and nano-tech research hopefully capable of saving Harmony. It was a law which would forever turn America more egalitarian and socialist, just as Stone' *Religious Liberty Amendment* could turn it back to the 1950s. Annie had to do whatever it took to win, even if half the stupid country actually now believed she was in league with the devil because of it.

Mark of the beast, my ass, Annie thought heading down the hall. *I'm no antichrist, just the only one with courage to do what's right*. The *Cyber-Care* plan required that micro-chip implanted in people's palms. ...*Right?* She felt a deeper chill ripple through her bones, and hugged herself tighter. *Fucking snakes.*

"Well, we should be able to get a feel for your speech's impact almost immediately, ma'am. Between Twitter, Bazzbark, and Hollerz, ma'am, there's over five million posts an hour."

"No feelings, Eli, statistics. Facts." She raked her long fingers through lengths of her blonde hair to sooth her thumping heart. "I need to know how it played, and where we can flip a state." She turned the first marble corner toward the garage entrance, her frantic mind going to the pink pills. "Or flip a single elector, or get House Republicans to switch to me if Stone doesn't fall for the threat. Something. Maybe Louisiana." Those Zennies had looked nearly translucent rose in her palm earlier, vibrant and peaceful pink like the eyes of that precious white rabbit from her childhood nibbling a carrot in her hand... before snakes and lies, sex and deaths. "Where's Henry?"

"I'm not sure. Mr. Corwich was in contact with our Louisiana operator, I believe."

"Find him." Annie's fingers scratched against the small wool pocket of her blazer trying to fish the bottle out. She was jolted by another good spark of pain as her now broken nail caught on the fibers. Henry Corwich was the only person

Annie still completely trusted, and maybe her only real friend anymore. "Three days until the vote and my damn Chief of Staff is missing?"

"Mozier thing, I believe," Eli said with a glance at his iPad. "There was a breakfast."

One more. Just one more pretty pink pill won't hurt, Annie thought with her heels clacking down the hall. Another Zennie would help her focus, keep the weird thoughts out of her mind. The chemicals in the Zennies helped attenuate the reuptake of serotonin in her brain, mitigate the excess cortisol in her blood and thereby achieve a more balanced, lucid thought pattern. Just science. It made sense, was the smart thing in these tense, sleepless last days, but she couldn't risk anyone seeing. A vice presidential candidate linked to non-prescribed, recalled sedatives could be a deathblow. She glanced to the right and left, wanting to make sure no one else was around before taking out the bright pink pills.

Annie rounded the last corner before the garage as she shook two shimmering pink pills into her palm. She tossed the Zennies into her mouth, and it was just as her head went back that she saw the woman looking directly at her—too late to stop.

Snakes. Annie swallowed. *Snakes fucking everywhere.*

"Senator," that same black woman with the glasses from earlier stated, a Miss Howe or something. "I insist on some time, Senator." She was standing before the doorway to the garage clutching a manila folder and wore a white blouse so tight around her neck, nose so high in the air, that she looked like a schoolmarm. And she surely just saw Annie take the bright pink pills. "Given the tensions, I'm concerned that the anti-religious tone of your speech—"

"Then you're fired." Annie slid past her into the garage, a

shoulder of her gray blazer thumping the woman's frail sternum on the way. "Turn your credentials in to Henry if you can't stop annoying me." Often a strong play was best.

"But ma'am," Eli whispered to Annie's back. "If you missed President Fuentes' email, that's—"

"Find Henry," Annie barked. "Now."

Three days, Annie thought as she marched through this superstitious, unscientific, cowardly world, toward a future of logic and peace, *just three damn days*. If she kept it together long enough to win. *I can't be the antichrist, right?*

***

Tweet from Governor Stone to country: *There's right and wrong in the world, and we now know what side the Democrats are on. How can they make America great again? Godless losers!*

***

National Terrorism Advisory System Alert: *Department of Homeland Security announces elevated risk of terrorist activity across the Eastern Seaboard of the US for the next 72 hours. If you see something, say something.*

* * *

Current new headlines in addition to Annie's "God Is A Lie" Speech:

Texas Gun-Rights Militia Standoff Enters 68th Day

Another Black Child Shot By Police

Mysterious Hacker Group Reboot.org Threatens Massive Internet Attack

whom she worshipped. Whatever stupid argument was forever going on between her mom and Uncle Amos was yet another example of adults being ridiculous. Harmony hadn't even gotten to speak to him since the prognosis for her mysterious ailment had turned bad, and she hoped smoking the off-white, illegal powder wouldn't cause brain damage or anything before she could.

DMT was no joke. Dimethyltryptamine (DMT) was a Schedule I narcotic, banned by the federal government as an incredibly dangerous hallucinogenic drug with no possible medicinal benefit, its use punishable with jail time. Some on the Internet claimed it took you to other dimensions. Some said you saw aliens, and others cited tales of demonic possession. A kid in New Jersey reputedly smoked it only once and became schizophrenic, but in the online tutorial they had called it a *doorway to God*.

The illness Harmony had contracted was being referred to on some parts of the Internet as the *stigmata disease*, which frustrated her mom to no end, and played into their decision to keep the illness hidden from the press. Some thought the bleeding from the forehead and palms of those sickened looked like Christ's wounds, while Harmony thought it was probably just from where she normally sweat a lot. So maybe smoking the DMT could help her know if her stigmata bleeding disease was really a sign from God, or even if God existed at all? Harmony had a hard time believing she could be chosen by God for anything though, especially after secretly getting the red rabbit tattoo at the base of her neck. *Did any saints ever get tattoos?* She sighed and glanced over at the glass pipe on her nightstand, trying to suck up some courage.

Bleeding was the main symptom of her mystery disease.

Disgusting, horrific, puss-strewn red blood dripping, oozing, and seeping from a normally clean girly-girl's forehead and palms. Harmony would feel completely fine one minute, looking as composed and radiantly beautiful as the daughter of Annie Daniels seemed destined to be, but then the next be so dizzy she couldn't stand. Stress seemed to launch her attacks. In less than a minute after her chest started aching she would feel the sticky blood sweat. Harmony would then uncontrollably lurch and hack, moaning from the dizzying pain as she doubled-over with coughs of blood-spittle. Maybe worse than her own horror of what was happening were the looks of disgust on people's faces.

Only 1500 or so other people worldwide had been affected by the mysterious bleeding disease over the past three years. Prior to being picked as Vice President Freeman's running mate, Harmony's mom had gotten the best doctors, and they'd run every test imaginable. They put Harmony on beta blockers, anti-anxiety meds, antivirals and antibiotics, but to no avail; nothing stopped the attacks. GMO food? Radiation from electronics? Exposure to some supposedly benign pesticide or chemical? There was no toxic or infectious agent that the doctors could find, and the best any doctor had been able to say was that it appeared to be a problem with her mitochondria. That particular doctor had called it *Hematidrosis Syndrome P31*, or "blood-sweating." She had also given Harmony a max four months to live as of yesterday.

Harmony dropped her phone next to a paperback of the *Bhagavad Gita* and told herself to not be a wuss. She checked her palms for blood, then leaned to the nightstand for the small glass pipe. Harmony felt shaky, almost sweaty, and she hoped she could keep it together enough not to bring on another attack. She picked the glass pipe up in one hand and flipped her long blonde hair over her other shoulder. Harmony had traditionally always been called a "good girl," never having even smoked pot and only ever drinking one glass of wine at Bobby Lagunda's going away party, but if her mom could scarf her recalled Zentanels anti-anxiety meds though, what really was the difference? Harmony patted around her hips for that tiny vial until her fingers eventually knocked against glass. Whatever was actually about to happen, it was terrifying.

Harmony kicked the blankets off to give herself more room. She raised the vial up over her chest and shook a bit of the off-white powder into the glass bowl like the video had shown, her heart beating faster in anticipation.

Breathe, she cautioned herself, *just breathe.* Harmony held the now full pipe with one hand and dropped the empty vial back to the bed.

She felt around for the lighter, noticing both hands were shaking a bit. She had reassured herself several times that nothing could possibly happen outside of her own imagination, but if she was going to die anyway, what was the worst that could happen? She wasn't going to get to grow up, fall in love, have kids and learn about truth the normal way like everyone else anyway. Even if the stuff burnt holes in her brain and left her bonkers it would only be for a few months tops. *Right?*

Harmony concentrated on slowing her breath, relaxing her muscles. She brought the pipe to her lips and held the lighter over the pipe, sucked in air until the flame shot down into the powder. Chalky smoke swept into her mouth and throat.

She coughed, yanking the pipe away from her mouth as her other hand lunged for the blood-speckled washcloth on the nightstand next to her Donald Duck clock. The coughing fit didn't fully develop though. There was none of the telltale pain behind her eyeballs indicating the onset of a full attack, so she breathed out again in relief. She was surprised at how harsh the smoke was, but was also sure that little, if any, had made it into her lungs.

She moved the pipe back to her lips. She sparked the flame again and inhaled smoke deep, squeezing her chest muscles hard against the heat, begging her lungs not to rebel. The smoke seemed to thrash and heave against her ribs like a hot living thing wanting to escape. It raced her blood stream, heat flooding the grooves and channels of her body from head to toe.

Eventually she couldn't hold her breath anymore and the smoke burst back out from her lungs, her eyes watering as she hacked phlegm from her nose and mouth. Her body tightened in pain and her head became warm and light like a balloon. She glanced at her palms, no blood.

She needed to relight the pipe at least twice more. Three deep breaths of smoke were needed in order to "break through" as they called it online.

She inhaled again, and swallowed hard, using all her will power to prevent coughing. Pain in her lungs, but less so, more warmth. Shapes in her room, from the television to the dresser, to the Donald Duck clock on the nightstand and the bathroom door all suddenly became sharper, brighter colors, more vivid. As she exhaled plumes of smoke, a buzz like a million bees rumbled beneath the floor and within the walls. The air particles began to vibrate. A red-orange hue seeped through the air above her, and she felt like her feet and legs were growing numb.

A few hours after Annie's speech, with a red sun hanging low in a hazed winter sky, nearly seven thousand Republican and Democratic protestors shouted at each other across the Bixley Recreational Park in Dayton, Ohio, either for or against the stopping of the Ohio recounts. Historians would long debate if Annie's speech, which would soon mysteriously replay on the park jumbotron, had been accidental, orchestrated by one party or the other, or some sort of divine, or devilish, act. One homeless person would swear an albino man with pink eyes and a snake birthmark had been near the jumbotron in the center of the park just before it started. Regardless of how or why, the replay of Senator Daniels' speech on the park jumbotron in front of the protestors would end up being the spark to a nationwide inferno.

One of the protestors in the packed park, clad in red, was sixty-nine-year-old Republican rancher Hank Thompson, who had shown up with his freckled grandson, Joey, in support of the Ohio Secretary of State's ruling. *Cyber-Care* was a dangerous leap toward big-brother government controlling everything, and maybe even something biblically awful. Wiry Hank wore a Stetson hat and carried a cooler of grape sodas and an American flag on a long wooden poll. Hank was supposed to be home recovering from a tooth extraction, his left cheek still throbbing, but felt it was important to show eight-year-old Joey how a proper democracy worked including peacefully demonstrating for what was right. Orange-haired Joey was all smiles.

On the opposite end of the Dayton park was Democrat Rosa Sanchez, twenty-four-year-old single mother and waitress at the diner across the street. Rosa was Latina, diabetic, and wearing a Democratic blue streak in her black hair to match her blue shirt. Even though her fingers were perpetually raw from working seventy-hour weeks, Rosa only had eleven dollars in her bank account, and she often had to skip buying insulin for herself so that her son could have even a leaky roof and a daily meal. Rosa was passionate about reforming immigration laws, and stopping the Republican's *Religious Liberty Amendment* so that her lesbian sister's rights wouldn't be taken away. If *Cyber-Care* passed, it might help her and her son to stay healthy, and raise the minimum wage so they could afford to eat.

"*What we have…*," Senator Annie Daniels' stunning visage suddenly blazed to life on that massive television screen towering above the center of the park as thousands of tense heads turned. "*Right here, right now, is a chance to birth this great nation anew!*" Annie railed like an old-time preacher, her blue eyes cutting into the camera with crisp certainty of a mother fighting for her child's life.

Hank Thompson, watching Senator Daniels on the screen with a bottle of grape soda in his hand, shook his head. He just didn't get her or the liberals in general. Didn't your actions, your choices, matter? America wasn't founded for freedom from religion, but freedom FOR religion. Was Annie Daniels really the ideal these people wanted to set for little girls? Hank had even heard Annie Daniels was some sort of nudie Internet model before she got into politics. Hank had honorably served in Viet Nam, believed in hard work and telling the truth, had never asked for help from the government in his life, and never called in sick to work. He sure as hell didn't understand how if you dropped your standards and told everyone it was okay for boys to marry boys, and girls to marry girls, that bestiality and pedophilia weren't around the corner. Or, if you let foreigners illegally come in the country and take people's jobs, how will people who play by the rules ever afford to have real families? Heck, now they even had to worry about the Arab-types sneaking in just to blow them up. Hank knew if Annie Daniels and Marcus Freeman continued to erode all the standards of decency that had made this country great in the first place, and push them into economic ruin with anti-free market policies, America would fall just like ancient Rome. Hank knew Governor Hampton Stone was a moral man, a straight shooter and economic pragmatist who would make America great again.

"America will only know lasting peace," Annie declared. *"Once we relegate the mythological fear-mongering and bigoted religiosity of Pastor Stone's and radical Islam's kind to the past. Once we fully embrace reality, logic and technology, instead of superstition and bigotry!"*

Hank decided he had to do something. He had to make a small, simple statement to show Joey what was right. Hank decided he would go plant his American flag directly beneath that big screen, and anyone watching that godless Senator Daniels would then also see the glorious stars and stripes waving and maybe be reminded of a higher ideal. Hank Thompson would show his grandson that good men, men of principle, didn't have to timidly sit by when bad ideas were being spread. In fact, it was their duty not to.

At the same time, Rosa Sanchez stood on the edge of the crowd of blue shirts and felt her heart rise in hope as she looked up at brave Senator Daniels speaking. If that vile Governor Stone was elected and able to push his *Religious Liberty Amendment* through any bigoted individual person or business would be able to cite religious beliefs as a reason for not respecting another person's civil rights, funds to stop global warming would be diverted to the military. Annie Daniels represented all of Rosa's hopes for a brighter future, and she truly cared about minorities and the dignity of same-sex couples to love whom they wished. Annie Daniels cared about immigrants chasing the American dream, and about Mother Nature surviving the soulless boot of capitalistic greed. Annie Daniels cared about women having the right to choose, and about stopping gun violence. *Cyber-Care* would finally ensure every American citizen's rights to liberty and the pursuit of happiness.

When Rosa saw Hank walk toward the base of the jumbotron with Old Glory fluttering in the breeze over his shoulder all her feelings of pride and hope went cold as the gray sky though. Why couldn't the old cowboy with the American flag be respectful and let Senator Daniels talk? How could a white man, who had been freely given everything for generations, still be so greedy? Rosa decided she was going to walk over to that old Republican with the flag and tell him point blank, without fear, that whatever hateful display he was about to make was not welcome, not on this day. Today was a day of acceptance and tolerance, not hate, she would say.

As Rosa Sanchez marched out from where the blue T-shirts were congregated, directly toward red-shirted Hank Thompson with his flag, Annie Daniels' last phrase, *"God is a lie,"* rang through the crisp air of the park. From there some would say Rosa tried to yank the flag out of Hank's hands, while others swore Hank shoved her first. Regardless of who raised their voice to begin with, or who touched whom, Rosa and Hank were soon grappling over the American flag, hands yanking on the wooden pole. In a flash, probably because of something rude Hank said while defending his flag, one of Rosa's hands flung loose to slap the man flush across his left cheek. It was the cheek that still hurt like hell from the dentist, and with that burst of pain Hank Thompson threw a reflexive overhand right, straight as an arrow, into Rosa's shattering nose. Blood sprayed and the young Latina woman tumbled to the ground with a shriek of pain. Dozens of partisans, depending on their point of view, either witnessed a crazy young foreign-looking woman attacking a patriotic old man, or a tall white man punch a young brown mother in the face. Individuals from both sides ran toward the American flag, a trickle becoming a tsunami, as two giant waves, one red, one blue, collided in the center of the park, fists and feet and sticks and stones flying from nearly seven thousand Americans.

Within thirteen minutes there would be a third-world anarchy to what was transpiring in that Dayton park, a rip in the social fabric unfurling beneath a shredded American flag. Violence reached a new level of unpredictability as neighbor was seen attacking neighbor over the color of their shirt. There was much blood, many hurt, and people were knocked down and trampled in the madness of surging crowds. Glass bottles shattered, rocks bounced off bodies, and fists cracked. On camera the cops beat and shot, water cannons raged, fluorescent-pink teargas wafted through the crazed groups, and eventually a long line of dark-clad riot police marched in lockstep toward everyone, young and old alike, with batons swinging as German Shepherds chased people down. By nightfall, nearly six hundred and fifty people would be admitted to area hospitals, four hundred and ten would be arrested, and one hundred and seventy one would die.

Going forward, video clips of the riot would run around the clock on cable news and social media. The liberal station highlighted the police brutality and the possible racial injustice of the arrests. The conservative station emphasized the deaths of the elderly, children, and white people. Republican had attacked Democrat, or Democrat had attacked Republican, depending on which five-second sound bite or headline someone decided to look at, and though the fight would be quieted, its dark frantic energy of fear, incomprehension, and hate would burrow like a virus into the country's soul.

One of the injured was eight-year-old Joey Thompson, Hank's grandson. The main conservative news station immediately started showing a still image of Joey Thompson crumpled in the street with his hips and back twisted at an unnatural angle and his freckled face staring numbly up at the sky as sad, mournful music played. His small white T-shirt was stained with red blood, and over their video, a graphic would read *Annie's Riot*.

(Various Locations Around County: Friday, 3:46 p.m. PST / 6:46 p.m. EST)

T*he right to swing my fist ends at another's nose*, thought the albino man. The part of his face not hidden by the sunglasses happened to have a distinctive, purplish snake-shaped birthmark slithering down from his left eye. *But who defines exactly what a nose is?*

He stood beneath a flickering, buzzing lamppost in front of Little Gumbo's seafood shack, located in an oily, rusted section of New Orleans. Little Gumbo was a Louisiana elector. A cell phone vibrating in his black suit coat stopped the well-dressed albino's ruminations. He wore sunglasses despite the fast approaching dusk. The man's face was square and flat with strong cheek and jaw bones, like he was possibly Native American despite having almost no pigment to his skin and his hair being an unnatural snow white. His build beneath the slim-cut dark suit stated he was, or had been, an athlete. The albino man removed the cell phone from his breast pocket and saw that it was the proper DC area code calling, followed by all 9s. The cell phone was black except for an embossed red silhouette of a rabbit on its back.

"Mr. Washington," the albino man answered into the phone. "We hold these truths…"

"To be self-evident," the voice on the other end replied. The voice was masked by an electronic audio device often used in radio or television interviews to disguise a person's identity, indistinguishable between male or female; metallic and chirpy. "New Orleans, Mr. Jefferson?"

"Affirmative, Mr. Washington. Just arrived from Dayton."

Louisiana elector Lawrence "Little Gumbo" Gatreaux's restaurant was nothing more than an outdoor garage with unpainted plywood nailed haphazardly around its edges pretending to be walls. A trembling clapboard room hanging on the side served as a kitchen, and rotting odors of sea life masked with gallons of rancid fat infected the already diesel air. This New Orleans neighborhood was not full of wrought-iron fences and well-heeled tourists, but of cracked concrete and lopsided tin roofs. At the far end of the block a group of people drank and sang off key in the quickly growing night around a squeaky boom box lit by the headlights of a parked car. The albino man answering to Mr. Jefferson had a single blue vein that protruded over his left temple when he was disgusted, and looking at the neighborhood of urban decay it throbbed between the edge of the cell phone and his sunglasses.

"Have you secured the asset, Mr. Jefferson?"

"Negative, Mr. Washington." The albino man glanced up and down the street once more, then back to Little Gumbo's paint-chipped front door. "Will return this evening when greater privacy can be obtained."

Mr. Jefferson clearly saw the fault lines cracking open across the country as if dry clay were splitting beneath a blistering sun. Their greed and lusts and egos, the rays of light splitting them apart faster and faster even as they clung ever more tightly to their silly reds and blues, their gods and facts, their phrases and T-shirts, all to keep the incomprehensible horror of their own mortality at bay. A purging was coming. And it was needed.

"1776, Mr. Jefferson," the voice on the phone said to him before hanging up.

"1776, Mr. Washington."

* * *

Annie had only slept three hours out of the past forty-five when her Chief of Staff, Henry Corwich, entered to wake her in the private quarters of the campaign plane. A phone was clutched in his thin, hairless hand. Annie was unaware the Dayton riot had even occurred.

Annie was on her sofa, still wearing her blue blouse and gray skirt, and had curled into a blissful nap with Harmony as they flew toward an evening rally in Arizona. The soft hum of the engines had lulled them to sleep. Harmony had been acting strange earlier, but now both their long yellow strands had spilled together into an indecipherable mass and Annie felt briefly at peace with her daughter in her arms. Annie had been dreaming of the serenity of when she was young, when she'd truly believed everything was going to be just fine, and when she and her brother Amos still got along.

In the dream, she and little Amos were splashing mud puddles in the creek behind their childhood home in Missouri. Five-year-old Amos had been laughing with abandon, like he used to before she felt he got tricked into judgmental religiosity, before being brainwashed into the military-industrial complex bravado. His cheeks were pink and he was holding his tiny ribcage with laughter as Annie tried to stick yellow flowers in his sandy brown hair. There was a nudge, and a black snake slithered menacing from the green weeds through the creek toward Amos' small cowboy boots. Annie trembled with horror at the danger to her little brother and knew she had to save him.

You're the damned antichrist, her father's voice sneered. *Whore.*

Another nudge and Annie gasped, her eyes fluttering from the dream word into reality. Henry was holding the phone over her, an unlit cigar in the other slender hand, its chewed end glistening dark brown. Henry was transgender—born a girl, but now the best man Annie knew despite his disgusting cigar chewing habit. He had a thick black beard he had undergone additional hormones and two grafts for, wore tweed coats like a professor, and purposely overate in order to be bulkier so people wouldn't notice his naturally thin bones. The cigar chewing was also part of his overt efforts at masculinity even though he appalled smoke. The irate Democratic president of the United States was waiting on the phone, and Henry's normally optimistic face was now grave.

President Fuentes' call to Annie lasted only seven seconds, and included the president stating the number of the Dayton riot dead, twice. The plane immediately changed course for Washington, DC.

Annie went to the bathroom to vomit.

* * *

1776? Amos wondered in shock as their transport plane cracked over an air pocket somewhere above the Gulf of Mexico. *What'd the Nicaraguan official mean, 1776?*

Amos' bad ear still rang from the blast of the guns. Stork had blown Thump's head apart in the hacienda. Friendly fire.

The Nicaraguan girl had been shot through the face by the official, dead before she hit the floor. All because of a single laptop, the contents of which Amos didn't even know. Questions haunted his mind like ghosts. *Why'd Stork shoot? What was on the laptop? And the election, 1776?*

Amos clutched the crucifix hanging from his neck with one hand, the rough bumps of the small pink stones jabbing into his palm heel. Blue moonlight flashed through the open door to light their faces like skeletons as the scene at the hacienda played over and over in Amos' mind. He was hollow and awful inside, gusts of wind ripping against his burnt ear. *How'd I screw everything up? My fault, all mine.*

Amos and his two living team members sat in the hull of the transport plane. They were flying low and fast over the gulf between Nicaragua and Florida, cold bursts of salty air smacking through the open door with each bump and jump of turbulence as they raced through the night to MacDill Air Force Base. Jacari sat at the far end of the bench, leaning his bald black head against the hull. He was chewing gum again, but now slow and methodical with his eyes closed and body tense. Amos sat at the other end with what was left of his best friend, Thump, zipped inside a thick black bag at his feet. Amos felt numb, suspected he was in shock. Lanky Stork stood holding on to a tether from the ceiling, looking out at the Gulf of Mexico as the plane squeaked, rattled and roared.

Amos' first real experience with death had been his father, and he had taken it hard, like the foundation to his understanding of life had been ripped from underneath him. Some days his dad had problems, sure, especially after he and his mom drifted apart and his dad had resorted to drinking. Other days though, his dad was the most inspirational guy Amos had ever known, his hero. If it wasn't for his dad encouraging him, Amos wouldn't have made it to Special Forces, maybe would have fallen down in a gutter and never gotten back out after the *incident* with Annie back when he was in high school.

Amos remembered when he was a little kid, when he and Annie had still been best friends and he'd dreamed of becoming a military hero like his dad some day. He had been trying to do a last push-up in the dirt yard behind their house, his thin arms starting to burn and wobbled with strain as sweat dumped off his forehead into dark plunks onto the ground, his heart and lungs wrenching for air. *Don't give up, son,* his dad called from the back porch. *I believe in you, don't give up.* Hearing his dad's voice Amos had been filled with a rush of new strength. He didn't just get one last push-up, but five more. *I should have saved him,* Amos now thought. *I'm failing everyone. Dad, Thump. I should have saved them.*

Amos had never had a friendly fire incident, never lost a man under his command before, but everything at the Nicaraguan hacienda had flashed with lightning speed. The official had jammed the gun to the girl's head. The floorboards had kept shaking, puffs of dust rising as the approaching boots grew louder. The official bellowed that he had told no one about *1776,* whatever that meant, and Amos just wanted the girl safe and no one to die. But those boots, those damned boots getting closer and closer. Another moment and Amos swore he could have gotten the guy to let the girl go, but Stork had burst through the doorway shooting.

Stork's first shot blasted into the back of the official's head, red blood and white bone misting the air. In the official's dying spasm his finger squeezed off its own bullet through the bottom of the girl's face and out the top of her skull, her long brown hair flying off in a single piece like a wig. Two dead before the flash of light cleared from Amos' eyes, dead before those blasts echoed into a singular ring, and yet two more shots still came. *Bam! Bam!* Stork squeezed off two more shots for some unfathomable reason, right over the dropping bodies, right through the bloody mist and rolling smoke, and right through the laptop into Thump's head.

That last shot into Thump's face exploded his skull into wet bone and blood splattering across Amos' cheek as everything become flashing lights and shattering noise, the stink of burning flesh and hair. "*No*," Amos had screamed. "*No, no, no!*" But too late.

Thump's body crashed to the floor, most of his head strewn over a dusty dresser.

How did God let it happen? Amos now thought, his left hand shaking. He clenched it tight once, then another time to squeeze the adrenaline out of it. Amos looked up, watching Stork take a sip from his canteen while staring out the open door at the chopping blue waves below. Amos couldn't be sure from the sound of the wind, but for a second he thought Stork might be humming. Humming?

Amos leaped to his feet, anger boiling inside him. But then immediately realized it was the vibration of the plane he heard. Stork was just silently staring, his face distraught too, sad. *Calm down. Relax.* Amos had been having trouble controlling his emotions ever since the Korpesh Valley, since he'd done what he had to do and the right side of his head had ended up scorched like burnt meat. *Breathe.*

"He was right there," Amos shouted over the wind at Stork though. Their word was their bond, and Amos knew Stork wouldn't lie to him, so Amos had to clear the air, make sense of things. "Why'd you take another shot? Thump was right there." Amos would be in front of General Harper in a few hours answering debriefing questions, their superior determining if a further Line of Duty investigation was needed about Thump's death. Amos hadn't even met the new general yet in person, but was aware of his fire and fury, his no nonsense reputation. General Mace Harper would determine if someone needed to face a court-martial. Most important, Thump deserved an answer.

"What are you asking, Amos?" Stork shouted back, shaking his sharp nose in hurt and disbelief. "There was smoke. Things fast." Stork looked down at his bloody boots for a moment, his big Adam's apple swallowing hard before looking back with watery eyes. "I'm sorry. I thought he was opposing force. I'm... I'm just so sorry."

Amos nodded his head, seeing the same emotions he felt in his buddy, feeling awful about his own anger. Mistakes happened. Tragic, but nobody's fault, just bad luck, real bad luck. Amos put a hand on Stork's shoulder, nodded, and tried to let his Lieutenant know he understood.

"That Nicaraguan was bad news, Amos," Stork added. "What with all the Muslim designs on the walls and him jabbering about that 1776 and election stuff. Who knows what kind of terrorist shit he would have done, ya know?" Stork shrugged and wiped at one eye with a boney finger. "At least Thump went protecting America, boss."

Amos forced a smile, trying to still believe that God worked in mysterious ways, and everything would make sense in the end.

* * *

Nationwide television advertisement playing over conservative station:

A young, brave United States soldier, camouflage face paint beneath his sincere eyes, looks into the camera and says, "Democrat Marcus Freeman doesn't care about Islamic radicals infiltrating our borders. He only cares about trees and pot." The screen then fills with the mushroom cloud of a nuclear blast as the soldier's voice ominously asks the viewer, "What do you care about?" ...*Paid for by Spirit of 1776*

* * *

Nationwide television advertisement playing over liberal station:

The same young actor who played the soldier now wears a female wig and lipstick on the liberal channel, mascara on his pained eyes. The transvestite lets a tear run down his cheek as he bravely looks into the camera to say, "Hampton Stone doesn't care about the right of people to be who they are, he only cares about Wall Street fat-cats getting rich." The screen then switches to an image of white-hooded KKK members dragging effeminate men and shrieking black women to burning crosses. "What do you care about?" ...*Paid for by Spirit of 1776*

* * *

@professorofplants: Why were two thirds of the people arrested at the Dayton riot black Democrats?

@jessejameskickass: Cause blacks the one's shooting! You can't keep playing the race card when the president is black!

@whoreads: Bullshit, it was a Republican gun that shot little Joey Thompson! Outlaw guns!

@axegrinder13: The whole system is corrupt. Only through revolution and technological decentralization can the country improve. Time to Reboot all this shit!

@archiesuperhero: Fools! Two party system is farce. Illuminati lizard-aliens controlling Pan-Continental Trade deal. I warn you again, wake up!

@mrsCee798: Positivity people! In a quantum world, your thoughts affect reality so be positive everyone, don't let the terrorists win!

@socialjusticewarrior: Demanding I be "positive" is a micro-aggression against the sovereignty of my mind. Please use trigger warnings, and the gender-neutral pronoun "Zee" instead of "he" or "she"!

@jessejameskickass: Trigger warning… I'm gonna kick your liberal ass.

* * *

The *Cyber-Care* Bill, as explained on Senator Annie Daniels' website:

Cyber-Care is nothing to fear. Cyber-Care will vault America into a future of increased security, universal healthcare, and drastically lowered costs for you and your loved ones. Cyber-Care will be the joyous fulfillment of America's constitutional promise to ensure domestic tranquility, provide for the common defense, promote general welfare, and secure liberty for one and all. The technology is here, wouldn't it be wrong for us not to use it?

At the core of this revolutionary solution to all of our country's modern challenges will be the Cyber-Care chip, a completely safe, tiny, bio-friendly data transmitter. It will conveniently be available for voluntary implant into every American citizen's palm. No one will be forced to receive the Cyber-Care chip, but once you see the amazing benefits gained from its use, you'll want to be part of the fun.

Upon implementation of Cyber-Care, government-licensed chip readers will become available at most stores, schools, hospitals, and governmental buildings in order to facilitate the cost-saving power of streamlining all American services. All future phones and computers will be integrated with your personal chip.

Imagine a new world without easily lost credit and ID cards, without hackable phones, where all of your banking, medical, personal, tax records, and forms of payment and communication are in one place—the palm of your hand! Satellites will make sure your GPS signal is never dropped, even allowing emergency services to immediately reach you whenever needed. And once everyone is on the network, anti-American terrorists won't be able to communicate secretly. Perfect safety and freedom for all, provided by Uncle Sam.

Your personal, secure palm chip will be individually linked to your existing social security number, and will route through an ultra-modern, unbreachable Internet cloud expertly managed and maintained with the full faith and power of the United States government. As more and more people sign up for the chip implant, savings will exponentially increase, providing vast improvements to us all. Most economists agree, once Cyber-Care has reached full capacity law enforcement will be able to act more efficiently, healthcare costs will dramatically reduce, and college cost will be eliminated from public universities. The Council of Economic Advisors projects billions in yearly surplus funds will be earmarked toward needed research in the fields of nano-technology and stem cell therapy, civil rights, education and infrastructure.

Imagine a new America where terrorism, hate speech, disease, and even potholes have become a thing of the past! An America where healthcare, education, Internet, phone access, and banking fees are minimized, if not entirely free. Imagine an America that finally reaches its full potential of freedom and justice for all. All it takes, fellow citizen, is a simple outpatient injection into your hand for a new dawn to shine. Love your country, love yourself, and love Cyber-Care.

Vote Freeman and Daniels, for progress!

Note: Those opting out of Cyber-Care chip implant could face up to a $25,000 yearly fine.

* * *

The *Religious Liberty* Constitutional Amendment, as explained on Governor Hampton Stone's website:

Threats to America's traditional way of life must be stopped. If not stopped, the Cyber-Care Bill will outlaw religion, free speech, and confiscate your guns. This is not a path to progress, but a road to perdition, the death knell of traditional American values.

America was founded by those brave souls wishing to escape religious persecution, to create a home of morality and freedom. The Religious Liberty Amendment to the United States Constitution will, once and for all, fulfill that noble dream of our Christian forefathers. Amongst other important rights, the Religious Liberty Amendment will allow Americans proclaiming Christian faith to voluntarily exempt from any federal or state laws they deem to violate their spiritual beliefs, including Cyber-Care. After all, what can be more important to our nation than to ensure the right of every citizen to believe as they see fit and to speak as they wish. You do not need government watching your every communication, outlawing your opinions and beliefs. Less government, not more!

Religious Liberty exemptions will necessarily include

Cyber-Care, as well as any and all attempts to force self-declaring Christians into participating in activities involving other religious customs, homosexual or deviant practices, abortion, or any commerce or public function involving sinful behavior, as determined by the Christian individual. Your forefathers did not fight and die for an America free of religion, but for religious freedom!

Note: As part of the Religious Liberty Amendment, all Muslims will be required to register with the federal government, and all funding for the study of climate change and universal health care will be re-appropriated to the Department of Defense.

Approximately 61 Hours Until Electoral College Vote

(Washington, D.C.: Friday, 8:05 p.m. PST/ 11:05 p.m. EST)

D*esperate times require desperate measures.* Annie tried to reassure herself she was still making the right choices as she and Henry marched down the skinny White House hallway toward the Oval Office, those broken red nails of one hand now clawing into her palm. *No one except Marcus and Henry know the Stone tape is garbled, I can bluff the president if necessary.*

Annie assumed President Fuentes was going to demand she leave the Democratic ticket. It was after eleven p.m. in Washington but the West Wing buzzed with hushed, serious whispers from aides rushing down the halls to douse Annie's fire. News of *Annie's Riot* had saturated absolutely every news outlet during her flight across the country, and President Fuentes' staffers now moved like well-greased gears in his typically flawless machine. Most of the suits at least flickered polite smiles at Annie before averting their eyes downward while others just swept by, ignoring the dead-woman-walking. One hundred and seventy-one now estimated as killed at Dayton, including poor little Joey Thompson, whom the whole country was cheering for. Annie felt horrible, and wished she'd thought to take another pill before entering the building.

Douglas Fuentes was a stickler for running his administration with precision and professionalism and could destroy Annie's career even more than her running mate, Vice President Marcus Freeman. On several occasions the president had expressed regret to Freeman on his choice of running mate, and this emergency trip to the Oval Office would be Annie's third such "issues meeting" since being added to the ticket. Being the first black-Hispanic to hold the office, President Fuentes was notorious for everyone respecting these halls where World Wars had been negotiated, where laws impacting generations had been devised, where life and death for millions hung on every tick of the clock. The president had claimed to never like Annie's youth, risk taking, and penchant for speaking off the cuff, even if she had been able to deliver the state of California and galvanize the liberal base. Innocent people had died, and now she was probably going to lose all she was fighting for, including *Cyber-Care* and her daughter's life. She imaged Hampton Stone's new America, where a conservative-tipped Supreme Court overturned legal abortion and once again outlawed same-sex marriage. *Religious Liberty* would usher in an even crueler version of the 1950s, with anyone not fitting the ideal of a male-dominated, white American becoming second-class citizens, or worse. Annie's dream of economic equality and social fairness for everyone would be gone forever, and she squeezed her hand into a fist to keep it from shaking, her frayed mind scrambling for the best plan to save her life's work.

On their way into the most powerful building in the world Annie and Henry had passed Marine guards and Secret Service, metal detectors and guard dogs, and Annie wondered if she could ever actually be making the decisions here. Within these walls, the impact of the slightest decisions crackled into the world like an untamed current of electric possibilities, and Annie's exhausted mind now spun with frazzled images of that young Thompson boy lying crumpled in the street. She couldn't really be responsible, could she? If there were any ideals Annie Daniels could be known for they were the health and well-being of everyone, for peace and tolerance.

"I can tell him the speech was my idea," Henry whispered in his tweed blazer and too-black beard. "That I added the language late?" Henry was as loyal to Annie as a knight to his queen. He was fumbling another half-chewed cigar into his blazer pocket, trying to get his iPhone to a new page. "You could even fire me until after—"

"No," Annie whispered, narrowing her glacier eyes ahead. Of anyone, Annie needed Henry, not only for his political mind, but also as her emotional rock. "Not necessary. Electoral projections?"

"Nothing new from Arizona or Michigan." Henry scrolled a small thumb over the information on his phone, cheap musk cologne wafting off him. "At least Pennsylvania and Colorado are still solid leads for us with recounts going, and Illinois legislature looks like it might appoint Democratic electors long as the governor doesn't fight it."

"But Louisiana?" Annie groaned in hushed tones, trying to shift her mind from the ax hanging over her head. "What about our guy?"

"Everything, unfortunately, still solidifying to the tie." He flipped his thumb faster and faster over the screen looking for some good news he couldn't find, his cheeks a worried pink above the black beard.

great country forward. We need Cyber-Care." The perfect tone would impress the new female intern with his courage and insight, yet also convey to her that he was a refined, nonviolent soul. "It is time for woman power."

Jesus, he thought in a rare moment of honest assessment as he reached for his grass-fed milk latte, *I really will say anything for the chance of getting laid.*

* * *

The illegal Zennie had a bit of a metallic bite against her tongue as Annie secretly sucked it while strutting into the Oval Office. Just before entering the Secretary's Annex Annie had blurted to Henry that she had to get something out of her eye, then darted around the corner to pop the pink pill. Just something to help her focus, to get control again. Science. Annie knew the entire potential for this great nation depended on her staying on the ticket. She had to be smart, clear headed. *Just one more.*

The Oval Office was never comfortable. All furniture within the world's most important room was rumored to be strangely angled in order to give a slight sense of inferiority to anyone speaking with President Douglas Fuentes as if he weren't intimidating enough on his own. Before the president's huge oak desk two white sofas contained overstuffed cushions that insisted someone perch themselves at a very stiff angle to keep their balance, then forced the sitter to strain their neck to face him.

Annie swallowed the Zennie, coughed as the president's brown eyes had latched onto hers, his face hardening into such a shade of disgust that his slight jowls seem to tighten. The ebony-skinned President Fuentes was six foot four and a former college linebacker. He had short white hair, a white mustache and small round spectacles that made him look like a black Teddy Roosevelt pre-chiseled for Mount Rushmore. The gold-trimmed Presidential Seal was perfectly positioned in the blue carpet between the sofas and the huge mahogany desk where the domineering statue of a man sat in a high-backed chair reminiscent of a throne. The American flag stood mounted on a golden stand next to the desk. There were two others in the room. The slim vice president sat tautly on one sofa in a gray shirt and yellow tie with sleeves rolled up. The other was the ancient lobbyist, Yanic Goran.

The vice president glanced at Annie and Henry, but then cast his dour eyes back down to the floor without a smile or greeting, brushing long fingers through his wavy hair, sighed. Vice President Marcus Freeman was a comparatively youthful fifty-six-year-old product of Northeastern Ivy League schools and was continually being compared to Kennedy, even after divorcing his wife of sixteen years at the start of Fuentes' second term and announcing to the world that he was gay and going to marry a man. Now though, he looked tense. Annie pretended a relaxed smile all around, but only oily Yanic Goran returned it, which made Annie feel all the more alone, and a little nauseous.

Super-lobbyist Yanic Goran was a frail, seventy-something man with wrinkling olive skin and a few greasy strands of silver hair over a shiny, liver-spotted skull. He wore coke-bottle glasses on his always-sniffling nose, and his body, draped in a $2,500 suit that seemed too large, twitched and trembled like a poorly constructed building in gusts of stiff wind though his thin smile was ever present. Yanic Goran revolted Annie and she was a little surprised to see him in the same room with Freeman since Goran controlled the largest Super-PAC in the country. Annie's threat against Stone had been to expose his very similar meeting with Goran. The few times Annie had the unfortunate luck of having to speak with him, she always thought of mating eels. Yanic Goran, however, was as fixated in DC as the White House itself.

Lobbying was about relationships turned into money, not things done on principle for the greater good, as Annie had vowed her life to fight for, but to line some already-rich guy's pocket further. A lobbyist's craft was to know as intimately as possible the publicly elected officials who created the laws of the land, as well as nurture relationships with the heads of businesses and special interest groups who wished those laws to be changed for their own benefit. The lobbyist made money arranging meetings and communication between those groups, selling their influence. To Annie they were all cowardly rats, sneaking within the shadows of legitimate government to nibble on crumbs and squeak greedy wishes to low-lying ears, and Goran was the worst of the worst. He was the super-lawyer at the top of the lobbying garbage heap rumored to make in excess of tens of millions per year, which he then had used to start his own political action committees. With his political action committees he was allowed to spend millions more on his chosen candidates each election, to perpetuate the cycle of him and his associates getting richer. Along with fraudulent religious guilt, lobbying and PACs were everything Annie saw as unjustly perpetuating the corrupt patriarchal American society, and what she wanted to remove.

Goran now nodded toward Annie, smiling like a manic little dog desperate to please even as he started slinking back from the president's desk. Annie knew he was negotiating the royalties for a book deal for President Fuentes as soon as he left office which was probably why Goran was still in the room even though she and Freeman were there. Election laws stated that a person working in an official lobbying or political action committee capacity shouldn't be in close proximity with official candidates actively running in order to minimize the possibility of a candidate promising political favors in exchange for campaign funds. In reality though, Yanic Goran went anywhere and everywhere in Washington he wanted, just switching his self-reported working status on disclosure forms between lobbyist, advisor, lawyer, financial bundler, or volunteer as was prudent. He was probably officially here now as the president's book agent, and he did after all, throw the best parties in the District of Columbia, so it wouldn't do for anyone to lose touch with him.

At least someone still sees earning potential in me, Annie thought from Goran's pathetic smiles as he slipped out the door. She tried to smile back at him, but it came out as a halfhearted nose wrinkle like she smelled feet. *I've just got to convince the president we are going to get Stone to concede based on the tape, that there's no need to replace me.*

"Mr. President," Annie said. "I'd like to apolo—"

"No." President Fuentes shook his large head in disbelief. "No." From behind the small round glasses his brown eyes looked genuinely bewildered. "Instead of confirming your trust in the system, telling the country you thought everything will work out, you're extorting the other side into quitting, Daniels? And equating religion to fantasy?"

"Sir, the tape will crush Stone's support—"

"Marcus already explained the tape is garbled dinner conversation with poor lightening, Daniels. Your days of shooting from the hip are done."

Has even Marcus turned against me? Her eyes darted to Freeman, but he only quietly plucked another cat hair off his lap. Annie's stomach dropped as she realized her plan A for diverting things away from an idea of kicking her off was already gone. *Snakes, snakes everywhere.*

"And, GOD A LIE?" The president spat it like an awful taste was stuck to his tongue. "Absurd. All you did was give Jews, Muslims and Christians something to finally agree on: hating you." It made Annie remember the look and tone of her father when he'd pushed her off the back porch, kicked her out of their home with the word *whore* spat at her back. "What were you thinking? I'm Catholic. And if the tape you obtained had the slightest admissible evidence to any actual illegal activity by Governor Stone on it, Daniels, you should be turning it into the Federal Election Commission or FBI, not using it for threats."

She wanted to rake her fingers through her long blonde hair to soothe her frying nerves, but concentrated instead on calmly lacing her fingers in front of her gray skirt. She had to appear composed, rational. She held the president's hard gaze even though she felt like screaming and running.

His eyes drifted down to her short skirt. "Sit," he snapped.

Jesus, I'm really screwed. She felt like ripping out the bottle of Zennies and chugging. *I'm off the ticket. They've already decided and won't even hear my side of it.* She sat down next to Henry and concentrated on not shaking, trying to subtly pull her grey skirt over her exposed knees. *There's got to be an angle to argue. Think, Annie, think.*

The four towering gold curtains of the Oval Office were currently shut, cutting off any distracting views into the nighttime Rose Garden. A grandfather clock, supposedly a gift from

Churchill to Eleanor Roosevelt, ticked mercilessly behind the desk as the president twirled the gold wedding band on his dark left hand, glaring at her. Annie didn't know which the president was more upset about, the threat to release the tape of Stone, or the *God is a lie* statement.

"Sir," she tried again, "please remember this is the most important election in our lifetimes, maybe in the history of America."

"PEACE is what is more important than ever." President Fuentes growled. "Not who wins." He straightened in his chair, pointed toward her. "This past summer America saw more riots and looting in urban areas than any time since 1968. Detroit. Chicago. Ferguson again. Tension between minorities and police are already at an all-time high, we're fighting ISIS secretly infiltrating our country every day, but now you're going rogue on us and inciting riots?"

"But sir, Stone's nationalistic rallies have been the cause of a lot of that violence. And honestly, the Dayton riot is even more reason why *Cyber—*"

"Stop," President Fuentes held a wide palm in the air. "No more with your sci-fi crap." His eyes burrowed into her. "Your idea of a chip implant in people's palms is exactly what rallied everyone to Governor Stone in the first place, allowed him to preach his fear." The president stood, two massive black hands brushing down the lapels of his crisp three-piece, navy pinstripe suit, his cobalt blue tie perfectly knotted against his neck. "Don't you ever think, Daniels?" Annie noticed it wasn't Senator, just Daniels. "I'm finalizing negotiations on the *Pan-Continental Trade Agreement*, potentially hundreds of thousands of US jobs on the line. Fifty-one countries. Trillions of dollars. Does economic prosperity not factor into your list of ideals for the country? Do you not get that the Russians and Chinese are using every negative to undermine our negotiating ability for the financial agreements that truly matter to the country's stability? Everything isn't about you publicly working out your daddy issues."

Freeman sighed, his lanky fingers stroking his yellow tie. "It was a devastating gaffe, Annie." Compared to the buttoned-up president, Marcus Freeman always looked like a rumpled business-casual, like a slightly weathered frat boy.

"Mr. President, Mr. Vice President, maybe I was wrong in my tone and timing, but I was right in my message. It is time to move our country forward, progress into the future once and for all, and *Cyber-Care* makes the most sense—"

"And what some call progress, others call mistakes," the president said. "Just because something CAN be done, doesn't mean it always SHOULD be done, Daniels. Sometimes we need to accept the status quo."

"Like racism?" Annie heard Henry softly groan in warning at her, but she knew if she could turn this into a debate about ideals rather than competence she could win. "Stone's crazed rallies use religion and false nationalism to incite idiots into embracing their own worst traits, promoting homophobia, xenophobia, and hatred of women or anyone unlike them. If people always accepted the status quo someone like you would never be in this position, sir. The *Cyber-Care* chip will finally ensure every individual's freedom, not just the rich and powerful, not hate."

"Do not cite racism to me, Daniels," the president stomped out from behind his desk. "And every word you can end with 'phobia' doesn't mean you have a point, it's not that simple." He glared back and forth between her and Freeman.

"Can't you see that some people have a problem with your idea to ensure their freedom by controlling them through a chip. Ensure freedom by government controlling them more—does that even make sense?"

"If the right people are in control, sir, government IS the solution."

"And what if the WRONG people are in control, Daniels? What then? What if the voters get it wrong?"

"I am a humanist, maybe I just have more faith in my fellow Americans than you."

"Well for being a humanist, you certainly seem to hate about half of them." The president glowered.

"Only the stupid half, sir. Which is why it's critical we win."

President Fuentes jabbed his round spectacles back up on his wide nose. "Well now I'm taking control of this situation, taking control of this fiasco you two are calling a campaign. It is time for a change."

"But gentleman, we're about to win." Annie's voice trembled despite herself at the worry that the president's demand for change would be forcing her to resign from the ticket. "We don't need to radically alter things in the closing hours." An image of poor Joey Thompson fighting for his life in the hospital sprang to her mind, and she thought how *Cyber-Care* could have prevented it. "Stone can't be allowed to win, he's corrupt to the core. This is for America's entire future. Now's the time to lead, not to give in to corruption or cower to fundamentalist bullies."

"Annie," Freeman gasped, "the president isn't SCARED. People died today. That boy Joey Thompson just DIED."

And Annie felt like she had just been punched in the gut.

She clutched both arms around her stomach and her eyes sank to the blue carpet. She'd never wanted an innocent boy like Joey Thompson to get hurt.

But she swallowed hard, she could not give up. "We can still keep the Electoral College from tying. We can flip an elector. Louisiana for instance—"

"We are NOT," the president's white mustache curled in partial sneer, eyes on Annie, "committing electoral fraud in addition to inciting a riot. There are rules, principles."

"It's principle I'm fighting for, sir. It's NOT fraud in any of the states that don't have laws dictating how an elector votes. Louisiana for instance—"

"No one from our side will so much as send a good luck email to any of the 538 electoral voters," the president growled. "My priority is in continuing the unbroken chain of peaceful transitions of power that have occurred in this county for over 200 years, not handing you two the keys to the kingdom at all costs. I'm president of the entire United States, not just Democrats."

"But we could make a deal with Governor Pullman in Ohio," Annie continued.

"You're not listening, Daniels." The president rolled his eyes, holding up three fingers. "Three days. Three days to get through with a happy country at the end of it, that's my only concern. Not who wins. So we're going to make a change." He pushed his round glasses back up on his nose and leaned over his desk toward his phone. "You're going to hear something, Daniels, so you can understand my decision." He jabbed a button located on a black control panel and spoke into it. "Send in Miss Howe, please." The president looked back at Annie and added, "Once you hear Miss Howe you'll understand why I've got to implement this change, Annie. I'm sorry."

Miss Howe? Annie's jaw tightened with a bad feeling she had heard the name before. *Miss Howe?* Things began to quiver inside her again and her arms went back to her stomach. *Shit.* Just when Annie thought things couldn't get worse, Beatrice Howe, the same skinny black woman Annie had demeaned only twelve hours earlier, strutted through the side door from the president's private annex. The same woman who asked Annie not to make her speech based on things being too tense. The same woman Annie dismissed so rudely in San Francisco's City Hall, and the same woman who had seen Annie take the Zennies right after the speech. *Shit. Snakes everywhere.*

"Good evening, Mr. President." Miss Howe looked from the president to Annie with the barest hint of a smile over her thin lips. She wore the same frilly white blouse cinched up to her neck and clutched a manila folder to her chest. In Washington proximity to the president equaled power, and Beatrice Howe's appeared to be skyrocketing as Annie's was plummeting. "Good evening, Vice President Freeman," she added with a cordial smile.

The pills, Annie thought with horror. *That's the leverage for forcing me to quit, the damned pills. Hell, maybe Howe is even my replacement?*

The president smiled at Howe warmly and explained to the room. "Miss Howe had been working for me over the last year in a classified capacity as my personal attaché to the CIA, NSA, DOD, FBI and Justice Department among others, and recently brought some information to me so important I can not ignore its potential impact on this country." The president looked to Freeman, then Annie. "So, as of twenty-four hours ago I dismissed Huxton and I've appointed Miss Howe my new National Security Advisor. Miss Howe is now going to bring you both up to speed on this classified information she has. Once you see the potential ramifications, you will understand why my change to the campaign is necessary."

Here come the pills, Annie stewed in silence, *the goddamn recalled meds.*

Miss Howe nodded to the president, then opened her folder to glance at its contents.

After getting kicked off, can I go to jail for them? Annie felt like the room was starting to wobble, the American flag and the towering gold curtains starting to sway. She put out both hands to either side of her on the smooth couch, breathed deep, and tried to regroup. *Whatever she is going to say, I'm smarter.* Annie was tired though, so damn tired. *I can still win this argument, save this country, and save Harmony. I can stop the snake.*

"I believe I have discovered evidence," Miss Howe stated looking at her folder, "that someone—"

"The pills aren't what you think," Annie blurted. "You're mistaken."

Miss Howe's voice slowed, eyes rolling up from her folder to Annie. "Someone is trying to illegally influence the election's outcome, Senator Daniels."

Henry groaned, and the president's mouth dropped open. Marcus Freeman's boyish face darted back and forth between Annie and Miss Howe as if he couldn't figure out whose statement was more shocking.

"What," the president growled at Annie while crossing his thick arms over his chest, "pills?"

I'm fucking losing it.

Senator Daniels Meets at the White House

(New Orleans, Louisiana: Friday into Saturday, 9:09 p.m. PST / 12:09 a.m. EST)

M r. Jefferson sat at a white plastic table across from the nervous Little Gumbo, the black phone with the red rabbit silhouette embossed on its back tucked safely into Mr. Jefferson's black suit coat.

"But what's you want?" Little Gumbo asked him. "Who you work for? The prisons? I seen on the Internet how rich them private prisons getting off arresting people like me, and that ain't right. It just ain't right."

"To fulfill your agreement," Mr. Jefferson answered. "Your contract, of sorts."

Louisiana elector Little Gumbo was a middle-aged black guy who had been so broken by life he appeared twenty years older than he was. He'd once been a good kid with the chance to play college ball, but had gotten arrested for weed and had his scholarship pulled. The two white kids with him had got off, and Little Gumbo began twenty years of being constantly harassed by the cops. His face now sagged like a deflated basketball. His red, watery eyes shifted to his greasy jeans, then to the curling beer posters on the plywood walls, and he wished more than anything he would never have to see this freaky albino Mr. Jefferson asshole again.

The albino in the dark suit had mysteriously shown up several weeks back to say Little Gumbo had been picked as a presidential elector and explained that it would help him raise his stature in the community. But now the freak had returned, and he was not being nice. Mr. Jefferson and his weird birthmark creeped Little Gumbo out, like he might be a demon more than a man.

Little Gumbo's entire skinny body was twitching from multiple days of booze and crack, everything popping and twisting inside him like the entire world was burning harsh. "But—"

"Things," Mr. Jefferson interrupted, "are no longer retractable."

"Retrac...?" Little Gumbo rubbed a trembling hand through his unkempt wool of grey-black hair. His voice was a mixture of Cajun twang and confused pleas. "Re—"

"You've already agreed."

Inside the closed restaurant an oily film had condensed on all surfaces like dusty sap on every chair arm, table surface and moist wall. On a paint-chipped wooden stool in the corner an old transistor-tube television silently flickered images of the Dayton riot from earlier that day. Shaky scenes of teargas plumes wafting through the park and of bloodied adults and wailing children had filled every particle of the airwaves for the past several hours. Mr. Jefferson's pale face occasionally shifted toward the images of the shot Joey Thompson as a graphic read *Thompson boy dead from Daniels Riot*.

Brassy big-band music scratched out from the poor excuse of a kitchen behind Little Gumbo. It overflowed with ancient greasy smells and smoke. A gray rat with a glistening black tail ran the baseboard edges of the tiny dining room through rotting crab shells. Little Gumbo looked to the rusted tin roof, and then anywhere else rather than into the freaky man's shades. "But wha yous really want, man?"

"Only for you to vote correctly on Monday," Mr. Jefferson answered. "All the country, all the world, is ready for the end. And your vote, just that one vote, friend, is the key. It's time to choose."

Little Gumbo swayed in his seat, almost like he was practicing the subtle movements of some hip-hop dance, if not for his teeth grinding. "Man, I know you helped getting the charges dropped, and with da elector thing, but I never even did most the stuff they keep arresting me for. Swear they just making money somehow by arresting me all the time."

"Louisiana has no laws dictating that an elector vote party lines." Mr. Jefferson's voice was stern. "You are legally free to vote as you choose, regardless of the popular vote in the state." Mr. Jefferson's words slowed, became more enunciated. "I am simply here to remind you of your preferred vote on Monday." He swallowed hard. "The correct choice to make with your free will, friend."

"But, I's got good reputations now, man." Little Gumbo's face wrinkled. "I can't—oh, God—" Little Gumbo collapsed forward, the cheap table wobbling as his greasy forehead thumped into it, his skinny dark arms wrapping around his stomach and his teeth biting hard as he groaned in pain, sucking for air. Withdrawals from the drugs and booze were brought on more intensely by the stress of Mr. Jefferson's visit. "Oh, God."

Little Gumbo strained one arm up toward the other man, pleading for sympathy. *Whap.* The bigger, younger man grabbed Little Gumbo's skinny wrist and crushed it to the table.

"Ow, man, ow," Little Gumbo whined. "What the hell?"

A full scowl ripped over Mr. Jefferson's mouth as he squeezed Little Gumbo's bones hard, pressing his arm down into the table until the frailer man and the table nearly toppled forward, the blue vein on the side of Mr. Jefferson's pale head bulging to near eruption, almost merging with the purple raised snake-like birthmark on his white cheek.

"Come on, bro," Little Gumbo whined. "Hurts."

Quickly, efficiently, Mr. Jefferson's free hand shot to his suit's coat pocket to produce a manila envelope. He thumped it down on the table next to Little Gumbo's pinned arm, the greenish edges of several US bills spilling from it. At its sight, Little Gumbo's eyes widened, his thrashing dwindling.

The man in shades nodded at the envelope. "Carrot." He released his grip from Little Gumbo's wrist and wiped that hand's fingers on a handkerchief.

"Ok." Little Gumbo's red-rimmed eyes went wide at the envelope of cash while rubbing his hurt wrist. A weary smile crept over his mouth. "Ok."

Mr. Jefferson's entire face wrinkled in deep revulsion at Little Gumbo. "Do not make us show you the stick."

"Okay, okay." Little Gumbo eyes flitted nervously from Mr. Jefferson to money, then back to the man. "I gots you man. I vote the way you want on Monday, no big." Little Gumbo's eyes settled on the envelope of money, American dreams of freedom and respect and shiny cars and clean women liking him filling his imagination. "No big."

The rat sniffed at Little Gumbo's toes.

"Rebellion to tyrants is obedience to God."
—*Benjamin Franklin*

*(Washington, D.C.: Friday into Saturday, 9:46 p.m. PST /
12:46 a.m. EST)*

There's a lot of crazy people in the world, Henry thought, hoping Annie wasn't becoming one of them. It was the first time ever for Henry in the Situation Room, to hear the secure details of Howe's possible plot by someone to illegally influence the election, but all Henry could think was, *is Annie losing it?* The speech, Annie blurting out something about pills in the Oval Office. *The campaign pressures, her daughter's diagnosis, has it all gotten too much?*

The Situation Room was essentially a subterranean vault directly beneath the Oval Office, impervious to electronic eavesdropping and nuclear attack. The Secret Service's counterterrorism war room was immediately next door, and two dark-suited Secret Service agents stood outside the Situation Room at all times. The president's iris had to be scanned in order for the hermetically sealed door to sigh open. Within the ambient glow was a long glossy table with leather chairs surrounded by three walls full of television screens. The screens were muted, showing ongoing scenes from volatile locations around the world including angry people at a Stone rally, flashing police cars still encircling the Dayton park, a gang shooting in Chicago, water cannons being sprayed on people in Egyptian streets, financial-market tickers from around the world, and Chinese warships sailing off the Alaskan coast.

I've got to help her, Henry thought with a nervous scratch of his black beard as they walked toward the long table. He felt his phone vibrate in his pocket and slipped his hand inside to silence it, sure it was from the individual he couldn't tell Annie about. *It's been too hard for her for too long, she needs rest.*

Over the fifteen years Henry had known Annie he'd developed an amazing respect for her commitment to the protection of all life no matter how small and frail, her compassion toward each individual having the absolute freedom to be who they wanted. Earlier, during their race from the airport to the White House Annie had even made them pull her limo over so that she could give her take-out dinner and a hundred dollar bill to a homeless woman pushing a shopping cart, reaching out through the window without hesitation to clutch the poor woman's filthy hands and reassure her that everything would soon be better. That was typical. Some days Henry admitted to himself that through the years his respect for Annie had morphed into complete and total love. But now, Henry wondered if the impossibility of saving the entire world was pulling her apart at the seams. *Pills.* Henry worried about her with an aching heart. *What pills?*

On the way down to the Situation Room Annie had brushed off the pill issue to the president and vice president. She gave a casual explanation that she was taking a prescribed antiviral as a safeguard against contracting her daughter's illness, and they had apparently bought it. Or at least, like most men when Annie insisted on something, they had accepted it.

The only problem was that Henry could tell when Annie was lying, even when he didn't know exactly what she was lying about. He noticed the way her flawless face got the barest whisper of crow's feet right on the edges of her glacier eyes, smiling just a mico-fraction too hard to be natural. She was up to something, he just had no idea what.

"Muslim sleeper agents," the vice president asked Beatrice Howe as he pulled out one of the leather chairs from the dark table. "Who? Where?" The vice president dropped down, video screen light flashing over one side of his hairless chin while he brushed a swath of that Kennedy-hair with a scowl. "Or a damned foreign government?" Freeman was a master of appearing congenial in public, but in private often lashed out. "And what on earth do they think they can do? They can't have some Manchurian candidate win at this stage, the damned Islamists."

Annie strolled to the other side of the table, her movements as smooth as a swan, her pink lips holding a soft smile as if everything in the world were sunny. He noticed the red nails on her right hand were torn and ragged though, almost like she'd shoved the tip of that hand in a wood chipper. Henry knew Annie's formidable mind would still be calculating an argument for staying on the ticket, and was hoping to somehow get reassurance that she was still mentally and emotionally sound as well.

"Not certain it's Muslim extremists, sir," Howe answered the Vice President. "The NSA's *Uncle's Eyes* matrix currently identifies over 5,000 individuals on US soil in the 15th percentile highest-risk of anti-government activity before Monday's Electoral Vote. In addition, there are 101 organized groups of concern of various sizes that could also pose an even more systemic threat to the public than a lone wolf." Howe placed her manila folder on the dark lacquer of the conference table, turning it to fit perfectly perpendicular to the edge. "The sheer macro-potentiality of violence, if a plot to steal the election somehow caused more chaos, is why I'm recommending the president enact *Operation Long Knives* this evening."

The president stared up at the television screens with his large hands entwined behind his back. "I haven't even informed the Justice Department of the suspicious communication patterns Howe's discovered. The whole key to *Long Knives*, Marcus, if I give the go order, is surprise. We'd send the Executive Order through Homeland Security, round up all 5,000 and put them in FEMA camps before the word can spread or the press finds out. Botching it could cause huge blowback."

"Whoa, whoa." Annie waved her hands, smiling. "Slow down, please. Rounding thousands of who up? And why?" Henry could see Annie was playing up her casual mode, leaning back in a chair across the table from the vice president and Howe and crossing one glossy kneecap over another like everything was fine. It was one of her favorite tactics to lull people out of actual arguments, so she could find weaknesses in their position and verbally tie them into knots. "I'm not hearing how any of this constitutes a specific election-stealing plot," she said. "Something to constitute such extreme legal action. And *Uncle's Eyes? Operation Long Knives?* What are those?"

Beatrice Howe glanced to the president, he nodding in authorization for her to proceed. Howe explained the secretive NSA program *Uncle's Eyes* had been running since the early 2000s. It was about metadata and microdata, the attempted collection and permanent storage of absolutely anything done within US borders by anyone, and then making it instantly usable by the highest security clearance levels of government. The government's most powerful computer servers then used the data to create predictive analysis of groups and individuals.

"Anything?" Annie asked.

"Everything," the president clarified, still staring at the television with the Chinese warships. "Almost. We reached over sixty-four percent of everything over the last year, should be at one hundred percent before the end of the next president's term." He rubbed the dark forefingers of each hand against his temples, just below the snow-white hair.

"But everything of what?" Annie asked the vice president across the table.

"*Uncle's Eyes* accesses all American cell and social media posts, pictures, audio of all phone calls, all phone texts," the vice president answered, clearly already deeply knowledgeable about the program. He tugged his yellow tie looser from his grey shirt. "All Internet searches and emails, everyone's banking information, everyone's credit card purchases, all medical records, television habits, as well as anything else it can get digital claws on. It then compiles it all into one master file on each person via a program cross-linking social security numbers and tax records with server IP addresses and facial-recognition software."

"Jesus," Annie said, all fakery lost. "Without court orders? No oversight or warrants required? That's not constitutional."

"In fact, Senator," Howe jumped back in. "Over sixty percent of every person's actual physical movements throughout each day in the US are now being GPS tracked and video recorded by a multitude of government-hacked cameras on every street corner, ATM, automobile, electronic device, and shop window. Most areas that aren't physically covered by local cameras are picked up by tiny drones and satellites, far more than anyone realizes, circling high up in the air and constantly recording activities below with high-powered cameras. All this information is constantly added to each individual's master file with a time and date stamp multiple times a day and kept on secure servers at the NSA." She cleared her throat. "Every, single, citizen."

"That can't be legal," Henry blurted out before he could stop himself, panicked at the thought of being watched all the time, of having his deepest secrets known. "The senator's right, what about the Constitution?"

"Strange how everyone always manages to cite just the parts of the Constitution or Bible they find useful," the vice president scowled.

"Yes," President Fuentes agreed. "Everyone wants perfect safety and perfect freedom, but no costs to get there." President Fuentes removed his coat to expose crisp white sleeves coming out of his navy vest. "*Uncle's Eyes* has been going on for years, you two, it has never stopped through many administrations of both parties despite whistleblowers and the laws." Fuentes carefully draped his coat over the chair at the end, smoothing out a crease. "It just keeps getting more powerful, closer to total information."

Freeman reached to the interior of the table and lifted up a metal coffee carafe. "If we don't use the potential, the bad guys will." He wobbled the carafe in his hand, then poured a steaming stream of coffee into a porcelain cup. "National security and all."

"But…" Henry's cheeks flushed red above his black beard, his forehead beading with sweat as he realized that everyone's most paranoid dreams of a society with no privacy and a government watching your every move was already here. "But if I'm inside at home, you can't see me there?"

"Well, Mr. Corwich," Freeman said with a smirk as he sank back into his chair. "Only if you don't turn on your cell phone, computer, television, or... toaster." The visibly exhausted vice president chuckled. Freeman held the coffee to his nose with both hands, inhaling. "The NSA enables backdoors into every computer chip in every electronic before it leaves any factory. Besides, then we'd just know you're at home not doing anything, and trust me, Henry, everyone in this room has already reviewed your porn file—it's only marginally criminal."

"Good God," Henry gasped.

"But this is the biggest problem people have with *Cyber-Care*," Annie happily exclaimed as Henry caught the renewed sparkle in her blue eyes. He knew she thought she'd found her angle for staying on the ticket. "If people knew *Uncle's Eyes* already existed, *Cyber-Care* wouldn't be a hard sell at all. Everyone's privacy is already gone, they just don't know it." She straightened. "Under *Cyber-Care* there will at least be some transparency and accountability, a real system accountable to the people with oversight and constitutional rights. Can't you see, this is our chance to win, by cutting out Stone's rallying cry at its knees. We've just got to come clean about *Unc*—"

"Nothing," President Fuentes jabbed a finger at Annie, "leaves this room, Daniels." The president's glare was harsh. "You're only finding out about this because of the election threat, if you start blabbing details it will only help those who seek to harm America. This is about peace and calm. People aren't ready to know about *Uncle's Eyes*, the opposition to *Cyber-Care* has proven that."

"Peace and calm by rounding up 5,000 Americans who

haven't committed any crime," Annie argued. "That's the most paranoid version of *Cyber-Care* coming true. This *Operation Long Knives* sounds like Nazi Germany."

"It's a failsafe created by the NSA," the president answered. "The protocol was originally designed as a contingency plan if we suspected Muslim radicals or the Chinese had secretly infiltrated the US government with moles." He shoved his hands into his pockets as his face sank in thought. "It works when I issue what's officially called *Executive Order 11316*. Howe then uses the *Uncle's Eyes* software to create a statistically predictive meta-analysis of anyone having an 85% or higher chance of divisive thoughts or actions toward the federal government between now and the end of the election on Monday. The names and current GPS locations of those persons-of-interest are then routed to the CIA and Homeland Security, who secretly round them up with the assistance of local law enforcement, and quickly deposit them in secure FEMA compounds at undisclosed locations." The president began to pace with his head down and white brows furrowed. "We'd hold them for several days until the election is over on a variety of trumped-up charges, then let them go once *Uncle Eyes* tells us the statistically probability of the threat has diminished. It purposely bypasses the FBI and Justice Department, in case those agencies had become compromised."

"And *Operation Long Knives* will only work to put down any potential conspiracy with the element of surprise, Ms. Daniels." Miss Howe still stood in the same spot, rigid as tree. "To neutralize any threat, people can't know the extent to which they are being observed. No one can know about the roundup until after the election, and no one can ever know about *Uncle's Eyes*. The fewer people know how much they are being observed, and how, the better."

"But arresting American citizens before they commit a crime." Annie snorted. "Without any attorneys or warrants, just because some computer thinks they might not be entirely loyal to the federal government?" She shook her head in frustration. "This isn't North Korea, this is an abuse of liberty. *Cyber-Care* is to ensure everyone's constitutional liberty, not take it away. If this roundup leaks to the press *Cyber-Care* will get killed, and there can't be 5,000 potential Muslim extremists within American borders—"

"To be clear, Senator," Howe cleared her throat, folded her small brown hands. "I'm not suggesting only limiting ourselves to potential Muslim radicals. *Uncle's Eyes* has identified 5,013 individuals of varying ethnicities and ideologies to quarantine for the next 72 hours. We'd use the *Long Knives* protocol to remove the risk of ANY sort of orchestrated conspiracy against the government or the election before it can end. I don't believe this is necessarily an Islamic plot. The high-risk communication I've observed went to a total of 101 different groups in various locations around the country. Everyone from the anti-immigration *American Defense League* to the global warming extremists *Earth Now*, to survivalist militias like the *Patriots of the Rising Dawn* and even some so-called anarchist groups like *Reboot.org* who have all been recipients of calls, texts and emails from the same nexus source I'm concerned with. I'm recommending to the president that ANYONE *Uncle's Eyes* identifies as having an above average potential to initiate domestic violence over the next couple days be picked up and quarantined."

"*Reboot.org?*" Freeman shook his head, now in apparent

confusion and seeming to briefly side with Annie's skepticism. "Isn't *Reboot* most likely just a bunch of bored flash-mobbing nerds who will stop hacking and posting their little YouTube videos as soon as they start getting laid? Are they really a threat? The tighter the *Long Knives* net, the greater chance we have of doing it with no one noticing. 5,000 is a lot."

"No way to know, sir," Miss Howe answered him. "That's why we strictly use the math, nothing biased, just data to prevent us making a wrong call. *Reboot.org* understands computer systems as well as our best techs, which makes them some of the few capable of staying beyond identification. As for ideology, they appear to be championing a mass decentralizing of federal and monetary power, basically anarchists."

"But we can't arrest thousands of innocent people," Annie protested again. "It's wrong, and this will doom *Cyber-Care*. Besides, *Patriots of the Rising* whatever are probably just a bunch of paintball playing truckers in camo gear, and *Earth Now* is less frightening than PETA. If there is an individual posing a specific threat, why not just arrest them and be done with it? Who's the source of this communication?"

The President sighed. "Howe only found the patterns of communication in the *Uncle's Eyes* reports, Annie. There are multiple phone calls going out to these high-risk groups and individuals, all sourcing back to the same DC origination nexus, but we don't know who it is, because…" The President took off his glasses to rub at his baggy eyes, adding gravely, "The calls are going over the *RedRabbit* system."

"*RedRabbit?*" The vice president's face dropped. "So the plot could be coming from within the highest levels of the government itself?" The president replaced his glasses and nodded sullenly at Freeman. "Lord," the vice president whispered.

"*RedRabbit?*" Henry asked, even more bewildered. "What's *RedRabbit?*"

"The only communication system left in the country that isn't monitored." The president lifted a black cell phone with the silhouette of a small red rabbit on its back out of his pocket. Vice President Freeman also pulled out a similar phone.

Annie and Henry looked at each other, dismayed.

"The *RedRabbit* secure communication system," Miss Howe clarified, "is currently granted to only those few people across all branches of the government and military with the highest *RedRabbit* clearance. Clearance to access anything, even the *Uncle's Eyes* master files, and in turn it also keeps their own conversations private. We can't listen to their calls or know their individual identities, only see it is being used. A system above the system."

A plot by someone within the government or military to steal the election? Henry was speechless as the frightening ramifications quickly fell into place.

"And if I have to set *Long Knives* in motion to suppress this potential plot, Daniels," the president said, "possibly rounding up thousands of people over the next few hours, then I think you should be able to understand the logic of my suggestion for that change to your campaign. We've got to calm things."

Annie's face went slack, a bit of worry creeping into her glacier eyes.

"Given your *God is a Lie* speech and the riot it caused," the President continued, "tensions are too high, Annie." The president's tired eyes suddenly looked empathetic. "I'm sorry, but it's time to put the safety of the country first. I'm instructing Marcus to—"

"Tensions?" Annie shot to her feet, her jaw jutting out.

"It is the closest election in US history, of course people are tense." The look in her eye had morphed to wildness. "This is absurd, you don't even have any specific plot you're just scared of some mathematical voodoo, and you think arresting a bunch of innocent people in secret, kicking me off the ticket, will calm everyone down?"

"What?" The president's ebony face tightened to disdain. "Are you insane? We aren't kicking you off. We couldn't, half the country has already voted for you, I don't even know what that would constitutionally mean." The president scowled at Freeman like it was his fault for picking Annie. "It's *Cyber-Care* that has to go, Senator. That's my decision."

Oh God. That's no better. Henry panicked. *Think. I've got to save her from herself. Think of something.*

"*Cyber-Care?*" Annie's face flushed with shock as she thrust both hands out to the table for support. "But... but you can't seriously be considering dropping *Cyber-Care* from the Democratic platform?" Her face morphed from indignation to embarrassment to horror. All of her goals in life were entwined with *Cyber-Care*, her singular effort to providing lasting change for America. She was it, it was she. "*Cyber-Care* is what got us here."

"No," the president snapped. "The idea of free healthcare and being safe is what got you here. A weird chip in people's palm makes half the country wonder if you're a devil worshipper, so I'm ordering you to publicly kill it, tomorrow." There was no room for questioning in the president's tone. "It's become anathema, Senator. Drop the bill from the platform and one of the main rallying cries for both sides is gone, hopefully any further chaos with it. The palm chip thing is weird, Daniels, always has been."

"And if we announce we're throwing out *Cyber-Care*, Annie," Freeman's voice was now tinged with optimism, "it might actually help us to win in the House. Take out Stone's main rallying cry against us. Or maybe even get an elector flip before the vote as well. Annie, it could actually help us win."

"No," Annie mumbled, her perfect face morphing into deeper shock. "No... no..."

Think, think of something, an alternate plan before she loses it.

"Kill two birds with one stone, Annie." Freeman stood and clapped his hands together like everything had been decided. "Calm the tensions in the country and possibly bring more independents to us." He grinned and stroked his yellow tie. "We can still do big things, Annie, just not with *Cyber-Care*, that's all. This is politics, after all, compromises and such."

"Marcus, no."

Henry watched doom wash over her face at the realization all her dreams and efforts were perched on a precipice. He knew he had to think of an alternative to save her quickly or she was going to do something rash.

Annie declared, "If you're killing *Cyber-Care*, then I quit."

Oh God.

"What?" Freeman's hands froze on his yellow tie.

The president's eyebrows rose. Miss Howe looked around, confused. For a moment there was no sound in the room, only two dozen video images of potential violent hotbeds around the globe silently flashing in all their eyes. Henry understood Annie's logic. They had just admitted how much it mattered that she stay on the ticket, so she saw her ability to quit as checkmate. Henry also considered she was possibly going crazy.

Pills, Henry also thought with pangs of love. *It's got to be pills.* "What if," Henry blurted, trying to get an alternate solution out before Annie's concession could possibly be considered real, "there's a way to keep *Cyber-Care* and still calm tensions?" Everyone eyes turned to Henry, even Annie's, although Henry wasn't completely sure she would like what came out of his mouth next. "Senator Daniels and Governor Stone could make a joint speech maybe? Show the country they've reconciled and are willing to accept whatever decision comes from the Electoral College and House on Monday?" Everyone continued staring at him as if they were considering the idea, though Annie's blue eyes froze on him like she was willing icy daggers into his heart. He knew she reviled Governor Stone, and would only marginally tolerate negotiating with Stone more than killing *Cyber-Care,* but it was maybe a way to keep things from self-destructing, maybe, if they would all go for it, including Stone.

"Interesting," the president said.

"You would have to privately apologize to him, Annie," the vice president thought out loud. "And agree to not release the tape you have of him."

"The Senator would just have to convince Governor Stone to do it with her." Henry smiled, as Annie's bitter stare hardened at him.

The president nodded. "If you could mend fences, Annie, a bipartisan speech between our side and theirs stating we're all in agreement on whatever the decision is would certainly go a long way toward keeping things calm. Maybe let me cast a smaller net with *Long Knives.*"

"Mr. President," Annie said, her voice a purr although her eyes still filled with muted rage at Henry. "Even though I would love to reconcile my... error with Governor Stone, he will certainly not agree to meet with me and broker a truce, no matter how much I would like that." Her voice was much too sweet. "Why don't we just stick to our guns and do what's right, just try to win outright?"

"The Thompson boy's funeral," the president said, ignoring Annie's argument in apparent enthusiasm for Henry's idea, and pulling up his sleeve to glance at his watch. "The parents insisted on doing it immediately, Stone invited by the family to give the eulogy. You need to be there too, Daniels. Apologize to him, convince him to do this joint speech of reconciliation." The president glanced to Howe. "So how much can we lessen *Long Knives* by if we count on Annie getting the speech set up for Sunday afternoon?"

"I would have to run the names and numbers again," Howe said. "But I would assume the reduction in the statistical risk would bring us down to only the most risky five hundred or so people."

"Five hundred, that's a big improvement from 5,000," Henry quietly offered at Annie, knowing by her hard glare back she was still furious at him. "And with *Cyber-Care* still having a chance."

"But, sir," Annie countered to the president. "Stone has no desire to meet with me; he probably won't even return my call. With such little time left, we need to simply focus—"

"Yanic Goran is both my book agent and Stone's," the president said, pulling his *RedRabbit* phone out of his pocket again. "I'll get him to set up a private meeting between the two of you."

"But Mr. President—"

"Either take your lumps and apologize to Stone, Daniels,

or I will accept your resignation from the ticket right now." The president glowered at Annie. "Either get Stone to agree to a joint statement to abide by whatever happens on Monday or I will endorse Stone myself."

"Sir," Freeman gasped. "You'd go against your own party, sir?" Then he spun an angry glare to Annie. "This is your only shot to keep *Cyber-Care*, Annie. Well?" The president, Freeman, and Howe all stared at Annie, awaiting either her agreement or the essential end of her political career and the anointing of Governor Hampton Stone as president.

She turned to Henry as she answered with a soft smile and too sweet tone. "I guess I'm heading to Dayton to apologize to Hampton Stone then." And as she spoke, Henry saw the crow's feet crinkling her eyes—she was definitely lying.

* * *

Tweet from Republican Candidate Governor Hampton Stone: *God hates communists, Muslims, deviants and Atheist Annie! Little Joey Thompson's death cannot be in vain! Let's make America American again, idiots!*

* * *

In his French Quarter hotel room overlooking the St. Charles River, a tired Mr. Jefferson hung his black Brioni Vanquish II suit jacket on a wooden hanger and carefully placed it in the closet.

He had two hours until he flew back to DC to implement the next step of *1776*, and he wished to relax, unwind, and maybe even take a brief nap. Mr. Washington had explained to him the country was like a ripe fruit, ready to be plucked, and that this election would change America and the world for the better, as long as the correct side won.

Mr. Jefferson felt he deserved a snack for dealing with these wretched fiends that scurried in the shadows of a broken world. He went to his black satchel and removed a Tupperware container. He popped the lid, held it to his nose, and took a long, lingering whiff, the scent ambrosial. The snack was not still warm, but by the tanned tone was definitely cooked to perfection, a soy sauce basting with a light panko dusting. Something to reward him for his labors, for beginning the purge of lies from this wretched world.

He lit a ceremonial candle and placed it on the table.

A heart is good for strength, Mr. Jefferson pleasantly considered sitting down, *but a ripe fetus, that is the secret to sleep.*

The Country Sleeps

T*he greatest trick the devil ever played,* Amos remembered hearing once, *was convincing the world he doesn't exist.*

Amos still heard buzzing in his half-destroyed ear, and placed a dirty palm to its crusty edge trying to mute the pain. The middle of the night newscast blared from the living room TV, something about another riot, in Dayton maybe, but Amos couldn't pay attention. A yellow, jelly-like substance clung to the fragment of his friend's skull that Amos had just found lodged in his boot.

Amos was sitting on his wife's ugly green and pink flamingo sofa in their family housing unit on MacDill Air Force Base in Tampa, and everything was tilted in his mind. It was hard to breathe. The bone fragment had apparently been blown there when Thump's head had exploded. Staring down at it, his wife yelling at him from the kitchen, Amos wondered for only the second time in his life, really wondered, if Satan was real. Not just in a metaphorical sense, but actually walking the earth, infecting souls with evil, and unleashing demons in the world.

"You're just a brute." Lynn's screams ripped through the

open kitchen doorway over the whir of the microwave. "Like your sister says, you're all Neanderthals." Amos had not even physically seen his wife yet, nor said a word to her. "Destroying the world with your toxic masculinity."

Over the past year, since Amos had been relocated from Fort Bragg to MacDill to oversee testing of the BRAHMAS-TRA system, Lynn had started sleeping through the days and staying awake at night. Lynn didn't work because of needing a "safe space," and she watched reality television thirteen hours a day. She had somehow heard him trying to tiptoe in, though.

"I deserve better. It's been there for TWO days." She was sobbing now

Amos turned his buddy's skull shard between his fingers, still trying to make sense of things. He tried to keep crazy thoughts like demons potentially possessing people out of his mind. Amos had only ever wanted to be a hero like his dad, to serve the people and country he loved.

"And don't try to give me any of your man-splaining bullshit!"

What is she even talking about? Amos felt a wave of exhaustion and blackness, numbness, lapping at his heart. It had been after the *incident* between him and Annie his senior year in high school when he had once before worried the world was too corrupted to save, that the devil was everywhere, or that maybe God had just turned His back. This could not be the way God wanted things, could it? *If He really existed, how could He want this?* He glanced around the living room full of tropical themed furniture and pictures he hated, a plastic fern in the corner. *All of this.* Amos had tried hard to make his marriage work, even giving in to Lynn when she decided to abort their child with all the consideration of taking a dose of aspirin because she didn't "feel ready," but it was all now crashing down in his mind. Not just with him and Lynn; something was completely off with society, like no one believed in anything bigger than themselves now. Like morals and ideals were considered passé, and Amos were somehow a freak from another time. Like everything in the civilian world was about self-promotion and social media bullshit, just a giant, lying, shell game to take for yourself at the expense of others. Maybe the core problem with modern society wasn't people being infected with the devil, but that it was just too easy to get food. There was just too much comfort, not enough struggles to keep people from becoming assholes. Maybe if we all had to spend our time hunting to stay alive all the rest of this materialistic, self-obsessed shit would resolve itself. All the modern bullshit would blow away like a nuclear blast. He looked down to the piece of bone in his hand, his buddy's brains sticking to his finger for fuck's sake.

"Why am I the only one that cares?" Lynn's shouts continued from the kitchen. "Up for two days!"

Amos realized only with great concentration now that Lynn was screaming about an Instagram photo she posted of her new haircut. He had apparently forgotten to publicly *like* it.

"I never thought I'd end up an abused housewife."

Amos had never hurt her, or even raised his voice to her, but he didn't give a fuck about publicly liking things. According to Spec Ops, Amos was not even supposed to get on social media, as Lynn well knew. *This isn't the way it's supposed to be.* He leapt to his feet in panic. *Everything's backward.* Amos' thoughts tangled down around that small, bloody piece of his friend's head in his fingers, it all seeming too hard. He was unsure if he needed to vomit, cry, or just run from this awful place, this pretend home. Maybe getting a truly religious, moral man like Governor Stone into the White House was the only way to correct this world. Stone at least seemed determined to get things done, to make real changes. *This can't be the way it's supposed to be?*

"You have no idea how hard it is." Lynn was now sneering from the kitchen doorway, spooning bits of pink snack cake into her mouth from a soup of melted vanilla ice cream. There was green frosting rubbed into her sweatpants, and her hips pressed against them like she were stuck in a tire. Her new haircut was a bad attempt at Jamaican dreads with little green beads in it and looked fucking ridiculous. "You think it's so easy, keeping this all together?" She chewed with her mouth open. "Me always being sexy and a perfect housewife?" Her haircut actually made her look ten years older than she was, her face grown puffy and fat. "All you know how to do is be a dumb BRO. A stupid jock soldier who never looks outside your own bro bubble." She sniffled. "I even had to restart that vacuum robot three times yesterday, it doesn't work right."

Amos just wanted to be away from her, for his buddy to still be alive. He wanted to have gone down the path in life that led him to being married to Shay with two kids, a black lab, and maybe some boring job involving pencils. Somewhere things made sense.

* * *

Amos collapsed into his deceased father's worn leather chair as soon as he shut the door to his den. He covered his ears to muffle Lynn's continuing tantrum, and reminded himself he'd made a vow to God when he'd married her. Keep his word and things would get better eventually, right? God would help him, right?

Pitch-black in the room, Amos gripped the leather arms of his dad's old chair. The one whose legs Amos used to play toy soldiers under, back when he and his sister still trusted each other, back when Amos wouldn't have been able to imagine anyone in the world being sad for longer than an afternoon. All Amos had ever wanted was to be good, to do good things, and have a wife and family that loved and respected him. Kids. Laughter. Peace and honor, but something had gone wrong. Sitting in the dark, Amos felt completely alone.

His eyes adjusted and he saw the small particleboard desk; books, a laptop he never used, and the Bible he had owned since junior high. A dusty bottle of Jim Beam sour mash whiskey. Amos never drank, and only had the bottle as a reminder of his dad after taking it from his father's kitchen once he had passed. For the first time, Amos seriously considered opening the bottle and taking a drink. What would Amos do with his life if the debriefing with Harper went bad this afternoon, if he was stripped of his command for Thump's death? But faith had always been an innate reflex to Amos, as natural as flight to birds, and even as he had those dark thoughts his fingers absently went to the crucifix around his neck. The cross Annie had given him when they were still friends.

The world has to be good at its core, Amos argued to himself. *God has to be real, because there just couldn't be any other way. Right?* He didn't reach for the bourbon, but the Bible, hoping to find comfort in its words. Instead Amos found Shay Wheeler's smiling picture from fifteen years earlier.

The picture of his high school girlfriend slid from its dusty pages, fluttering into his lap. Amos smiled. Shay Wheeler had been the love of his life. He had forgotten he put the photo there, but it reminded Amos of when his soul and the world were still perfectly aligned. Looking down at her gorgeously lopsided grin, the rivers of long ink-black hair and light-brown skin, Amos remembered the purest peace and passion he had ever felt. He hadn't seen a photo of her in a decade, and was simultaneously haunted with joy and sadness at the thought of her probably married with kids. *How lucky that guy would be.* Amos had heard that she was an up-and-coming political reporter for some news magazine, but in an effort to give his marriage its best shot, he had always avoided hearing too much about her.

When they had been together in high school the world had seemed flawless, and love had burst through his heart as natural as the sun's rays through a cloud. Eyes like a doe and skin the color of coffee with just the right amount of cream, she had the blackest, straightest, longest hair. Her dad was Iranian, and her mom was an Ethiopian-hippie-English-Taoist, whatever that was. Shay always jokingly referred to herself as a Muslim mutt. She had a laugh so genuine it seemed to warm the world. For young Amos, Shay Wheeler had been a luminous beauty to spur armies; near her he felt like Lancelot, Beowulf, Hercules. The peace he had felt falling asleep in her long dark hair, the fire he had felt with her lips against his, and the truth he knew when her warm whispers were in his ear were all the proof he would ever need to know that God was real.

Amos breathed deep and pulled his crucifix out from under his shirt. He took it off his neck and clutched it in both hands, looked down at its tarnished silver and its tiny pink stones. Amos dropped forward out of the chair, knees down onto the rug to pray. First for the Lord to forgive his sins, his own failings, and then for guidance to help him make the right choices in the future. Then he prayed for everyone, that their burdens might be eased, including and most especially, Lynn. Last but not least, he prayed for Thump's family, and for Stork. Prayed that Stork wouldn't be too distraught over the accident—

Amos' eyes opened wide. His hands dropped to his sides as illumination sparked across his brain.

Stork, Amos realized, had been nowhere in the room when the Nicaraguan official mentioned *1776*. Stork also could not have heard that term in the transport plane home either—no one had mentioned *1776*... until Stork did.

Stork, Amos realized as he climbed back to his feet with his crucifix clutched so tight it cut into the flesh of his closed fist, had lied.

Approximately 51 Hours Until Electoral College Vote

(Washington, D.C.: Saturday, 6:03 a.m. PST / 9:03 a.m. EST)

Morning News Headlines:

Country Torn Ahead of Electoral Vote

Joey's Thompson's Death Must Bring Gun Control!

Chicago Muslims Begin Protest to Stop Racial Profiling

Mississippi Republicans beat up Dems in 'Retaliation for Dayton'

Black Lives Matter calls for urban gangs to 'Protect' fellow Dems

Kardashian/Jenners Dedicate All-Nude Photo Shoot to "Jesus"

* * *

What if I'm actually still tripping, Harmony wondered just prior to seeing the albino man in the dark overcoat with the snake birthmark on his cheek. It was déjà vu, like remembering him from a dream maybe? She glimpsed porcelain white skin, strange pink eyes, and for moment thought it was almost like a white bunny had morphed into a man.

The albino passed her on the sidewalk of downtown DC and she smelled strange spices, her heart skipping a beat. He appeared to have just emerged from the storefront of a US Military Recruitment Center and was now walking at a brisk pace up ahead, efficiently slipping in and around many other well-dressed professionals hustling through the chilly dawn. She hadn't been able to sleep, and was definitely groggy as she walked through the misty morning light to find an early morning cup of coffee, but the side of his pale head with the weird birthmark caught her attention like a beacon. Like she had seen him somewhere before.

I can't still be tripping, can I? Did I dream about someone with pink eyes last night?

She'd been feeling weird ever since yesterday's DMT experiment back in Cali, mostly unable to remember its details, but then was suddenly overcome with bizarre fears that if hallucinations could be so real, maybe this too, all of life, was still a dream? *How do I know this is real?* Her heart fluttered. *What if the drug from yesterday really hasn't worn off and I'm just imaging all this?*

She halted on the icy DC sidewalk, glanced through the morning half-light at her palms to make sure there was no blood, then told herself to relax. *You're fine. Breathe.* A quick touch to her forehead—no blood. *Thank God. He probably works for Mom's campaign or something, that's where you've seen him before.*

Frantic Washington suits crunched past Harmony over the dirty sidewalk ice-films, scurrying to some silly meeting or job and Harmony imagined how they'd stare at her in horror if red blood started streaming down her face. Harmony had never liked Washington, DC. It reeked of manipulation, of adults selling out ideals for the slightest smattering of applause, or another pocketful of money they would spend on stupid materialistic stuff they didn't need. Washington seemed a ridiculous place of supposed grown humans arguing over the smallest minutiae of laws and policies to keep everything negative rather than ever just embracing the bigger positives that could help everyone get along. With angst, she suddenly imagined dark tendrils, like smoke, creeping into the hearts of all the people passing her. She imagined it infecting their souls and turning them all on each other, wearing red shirts or blue shirts, attacking each other in the streets with knives and bricks and bats and fists. *Breathe,* she told herself again. *Think positive. You're not still on DMT, just tired.* She clutched her black handbag tighter against her red coat, and forced herself to smile. *Just fine.* Luckily, the albino guy up ahead was oddly attractive. Odd being the prominent part. She followed him. *You only live once after all.*

Love was what had woken Harmony in her DC hotel room before the sun rose this morning—the fear of dying without ever knowing it. Harmony had already out negotiated her exhausted mom to let her wait in DC rather than getting back on the plane for Annie's short daytrip to Ohio. She had easily snuck past the Secret Service at the hotel in search of good coffee. She had twisted her blonde hair into two long pigtails, threw on her favorite red pea coat, and wrapped a plaid scarf around her neck. With each precious second of her life seeming to tick away faster and faster, she would wander the streets of DC by herself and attempt to find something at least mildly true with whatever breaths she had left. Or, maybe love?

She darted around the occasional suit headed in the opposite direction keeping her eyes on the pale guy's back and trying to think good thoughts. He couldn't have been older than twenty-seven, thirty tops, and there were plenty of couples with a fifteen-year age difference. His hair was cropped close and white, and strangest of all there was that prominent snake-like purplish birthmark running down one cheek. Even more than his looks and his sharp black suit, it was something about his ultra-serious way of marching through the crowd, intensity radiating from him, which made him weird. Violent. Primal. Thrilling? As Harmony followed she pulled a pen and a piece of paper from her purse, began to jot down her name and number to give to him. *Nothing to fear, dead girl, except fear itself.*

She was relieved when he finally darted into the Pandu and Sons Coffee shop to put both of her morning goals in one spot. The coffee shop had rickety red shutters and a big red metallic coffee roaster in the corner of the skinny space. A sign in the window read, *roasted here*. It had just a small stainless steel coffee bar with simple hardwood stools, warmth fogging against the big windowpane, and it sang out all the no-nonsense Harmony loved and respected. No mass-produced chains with their evil greedy ways for this girl, the place hit her right in the feels. Some of the stools even looked broken.

She entered the paint-chipped door with a tiny bell jangle. The choco-woodsy smell of fresh roasted beans sizzled a thin stream of bliss to her cold nose, her achy body heating at the thought of a crisp caffeine spark on this chilly winter day. The line was about four deep, and Harmony tried to finally suck up her courage as she sidled in behind the unique-looking man. She reminded herself that with every action, an entire new timeline of life events opened up.

"Knock, knock," Harmony said to his back, a nervous girly pitch to her voice she immediately regretted.

He peered back out of the corner of his eye with what could best be described as mild disdain, his irises pink.

She flashed a radiant smile, her heart thumping with fear, but incredibly alive. He was so weird, spooky even, with the snake birthmark on his cheek. He was badass. But he turned back without saying anything, took a step forward in line.

What the? Prior to getting sick Harmony had never been shy, and in fact had objectively realized from an early age that almost everyone really appreciated her presence. She knew she was beautiful, knew she was positive, knew she was nice. So genuinely nice in fact, she often honestly tried to forget that she was beautiful. *What I'm not though, is okay with being ignored.* "Who's there," she stated to his tall back with a following step. "That's how you answer when someone tries to tell you a knock-knock joke, you ask, 'who's there?' And then, see, I would say—"

"Harmony Daniels," the albino stated before continuing on to the counter.

Harmony's stomach dropped like she was about to go over the crest of a roller coaster. *So I do know him?* She was both a bit creeped out and intrigued. *How do I know him?*

Watching the weirdo place his order, she couldn't help but smile trying to remember how they met. He had an utter lack of courteous expression or any friendly words or movements, and even though Harmony loved when people were nice, she also knew the ruder, colder people often turned out to be the most sincere if you could break through their shell. Besides, think of all the clichéd times they used albinos in books and stories as bad guys for nothing more than a pigmentation problem, he had a right to be a little pissed at society. She waited for him to turn back to her and explain.

He did not. After placing his order, he glided past her to one of the hardwood stools that faced out the big glass window onto the sidewalk. With his green bottle of mineral water in hand, he sat at the open stool farthest from any other person, staring out the window as if he were waiting for something to happen.

Jerk, Harmony playfully thought as she stepped to the counter. She placed her order with her eyes continually darting over to him. He never turned back from watching the hustle and bustle of the sidewalk outside though, the cars passing in the DC street. By the time the barista handed Harmony her coffee in a big red cup, she had also noticed the guy hadn't bothered to even twist the cap open on his bottle of water, the one he'd just spent five minutes waiting in line for. *What a freaking weirdo. A wonderful, amazing weirdo.*

She strolled up behind him, and coughed.

Nothing.

Don't waste time you don't have, dead girl. Give him your number.

She exhaled, bolstered her courage.

"Look, sorry if I was being silly," she said with a smile. She placed the paper with her number on it on the counter next to his arm. "You'll probably need the digits to go with the name." Harmony sat down on the stool next to him. "So what's yours?"

She leaned over into his view with a bigger smile. She looked directly at the side with the prominent birthmark to let him know it was okay. It looked so much like a snake, head and tail slithering down his cheek, it could have almost been a tattoo except it was raised flesh. "And remind me, where do we know each other from?" She wondered if it was possible to fall in love over a single cup of coffee. There was an automatic termination date to their passionate love story with her impending offing anyway, so neither of them could weird out over anything getting too serious. It was only shyness over his condition that made him distant, she was sure, and she could certainly relate to that. "Are you involved with my mom's campaign, or—"

"What if," he still stared out the window, "you ARE chosen by God, Harmony Daniels? Your affliction, the stigmata bleeding, how do you know it is not a sign from God? Or… the devil?"

"What?" Harmony's heart began thumping harder. "How…?" No one knew Harmony had the disease except for her mom's innermost circle, a few doctors and nurses sworn to secrecy. That was one thing they had been extremely careful about. The vast majority of people working on her mother's campaign had no idea Harmony was sick, so how could this stranger know one of the most intimate details of her life. "Look, I truthfully don't—"

"But what do you know of truth?" the man interrupted her, his face turning with a scowl, his pink eyes torching into her. "Is truth absolute? Subjective? Your arrogance only feeds the guna of rajas."

"I… ?" Harmony was a little scared, and a little offended. "My arrogance? The guna—what?" *Is there still DMT in my system?* Looking into his weird pink eyes she suddenly remembered a time when her dad had been teaching her to drive. With her dad in the passenger seat of their jeep she had realized it was completely within the simple flick of her wrist on the wheel to send them careening over the Pacific Coast Highway cliffs and into the ocean. It had been a strange, horrifying pull toward her own destruction, for no reason but an instinctual urge to know the truth of everything once and for all, even death. *The DMT must still be messing with me.* "Who... who are you?"

"Truth which can be spoken," he whispered closer to her, "can never be eternal truth." She suddenly smelled the pungent spices again, like cinnamon and cloves and coriander and things she somehow thought she remembered even though she had never experienced them. "Decide, Harmony Daniels, just decide. Are you chosen or not?"

Harmony's heart quivered again, unsure if it was love or fear. It was like he was looking into her with those bizarre pink eyes to see everything she thought she could cover, and she was unsure if she wanted to run from him, or follow him into oblivion. Her breath shallowed, her lungs tightened. "I... I don't know." Her heart was beating faster, and she was beginning to feel dizzy, desperately not wanting to have another attack in public, desperately just wanting normalcy. "My condition is..." She put a hand to head to stop the swaying. "I'm... I'm just sick."

"Nothing is JUST." He said. "All has meaning and soon, dead girl, you will help us burn the lies from this world."

"What?" she gasped, the room spinning.

"Truth comes." He snatched up the paper with her cell phone number on it as he stood, the stool squeaking against the polished stone floor. "Truth does come."

"Wait." She gasped for breath, her heart thumping wildly with the overwhelming sense of déjà surging over her again. *The DMT? Or have I dreamt this? Or...* She felt the wave of panic, unsure of what was real, hoping the blood did not begin to pour. "How do you know..."

But the strange man was already gone. She rocked with dizziness and threw both hands out to the counter for support, accidentally knocking her cup off in the process. Coffee splattered on the stool and over the floor, the cup bouncing and rolling across it. The albino's departure was so fluid and quick that by the time any customer bothered to look at the sound of the bouncing cup and the dripping liquid it simply seemed as if a silly young girl had spilt her drink.

Harmony Speaks with the Serpent

(Somewhere Over Pennsylvania: Saturday, 6:46 a.m. PST / 9:46 p.m. EST)

"Christ, stop bothering me, Henry," Annie grumbled over the drone of the plane's engines. "I've got something up my sleeve for Hampton Stone."

Henry was in the doorway to her private cabin on the campaign plane, his thin frame still draped in the ugly corduroy slacks and bulky tweed blazer, beard so black it looked like someone had dipped it in paint. "Up your sleeve?"

Annie couldn't stand when he got the self-righteous whine to his fake male voice.

"You lied to the president's face?" The papers he clutched trembled in agitation. "Why agree to the president's reconciliation plan if you were just going to come up with your own?"

"Don't you mean YOUR reconciliation plan, Corwich?" Annie was already feeling claustrophobic the way he was crowding the door. The private cabin on the plane wasn't very big, only large enough for the laminate desk, a chair, and a sofa that could be pulled out into a tightly fitting bed for overnight trips. Annie had known Henry for nearly fifteen years, and she was pretty sure he had been in love with her the whole time. Maybe if he had stayed a lesbian named Henrietta though he might have had a better chance in those wild college experimentation days? "Can't believe I'm now having to meet with that scum, Henry," she grumbled. Annie was more than a little pissed off at Henry for putting her in the position in the Situation Room of having to agree to fly to Ohio and meet with Stone in the first place, and she couldn't decide if she felt more like manipulating his schoolboy crush into winning the argument, or just swatting him like a fly and kicking him the hell out. She turned from him to wrangle her blonde hair into a loose bun and jab a pencil from her desk into its heart to make it stay. She could feel his longing eyes tracing the curves of her breasts and ribcage beneath the blue blouse. "Thanks."

"Regardless, the president and vice president are now counting on you. Do you mind letting me in on what plan you could have possibly formulated so brilliant as to betray the Executive Branch of the United States government?"

"I said I've got it under control." She crossed her long legs, purposely letting the gray skirt inch just a bit higher up her taut thigh as she propped an elbow on her small desk. She glared back into his forever worried face with her icicle eyes, wondering where the hair came off his female body to originally make the beard. *Pubic?* "Letting Fuentes think I'm doing what he wants keeps the *Long Knives* Operation minimized. I couldn't disagree without him dishonestly rounding up thousands of Americans and killing *Cyber-Care,* overtly or by public perception, in the process."

"And what about keeping your word, Senator? Is there any dishonestly there?"

"You look nice today." She fluttered her eyes over his crotch to purposely scratch his longing mind with naughty thoughts, then inhaled with a bigger smile as she looked into his worried eyes. Seduction or destruction, whichever served the greater the goal. Her red lips parted and her chest expanded with a gentle inhale as her body language cast the subtlest of sexual clues toward him. Secretly, Annie could never imagine being with a man recently morphing into existence from a witch's brew of hormones and the slicing and dicing of flesh. *What the hell could possibly be going on down there anyway?* "New blazer?"

"I haven't worn a different blazer in two years." Henry's tone was too frustrated to give in to her veiled flirting, his bloodshot eyes strained. "Lying is—"

"Smart. If it serves the greater good," Annie was suddenly more exhausted than ever. "I'm not going to lose the most important election in modern American history based on misplaced ideals of moral absolutes. We aren't children for fuck's sake." On the days she wasn't feeling deep friendship for Henry there was a mild disgust at his pathetic loyalty, like a dog that would wag its tail at her no matter how often she beat it. And in the rare times he proved difficult, showed a backbone, it really pissed her off, like that dog unexpectedly biting back. "I will do what is necessary to win and get this country changed for the better, that's what's right. Now drop it."

"It's just..." Henry took a deep breath, his tone annoyingly concerned. "It's just that you've been acting a bit erratic, Annie. What with the speech, and now lying to the president and Marcus Freeman. What if Howe is right and—"

"Howe doesn't have shit, and I refuse to see bogeymen in every corner, Henry. It's two days to go, that's it, two days. Whose side are you on?"

"But are there really pills, Annie? Are you taking something you shouldn't be? How are you going to pull off a plan—"

"How dare you." Annie's lip curled in a feign of self-righteous insult. "Of course, not." She swiveled her chair away from Henry's pathetically concerned face toward the tiny window. She looked out at a massive cloudbank, wondering if she might as well just pull the bottle of Zennies out and gulp a couple right now. She needed something to take the edge off, help her relax and to feel confident in herself that everything was going to be okay, especially now with the risky plan she had come up with. She just needed to keep it together for forty eight more hours despite her exhaustion, her thoughts splintering sadly to Harmony, as they did every few minutes. "Now you're suddenly accusing me of being on drugs just because I'm the only one with the balls to actually still try and win this election?"

"You're lying, I can tell," Henry surprisingly snapped back. "You get crow's feet."

"Fine. Get lost then." She glanced at the bottle of Jim Beam whiskey on the far corner of her laminate desk and considered chugging it.

"Twelve Congressional Republicans." Henry leaned in to drop papers on the edge of her desk like they bolstered his point. "They've written an op-ed in the *Wall Street Journal* calling on YOU to quit, because of your *God is Lie* thing and the riot."

"Oh, so sweet of them." Annie rolled her eyes to the low ceiling. "Seems no one ever takes the time to actually write anymore."

"They've detailed every divisive word you've said, every questionable action you've ever made, listing them all in chronological order back to your college thesis."

"So?" Her eyes drifted back out the window ignoring

him, wishing he'd vanish. *Just two more Zennies won't hurt,* she thought, looking on the endless sea of sunlit white clouds, so craggy and motionless they almost looked like an inviting mountaintop to escape across. *Why does it matter if Henry knows about the pills, he'd die before betraying me.* She imagined stepping off onto the cloudbank, walking away barefoot over a craggy white landscape illuminated in golden rays. *Two more won't hurt.*

"Annie, they've even got the college sex tape on here." Henry thumped a thin finger at the papers.

Annie put her hand with the ragged red nails to her temple, blonde strands swinging down from the bun as she dipped her head. "I never put that tape out to the public. Everyone knows it was my lying ex-boyfriend who did it, and it's men who are the ones beating off to it. If anything all those old senators should be writing me thank you letters."

"The point is...," Henry let a barely audible sigh escape. "In response to the op-ed, the *Civil Liberties Union,* several collegiate and atheist and LGBT groups along with the *African-American Equality League,* are already calling online for public rallies of support for you."

"Well, isn't that a good thing? Sounds like problem solved." Annie's blue blouse clad shoulders shrugged. "Let's get drunk. By the way, did you buy Mr. Daniels a birthday tie?"

Annie's husband had taken Annie's last name in a show of feministic support. The real reason she had even started to date her Chinese basketball star husband in the first place was because he had been collegiate captain of the basketball team and it had helped raise her profile to win her first Harvard election. The pregnancy had happened though, and despite being pro-choice to the core Annie had decided to keep Harmony.

Annie regularly imagined divorcing her husband after the start of her second presidential term. It wasn't that Mr. Daniels wasn't nice, he was possibly the nicest man she'd ever met, but besides for ticking off a public-electability issue for her, that also made him utterly boring to her.

"My point is that further rallies, even in support of you, will cause other rallies against you by the Republicans and raise the risk level Fuentes is worried about."

Annie yawned. "So did Mr. Daniels like it?"

Henry shoved his hands in the ugly corduroy pockets, his dark brows, like two black caterpillars, furrowed. "Word is Buddy Dukes is heading to Texas tonight in a show of support for those ranchers claiming we're going to repeal Second Amendment gun rights if we win and use imminent domain to scoop up all their land. With Dayton, if anything else goes wrong between now and Monday something awful could happen, especially if Howe's suspicions are correct." He yanked the cabin door shut, spinning back like he was really ready to argue now. "If you're not going to take anything but your little secret plan serious, would you at least mind updating me as to what the hell it is now?"

"So you can talk me out of it?"

"Yes. You PROMISED the president and vice president."

"I am not," Annie growled, "apologizing to that repugnant, fraudulent, Hampton Stone, Henry. Any joint speech with me and Stone only plays into their hands, lets Republican hate mongers stealing this election seem more legitimate. If I've got to lie or deceive to win the war, so be it."

"Breaking your word to Fuentes or manipulating people isn't just trying to win, Annie, it's wrong."

"Wrong?" Annie snorted, her thin blonde eyebrows rising

in genuine fascination. "According to who? You? Men? The Bible? This is about logic versus hate, about right versus wrong for generations, Corwich, and I have a way for us to win outright without an electoral tie. That's what's right, not how we get there."

Henry's mouth dropped open. "You can't be serious, Annie. You can't really give up on morals just because you believe ALL Republicans are bad."

"Whose morals, Henry? In a logical world the end always justifies the means, abstract ideals are for the sentimentally weak and the hypocritical con men like Stone who manipulate them. There's nothing smart about living by rules your opponent doesn't. It's simple: Republicans ARE bad, and it's our moral imperative to win."

"Come on." Henry threw his hands in the air, "you can't believe that. All Republicans aren't bad, just like ALL Democrats aren't good. The two-party system is just bullshit T-shirts and simple slogans—a sales pitch so we all get to keep jobs and make money, not an actual demarcation line between good and evil."

"Are you saying there's no difference between intelligent progressives and bigoted right-wingers?" Annie scowled in disbelief at her most trusted aide's declaration. "I've certainly never been in politics to make money. The very idea of freedom could be a thing of the past if Stone gets his hands on the *Uncle's Eyes* power."

"Whose freedom? If you insist on going your own way, then at least explain who gets to decide what's protected, what's limited? In a world where everyone is monitored by *Cyber-Care* or *Uncle's Eyes*, who gets to decide where the line of right and wrong is? You?"

"Logic does," Annie snorted in surprise. "We're the good guys. We're fighting for science, for logic, for... progress."

"And what if we aren't as smart as we think we are, Annie? What if there are things we don't understand? Like the president said, just because we have the technology doesn't mean we always should use it."

"I don't know where you're going with this, Henry, but technology is obviously good." Annie's spine straightened and she crossed her arms over her chest. "In fact, intelligence might be the only absolute good. It evolves society."

"Like the Internet enabling ISIS to recruit American teenagers in their own bedrooms? Or genetic manipulation systems like CRSPR creating a super race only the wealthy can afford? Or... artificial intelligence potentially turning on us, or... or *Flakka 3.0*?"

"What are you babbling about?"

"*Flakka 3.0* is a drug that can be made in any American garage, with technology easily obtained over the Internet. It's tasteless, odorless, and not only gets you high for cheap, but you supposedly never come down. Some people in Miami even getting cannibal urges from getting inadvertently dosed with it in weed. Is that the way you see technology and science always being good? That progress? If we can create it, we should do it, regardless of any moral consideration?"

"What the hell that has to do with *Cyber-Care* providing healthcare and stopping hate mongers? You're just irrationally scared of the palm chip too? How about the forehead then?"

"Because what if there are things in the universe we can't yet understand? Have you ever considered that SOME Republicans might be right about SOME things?"

"Like what?" Annie smirked in disbelief at the words

coming out of her oldest friend's mouth. "Believing in an old white man in the clouds, or denying the overwhelming evidence of climate change for more oil profits? Maybe that birth control is the same as murder? Maybe, Henry, you want some pedophile priest telling us all the right way to live, is that it?"

He slapped two hands to the sides of his beard in exasperation, groaned. "There doesn't have to be just binary choices between everything, Annie, like Republican OR Democrat. Why do we have to choose between big-brother government controlling everything OR only corrupt capitalism for the greedy one percent. Red OR Blue, black OR white, either science OR God. Maybe we don't need to throw out the idea of a higher power just because of some loudmouthed perverts claiming to speak for it. Why does everything in this country have to be extreme? What if there's SOME truth in all of it?"

"Some truth in what?" Annie chuckled. "God?" She cocked a quizzical eyebrow at him. "Did you get cornered by those Jehovah Witnesses at the airport? They buy you a smoothie or something?"

Henry's face hardened. "Whether or not something exists after death is probably the most important question we can ask?"

"Not in politics. God has no place in American politics."

"Correct," Henry crossed his arms. "Unless God exists, and then it pretty much has a place in everything. All I'm saying, is just self-identifying with the word science or wearing a blue Democratic T-shirt doesn't mean you understand everything in the world. You might want to remember that you aren't God either, Annie, and you don't have all the answers."

"No, because God doesn't exist." Her eyes burrowed

into him. "But science does, Henry, and it DOES have all the answers."

"Then explain consciousness to me." Henry nervously pulled out one of the gross half-chewed cigars from his coat pocket and began twirling it in his fingers. "Or the Big Bang. Can science explain those? Something just exploded from nothing? And science hasn't come close to explaining how we actually have consciousness from a bunch of chemicals swirling in brain matter. You're putting your FAITH in so-called 'science' despite not having any evidence. Not very scientific."

"Using Philosophy 101 arguments against me?" Annie rolled her eyes and reached for the bottle of bourbon. "So science can't answer that... yet. So what?" She poured a couple fingers worth of the bourbon into a glass.

"It matters because they are a core factor in determining what the real world is. If you can't answer those core questions, then the scientific method would state we DON'T fully know exactly what reality is. Whether God or some other worldly things are actually true or not. It's about avoiding arrogance."

"Jesus fucking Christ, isn't it a little late in the game for you to be becoming a fundamentalist?" She slugged some whiskey into her mouth. "We don't need God, Henry. And we all know what's real, Henry—REALITY." Annie pushed her seat back to get a few inches further from him and touched fingers to the pill bottle hidden in her skirt pocket. "Hell, I'll even admit when I was a kid I prayed, like every kid, but no supernatural things ever happened, no God appeared to change things for the better, shit still went bad regardless." Her voice dropped lower and she squinted one eye to kill the whisper of a tear as she thought of her sick daughter. "I waited, and waited for a long time, Henry, waited for just one miraculous thing, one unexplainable thing for a loving God, so I could have faith, but no miracles have ever happened. My dad still did what he did, my brother and I still don't speak, and Harmony might still die." She shook her head, two stray blonde strands from the pinned up bun swaying over her shoulders. "So what, if we can't explain how we have consciousness or the origin of the Big Bang, yet."

"Because something from nothing isn't a math problem, Annie, it IS a miracle." Henry's voice got softer and his eyes kinder. "There are potential miracles all around us, every day, if we chose to see them."

"Fuck off," Annie snorted. She pulled the Zennie bottle out of her pocket, shaking the last two pink pills into her palm, surprised that was the end of the bottle. Hallucination. Seizure. Foot rash. Possible Stroke. Those were the list of potential side effects on the Zennie bottle, but their pretty pink gave her comfort, and the FDA did approve them once after all. "I need to relax."

"Are those," Henry's voice became shrill. "Are those the PILLS you mentioned? What are they, Annie? What are you taking?"

"Science and booze," Annie said with a smirk as she popped the shimmering pink pills into her mouth and chased them with a gulp of Kentucky bourbon. "Only saviors I know of."

"Annie." Henry's glare went hard. "You can't afford any more mis—"

"Calm down," she snapped. "This fucking campaign's been going a year and a half, I deserve some enjoyment too occasionally. And they're prescribed." For Harmony, of course, and recalled, but she was sick of people telling her what to do, especially a fake man.

"With whiskey?" Henry stammered.

"Good Lord," Annie growled, slapping the glass down on the desk. "You're so boring, Henrietta. When they globbed a fake dick out of your ass fat, did they also give you an instruction manual on how to be an overbearing bully or is that just a side effect of the pig testosterone?" And Annie immediately felt guilt at the harshness of her words as Henry's face flushed red. She just wanted to relax for a bit though, not think about all this shit for at least a couple hours when nothing was likely to go wrong. "I am the one in charge, I'm the one running for office, and you best not forget that." Then she thought about the empty pill bottle in her hand. "As a matter of fact, get this refilled for me." She tossed it at him.

Henry reflexively caught the bottle, and glowered down at it sadly, sheepishly.

"And yes, I did lie about them being prescribed for me, but figure it out, dammit. I want more by the time we get to the fucking church."

"Annie," he whispered, "I just don't want things to go wrong for you. I care about you and what if everything matters, just in ways we don't fully under—"

"Thank you, Henry," she interrupted as she brought up one hand to pull the pencil out of her hair, blonde lengths spilling over her shoulders with a shake of her head. She unbuttoned the top of her blue blouse, and started to slowly massage the side of her long neck with one hand as she felt the pathetic pressure of Henry's needy, love-struck eyes again, the weakness of his spiritual longing. "Now send in Eli. And tell Castor to watch the door on your way out."

Henry's face hardened to crimson, his narrowing eyes now a bloodshot combination of hurt and wrath.

"What?" Annie scoffed. "You can turn yourself into a man but I'm supposed to always be a sweet, polite, truthful lady because society demands it?" She looked out the window, absently twirling a finger in her hair like a little girl as she brought the bourbon glass up to her nose again with the other. "And tell Eli to brush his teeth." Nothing infuriated poor, sad Henry more than when Annie fucked the help.

Senator Daniels Flies to Ohio

(Various Locations Around Country: Saturday, 7:21 a.m. PST / 10:21 a.m. EST)

M r. Jefferson used many aliases on the Internet, including *@whoreads*.

On one of the numerous blogs, forums, and social media sites Mr. Jefferson anonymously participated in was man who went by *@jessejameskickass*. Without provocation, Mr. Jefferson privately sent a message to *@jessejameskickass* that read: *The government is secretly controlled by Muslims and they're coming for your guns. Look outside.*

* * *

@jessejameskickass was a thirty-two year old steelworker in Birmingham, Alabama. He preferred to wear a trucker's cap with the words Get Some bedazzled on its front. He was white, had one brown tooth, lived in an apartment from the 1980s that reeked of fungus, and every night saw examples in television beer, car, and phone commercials of how glorious his life was actually supposed to be. Despite being a loyal, dedicated worker though, *@jessejameskickass* had not been able to get a raise in six years and had therefore not been able to get the fungus smell

out of his apartment or get his one brown tooth stained white. His girlfriend left him for something less 'ghetto.'

He had never considered himself a racist, but did have a Confederate flag on his main social media page, a symbol of his favorite country band. Over the past two years he'd grown increasingly more bewildered and frustrated as strangers sought him out online to call him a bigot and try to bully him into taking the flag down. They claimed, as a white man, he should be more grateful and respectful for everything he had in life, but *@jessejameskickass* was pretty sure what he had sucked. He was beginning to suspect someone was intentionally screwing him, but he didn't know who. Black people? Liberals? Foreigners?

When *@jessejameskickass* received the mysterious message from *@whoreads* he was at home. His work hours had recently been cut due to something management only explained as 'Chinese competition.' He was lonely, missing his girlfriend, bored, and broke, trying to tune out the brown-skinned family's foreign language jabbering next door, so he could just enjoy some MMA fights on TV. Upon seeing the strange message from *@whoreads*, out of curiosity, *@jessejameskickass* put down his bowl of grits and leaned from his sofa to peer outside through his white blinds.

Across the street from his shitty apartment complex was Ashby Guns, a gun store he often frequented and whose owner he considered a friend. It was also where their area's monthly *Oath Keepers* meeting was held, which was a conservative group of volunteers that carried firearms to public events in order to provide additional security for members of churches, the military, or people trying to demonstrate for their constitutional rights; one of the few things left in life *@jessejameskickass* could do that made him feel like a useful man.

Now though, at the entrance to Ashby Guns, two of President Fuentes' black, window-tinted, *Long Knives* ordered vans had pulled up, red lights ominously flashing. *@jessejameskickass'* heart skipped a beat. Several imposing men in black suits and shades, some with brownish-skin, like the suspicious foreign family he could never understand next door, were leading the protesting gun store owner into one of the van's back doors, his hands zip-tied in front of him.

Holy shit. *@jessejameskickass* dropped back from the window, the blinds snapping closed as his heart thumped in increasing panic. Is what the weird text said right? Were some of the more crazy conspiracies he had read online true? Was someone trying to warn him that he was about to be hunted down and arrested for simply being a white, Christian man, the government already in the clutches of the evil Muslims or worse? *Those motherfuckers,* he thought with a deep whiff of that damned fungal smell in his apartment. *Those goddamn motherfuckers have always been trying to screw me.*

Suddenly incredibly angry *@jessejameskickass* ripped his trucker's hat off and threw it across the room at his Kate Upton poster. He thought about going outside and finding someone to punch in the face, but knew it was better to use your words, if you could, than resort to violence. Before he'd thought much about it, *@jessejameskickass* fired off a private message to a loudmouthed liberal black guy on the forum, *@professorofplants.* He often suspected *@professorofplants* was a Muslim, and *@jessejameskickass'* unsolicited message to him read: "*Y'all better watch your dumb dark asses, or swear to God I'll start shooting!*"

* * *

@professorofplants was actually a forty-two-year-old female

professor of botany at a large university near Chicago, Illinois. She was Kenyan by heritage, but was born and raised in Chicago.

Chicago had a horrible violent crime problem, with one person shot every three hours, nearly 800 people murdered each year, and the vast majority of them were black. She was very troubled by the recent racial and religious tensions across the country, and during the heated election campaign had sadly started to wonder if some problems just couldn't be solved with communication anymore; if there were simply too many ignorant, dangerous people in the world to ever completely talk things out. She suspected they all lived in the south. She also saw a lot of beer, car, and phone commercials each night that let her know what her life was supposed to be like, and suspected she was getting screwed by someone. *@professorofplants* was on her way to class to give a lecture on medical marijuana research to about three hundred students when she received the unsolicited, unexpected, and altogether horrifying private message from someone called *@jessejameskickass.* As she walked she decided she must do something to warn the youth of this country, before it was too late, that racism was alive and well. Wasn't that her duty as a teacher?

By the time *@professorofplants* began her lecture, she had decided to forgo the talk on medical marijuana and start a much-needed discussion about race relations in America. She started by citing how white men were the ones historically instigating mass shootings around the country, far worse than any minority or foreign terrorism. Surprisingly, the main question she found herself asking the students several times was, *is maybe the solution to modern America's ills not gun control, but for students of color, minorities, and women, the victims, to* *just begin carrying guns themselves?* Several students in her class were broadcasting her lecture via Periscope, uploading it to the Internet in real time.

* * *

@socialjusticewarrior was a young, Buddhist, semi-pro Frisbee player in Seattle, Washington, who tried to stay current on the most enlightened, progressive, and socially redeeming thoughts and trends despite the incessant rain. He often saw beer, car and phone commercials showing how his life was supposed to be, and suspected he was getting screwed. It was when he happened to watch a Periscope broadcast of a brave Chicago university professor encouraging her students to stop being bullied and carry guns that he was finally inspired to action.

With the noblest of intentions, he started tapping the keys of his computer, feeling a warm rush of pride as he quickly made an Internet meme of a picture of broken-nosed Rosa Sanchez immediately after the riot in the park, just after she had been attacked by that bigoted white man. *@socialjusticewarrior* typed the words *Hate Against Muslims Must Stop* at the bottom of her picture. Even though he considered she might not actually be Muslim, she certainly looked Muslim enough with her dark hair and skin, and how could trying to raise awareness against intolerance ever be wrong? He began posting the meme online.

* * *

@mrsCee978 was a Jewish, fifty-five-year-old elementary school teacher in Burlington, Vermont, whose well-off husband had recently left her for a young stripper with duck lips and pain pills. Oddly, that never happened in all the beer

commercials that showed her the way her life was supposed to be. For a while, in fact, things had seemed off. Despite Burlington, Vermont, being a largely middle-class, white, historically sensible community, everyone now seemed to be hooked on pills or heroin, including her husband and his duck-lipped stripper girlfriend.

@mrsCee978 had recently been introduced to The Secret through her hot seniors yoga class, and realized it was her own negative thoughts creating all of her misfortunate. The Secret explained that everyone's thoughts were actually creating reality on a quantum basis, so it was incredibly important, critical even, for everyone to be positive. When she saw the Internet meme of that poor young Muslim woman getting attacked by a white man in the Dayton Park it tipped the balance for to be more proactive in spreading a message of positivity to the world. @mrsCee798 decided to post several heartfelt, direct, private messages to some of the people on her favorite forum, to make them feel special and loved. As she typed she even wiped away a tear, imaging how her words of encouragement and love would help someone like herself.

Believe in yourself, her first unsolicited private message to someone named @archiesuperhero read. She was pretty sure he was a young, impressionable, geeky boy by the things he posted on the forum. *Trust your instincts, and don't let people discourage you!*

@archiesuperhero needed the encouragement, as he was just about to shove a cattle prod down someone's throat.

* * *

Cold sunlight sparkled the snow hanging in the Idaho valley's pine trees around @archiesuperhero's compound. White clumps in dark green stretched up a powdery mountainside as dawn light burned the shadows from those trees of the *Patriots of the Rising Dawn's* location. Fresh snow from the day before blanketed the jagged northern earth, muffling everything in swaths of white except for a single coyote casting a last howl somewhere in the woods before curling up for a morning nap and, of course, the sharp crackle of an electric cattle prod followed by a man's anguished scream.

The compound was located in a tight valley below three Idaho peaks. Seven log buildings of various shapes and sizes, all lined with tinfoil to disrupt the drone's technology, and two large camo-painted metal hangars were nestled within the dense 168 acres of forest. Mr. Jefferson had not only warned *@archiesuperhero* that the drones were circling high overhead, but that the noose was tightening, and that the Illuminati lizard-infested government would soon move against them. *@archiesuperhero* had even been warned of those suspicious dark vans at a gas station in town this morning, just before reading *@mrsCee798's* nearly prophetic message of encouragement to him that it was time to take the next step. If he'd ever had any doubts, he must surely now admit that his visions were real, and it was time to act, God bless her.

The human wail came from the smallest of the log buildings, known to the members of the militia as the meat locker. It was off a ways from the main lodge of the compound, near a snow-stuffed ravine. The meat locker was ten by twelve of rough-hewn pines and no windows, a single wood door. A thin trail of crimson blood led through the snow to its cinder block steps.

Inside the meat locker deer in various states of being butchered and drained hung from black iron hooks. Their suits of fur were sliced in different levels of undress from their glistening bodies, and some were altogether frozen bare and pink-marbled. The sweet rot of dead flesh overpowered even the crisp winter pine in the room, and older blood had stained the wood floor in shades of purple. Three men, in camo and bulletproof vests, stood in a small space in the center of the room between the hanging carcasses.

The center of the three was a bear of a man, holding an electric cattle prod—Lawton Smith, who had been going online for months under the handle *@archiesuperhero* to anonymously warn people of the coming Illuminati threat. Lawton had long and stringy silver-black hair spilling over massive shoulders. He had a salt and pepper beard that had been growing without concern for several winters, and his head twisted in violent intensity with every word or movement from the sobbing man tied in the chair. To his left and right stood Buck and Slicker. Both were younger, skinnier, and obviously deferential to Lawton's simmering ferocity. All three glared down on the man in the chair, whose broken nose dripped bright red blood to the floor. The beaten man had a stubble of dark beard growth and short dark hair over a purple-bruised and swollen face.

"Show yourself, creature." Lawton Smith's voice was a rusty whisper, like a man whose vocal chords had once been sliced by razor wire, then healed. "Let me see the TRUTH."

"Lawton," the beaten man sputtered, "please?" Flecks of blood and saliva sprang from the man's busted lips, but he still managed to keep a steady tone. "I'm telling you, Lawton, this can be worked out, it doesn't have to go down like this."

"I said, show yourself." Lawton tapped the end of the sparking electric cattle prod to the beaten man's shin. Blue light sizzled from the cattle prod to clench his body tight, every muscle fiber uncontrollably seizing, the man's jaw clamping on his own tongue and he trashed in grunting pain, his eyes bulging. "Think us fools, eh?" Lawton smiled. "But I already seen you, creature."

"I don't understand." Tears ran down the man's cheeks. "I admitted I'm CIA, Lawton. What—fuck. What more do you want?"

"We'st known that already." Slicker, thin and greasy, spat brown juice on the floorboards behind Lawton. "Thomas Jefferson done told us, pig! You slimy alien or not?"

"Hush, now," Lawton snapped back at Slicker. "I'm conducting this cleanse, not you."

"Yes'm, Colonel." The younger man dropped his boney frame onto a stack of wooden crates marked *grenades* by the door. "Apologies."

"And that means both yous." Lawton glared back and forth between Slicker and Buck with a single raised finger, the finger yellow with untreated nail fungus. "I got the sight, youns just need obey, hear?" The shorter, thicker one, Buck, looked sheepishly down at the floor and started chewing at his own oily nails. Lawton spun back to the beaten man, his eyes knotting into a piercing stare and took one step forward with his big black boot, the entire cabin reverberating under its thump. "War's coming," Lawton rasped at the tied man. His eyes devoured every inch of the beaten man's face. "Final battle twixt Illuminati and free man."

What the beaten man, CIA Agent Charlie Pough, didn't exactly understand was what Lawton Smith saw while looking at him. Lawton looked at Pough's broken and bruised all-American face and saw glints and glimmers of a six-foot-tall lizard-man. After each blast from the electric prod, Lawton had caught the tint of green rising in Charlie's pale skin, saw his alien cloaking technology wane. To Lawton's special vision he saw Charlie's eyes morph to jet-black, the whites bleeding to coal with thin vertical slits of yellow slicing up their centers. The cheekbones and forehead of Charlie's face thickened and sharpened, and Lawton caught the nubs of those weird horns, tiny pointy tips sprouting from the top of Charlie's skull, his too-white teeth growing longer like an alligator's. It was all for only an instant, and as soon as Lawton removed the electric surge the son of a bitch was able to use his alien cloaking technology to conceal his true nature once again. Lawton had almost doubted his own ability earlier, but luckily had received *@mrsCee798's* text of positivity.

"Please, Lawton," the CIA agent whispered. "You've been showing psychotic tendencies for a while. You're ill, but I can help you, I can get your grievances against the Fuentes administration heard, get you a doctor."

"Don't believe him, Pa. He wretched evil liar through and through!" Buck jumped from around Lawton's back, jabbing an angry finger at Pough. "Yous was my best friend, Charlie!"

"Shit," Slicker scoffed. "Twern't my best friend. Always smelling like lady vagina and such, I'd just as soon shoot the—"

"Hush now!" Lawton glared back at Charlie. "Entire government's already in the Illuminati's clutches, creature, ain't no Democrat nor Republican, just childish lies for childish minds. You watch our every step to stamp and number us like livestock. There be no more time for weakness, no more peaceful marches and protests."

"Lawton," Charlie begged, "there's no alien invasion coming, there is no government official named Mr. Jefferson that you've been speaking with. You're having a psychotic break, and I can help you get better."

Lawton couldn't help but smile. Smile at their same old tricks of doubt and fear. He caught another flicker of reptilian spookiness peeking through the CIA agent's skin—scales and fire, claws and black death all oozing from the wicked creature—and Lawton chuckled down at him. "Not what Mr. Jefferson said, fork-tongue." Lawton glanced back at Buck and Slicker. "Bring me mine sloppin' hand, boys." Slicker and Buck both grinned, then knocked into each other trying to get out the door first.

A blast of fresh icy air rolled in from their wake. Air that made Charlie think of the outdoors, of the perfect freedom of an endless wild land. Air that made Charlie Pough breathe deeply, longingly, and start to softly sob for the next dawn he realized he was probably never going to see. "Lawton, please, I'm not an alien."

"Mine sloppin' hand, boys!"

Slicker burst back in first. He clutched a big yellow rubber glove covered in dried intestines and blood, and Buck hurried behind trying to reach over and take it from him. The cabin rocked and jostled as Lawton snatched the glove from them with a simmering glare. Buck bashfully retreated behind a hanging deer carcass while Lawton slipped the glove over his left hand, disapproving eyes latched on his son the whole time.

"Lawton," Charlie pleaded, "my girlfriend, she's pregnant. There's no aliens. I'm going to have a son. Please?"

"Figures," Lawton snorted, tapping the cattle prod twice with his right forefinger to test the strength of the crackling blue jolt. "Trying to breed us out." Lawton took a giant step forward toward Charlie. "Sir Stephen Hawking has assured us," Lawton stated calmly as the cattle prod rose high in his right hand, his gloved left scooping the back of Charlie's skull, "that the mathematical existence of aliens is all but certain." Lawton's body felt a surge of righteous power as his finger contracted down on the trigger of the cattle prod. "'Merica ain't fer you, lizard."

Charlie's screams and terrified pleas ceased once Lawton rammed the sparking cattle prod down into his mouth. The jolts of electricity exploded throughout the CIA agent's body in spasms. Thrashing, Charlie's eyes bled, his cheeks charred.

His left eyeball popped from his skull, dangling. There was so much snot and blood and eye stuff flying and sizzling that Slicker flung the door open and tumbled outside to start dry heaving on the snow. Buck hugged the dead deer with only half his face peeking out from behind, pressing his nose into the frozen carcass rather than smelling the awful burnt flesh and hair scent.

And then, it was over. The alien was dead, and Lawton breathed deep with satisfaction. One more exterminated, only about 1500 more to go. The number was the best Lawton could figure according to the Internet facts he'd accumulated regarding some new bleeding disease around the world, which he was pretty sure was part of the lizard infestation. Of course, there were tens of thousands of traitorous humans who were surely helping them too.

"Slicker," Lawton barked out the open door, yanking on the cattle prod fried into Charlie's throat. "Stop being a dern girl." Lawton yanked harder, snapping several of the dead man's teeth in the process of getting the prod unstuck. "Get yourn backside in here to dispose of this thing properly, and scrub Mama's chair with the smell-good."

"Pa," Buck whispered from around the deer carcass, his nose buried in the crook of his arm. "What we do with him?"

"What do you think we got them dern pigs for, boy?" Lawton used the gloved hand to knock the stuck things off the cattle prod before they became hardened with the cold. "And once y'all got that done, get on the two-way and make sure Mr. Jefferson is still sending us instructions for the dirty bomb." Lawton lifted up the glove that had some fried meat on it and took a whiff. He was curious if his sniffer was as sensitive to aliens as his eyes were.

* * *

That morning Mr. Jefferson would send one more message through his @whoreads account.

@axegrinder13 was so brilliant he had gotten into Stanford at sixteen years old despite growing up in a trailer park outside of Mesa, Arizona. Working with computers was all he ever did after developing a rare genetic disorder in grade school that made his body order smell like rotting fish. No matter how smart, nice, or well groomed he was, no one wanted to be around someone who inevitably smelled like rotting fish thirty minutes into the day. There was no cure, and no deodorant that could help. In Arizona it was so blazingly hot that he always sweat, so @axegrinder13 had become accustomed to immersing himself online for all social contact, where no one knew to make fun of him.

Online was where brilliant, lonely @axegrinder13 had stumbled across the political ideology of 'anarchy', whereby the best solution for America, and the world, was to use technology for a massive decentralizing of all power. The end result of technological-induced anarchy would actually be democracy in its purest form, destroying all existing power structures to truly give the power to each person. Technology and the internet could make it viable for every single law to be voted on directly by every citizen, and decentralized forms of electronic payment online could do away with federally backed funds and banks. That was why he had started the anonymous hacking group *Reboot.org*, to usher in a revolution to the world as important as America's original one from the British in 1776. And to make friends with people who didn't know he smelled like fish.

Of course, still being a genuinely nice, shy, nineteen-year-old kid, *@axegrinder13* really didn't want anyone to get hurt either. So far he'd just directed the other brilliant, lonely, Internet activists comprising *Reboot.org* into hacking a few online dating sites and the naked photos of a judge, but to no real results. Unfortunately, no one was even bringing up "decentralization" within the presidential election as yet, so he had been wondering if he needed to do something more extreme.

Additionally, some of the other activist groups that *@axegrinder13* regularly hacked into and eavesdropped on were spreading troubling gossip of numerous black, government-looking vans showing up at activists' locations around the country and quietly taking people away. What if they actually figured out he was the leader of *Reboot.org* and found his location, *@axegrinder13* wondered? What if he never made a difference, and just went to jail? That was exactly when Mr. Jefferson used his *@whoreads* account to send the last unsolicited private message of the morning. It said: *So do you have the balls to actually do something that makes a difference or not, you fish-stinking freak?*

> *"We must guard against... the*
> *military-industrial complex."*
> *—President Eisenhower*

(Tampa, Florida: Saturday, 8:10 a.m. PST / 11:10 a.m. EST)

M*aybe there's just too many lunatics now.* The Florida sun was high overhead as Amos walked down the sidewalk on MacDill Air Force Base with his mind churning, the back of his neck warming, it too hot on the tender pink flesh of his marred ear. *Truth, honor, morality, that's what's missing from America. Maybe Governor Stone really will help set things right? He at least believes in God.*

Amos gave acceptable nods or salutes, but found it difficult to concentrate. He was still grappling with whether he should bring his concerns of Stork's dishonesty to General Harper. In the past few hours he had caught more extensive coverage of the Dayton riot as well. He'd seen how they were spinning Annie's speech as the causative factor, and it was dredging up all sorts of conflicting feelings within him. On the one hand Amos knew his sister to be a crafty manipulator, but on the other he knew she was passionately idealistic about protecting the lives of innocents. Long-dormant instincts to protect his older sister fired to life in Amos' belly, but then almost as quickly flashbacks to what had occurred in his senior year of high school, and what she did to their dad, shattering those loving thoughts. *Forget it. She made her own bed, she can lie in it.* His mind went back to the more pressing concern, the probable end of his career.

MacDill Air Force Base was nearly 6,000 acres of various operations facilities, training ranges, family housing, a school for kids, an airfield, and hangars. Around 15,000 active duty soldiers worked on the base, with more associated civilian contractors and intelligence personnel coming and going at all hours. MacDill was home to the 6th Air Mobility Wing, but far more relevant to Amos it was also the location of CENTCOM and SOCOM.

SOCOM, United States Special Operations Command, is the centralized leadership for all Special Forces divisions across all branches of the United States military. The new Combatant Commander (CCDR) in charge of SOCOM was General Mace Harper, one of only nine active CCDRs in the country, who were arguably nine of the most powerful people in the world.

Each of the nine Combatant Commanders answered only to the Secretary of Defense and thereby the president of the United States through the chain of command, no one else, each with a specific area of responsibility. All except Harper's Special Operations umbrella were designated to a specific geographic region worldwide. SOCOM's area of responsibility was pretty much wherever its current Combatant Commander believed deadly, clandestine force was needed. As the nature of war had changed in the 21st century, Special Forces had almost evolved into its own branch, a super-wing of the military comprised of the best of the best of the traditional four. SOCOM had access to intelligence and weaponry unavailable to typical boots on the ground. The daily orders coming out of SOCOM, although rarely known to those outside of Special Forces, often swayed the fate of lives and countries. And General Mace Harper called the shots.

Amos and his ODA team were stationed out of MacDill to assist in overseeing a top-secret weapons project called BRAHMASTRA expected to be of use in urban warfare. If not for the BRAHMASTRA project, Amos would be reporting at Fort Bragg in a little more relaxed state to his direct mentor, Colonel Wally Jackson, who would then relay a report to General Harper. As it were however, Amos was stuck explaining himself to the infamous four-star general.

Amos was more than tense as he headed toward the main door of the off-white, non-descript Central Command building. Given what Amos had heard about the general, and knowing that Amos had definitely broken Section 892, Article 92 of the Uniform Code of Military Justice by defying a direct order and initiating contact with the enemy, he realized this first meeting with Harper would likely be the beginning of a court-martial proceeding.

It was rumored Harper actually considered himself the reincarnated soul of King Leonidas of Sparta and, yes, Amos worried Harper might be that nuts. What was myth versus fact was a bit hard to decipher when it came to the infamous general. The man's public presence fulfilled the most extreme description of his reputed bravado and swagger, but at times the stories around him approached near-absurd myth. He was as old-school military as old school could get, and another rumor about his mental state claimed he actually thought himself unable to be killed as long as he wore his Marine Dress Blues. Whether or not that belief was accurate, he was almost always seen in them, dripping with medals and ribbons, a glinting saber and oiled sidearm strapped to his hip. He dressed like he was ready for a military parade, or a duel, and behind closed doors many made fun of the spit and polish swagger. No one, however, made fun of Harper to his face.

Amos passed the first sentries with a salute, and turned down the hall toward SOCOM's command floor with disappointment in himself. *Of course I shouldn't say anything about Stork.* He needed to confront Stork in his lie man to man, and then deal with it however was appropriate. No matter what poor choice Stork made, it was a separate issue from Amos' own screw-up, and Amos needed to take his appropriate lumps for that with honesty and courage. *I was in command, and everything that happened is my fault.* He would tell the general exactly what happened as he factually knew, and take full responsibility for having Thump in the situation that got him killed. *My burden to bear. Mine alone.*

"Major." A voice like honey interrupted his glum thoughts, and a surge of comfort flooded Amos' tense body as Corporal Ashley Kline sidled up next to him with a clipboard. "Signature, sir." She tilted her dark pony-tailed head to the side and held out a clipboard full of papers with that flawless smile, always smelling like summer vacation. "For last Tuesday's BRAHMAS-TRA run."

It was crazy how much she reminded him of Shay Wheeler. The long black hair, a twenty-three year-old-body, and clear eyes that sparkled with belief that everything in the world was going to turn out fine. Or maybe, he just still loved Shay? Either way, Corporal Kline was a subordinate, and he was married. Amos took the clipboard from her, flipping through the pages.

Her voice dropped into a bit of a gentle whisper. "We've got some people headed over to The Dub tonight, if you could use a beer, Amos?" As they turned the last corner he ignored her flirting as he double-checked the dates and dispositions he was authorizing. The steel doors to SOCOM Control became visible as Amos scratched out his signature on the appropriate lines. Two armed Air Force sentries stood guard to either side. "Game of darts?" Corporal Kline continued.

The guards would stop the Corporal since access to SOCOM Control was the most restrictive on base, and take Amos' cell phone if he had one. SOCOM Control was an ultra-secure SCI (Sensitive Compartmentalized Information Facility), or "Las Vegas zone" as it was nicknamed, meaning whatever happened in SOCOM Control, stayed in SOCOM Control.

"Loser buys the first round?" It was amazing how a beautiful woman's affection could even make you momentarily forget you were headed to a firing squad though. He signed on the last line, and as they neared the doors Amos flashed his wedding band at her.

"Shame," she said with a pout. "Think everybody needs a break from their oaths occasionally."

"If you take a break from it," Amos slapped the clipboard back onto her palm, "then it was never really an oath, Corporal."

***

Amos rapped twice on General Harper's doorjamb, prepared for an onslaught of tidal venom to rival his Basic Training Drill Sergeant. Botching a mission and causing a soldier's death were not received well by brass.

"Come." Harper's voice was blunt, hard. His back was to Amos in his full Dress Blues, and he was cradling his white hat under one arm. He was glaring out his one window.

Amos took two steps in, snapped to attention and saluted. "Major Amos Daniels reporting, sir."

"Fucking faggots," the general growled, not turning back to look at Amos.

Amos swallowed hard, held his salute quietly. "Sir?"

"Gonna cut our funding again." The general spun from the window, glaring across the small, bare office at Amos. Harper was a gnarled stump of a man whose stare could wilt concrete. His eyes methodically ground over every millimeter of the major who stood frozen with shoulders back, head straight, hand snapped into position against his brow. "We'll be up to our eyeballs in sand niggers with plutonium up their dicks if those damned liberals win Washington again." Harper was easily six inches shorter than Amos, but had ramrod straight posture, and deep vertical lines etching down either side of a face in permanent scowl. Few people had ever seen the general laugh, and those who had said it was unsettling. "That pansy Freeman would prefer to completely do away with the military, as if Fuentes hadn't snipped our balls enough already. Know what I'm saying, son?"

"Sir," Amos said, still holding his salute, "I'm not privy to funding concerns—"

"Since the dawn of civilization, boy," the general stepped even closer to Amos, his growl not betraying if he were asking a question or stating a fact, "there have been goddamn cunts like Freeman who refuse to fight, but then expect us to risk life and limb saving their cowardly asses when the shit hits the fan." Hot cigar-smoke breath rolled up over Amos' face, the general's eyes never ceasing their blatant inspection of him. "But then those excuse makers, those thumb suckers, once we've slayed the fucking dragon for them, those queers don't want to see us anymore, try to hide us away from the civilized, take away our livelihood, and downsize the shit out of our military and resources to cut our pay, call us barbarians. Know what I'm saying?"

"Yes, sir."

"Son of a cunt, right." General Harper snapped his hand in return salute as if that settled it, turned to his gray metal desk. "There's a goddamn third world war brewing out there with the towel heads, boy. Upward of over one thousand of those potential jihadists already slinked into the country and Freeman would rather just drop our borders like dungarees, great them with blowjobs instead of guns." The desk only held a single manila file and a map of the east coast unfurled on it. There was a metal coat rack and chair, but nothing else, nothing on the walls. "Heard there was a bit of a dustup, son?"

Amos let his salute relax and breathed a little deeper. "I messed up, sir. There was a civilian girl, sir, and—"

"It's alright, son." General Harper glanced back at Amos once, as if he found whatever the major was about to say acceptable, nodded. "Shit happens." The general took his white hat and placed it carefully on the metal coat rack. "Let it go."

"Let it go?"

The general's voice dropped to almost a whisper. "Lieutenant Stoughton already explained the situation to me, son. We're gonna let this go."

"Lieutenant Stoughton?" Amos' nervousness about his position now evaporated. Stork speaking with the general before Amos was a fairly blatant circumvention of the command structure, not to mention a bizarre stance from a commander regarding his soldier's death. "You spoke with Lieutenant Stoughton, sir? Stoughton came to you instead of me?" Amos was bewildered.

"The important thing," Harper's tone almost became gentle,

"is that the mission objective was achieved, son, the laptop destroyed." The general reached for the manila file. "I'm going to go ahead and clear your man's death as in the line of duty, no LOD investigation needed."

"Clear?" Amos' friend had died under his command; this wasn't something to be cavalier about. And the fact Stork had already given the general a debriefing was more than a little unsettling when put on top of the lie. "But Weapons Specialist Bills was shot by Stoughton, sir. In all honesty—"

"Drop it." The general's eyes shot up from the open file to Amos, hard and fiery. "Gary Bill's death will be recorded as KIA, there won't be any investigation into how it occurred. Full honors, a hero's death, I'll make sure of that. Just... drop it."

Amos was stunned. "What was on the laptop, sir?"

The general's face hardened. "Standards," the general eventually stated, as his cold eyes drifted back to the manila file. "This country is losing all its standards, Major, you'll do well to remember the forest despite the trees."

"Yes, sir." Amos' mind wrestled with the odd nature of this conversation, and if the phrase *1776* had any part in it.

"You know your sister and that homo Freeman are actually talking about closing Fort Bragg if they successfully steal the election, Major? Close the home of the fucking Green Berets." Harper shook his head in disgust, his tone relaxing a bit but his eyes never leaving Amos. "Like the hippies flushed the toilet back in the sixties and that piss-water is still sucking us all down, know what I'm saying?"

"Sir," Amos sighed. "Regarding the Lieutenant and the lap—"

"Major, I respect the fact you've stayed in the field as long as you have. You could have easily taken a desk job by now but you didn't, and that shows grit." The general stepped around his desk closer to Amos again, his breath raking over Amos' charred ear. "And what you did in the Korpesh Valley was nothing short of brilliant." Something in the general's voice resonated with true respect, his eyes now softening. "Guts and honor, no other way to say it, soldier."

Amos glanced down at the mention of the Korpesh Valley. Years later, he was still unsure if he felt pride or humility, or simply regret, for what happened in Afghanistan. "Thank you, sir."

"That was real shit there, son." The general put a hand on Amos' shoulder. "You performed courageously, saved many lives. In fact, I see a lot of myself in you, Major. Hell, you might have even made a decent Marine." Something in the general's face twisted like a person with a facial nerve damage trying to smile. "Four with your hands? Maybe sometime we'll have a drink and you'll tell me about it."

"Certainly. Thank you, sir."

"We need real soldiers more than ever." The general slapped his brick-like palm to Amos' shoulder, then stepped back to the window as his voice returned to a disgusted growl. "The world's a dangerous place, Major, and it's only men like us that can keep the wolves from the door. Can make America great again like it started out in 1776."

1776? "I know it's not my clearance to know what was on the laptop, sir, but—"

"No, it's not," the general snapped. "Can we count on you, Major?"

"Yes, sir, definitely, sir."

"Who can?"

"I serve… um… the orders of the president of—"

"Come again, son?" Harper's eyebrows raised.

"I said I serve the president of the United States of America, sir. In whatever capacity they need me to—"

"You mean you serve the CONSTITUTION, don't you son?" The general's eyes narrowed. "The oath you took when you enlisted was to protect the Constitution of the United States, correct? Not a title, not a person, but the CONSTITU-TION, from all enemies, foreign and domestic. Wasn't that what you promised, son? Your dad's promise too?"

"Yes, sir. Of course, sir."

"Good." The general snapped off a dismissive salute before turning back toward the window. "Now get the fuck out of my sight."

By the time Amos walked back past the guards of the SOCOM Control doors his mind was creating questions he would have never imagined forty-eight hours earlier, wondering if there was more to Thump's death than an accident, and what the phrase *1776* had to do with it. His guts clinched tight at the thought of questioning the military, of questioning the backbone of America that he had devoted his life to, but he had to know the truth, because beliefs mattered. The bitter image of Annie's face from just before their dad died flashed across his mind.

It was time to find a reporter he could trust. Shay Wheeler, hopefully.

Operation Long Knives Secretly Continues

(Dayton, Ohio: Saturday, 11:03 p.m. PST / 2:03 p.m. EST)

"You've got to be kidding me." Annie leaned back from Eli in shock. "You're like, what, twenty-five?" Annie glared in disbelief that Eli couldn't get it up again. "And black. Come on, where's the animal instinct?"

"That's pretty racist, ma'am."

They were sitting on either end of the tiny sofa in Annie's private quarters of her campaign plane. Annie wore only her glossy, bright-blue panties, the ends of her long blonde hair clinging the bottom of her breasts like damp ivy tendrils hiding from the sun. The black, white, and red skeleton tattoo arched up Annie's long back and around the taut curves of her slim body, like she were being hugged by the dead. Naked, even more so than clothed, Annie was damn sure used to getting her way.

"Screw you, I can't be racist." Annie snatched the bottle of Beam off the tiny table, shoved it toward Eli. "I'm banging a black guy."

Eli was sitting upright at the other end of the sofa. His light blue suit pants were back on and he clutched a White House-issued blanket up to his chin. He shook his head at the bottle of alcohol. "I'm only twenty, ma'am." His face twisted in concern. "I won't be able to legally drink for two more months."

"Jesus, that might even be hotter." Annie took a swig out of the bottle, gasped. "Let me see if I have any of my husband's dick pills in my purse." She slapped the bottle back down on the table and stood. She stretched her arms high above her breasts with a soft girly squeal, squeezed her ass to get the blood moving again, then reached for her purse. "Once your cock is fixed we'll toast your upcoming birthday."

After she had been named Freeman's running mate and issued a Secret Service detail, Annie had quickly discovered the agents were extremely good at assisting with professional breaks like this while keeping their mouths shut. The good old boys had been doing this kind of shit back to Kennedy and before. Hell, men in power had been using it to get laid since the dawn of time, so why not her? The private quarters on the plane were completely soundproof, and Castor now stood just outside the door. Her primary Secret Service agent was big and serious, like a pile of bricks, wore a crew cut, and with his earpiece in and gun holstered beneath his dark suit no one would question that Senator Daniels was in a high-level meeting with one of her chief aides.

"Ma'am, I…" Eli stammered as Annie dug through her purse looking for her husband's erectile dysfunction meds. "I don't know if this is a good idea, ma'am?"

"You're right, you having a limp dick's about as good as a broken pencil—horrible idea, Boze." Annie snorted. "Try being a man."

"But isn't this wrong, ma'am?" Eli asked. His voice was a whine, his chin trembling. "I mean, we're not married, or… even really dating."

Annie looked up from her purse into his watery eyes and couldn't help but be moved. To disgust. "Jesus, you can't be serious," she groaned, "this shit again? What's wrong with America's youth?"

"Ma'am, I don't want to make you upset—"

"Wrong, Eli? It's sex." She shook her head, completely bewildered. "It's what humans are genetically programmed to do, trust me, I've got a degree." She put her fists on her sharp hipbones and tilted her head, her breasts jiggling slightly from the movement. "Is it the black-white thing, are YOU actually racist?" *What buttons to press?* "Or are you gay, is that it? Because if you are, we're going to let people know. Not coming out is as good as condoning prejudice." She jabbed a finger at him as if suddenly enlightened. "Or then again is it that you're threatened by a woman's sexuality, you misogynist son of a bitch?" She threw up her arms. "Maybe all these things need to be made public, Eli, and let social media decide for us; I don't like covering things—"

"No." Eli's eyes went wide in panic, curling the blanket tighter to his quivering face. "I completely respect women's rights, and love girls. White ones! But, uh, shit, I mean in a very respectful, um, appropriately romantic way, regardless of race, of course, ma'am, and—"

"Then get those goddamn pants back off." Annie snatched the blanket from him, throwing it in the corner. "If you want to keep this job, you've got to learn to work on a goddamn schedule."

"But you're married," he pleaded, "and you're my boss, and we're not age appropriate, and I prefer to be in a committed relationship, not just—"

"You've got to be kidding me." Annie dropped her

forehead in her palm for a moment, groaned, long blonde hair tumbling forward. "Marriage is about tax breaks and raising a kid, not love, what is wrong with this country?" She shook her head in exasperation. "It's like you're a generation of dudes turning into women, why's that happening?" she wondered, picking up her cell phone.

Knock. Knock. It was two raps to the cabin door, Castor's way of letting Annie know she was requested outside. "Shit." Annie glanced at her phone's clock. "Pilot must have made good time. Grab your shit and get dressed." Annie started looking for her bra. "Oh." She smiled up at her young black aide, her voice suddenly tender. "When you're at the doctor for Viagra, babe, make sure to schedule an appointment for that vasectomy we discussed." She used the smile and tone that had launched countless male dreams into flight through-out her life, then dashed just as many to the rocks below. "I wouldn't want your career getting derailed in any way."

* * *

As long as my plan works, Annie thought, *it will be game, set, match for progress, no time left for the president to even get pissed off at me.* She silently gazed out the window of the limo, feeling the burn of Henry's glare but pretending not to. *It will be such a deathblow to Stone, it will even take the fire out of any of his supporters to riot.*

But she also felt strange, exhaustion soaking into her bones like heavy grease. Her mind wandered to odd places as she watched the white-dusted Ohio landscape yawn past, like she was watching a film through the limo's window. Sometimes she almost felt like she were reading a book about a woman running for vice president rather than actually doing it herself, and she now caught her mind drifting back to Henry's bizarre conversation with her on the plane. *How do we ever know what's actually real?* Particles of some energy called light hit something called your retina and cause a cascade of chemicals bouncing around in a mass of gray matter, generating images in something called our mind, and each of us swears it's real even though it's got to different than what other people experience. *What if we are all just characters in a book?* She wondered, her fingers brushing over the cap to the new bottle of Zennies Henry had gotten for her upon landing.

After a quarter mile of gravel road they came to a patch of rolling hills. The church looked like it had been constructed in the 1800s, without much upkeep since. Barren trees and dead shrubs looked like balls of iron yarn dotting the snow dusted horizon behind the church. Annie's eyes widened as the limo slowed to a stop at the First Baptist Church of Greenfield, surprised by both the tiny size, and dilapidated state, of the old church. Even more so by the massive carnival of would-be political players, activists, press, and curious onlookers trying to squeeze into it.

Built of sturdy gray stone, it was a tiny chapel with no adjoining rooms or halls, its roof rotting wood. The precarious steeple rose high into the sky over a large red front door and looked as if it was leaning slightly to the left and might tumble backward through the flimsy wooden roof at any moment. Except for the bright red paint on the door, the exterior of the structure looked tired and ashen, with visible cracks and holes in the stained-glass windows. The stone steps leading up to the front door sagged and crumbled with a split down their center. White snow blanketed the rolling ground in every direction, broken only by those occasional leafless trees and lopsided tombstones from a surprisingly large graveyard behind the church. There were few other buildings in sight except for distant farmhouses. Annie figured the church had been designed to hold one hundred people at best, and there were near a thousand now surrounding it. Annie dug the jagged red nails of one hand into a bit of fat she could find on her thigh to awaken and clear her head, clenched until the liberating pain scorched up her side. Annie had already swallowed seven of the Zennies Henry had gotten refilled.

The suddenness of the event by the family, the poor choice of the tiny church, and an ill-prepared understanding of how politically symbolic the death of their son might become had obviously led to the circus-like atmosphere. Thankfully, the local police had already set up a barricaded perimeter to keep the general population out. The Secret Service was limiting actual access to the church through an interior circumference.

On the outer edges of the crowd, Annie's limo parted a crowd of onlookers. A group of about twenty people cheered and clapped, raised their fists in the air in support as Annie's vehicle passed them. They carried signs that said things like *religion = idiots*. But there was another, much larger sea of protestors waving signs as Annie's limo passed too, saying things like, *no mark of the beast for me*, and *warrior for God*. A kindly-looking elderly woman held a sign that read, *Daniels is the whore of Babylon*. A handful of greasy cow dung slapped Annie's window and she jumped. It partially stuck, partially slid, Annie watching as an awful brown film was left on the window, and she remembered again her father laughing wickedly, *Ya never know you're right, unless someone's shooting at you.*

Once past the first barricades, it seemed like every news station in the country had a van parked with an antenna raised. Telegenic men and women spoke into cameras and microphones, busy adjusting their blouses and ties until Annie's limo pulled past, then all the cameras and all the people turned toward her vehicle.

Annie's limo finally pulled inside the Secret Service's perimeter, where a sea of politicians, staffers, lobbyists and analysts were going in and out of the church. Annie suddenly felt sick to her stomach. Everyone was desperate to get on camera, to appear a respectful and grieving public figure or trying to use the event to get face time with one of the political principles there. She wondered if there was even room for the poor family. She glanced across at Henry, craving the reassurance of his bearded smile, but Henry would not look up at her. Governor Stone was supposedly inside waiting for her apology, and Annie wondered if her secret plan was inherently immoral, if she was maybe going too far. If maybe she had been making wrong calls ever since that damned rabbit?

Snap out of it. She quietly dug the broken nails into her thigh flesh again. *No such thing as moral, only smart or dumb. Win.*

Hampton Stone Begins Joey Thompson's Eulogy

(Various Locations Around Country: Saturday, 12:38 p.m. PST / 3:38 p.m. EST)

Twenty-eight miles outside Killeen, Texas, a middle-aged man with a bushy orange mustache and a stiff cowboy hat held up two photos in his gloved hands. He held them over a barbed-wire fence, displayed to eleven chilly reporters. The rancher was the de facto leader of thirty-seven individuals who had been hunkered up inside the dirty-white ranch house in the distance for the past several weeks. They refused to leave so that the federal government couldn't take their land over through an eminent domain declaration and make it protected area for a recently discovered rare muskrat population. Republican vice presidential candidate Buddy Dukes was rumored to be traveling to them the next morning in a show of support.

"Hank and Joey Thompson," the rancher boomed out of a mouth half-filled with chewing tobacco, "are just the first casualties in this war." The pictures of the Thompsons shook while he glared at the reporters' cameras, heated breath puffing from his open mouth. "That's right, I said WAR." He angrily folded up the pictures of the Thompsons, shoving them into the pocket of his orange hunting vest. "I have it on good authority that the black helicopters endorsed by Fuentes are rounding up good people.

Decent, hardworking, liberty-loving American people this very morning are being locked away in the secret FEMA concentration camps. You can claim I'm a nut, but I won't take it anymore!"

The rancher ripped off his orange hunting vest, grunting and groaning as he twisted out of it and threw it to the brown grass. He snatched off his cowboy hat and hung it on the fence, then snatched up a bright red T-shirt that said *Make America Great Again* on its front in white cursive. He wriggled it over his head, copper strands of hair dancing long in the wind. "A WAR, I say!" Once he had his Republican T-shirt twisted over the bulk of his flannel shirt, he jabbed a finger at one of the cameras. "And we're gonna fight!"

* * *

News Headlines:

12 Terrors Cells Predicted Hiding Within US

Flakka 3.0 Causes Cannibalism?

Confederate Flag Rally in South Carolina
Turns Violent

Mysterious 'Stigmata' Disease Spreading in Liberia

Man with Possible Fertilizer-Bomb Shot at
Oregon Airport

Occupy Wall Street Protests Clogging New York

* * *

Tweet from Governor Stone: *Let's just be honest, minorities are typically less Christian than normal people! Obvious. And less American too!*

* * *

@wallstreetwizard: Too many nutjobs out there. I hope atheist Annie has sense enough to avoid Thompson boy's funeral, not make a photo-op out of it. Occupy WS nutjobs don't even get what they're protesting. Everyone needs economy to work.

@jessejameskickass: I would flip the f********* out if that Satanic slut showed up in a church at my murdered boy's funeral. Down with devil worshipers!

@professorofplants: Another example of a peaceful Christian. Ha. For any rational people, we will be planning sit-ins in various locations across the country to show support for Freeman and Daniels in the coming days. Only requirement is respect ...not being a hillbilly idiot!

@socialjusticewarrior: The attacked Muslim woman is the real victim, the boy was an accident! Islam is a religion of peace.

@archiesuperhero: Sheep!!! Everything orchestrated by the Lizard Illuminati. Pan-Continental Trade Deal start of one world government! Heed my words!

@mrsCee798: Positivity people!

@hotpancake: Exactly. Love, not violence. Why not orgy in Dayton park instead of fight?

@mrsCee798: Please stay off my feed, you pervert.

* * *

Within fifty minutes of the *Reboot.org* video being released it had over 750,000 views worldwide, increasing rapidly. The video showed two young males with shaved heads. They stood militantly in front of a brick wall. One man appeared to be black, his entire face painted in white make-up, the other Caucasian, his face painted completely black. Both wore black sunglasses and black T-shirts, with black pants. They looked like mirror images of each other, from the face paint and exposed skin of their arms, and were utterly unidentifiable. They took turns speaking.

"Be warned, false kings," the one in the white face paint began. "Those you enslave will no longer accept your chains."

The black-faced one said, "This is not Republican versus Democrat, nor black versus white. It's not male versus female, gay versus straight, young versus old, or Christian versus Islam. This is about those who have, versus those who have not."

"It is about corruption versus justice," the white-faced one continued. "About overturning this American system of greed and lies, and stopping a two-party political system which only serves the rich, at the expense of the honest, the poor, and the earth."

The black-faced one said, "It is about good versus evil."

The white-face one ended, "Be warned, corrupt kings," and then used his right hand to pull a sword from behind his back and point its glinting tip at the camera. "The time soon comes when you can ignore us no more."

* * *

Only story trending faster than *Reboot.org* video: *Kardashian/Jenners Cancel All-Nude Photo Shoot Due to "Security Concerns."*

"Question with boldness even the existence of God."
—Thomas Jefferson

(Dayton, Ohio: Saturday, 1:07 p.m. PST / 4:07 p.m. EST)

B*ody odor and bullshit,* Annie sadly thought as she entered the church, her lungs straining to breathe from the electric heat, putting a hand to Castor's broad shoulder for brief support from a wave of vertigo. Inside, people were sweating like they were at the beach. Governor Hampton Stone had been at the church all afternoon, hugging the bereaved and leading prayers, and just seeing Stone's fake-tan hypocrisy, Annie had started to fume inside again. She did not see a man of passion and God but a charlatan weaving the weak minded to his gain, and as always was shocked anew that people fell for it.

Annie had heard words like Stone's all her life, and all Annie ever saw when someone spoke of God was a con man, a liar trying to make themselves appear more righteous by highlighting everyone else's inherent humanity as a flawed sinner. God was a lie, Annie knew in her bones, and it was the core problem with humanity.

The church seemed ready to burst at its old walls. All the pews were packed, the aisles to the left, right, and center filled with well-dressed men and women brushing uncomfortably against one another. The claustrophobic crowd was pressed up to within a few feet of the Thompson boy's small casket, it draped in an American flag, everyone desperate to be seen and counted among the attendees for this sudden political who's-who. All the obvious players were there. Prominent senators and governors who were considering a national run in four years, or jockeying for a cabinet position in the next administration. Some state politicians too, and a smattering of diplomats and think-tankers, most likely using the opportunity to get closer to someone they deemed valuable. Staffers and assistants were in tow, and then the lobbyists and the press, whose jobs dictated they perpetually be hunting all of those here. Within all of it, Annie wondered how many of the actual friends and family, neighbors and schoolmates of the poor deceased boy had been allowed in. It seemed like the bullshit started at the top in America, and trickled down into everyone's lives.

By the time Annie entered, with Castor and Henry to either side of her, the charismatic Stone was already reaching the crescendo of his eulogy and Annie was relieved she would not have to hear him drone on through the whole thing. Stone could slap a back with his tiny hands, and give a wrinkled wink while telling a dirty joke, but somehow still toss in a Biblical quote to make everyone feel morally enlightened at the end. All of which many saw as a blessing, but caused Annie to seethe. Governor Stone now stood on the dais above the small casket, the former pastor's jowly orange face somber and his voice stern as he finished manipulating a boy's death into votes.

"A return to morality," the Governor called out to crowd, "is the only hope America has."

Annie felt nauseous.

* * *

I just want this to all make sense, Henry thought. As Stone neared the end of his eulogy Henry stood to the right of Annie, putting his hairless hands in his trouser pockets before anyone stared. In public, Henry often wondered if people could tell he used to be a woman. More than anything in life, he someday just wanted to know what it was like to be free from doubt, laugh without the worry of being judged. *To feel like life has a purpose.*

He watched Annie's tense revulsion and compared it against the trusting, hopeful expressions filling the sea of parishioners. Henry wondered if any of his discussion with Annie on the plane, his attempt to make her think about things in new ways, had actually stuck. He wondered if she was going too far over whatever her plan was.

"Over two hundred years ago, in the first presidential address ever given by that great man George Washington, our founding father prophetically warned us that if we were ever to 'stop following the eternal rules of good order that God hath ordained, we shall lose the smiling favors of heaven.'" Governor Hampton Stone's trademark wispy blonde hair was swaying as he spoke, his old spray-tanned neck sagging over a pinstripe suit. He carried his massive girth with a bounce of a man half his age. "Second Chronicles 7:14," Governor Stone bellowed in a baritone that rattled dust from the old crossbeams overhead. "*If my people WILL humble themselves and pray and seek my face and turn from their WICKED ways,*" Stone's firm eyes worked their way slow and methodical over the packed pews, "*then I WILL hear from heaven, and I WILL forgive their sin and WILL heal their land.*" Stone paused, looking down at the casket with a deep sigh. "So I ask you, when will we take that first step in God's proposal? When will we turn from our WICKED ways so that God can in turn fulfill his promise to us and heal this land?"

A few *amens* and *yeses* were uttered in the congregation while Stone breathed deep for his next burst. "And do not misunderstand me, do not let the liberal press bend and twist my words into something they are not." Stone wagged a tiny tanned finger to the world. "What I speak of is simply a call for common sense, a return to the eternal principles and ideals of absolute goods that once made this country the most powerful, and glorious, in the world... before it is too late."

Henry saw one elderly woman in a large frilly hat dab a handkerchief to the corner of her eye, nodding softly at every thing Stone said. Henry was reminded of his grandmother, the sweetest person he had ever known, and felt a twinge of despair over the futility of the human condition, how we were each, one and all, already sentenced to death. Henry's eyes went from the older woman to Annie, wondering if she were thinking the same. Instead, he only saw her defiant glare, and smelled a repulsive hint of the sex from the plane wafting off her. Nothing in Annie's eyes said she was willing to entertain an alternate view; she just looked perpetually ready for a fight.

"For if we do not follow God's word, all we then have left to follow is MAN'S word." Stone shrugged his shoulders in mock confusion. "And can not man be corrupted by money, by flesh, and power? All humanity is fallible, just look at the black man who killed this poor boy for instance."

More *amens* and even a *you tell 'em, Hampton* was shouted from the crowd.

"But these days, I see people are afraid to speak their minds because of the politically-correct police, as I call them, afraid to call someone out for killing an innocent child because everyone is being called racist. It was a black man's gun, that's for sure."

Speak truth, pastor!

"The liberals with their big-brother government, want us to believe MAN is perfect, not God. Those liberals that control our media and our schools, tax us to death, and want to control everything else with chips and such so they can make the common American person of faith afraid to profess their morals for fear of being ridiculed… or worse." He shook his head sadly, the long blonde strands hovering like spider webs over his eyes. "But I say we cannot let this happen, for if we don't fight their technology and warped ideals they will finally outlaw religion once and for all, and is that not EXACTLY what Satan wants?"

Heck no, we fight!

Smatterings of applause and enthusiastic whoops erupted, but Governor Stone held up both his small pink palms, guiding his listeners to remain calm and respectful. Henry peered over at Annie to see her grinding her jaw, shaking her head as she glared at the governor. When Henry looked back to the man on the pulpit, he noticed a shaft of sunlight now streaming down onto Stone from a small hole high in that ancient roof above.

"Psalms 33:12 states, *Blessed is the nation whose God is the Lord.*" The Governor's baritone rolled over the people like a brewing storm. "Not greed. Not lust. Not mammon. Not computer chips with a socialist promise of every comfort here on earth without working at it, or living by any standards, with only the simple cost of your soul!"

That's right, people shouted. *Save us, Hampton!*

"Moral decay, fiscal irresponsibility, a weakened and demoralized military. These are the same things that have self-destructed every pinnacle nation to come before us, that simple act of a people losing their way between right and wrong. Morality is what is missing, my brethren! Immorality is what caused this poor boy's death!"

His voice bit with indignation, and his gaze focused so hard suddenly to the back where Annie stood that several of the parishioners actually turned their head to glare in disgust at her.

"Nearly half of our children are born out of wedlock in this country today. Sixty percent of our most innocent and vulnerable missing the innate blessing of a natural childhood guided by the loving hands of both a mother and father." Stone shook his head. "Never before in America's history has divorce been as high, poverty as high, murdering our unborn children as high, drug use as high, and don't get me started on the rioting and violence over the past few years, the ever-increasing threats from foreign shores. If we want to solve this country's problems, it is not by looking to some godless government to grow bigger and bigger, it is by re-instilling God-given family values into our country. Reestablishing one man and one woman families, and not telling women it is okay to have promiscuous sex because it's just a scientific procedure to kill their unborn child. Moral traditions are our savior." Stone looked to the church's rafters as if seeking guidance as that ray of sunlight basked down bright over his face and sighed. "Yet those in the Freeman and Daniels' camp wish you to believe we are on the right path. More government control, but less moral control."

Someone in the audience shouted *heck, no*, and Henry saw Annie's face turning pink with rage.

"What happened to our morals, America?" Stone looked toward the rafters again and outstretched his arms even higher and wider, his voice trembling with emotion. "When did the belief that nothing matters except for your pleasure become mainstream? What happened to God's laws and those smiles from heaven the great George Washington believed in?"

More *amens* and more applause, but this time Stone didn't quiet anyone.

"We need to have the courage of conviction to speak and act toward the highest ideals we can be, not forgive our way into mediocrity and self-destruction through a hedonistic liberal doctrine and mistake darkness for light."

Louder applause and cheers.

"Not bow down to the false gods of money, or lust, or political correctness, or any manmade thing!"

As the applause and cheers grew further, Stone's voice rose higher, the light on him seeming to Henry to somehow grow brighter still as Stone jabbed a finger across the sea of people.

"Government does not need to get bigger, morals do not need to get looser, more innocent children do not need to be corrupted and killed by fatherless ruffians! Government needs to get out of the way to allow a society of moral individuals to thrive!"

Yes, Lord!

"What we need to ensure is exactly what our founding fathers fought and died for—not freedom FROM religion, but RELIGIOUS FREEDOM!" Stone stomped up and down on the dais and shook with energy as he glared down at the casket, a tear forming in one eye.

Yes! Amen! Yes!

"Brothers and sisters, young Joey Thompson is no longer just a boy, he has become a martyr. He has become a reminder for all the Lord's people that Godless reasoning is like a fast boat with no North Star, racing toward the depths of a dark ocean." Stone raised a pink finger toward the back of the room now, directly at Annie. "We do NOT need Satan's stamp, we need to restore AMERICAN VALUES!"

Amen, Lord! Applause and foot stomping. *Amen!*

Henry watched Annie's red face harden in determination, her blue eyes looking straight back at multiple stares from the crowd, almost as if she were ready to physically fight them each and all.

"This innocent child can not, shall not, have died in vain," Stone bellowed. "We must return this country to GLORY! To HONOR! We, my brothers and sisters, must return this great land's soul to good men and women who still believe in something greater than themselves, who believe in God." And as Governor Stone let his words burst from his deep chest one last time, echoing over even the applause, the church seeming to vibrate with a palpable energy, *amens* roaring in approval and the sunlight streaming down over the man like heaven itself were warming him, Henry felt something move within his heart. "GOD BLESS AMERICA!"

* * *

The idea of evil, that's the fucking root of all evil. Annie knew churches, just like overt patriotism, had been constructed on fantasy and guilt to manipulate the masses, and the man lumbering down the steps in front of her was just the latest bastard in a long line of those trying to use religious and nationalistic lies for their own gain. But Annie Daniels could outsmart any man and she would prove Stone was a fraud once and for all, she just needed him to drop his guard and say the right words. *But what happens down here will finally put things right. I'll make things right.*

As she descended the wooden stairs into the basement Annie mentally salivated at the chance to expose hypocrisy, but also felt another wave of vertigo from the stuffy electric heat choking her. She undid the top button of her blouse. She had two goals: to get Stone to agree to President Fuentes' more pedestrian concerns of the joint speech as backup, and to get the fraudulent pastor to clearly admit that he didn't believe in God, while secretly taping him. She wouldn't, of course, actually make the joint speech unless her first plan fell through, but getting him to agree to the speech would placate her side and theirs, allow her adequate time to release both recordings of Stone and doom him to political oblivion before the electoral vote. Once she was able to clearly prove he was a fraud it would be too close to the end for anyone to do anything about it. Her phone was secured inside her blue blouse's right sleeve, microphone app already on.

The stairs creaked and swayed a bit under Stone's girth while dark-suited Goran scurried down into shadows ahead of him. It was ironic; the very thing she had originally tried to threaten Stone with, exposing his meeting with Yanic Goran, she had now been involved with herself twice in the last twenty-four hours.

The basement was dank and hummed with anemic light. The cinderblock walls were clumped with dark swaths of mold. A single flickering bulb hung from an electrical wire in the center. The floor, which was difficult to see in the weak light, was probably old brick with a thin film of mold clinging to it. The whole area was no bigger than a guest bedroom, and appeared to be used mainly for keeping boxes of extra Bibles and hymnals, crumbling and decaying from wet time. The small chamber reeked of fungal life, and Annie thought it a fitting little hole in the ground to meet with scum. *I just need to keep my head on straight, manipulate this conversation so he says the right words.*

"This privacy?" Stone outstretched his arms at the bottom with a glance up at the pinprick holes in the ceiling.

The three had stopped under the weak glow from the bulb, Annie's eyes and ears gravitating toward a drizzle of dark water running down the wall to disappear into cracks in the floor.

"No press can hear, right," he asked Goran. "No cameras?" The ceiling and the main room's floor above were one and the same, just one level of ancient wooden slats. The sad music from the organ and muffled voices barely wafted down on tiny shafts of light from the pinprick holes above, the entire ceiling seeming to pop and clack with every funeral attendee's step. "Too many Godforsaken cameras everywhere these days."

It was dark enough that Annie was still having a hard time reading the facial expressions of the other two, even in making out Goran's shape off to the side.

"I assure you, sir," Yanic Goran said, "I find no cameras down here. And I pay the organist upstairs to play loud."

Stone might have turned to her in the gloom. "We wouldn't want any competition for the little tape you've already got on me, Senator, now would we?" She could barely see Stone remove a white handkerchief from his pocket, wave the stale air from his nose as he glanced again toward the ceiling. "Now what the hell do you want? Whatever you're proposing better involve your promise to destroy that tape, Daniels. It's the fundraiser dinner, right?"

"Of course it was the dinner," Annie purred. As her eyes began to adjust to the gloom she thought she could now make out Stone's beady eyes narrowing at her under his wispy blonde tuffs of hair, suspicious. "I'm sure a man of your honor could only have one transgression, Pastor."

Stone sighed, ignoring her passive-aggressive insult. "And it doesn't trouble you that with Mr. Goran here you're potentially breaking the exact same campaign finance rule, Daniels? Little hypocritical, no?"

Inside her stomach churned at being alone with these two men, and she wanted to add, *I'm not here to sell my integrity for power*, but she had become a master of hiding her emotions when she chose. Her father had made sure of that. "Hopefully, Governor, we can reach a beneficial understanding. For the good of the country."

"Understanding," Stone scoffed back. "You called me a hypocrite on national television. Six times. And are blackmailing me to quit. I think I understand your stance already. Fuentes must be pissed about the Dayton riot, huh, for you to come groveling to me?"

"Maybe I find some Communion wine?" Yanic Goran leaned a little forward from the dark, his rodent eyes twitching nervously between the two. "Help us relax?"

"Leave," Annie snapped at Goran. She took an angled step closer to Stone to cut Goran from the conversation, determined to use any resource she could to out-smart Stone. "We prefer to be alone."

The tip of Annie's tongue crested the top of her lip within the half-light, licking for just a moment before going back in.

Nothing overt, just enough to rattle the synapses in his Cro-Magnon male brain a bit.

"But Governor, would you not like me—"

"Get out," Stone confirmed to Goran, curiosity dripping from his voice as he looked the svelte senator up and down.

"Of course, of course." The super-lawyer backed away toward the stairs, all apologetic bows and nods, sniffles and whines, like a subservient pet. "I shut and guard the door above."

But Stone's tone was still harsh. "Sixty seconds, Senator. What do you want?"

"To…" Annie tried to make hers sweet, using both hands to scoop her blonde strands off her shoulders now and twist it to one side, her long neck sweating even more in the stuffy basement. "I just want to…" She swallowed, finding it harder to say those words than she'd even imagined as Goran's footfalls receded back up the steps. "To apolo—" she coughed, and suddenly felt a wave of dizziness again.

"Ha." Stone chuckled like he was speaking to a carnival barker trying to con him out of his last dime. "You can't even get the words out." And as her vision further adjusted to the light she now found his massive girth almost towering over her, the door at the top of the stairs clapping shut. She suddenly felt vulnerable, as if she were wading into deeper waters than she had first suspected. His eyes were now drifting up and down her in the dull light and she felt hotter and sicker, his close proximity making the room feel like it was getting smaller. "Cut the bull, Senator. Are you really this desperate?"

Careful, she cautioned herself, *careful*. She had to strike exactly the right balance of seduction and threat to get the words she wanted recorded, just like Stone coaxing wallets into collection plates. Stone's huge body was so close she felt the rancid humidity of his perspiration and was overwhelmed with physical revulsion. She glanced around the edge of him toward the stacks of decaying cardboard boxes against the wall, to stall, to calculate. But the room was too hot, muggy, and her mind suddenly didn't feel sharp. "Okay, you're right, I'm not sorry. You disgust me."

Stone chuckled. "What makes you so blind to your own immorality, Senator? I suspect you'll do anything to win."

"Me?" Annie subtly leaned back from his creeping girth. "You claim a public morality you don't even believe in. You're a hypocrite… at best."

"You don't know my faith, woman. What if God works through individuals in ways you don't understand?"

As her vision was adjusting to the low light she now noticed the brick wall behind him had a crude mural painted on it. It was the classic male-constructed scene of Eve being tempted in the Garden of Eden. That painting had an overtly innocent man standing off to the side of a tree, watching in horror as a voluptuous naked woman reached for an apple while a black snake coiled menacingly around the trunk. *Typical patriarchal bullshit. The man so fucking noble, the woman only a wicked, dumb slut.* The snake's eyes, she realized with a shudder, were strangely bright and translucent, almost a living pink cutting through the darkness to her, just like the Zennies. "I had a calling," Stone continued. "You know nothing of having a code of—"

"Please, you're a fraud, in bed for any corporation that can write you the biggest check."

"How dare you."

"Everything in your platform is about helping the rich get richer, Hampton."

"Corporations ARE America, Daniels. The only way to keep a democracy alive is to support free market businesses to make money so the entire economy stays healthy, so even your lazy low-achievers can still eat. You can't just give everyone everything, it's why socialism is never feasible. If you want to help someone you teach them to fish, not just give them... weed and porn."

"A free market without morality is fascism." Annie did not feel normal, dizzy. She was distracted by the odd fluorescent color of the snake's pink eyes, and her brain was getting foggy. "If there's no moral component within free markets then only the corrupt wealthy win, everyone else is crushed beneath their greed. Where's God in that? Morality?"

"Ha, a declared atheist who I could pull up having sex online right now, arguing that the problem with a free market democracy is missing morality? Certainly you're not the judge of what's moral or not? That's why humanity must appeal to tradition, scripture, for ultimate guidance."

"Admit it Governor, you're just the latest politician to be dispensing religious opium to the narrow-minded masses."

For a surreal moment, she swore she saw the snake's black tail flicker in the gloom. *What the fuck?* She tore her eyes from the weird mural in a wave of panic, folding her hands in front of her with a deep breathe as she focused back into the governor's scowling face as another wave of vertigo rocking her. *Keep it together. The snake didn't move. Hissss.* Annie suddenly thought she heard a hissing in the room and her heart fluttered. *The pipes, it must be old pipes. It's not a snake. Keep it together.*

"Fitting," Stone growled, "for someone like you to quote Marx. How has every equality-based state-controlled communist country faired in the past for its people, Daniels?" Stone wiped a tiny orange palm over his glistening upper lip. "Ten seconds before I walk."

"A deal," she gasped, forcing herself to hold his eye contact even though it felt like the room were starting to wobble. She gently pressed the phone secured beneath her blouse to her ribs to reassure it was still there, recording. "After Dayton, we've got to put a lid back on things, for the good of the country."

"I'm listening. But destroying that tape is non-negotiable, Senator," Stone said, his eyes drifting again from her face to her body, more blatantly this time.

Hissssss.

"Okay." She rubbed the sides of her sweaty neck, pushing her blouse open a bit to get more air, reassuring herself again that it was just the sound of old water pipes she was hearing. "But we've got to agree to making a joint statement, both camps." Her breath became shallow. "All four of us standing side by side, publicly agreeing to abide by whatever the electoral vote Monday is, in order to keep the country calm."

"Why would I help publicly redeem you before the electoral tie? Your Dayton speech backfired."

"Because it won't tie." Annie heard herself blurt, eyes squinting in the low light, crow's feet crinkling beside them. "You're going to lose the vote outright. I know."

Hisssssss.

"What?" The Governor's eyes shocked. "How—"

"Louisiana will tip to us." Annie tried to sound confident despite the heat, despite the vertigo and her groggy head. "I'm just trying to ensure that all of your less-than-intellectual followers are willing to accept the verdict without disruptions." Despite the *hiss*.

"You flipped a Louisiana elector?"

"How and why is for me to know," Annie answered. "Your only task is to make the smart move now. Do what I ask and I'll make a spot for you in the next administration. Attorney General maybe?"

"No." He shook his wispy blonde head, a smirk breaking over his lips. "I don't believe you." His face was confident, too confident. "You're bluffing. I hold cards you don't even know exist, Daniels. Forces you don't understand. Ohio is mine. Louisiana is mine, and the tie will happen. You're going to lose." He leaned farther toward her and inhaled, like he was smelling supper. "I'm destined to win."

"Destined?" Annie willed herself not to step back, even though his nearness was roiling a primal disgust in her, his stench like wet, horny dog. *Concentrate, Annie, concentrate. Get him to say the words.* "By God?" Things were swaying; too hot, cramped, Stone pressing too close. "You can't tell me you actually think God is real, Hampton. That some kindly old man is sitting up on a cloud watching us and that he wants you to take money from hedge fund managers and gun dealers, pass your Religious Bigotry Amendment? To arrest poor people using a natural herb of the earth, but uphold the carried interest loophole for Wall Street bankers? I guess your version of God doesn't like civil rights, huh?"

Hisssssss.

"There is actual right and wrong in the world, woman, everything is not relative."

"You're too smart for religion, Hampton, just admit you

don't believe, and I'll make a deal to give you whatever you want." *Hiss. Hiss.* Annie put a hand to her throat, tugging at her blouse a bit as sweat trickled down her collar bones. *It's the pipes, the hiss is the pipes.* "I bet you'd forget your morals right now for a sweet enough temptation." Her balance lurched, and she jutted one foot out wider, reflexively throwing a soft palm to Hampton Stone's dark lapel, resting her fingers against his barrel chest for support. "Do... do you hear that?"

"Jezebel." Stone's eyes were wide in bewilderment at her hand clutching his shirt, his lips trembling in indignation. "You, you... whore."

"God is bullshit," she panted. Her wobbly eyes glared up into his, her hand still on his chest to steady herself, trying to focus her foggy mind. "Say it." Her woozy gaze flickering downward, resting for a moment on his silver belt buckle as the snake only she could hear hissed louder. "Just say it, daddy... before the snake..."

He snatched up her other hand in his and ripped her closer.

"Lord," he growled, "forgive me."

* * *

True morality, Henry remembered hearing once, *was what you did while no one else could see.*

In the back of the limo Henry watched Annie emerge from the church and wondered what he was actually seeing. She seemed flustered, sad.

Once technology allows us to watch each other all the time, will we all become more moral, or just give up on the idea altogether?

Henry had just erased the text message he'd received from Harmony, feeling guilty about keeping these communications with Annie's daughter a secret. It wasn't anything nefarious, he had just been helping to arrange for her to visit a holistic doctor in Denver, a last-ditch effort Harmony desperately wanted to find a cure for her disease. Harmony had asked Henry to help after Annie had immediately written the man off as a witch-doctor and forbade her daughter from getting sucked into false hopes and 'pointless spiritual mumbo-jumbo.' Henry hated covering things up, but where was the line that made deception okay if you were trying to achieve a greater good? He wondered the same thing watching Annie walk toward the limo, and suddenly concluded that maybe there was never a cause to deceive, and any justification to was just selfish and cowardly.

The sun was starting its early winter descent, and shadows and murk were already casting the church grounds in dark claws. Henry thought he maybe caught a flash of despair creep over Annie's face as she passed through a branch's long shadows, as if she was fundamentally unsure of something. She adjusted her blue blouse as she approached the car, then wiped the corners of her mouth before opening the door and sliding in.

"Talk to me, Henry," she stated confidently though. No doubt in her at all now, and Henry considered he must have processed her look of confusion incorrectly.

"Well," Henry glanced at his iPad, wondering if she had reached the deal with Stone. "A fight between some kids broke out in front of a Georgia abortion clinic, ma'am. No one seriously injured, but four arrests and the national news spinning it in obvious ways."

"That *Tifton Church* Group?"

"Yep." Henry scrolled further down the news feed. "And in addition to the *Reboot.org* thing, the FBI has announced they might have thwarted a radical Islam sleeper cell discovered in New York."

"Any backlash to *Long Knives*?"

"Only the few whackos that always cry conspiracy seemed to have noticed, and the White House is easily covering things up with some disinformation about heroin and terrorism busts." Henry glanced up, studying her face for clues to the meeting with Stone, clues to what was really going on in her mind. "Total of 478 individuals that Howe pinpointed have successfully been detained in FEMA camps, the president saying no more are necessary as long as the public reconciliation speech between you and Stone happens."

She glanced out the window now, her blue eyes seeming to focus on a point far over the horizon.

"So," he asked, "how'd it go?"

"Stone agreed to the speech." Annie exhaled, dropping her head back against the black leather. "I'll need you to coordinate with Parker in the governor's camp. Make sure to set the joint speech for sometime tomorrow night, as late as possible. Think I might actually be able to sleep tonight."

"Good." Henry nodded, relieved. It was the safest move for the country. It was at least a sign she could still be rational. "But wouldn't you want it in primetime, so—"

"I won't be making it though, Henry." She sat forward and reached for a glass tumbler on the limo bar. "The later the time, the longer we have to maneuver though."

Henry's heart sunk. "Not making it, ma'am? Do you think it's wise—"

"Don't patronize me." Annie plunked two ice cubes into her glass. "Let's go home." She splashed Beam into the glass, leaned back in the seat with a sigh, and took a sip. "Jesus, I'm going to enjoy sleeping in my own bed for once. Even if my husband's there." Her gaze drifted out the window toward the church as she talked to herself, dreamily. "I wonder how easy it will be, once *Cyber-Care* is installed in everyone, to actually outlaw religion? Imagine a world, Henry, where no one ever had to feel guilt again."

"What did you do?" Henry growled. "You promised the president you were going to make the speech with Stone, Annie. You've got to make the speech. Truth matters."

"Joking. Relax." She shot a hand up the arm of her sleeve, fishing around in her suit jacket for a moment, then pulled out her cell phone from where she had it taped and recording. She tossed it to him. "Somewhere on there I've got Stone declaring stuff like *God is a sham* and *of course I'm just using religion to get votes.* Find his audio and isolate it, erase everything else." She sighed. "We'll need to take it completely out of context, but that statement paired with the video at his fundraising dinner should push him over the edge, make him toxic to everyone, even the Republican House members." Annie rolled the icy glass over her forehead. "A little insurance. It's the smart thing."

"Something up your sleeve." Henry glared down at the cell phone in his palm. "Annie, this isn't ethic—"

"I said it was only insurance, Corwich. I just need to make one more call. Then let's head to San Fran."

And looking at her, Henry wondered if he had been wrong all along. He thought about the warmth he'd felt watching Stone speak, and wondered now if the antichrist really existed. Wondered if she was sitting in the seat across from him.

A*true solution for a temporal world,* Mr. Jefferson thought, *can only come from a timeless place.*

Mr. Jefferson knelt on his woven meditation rug with his white, Sea Island Cotton dress shirt carefully draped on a wooden hanger on the closed door's knob. All his red and blue scars, the welts and lava-like burnt skin were exposed across his translucent pale flesh. The single window's drapes were drawn tight, and Mr. Jefferson's pink eyes gazed softly in the dim light to the iPad on the floor before his knees. The infinite streaming numerical calculation of Pi ran across the screen like tiny starbursts from deep space, left to right, top to bottom, never-ending white blips on black, forever.

Mr. Jefferson repeated the mantra with straight spine, rhythmic breath. "*Om, pishlay doth. Hey, pishlay ashta.*" It was the oldest language—far older than Sanskrit, or Tamil, or Sinhala, or Khoisan—and the sacred words prepared him for the next choice. "*Om, pishlay doth.*" Without taking his eyes from the numbers on the screen, Mr. Jefferson picked up the handgun and raised it to his temple, expectant joy surging in his heart. "*Om, pishlay doth. Hey, pishlay ashta. Om, pishlay doth.*"

Quantum suicide. Everyone was immortal, as the reality of quantum mechanics was there were multiple worlds, infinite branches of reality forever splitting apart with every choice made. Consciousness was energy, and energy could never be destroyed, only shift. So, the facts of quantum suicide dictated that no one ever died, they simply appeared to die for those observers left in one timeline of reality while an individual's true consciousness would go on living, unaware of death, in another. When the bullet entered Mr. Jefferson's skull in this timeline he would actually know nothing of it, just seamlessly shift to an identical timeline elsewhere. The only fact in his reality would be that the gun had simply jammed rather than splattering his brains across the carpet. *"Om, pishlay doth. Hey, pishlay ashta."*

This act was a way to harness courage for the true work, the eternal work, to free his mind from petty concerns like trying to live. To destroy the core fear. He had preformed the ritual twice before, and both times the gun had correctly jammed. *"Om, pishlay doth."* He pressed the gun's muzzle tighter against his temple, his forefinger beginning to squeeze. *"Hey, pishlay ashta."*

The *RedRabbit* phone rang.

Mr. Jefferson stopped chanting.

The phone rang again. Mr. Jefferson set the handgun to the side, picked up the black phone and answered. "We hold these truths, Mr. Washington…"

"To be self-evident, Mr. Jefferson," the metallic voice chirped. "Plan B. Make the call."

"Certainly, Mr. Washington."

"1776, Mr. Jefferson."

"1776, Mr. Washington. All is connected."

"Uh…" Amos stuttered on the phone call with Shay.

He hadn't actually expected her to pick up. In the couple hours he'd debated making the call he'd imagined himself being much cooler, much more businesslike in his tone. Then he'd heard her voice and every cell in his body vibrated with excitement, trepidation. They'd already gone through minutes of awkward chuckles and long silences as Amos had asked general questions about her life, her job. "Well, it's just a favor I need, someone who can look into some names for me. Like a reporter, but someone I can trust." He switched the phone from his bad ear to his good. "Lieutenant Ty Stoughton, General Mace Harper, and a Nicaraguan official, Deputy Lupe."

"Amos…" she said for what must have been the tenth time, her tone seeming to oscillate between a half dozen emotions: joy, fear, annoyance, confusion, and hearing the tickle of her breath against the phone surged fire through him. "Wow. It's strange to hear your voice." Did she still care about him? Hate him? Or maybe worst of all, was he now nothing to her, just a faded memory? Fifteen years was a long time.

"You used to cover the Pentagon for a bit right," he tried to sound relaxed. "DOD? I thought I read that somewhere."

"Yeah," she answered. "But Amos, I don't know if—"

"Sounds like your job is going well." Amos wanted the conversation less awkward, didn't want her feeling pressured, and his mind raced with images of what she might look like. Did she still have the ink-black hair? The quizzical crinkle over her nose? He pictured emerald eyes, the dimples, and the dusting of pinprick freckles over the bridge of her mocha-skinned nose, like God knew he'd created too much of a masterpiece and splattered his paint brush at the end just to add more character. "What's the story they've got you racing all over for?"

"Electoral College," she answered. "With all the debate about potentially tying we're trying to get an article hammered out on some of the individual electors for tomorrow."

"Who?"

"Ha. Exactly. Just 538 people picking the president for the entire country, and no one ever really ever knows who they are. I'm trying to interview at least a couple from states that don't have laws demanding an elector vote in the way that matches with the popular vote. Maybe we can catch a faithless elector before he actually cheats on his party."

"Faithless elector?"

"Yeah, it's actually happened over 150 times before, electors voting a different way than the popular vote. It's never ended up mattering before though, because the electoral vote total wasn't close enough, but if it happened this time, well, it would be a BIG deal. Every elector counts."

"Seems a silly system. Why don't our individual votes just count?" Amos breathed deep, wanting to talk about them, about where things went wrong, not about their jobs or his fears of something wrong on his own team. He wanted her.

"Because as much as they talked out a government run by the people, the founding fathers were actually pretty afraid the average American was too dumb to actually understand the issues." She chuckled.

"Someone died," Amos blurted out, realizing he was handling this all wrong, but just needing to get to the point, then maybe be able to say even more important things, like that he was sorry. "There's something strange going on with it, Shay, and I'm not sure what. That's what I need your help on… the names."

There was a pause, and he could hear her breath, soft and slow just like when she used to lay next to him. "Okay. So, you call me up after fifteen years and want me to look into something, but can't tell me what it is? Just some random names?"

"Being Spec Op, I'm not supposed to speak with press. Someone like you could look into those names, cross searching them with the phrase *1776*."

"You want me to get you information on the American Revolution?" She laughed again and at the sound an uncontrollable smile stretched across his face. "Do they not let you top-secret types use Wikipedia?"

"I can't look into it on my own, they monitor me. And I really can't say more, but could you maybe please call me if you find anything?"

"Well, the reason I don't work DOD anymore was because I asked too many questions about Harper and some others higher ups. I often saw them bringing military-industrial reps into meetings. You know, Boeing, Lockheed, Raytheon and others. Harper didn't like me prodding."

"Yeah, that happens. They advise on the equipment."

"Except, I think they were doing more than giving instructions on hardware. There were some rumors that they were helping the military actually devise strategy on where intervention was needed. Everybody getting more rich for each bomb dropped." Shay sighed. "Look, I'm going to be in Tampa tomorrow for the elector story, landing late afternoon. Want to meet, maybe grab a drink?"

Amos felt a rush of adrenaline, a combination of dread and rapture like the first time he'd been under gunfire. It was strange how cold and certain Amos' nerves could get in the heat of physical danger, yet how much of a jittery wuss he felt in some social situations. Another reason why he felt more at home in the field than trying navigate through all these murky complexities of domestic life. He wanted to see Shay again, more than anything in the world, but he also felt dread over something inside his heart getting torn to shreds like before, and guilt thinking about his wife. He looked down at his hands and saw his wedding band on his finger, swallowing a lump in his throat. He had made that vow before God and had never broken it, and for a second he didn't say anything. Then two. Then three.

"Okay," he said.

If God was going to give him the chance to correct all the mistakes of his past, maybe he just needed not to squander it.

* * *

Just before his newest patient Harmony Daniels arrived, Dr. Mokeba saw a sad news update on the death of the boy from the Dayton Riot as well as several tense political protests from both sides in large cities around the country. Dr. Mokeba was first generation Batswanan and to him it seemed American politics and its press had reached an absurd state of dishonesty and farce. Dr. Mokeba flashed his gold tooth in a relieved smile though when he saw how simple and genuine the political daughter was. "Welcome, Miss Harmony," Mokeba beamed, making sure he spoke his second language slowly and with the proper words. "Welcome."

No Secret Service, no assistants, just the yellow cab pulling up with a beautiful young woman. More stunning in fact than any pictures he had seen of her; tall with long blonde hair twisted into a pony-tail, a hint of Asian features to her face. She was obviously nervous, her eyes darting over him and the exterior of paint-peeling house, even as she cast the most courteous smile of bright white teeth at him with an extended hand. Under a tan wool overcoat she wore a purple sundress with flowers on it and open-toed sandals, and as she leaned back into the taxi to grab her one bag, he noticed the tiny red rabbit tattoo at the base of her neck.

Genuine, brave, kind. That was Mokeba's initial assessment. *An open heart of youth.*

He gently took her hand again and held her eyes as his own smile basked back. "Are you ready to heal, my dear?"

"Yes." She smiled and the tightness of her body seemed to melt. "I saw your ad mentioning something about the *guna of rajas*, and I just had an instinct you were the one who could help."

She did, however, let out a soft gasp of shock as they entered his office though. It was a shithole.

* * *

"All is entwined, interrelated, and connected," Mokeba attempted to explain once he had completed their initial conversation about his healing methods and explaining the guna of rajas. The most telling thing he had found in the initial part of her conversation was that she feared being alone most of all, of dying before she felt like she were completely connected to the world. "From our cells to the stars, from quantum twitches to coronal explosions, this illusory material world is inextricably woven into an eternally shimmering web of causes and effects playing out across our collective consciousness—as above, so below. And your body is essentially breaking at its seams from all the… the…" He rolled his eyes toward the sagging ceiling above him and tried to remember the right American slang. "Bullshit." A soft trickle of snow gently drifted from a hole in the roof down onto one of the numerous piles of yellowing papers cluttering the floor. "Depression, hate, anxiety, extremism, they are all *Kali Yuga* symptoms of the same disease... materialistic bullshit."

They were sitting in his ruined office, he on one side of the lopsided desk, she on the stool across from him. On the wall behind him there hung no medical degrees or photos of him shaking hands with important people but only a single green poster, one corner torn. White lettering on the poster read *Say No To isms*. He pushed stacks of books and crusty papers off to either side in order to see her from where he sat, and two empty coffee mugs had clunked to the stained carpet in the process. He had just explained she would need to fast for twenty-four hours at his home, then drink the hallucinogenic plant medicine, *Soma*, tomorrow.

Mokeba had already given her an explanation of the *Soma* drink. He had explained the drink was something that had been revered in the ancient times as the healing elixir of the gods, but whose ingredients were forgotten through the modern age until Mokeba's uncle, a one-eyed Bwiti shaman in Arizona, had rediscovered them. The drink was made of a number of hallucinogenic plants, including Ayahuasca from the Amazon and Iboga from Africa. Ayahuasca was the mother plant, revered as a scared healer of mind and body with numerous modern anecdotes about it curing a myriad of illnesses from depression to cancer to multiple sclerosis. Iboga was the father plant, and was said to be able to beat your way of seeing the world back into shape, supposedly curing addicts of heroin, alcohol, and many other substances in a single dose. Mokeba said the *Soma* also contained small portions of peyote, mushrooms, and huachuma, as well as trace amounts of many ancient alchemists' tools like mercury and gold. He started to name several other ingredients, all supposedly combined in exact portions and in an exact cooking order, having names like *snakeroot* and *dragon's bone* and *eye of Trismegistus*, but eventually, Harmony had held up her palm and asked him to stop. The nervous tightness had returned to her face.

"And this *death drink* is the cure to my stigmata disease?" She pulled shoulders back, trying to remain composed and ladylike even while discussing her own mortality.

"Sort of." He nodded, shrugged and sighed, then nodded again. "Kind of." Explaining the way the universe actually worked to modern Americans, the enternal-ness of impermanence, had proved the most difficult part of his practice here. What did they mean exactly by cure, for instance, when everyone would eventually die? If Americans couldn't see it and touch it, have someone with a degree tell them it was okay to believe, they had been thoroughly indoctrinated with not trusting in the universe. "You see," he started, noticing his half-eaten avocado sandwich wilting brown on the side of his desk and quickly tossing it in the wastebasket. "The drink will pull back the veil of this material world to let you interact with more eternal truths, beyond the life and death of this world, and in that you will, hopefully, get cured."

"Hopefully?" Harmony tilted her blonde head, as if she were unsure if *hopefully* was the word she wanted to hear.

Mokeba decided to try explaining from a different angle. "The connection between all things is growing tighter and tighter." He pointed to the cell phone still clutched in her thin left hand by way of example. "Like the cinching of the universal knot, both the good and the bad of this world, whatever we originate, infects those around us with greater speed, greater saturation. We clutch tighter, chatter more, yet this simply makes change accelerate, the bullshit spread faster." He raised his eyebrows at her hopefully, smiled with his gold tooth sparkling.

Harmony sighed. "I'm sorry, I don't think I'm following after all." She pointed at the poster behind him on the wall that read 'say no to '*isms*'. "What's that mean?"

Dr. Mokeba grinned, excited that she had already asked. "It means that the greatest form of disease currently spreading through this macro-organism is believing that you already know what the truth is. Liberalism, conservatism, feminism, patriotism, racism, spiritualism, etcetera, etcetera, they are all forms of the same error. If you believe you have solved the equation of truth with a reality-based ideology, and therefore defend that ideology from any new information rather than embrace growth in an ever-changing reality, you are certainly always wrong. One truth is never THE truth. The truth that can be spoken, can never be eternal truth, my dear. Do you understand, Miss Harmony? Your best, maybe only shot of being cured, is to reintegrate with eternal truth, to escape the modern bullshit."

"I guess. Except, I like reality, its not all bad." Tiny creases at the bridge of her nose furrowed though. "So... does the drink send me to the spirit world then?"

The doctor folded his hands over each other and smiled softly, but could not find the English words to accurately answer her. She was so pretty, so naturally beautiful and perfectly innocent it always made him a bit sad to think of children having to come terms with what this life truly was. "Truth comes, no matter what, my dear. Truth does come."

And at those words Harmony seemed to become more

stiff, nervous again. "This… maybe my mom was right, maybe this has been a mistake?"

"But you can't give up yet, my dear," Mokeba grinned wide. "We still need to kill you."

Overnight

(New Orleans, Louisiana: Saturday into Sunday, 11:45 p.m. PST / 2:45 a.m. EST)

In a dimly lit Alabama bar, *@jessejameskickass* took off his bedazzled trucker's hat and set it down next to his and his buddy's half-drunk beers. A John Mellencamp song played on the jukebox, singing about the way American life was supposed to be, about love and loyalty and simple good things. The two friends hunched on their barstools, as weary with life's defeats as two old men. *@jessejameskickass* was getting tired of everyone saying he was bad and wrong, and got more than he deserved just because of the color of his skin, and because he happened to born with a penis. "White privilege? Shit, the nicest thing I own is this damn trucker's hat."

"I don't know either," his friend said, two grease-stained fingers pulling against his red *Make America Great Again* T-shirt. "I'm just starting to think it's us versus them. Jesus-loving normal people against the weirdoes, and they keep winning because we don't fight anymore. That rancher said it was a war. My dad wouldn't put up with this shit."

@jessejameskickass took a sip of his beer, and nodded in thought. "Shit, I heard zombie cannibals might be a real thing now."

I never knew no dad, Louisiana Elector Little Gumbo sadly thought, his hurting head resting on one arm on the plastic table, trying to focus through his hangover on the reassuring, although quick, beats of his heart. *Maybe if I'd just had somebody I coulda talk to when young, somebody to really trust, they could have shown me the way?* The muscles around his eyes ached, and outside the honks and shouts from Saturday night New Orleans traffic burst in his ears. Little Gumbo couldn't remember the last twelve hours too well. *I wanted to be good.*

He slowly concluded the bowl of red beans and rice two rats were gorging on must have been spilled sometime yesterday. Maybe he'd had a customer, maybe he'd been eating red beans and rice and dropped it himself? His breath reeked of tequila, and he felt like a doom of Biblical proportions was bearing down on him, like he was a broken piece in a game no one had ever told him the rules to. The one rule he did know: if you were black in America, then creepy white people always fucked with you.

It had been all those big bills. Mr. Jefferson had given him the cash, and it had smelled crisp and powerful, like freedom, and it had lit the fuse to one hell of a party. Or at least, Little Gumbo assumed it had been one hell of a party.

After the weird Mr. Jefferson had left, Little Gumbo could remember telling himself that the money was a chance, a last chance to finally turn the tide into positive things. He had counted the bills once, twice, and a third time, his hands trembling with excitement. He imagined paying off the pawn shop loan he had gotten to fix the stove in back, catching up the back rent, and maybe even getting some of the worst tables and chairs replaced. He could send money to Darlene in Baton Rouge to help with the kids, maybe? But that kind of talk only lasted for a bit, and soon all the other emotions starting eating at him like a cancer. No aging black man with a past would get a break in America, not a real one, and everything in him got tangled and tense. His heart started cramping up on him from too many possibilities, too much stress, and too many choices. He felt shaky and weird and scared, and that's when he'd realized he just needed to take a break from it all, get his mind clear. Maybe have a drink? *Everybody needs to relax*, Little Gumbo had thought as he lit the crack pipe over all those fresh green bills. *Hell, bet Annie Daniels even relax sometimes.* That had been over twelve blacked-out hours ago.

Little Gumbo now pushed his head off the table and the world lurched in pain, like a steel spike being driven through his skull. Had there been something else he was supposed to do for that freaky Mr. Jefferson. Check in with him? The vote was a day away, right? Little Gumbo couldn't remember. His vision wobbled and he felt like he might throw up. He used two fingers to lift open the manila envelope on the table, and tried not to cry. Only a day ago it held the $15,000 cash, but inside it now was only a $20 bill and an unopened condom. His hangover was so bad, the gloom so thick, that he didn't even hear the police until they were standing inside his restaurant's doorway staring at him.

"Lawrence Gatreaux?" the fat white cop asked, repositioning his big black belt with the gun and nightstick on his wide hips. "You Gatreaux?"

Sitting straighter in his chair, everything in Little Gumbo tingled danger. Both were beat cops. The sweating white guy, pudgy and with a bushy cop mustache intact, and a black woman with a sprinter's ass, hard eyes sick of Little Gumbo's kind bringing their race down. They were decked in their cop-blue uniforms and already carrying looks of disdain.

"I's Gatreaux, but ain't no Lawrence," Little Gumbo lied. "Darryl Gatreaux."

"Funny," the black cop said glaring at a picture she held in her hand, "look like Lawrence to me." The white cop took a couple of steps to the side, spreading out the distance between him and his partner to either side of the doorway. Every twitch inside Little Gumbo told him to run.

"Nah," Little Gumbo said as casually as he could, getting up from his chair like it wasn't no big deal. "I get my cook. He tell yas, I Lawrence's brother." Little Gumbo turned, started walking the few feet back toward the kitchen before the cops could say anything. Little Gumbo knew cops, and calm ignorance was the only card he could play. "He right here with my ID, hold on."

"Hold up there, Mr. Gatreaux," the white cop called from behind him. Little Gumbo knew better than to look back though. "Mr. Gatreaux, hold up now."

"He right here." Little Gumbo raised a finger over his shoulder and stepped into the kitchen doorway, then around the corner out of sight to start calling for a cook that did not exist. The kitchen was narrow, cramped, a fifteen by nine space at best, overflowing with dirty pans and plates in all three sinks, piles of food in various stages of decay crowding the stove and counter and cabinet spaces. Importantly though, there was a rickety screened backdoor into the brick alley behind. *Think. Think. Think.* Little Gumbo paced in that min-iscule space before the open doorway leading into the dining room and the cop's line of sight, trying to determine through his hangover what he should do. The screened door led to freedom, or a potentially huge mistake by running from the police. He grabbed his hair with both hands and tried to calm down, to think. *Make the right choice, dammit. For once, make the right choice.*

"Mr. Gatreaux," the white cop called again, obviously closer to the kitchen door now. "Come back out here, please, sir."

Think. Could they be here regarding his child support? Of course, he couldn't remember the past twelve hours, so maybe something horrific had happened. Maybe they knew, or would find, the crack rock he had hidden in the pantry. *Jesus, that rock! I got that fucking rock!* Little Gumbo's eyes went wide toward the coffee can in the pantry. That tiny crack rock would send him away for years. *I was born guilty.*

"Mr. Gatreaux," the white cop's tone was now firm. "Please show yourself, Lawrence." Little Gumbo heard a gun pulled from its holster, steps cautiously nearing the kitchen door.

And there was nothing left for Little Gumbo to do but run. Run for his freedom, run for his life, run for his soul. Little Gumbo burst out through the squeaking screened back-door into the alleyway, his legs flying fast, fast as his wheezing lungs could power them, down the dark brick alley toward the light coming from the open street. Freedom. Escape. A new life.

But behind him was the clap of wood on wood; the screen door slamming shut, then bouncing open once more to slam shut again, just before the shouts of two chasing cops. "Freeze!"

Twenty-Five Years Earlier

(Gainesville, Missouri: 11:51 a.m. PST / 2:51 p.m. EST)

The way Annie remembered it, when she was eleven it had taken her prodding her teacher nine times to mention to their mother the importance of having a computer with Internet access in the home, before Ray Daniels, Annie and Amos' perpetually angry father, would allow it. In Ray Daniels' defense he was actually only angry if he was too drunk. Or too sober. The nice buzz he managed to keep between ten a.m. and one p.m. was when he'd sing Marine chants and make pancakes, everyone laughing. It was nearly three in the afternoon though, the day Annie was showing Amos how to pull up Wikipedia for his first real school report.

"Get the fuck off it," Ray Daniels slurred. "It's infected with bad shit." He grabbed Annie by her upper arm and yanked her back from the table in the room they called the study. "Besides, I don't pay hundreds of dollars a month for you to be screwin' shit up fer games." At this point, Ray Daniels had not yet taken his wife by the throat and knocked her head off the sink. At this point, their mother had not left with the youth pastor from her church, and the kids had not spent nights sitting out in the cold pouring rain waiting for their drunk father to pull his shotgun from his mouth and stop sobbing. At this point, Ray had not come into Annie's bedroom that night. "You're being dumb, little girl." This was the time period between Ray Daniels being a supposed 'war hero' with PTSD, and before he had given up the drink for God through Alcoholics Anonymous.

The study was actually a dusty closet in their double-wide mobile home in Gainesville, Missouri, and the 'table' the computer monitor sat on was actually a wobbly stack of cardboard boxes holding several gallons of motor oil. Amongst much broken furniture and strewn auto parts, the only things Ray Daniels tried to keep crisp and clean inside the mobile home were the five American flags mounted to different walls, and the glass case holding his bronze star for heroism. Ponytailed Annie smacked into the hallway wall, dust swirling and the mobile home trembling.

"Damn, Ray," she grunted, but otherwise didn't flinch.

Instinctively, Amos leapt for the stack of boxes, putting his small hands up to keep them from toppling. In and of itself, Annie getting yanked backward into a wall by their cursing, swaying father was nothing to cause alarm.

"It ain't games." She bounced back into a stand. "It's for Stubb's class report." It would take a year of speech therapy after leaving home for Annie to lose her country twang.

Ray Daniels didn't bother to turn to Annie. "Watch your sass, girl." He took a slow sip of the Jim Beam bourbon he perpetually drank from a sterling-silver mug with the Marine Corp crest on it. His yellowed eyes squinted down in cloaked confusion and blatant distrust at the computer that young Amos carefully righted. "This thing ain't good," Ray whispered. "Ain't no good. Too much bad out there."

"It's the Internet, Ray, we need it," Annie countered. "The

whole world's already on the Internet. It's a big, beautiful, fucking world." Annie had been calling her father by his first name for several years now, and he turned back at her with the typical snarl. It was obvious to everyone that Ray Daniels thought his young daughter calling him by his first name was a sign of disrespect. It was also obvious to everyone that it pretty much was. No one except Annie knew exactly when and why she had started doing it, that it was all about a rabbit with pink eyes, and a snake. "Ms. Mullins already explained it all to you and Mom, Ray, get with the damn future."

"I seen shit, girl." Ray jabbed a long boney finger down at her. "I've seen shit on TV 'bout how every psycho and pervert is lurking out there on the web world, waiting to scoop dumb little fuckers like you up in it. There's probably Arabs on there, drug pushers and porno producers, so am I not supposed to protect my family?" Ray Daniels gulped down the rest of his bourbon, then shoved the empty mug back to a proud nine-year-old Amos. "It just might be, girl, that I know a thing or two more than a fucking six-year-old lady." Ray gritted his scruffy jaw.

"I'm eleven."

"Jesus fucking Christ." Ray Daniels threw up his scraggily arms in exhaustion. "Tomatoes, potatoes, you're a kid." Ray rubbed both dirty hands through his greasy hair, knocking his trucker hat to the floor. "You two get your asses outside and play like real kids." He gently used the back of his hand to guide young Amos from the computer and toward the door where Annie stood. Ray, for whatever reason, was always more gentle with Amos. Down the hall, the side of Ray's boot went to thin Annie's ass a couple of times. Not hard, but not soft either, shoving and prodding the two siblings toward the front like he was trying to herd stubborn donkeys. "Out!"

The flimsy metal door to the mobile home clapped shut behind them as a last kick to Annie's ass helped her down the rotting steps and into the dry red clay. Amos was already down at the bottom of the steps clutching his dad's empty bourbon mug in two hands like a priceless relic.

Annie barely had the time to stand back up and dust herself off before the door squeaked back open. A handgun thudded to the ground between her and her brother, a pink puff of clay dust rising. "Play with that shit," their dad grunted from the door with a wave of his dirty hand. "It ain't loaded." Then the door clapped shut again.

"Jesus fucking Christ," Annie said with a shake of her head down at the gun between their feet. "You know Dad ain't right in the head, don't ya, Stubbs? Jesus fucking Christ."

"Mom says you shouldn't curse, Annie. Taking the Lord's name in vain and all."

"Oh, fuck me, Mom just has a crush on the pastor."

The door would open two more times. Once for the computer, monitor and tower, to come flying with white extension cords spinning like airborne snakes, crashing into the hard dirt with plastic and glass spraying. Then another time for their father to stumble down the steps and gently pull the silver mug back from Amos' hands, drunkenly dropping his half-empty bottle of Beam in the dirt as he stomped back up the rickety steps. "Y'all play now. Find some toads or something," Ray mumbled, then locked the door from the inside.

"Damn. What a shit show." Annie shook her head at the mobile home, the gun, the bottle, and the computer parts strewn across the clay. "This ain't a home, it's a goddamn lazy-eyed carnival."

"You shouldn't swear so much. Mom says swearing is a

whistle for the devil." Amos leaned over the gun. "Dad's a war hero, he don't mean nothing bad. People say he's just seen stuff, Annie."

"Ray's seen the bottom of a bunch of those bottles, that's what."

"Dad's not bad, Annie, he's just feeling bad." Amos stepped toward the handgun. "We need to support him."

"Don't you dare pick that up, Stubbs," Annie cautioned her younger brother. "Dad ain't right in the head. Time people stop making excuses for bad behavior, and using guns and stuff." Annie took the handgun and placed it under a heavy rock behind the mobile home, instructing her little brother to never get near it. The half-drunk bottle of Beam, however, came with them on their walk into the woods, Annie curious as to what her father found in it.

"So Ray don't find it," was what Annie said as they walked down the dirt trail, but her eyes were fixated on the sloshing brown liquid inside.

* * *

A quarter mile down the wood trail, speckled sunlight breaking through the leaves above, Annie titled her head back and let the smallest sip of bourbon pass her lips. "Gawd damn." Her face wrinkled, and her eyes widened. "Shit, but that's bad," she gasped.

"Annie," Amos stammered with worry. "Mom says God says getting drunk's sinful and—"

"Don't be a tard, man, you're too old to be believing everything they try to manipulate you with," Annie scoffed. "Use your brain. The Internet said it would take at least two ounces of liquor to get my body weight intoxicated." She held the bottle up before her eyes and peered hard at the level of brown liquid left. "Long as I don't drink two ounces I'm fine." Annie tilted her head back and took another sip, this one more like a gulp, and wrenched her face with a shiver as it went down, then opened her mouth wide and exhaled hard. "Damn gawd."

After a moment Amos asked, "Ya feel more evil?"

"Nope." Annie rolled her eyes toward the sky. "In fact, except for my stomach rumbling, I feel pretty damn good." She held up at the bottle again, smiling at it with wonder. "I'm pretty sure I've had one ounce now, so as long as I make sure to keep drinking smaller and smaller amounts, I can't ever get to two. That's math." Annie took another sip, about half of her last one, and kept walking.

"Well, Mom said you got to be extra careful," Amos cautioned as he continued down the trail. "Since as a girl with unruly blood, you're destined for evil."

"What?" Annie said, her face flashing a glimmer of true shock. "Mom said that? Thought Mom loved me at least."

Amos' stomach dropped at the flash of pain he saw in Annie. Annie was everything that Amos depended on, the one he looked to for guidance and stability, the one he could trust with 100% of his being, and at the sound of her slightest hurt, he was engulfed in worry. "But... but...," Amos stammered, trying to backtrack. "She talks about everybody when they're not there, Annie. She just talks, you know that, she don't mean nothing. They both love us."

"Welp, they make me wonder if there isn't a better kind of love out there." Annie cared for her little brother more than anything, so at the sight of his worry about her, she immediately let go of the pain she'd felt. Annie chuckled, rubbing a soft hand through Amos' mesh of light-brown hair. "Don't worry, Stubbs, I'm okay." And she meant it too, feeling warmer and the whole world wonderful suddenly, even if it was getting a little more difficult to walk in a straight line.

"Look, I've been meaning to give you this." She smiled, and with one hand pulled the sliver crucifix with the pink stones from beneath her shirt and out over her head. "I think you should have it." She handed their mom's crucifix to Amos, who reached for it with excited eyes. "That pastor gave it to her to give to me, but I don't want it. Pretty sure they're sweet on each other."

"Wow, thanks, Annabel."

"It's starting to rub my skin raw. Just don't let it get you more caught up in her silliness, it's just jewelry is all." The bourbon bottle swung by Annie's side and she smiled down at her little brother so tenderly it made him blush. "All her prayers ain't gonna help. Mom's problem is Ray. She needs to learn to stand up for herself. This ain't the 1950s anymore."

"Well, let's you and me promise to always love each other, okay, Annie? For ever and ever we'll be best friends, no matter what Dad and Mom do."

"Sure, Stubbs, that sounds fine."

"Swear to God?" Amos asked, his brown eyes deep with sincerity. "I swear to God I'll never hurt you, Annabel, I love you more than anybody. You swear to God we'll always look out for each other?"

"Sure, Amos," Annie said, feeling her own cheeks blushing red now at her little brother's tenderness. "I swear to God."

* * *

Things got progressively worse over the next three years. No one would ever be able to determine if Ray Daniels started punching for real because his wife started sleeping with the youth pastor, or if Mrs. Daniels started sleeping with the youth pastor because Ray Daniels started punching. Regardless, Ray Daniels' slaps to their mother grew progressively harder and more frequent as time wore on, although they were often followed by his wailing tears of regret over the bourbon making him do it, and crappy presents from the dollar store that only Amos would bother to like. Throughout it all, despite Annie's insistence that their dad was bad, Amos would help his father stumble into bed at night, and bring him food on the days he was too hung over to move.

The night Annie crawled from her room to see her dad cracking her mom's head off the sink was the last time Annie would see her mother. Their mom would take her toothbrush, a dress, and one black and white photo of their grandmother before leaving with the youth pastor for California. When Annie moved to California after Harvard it was with a secret hope to find her mother and fill some holes that had been left gaping from when her mom had escaped, but by that time Mrs. Daniels would have already overdosed from pills in a different trailer park. Annie never blamed her mother for how their family was, instead only ever felt pity when she thought of her. Pity for a woman who was too weak to make it in a world rigged by men. Pity for a woman who never learned to stand her ground. Pity for a woman who wasn't smart.

It was always Ray's stinking breath and vile words that Annie remembered from that night he came into her room. She was almost fifteen, and had already blossomed into enough of a radiant beauty she made grow men, and some women, turn their heads. Their mother had been gone a few months by that point, the realization that she was never going to return settling in for all.

The flimsy particleboard door to her room cracked down the middle as a drunk Ray kicked it open. "Your fucking fault," Ray had sneered with a boney finger pointed down at her.

Annie jolted up into a sitting position on the lopsided futon she considered a bed, knowing it must be just after two a.m. in order for her dad to be home, the bar closed.

"She wouldn't have left if you hadn't filled her head with all that lady empowerment crap."

"Get out, Ray," Annie snapped, throwing hands to her eyes, trying to blunt the sting of hallway light. "My room. Get out!"

"All your Internet bullshit." Ray stomped two feet to her bed, the mobile home trembling. He leered over her with waves of humid whiskey and rancid sausage scent washing down, his right hand clutching his bottle of Beam by the neck. "You've never respected nothing. You was born bad and infected her."

"You're drunk."

"Empowerment to no longer believe in nothing, that's what." He leaned farther down, sneering into her face with his awful breath panting hot. "Empowerment to break all your vows and do whatever the fuck you want, right? Be a goddamn whore! You're the fucking antichrist, if any of that shit even exists."

"Get the fuck out," Annie snarled. Her fighting blood was boiling, and before she realized it her palm leapt out to crack across her father's greasy face. "Out!"

It was the first time, and last, that Annie ever struck her father. His left hand shot to Annie's face and harpooned the back of her head deep into the futon's cushion. She would always remember the claw-like grip of those boney fingers as they latched around her jawbone, a fear she'd never known surging within her as she tried to scream and thrash, innocence betrayed into violence, but because of his hand it was only a muffled whimper. The hand smelled like sweat and shit.

"Ya never had no damn respect for nothing," Ray sneered, thunking the bottle of Beam on the nightstand. "I always been too lenient because you were a girl, too kind," he whispered. "And you took the kindness for weakness."

Annie, her heart beating a thousand times a second, tried to kick and squirm and use her hands to pry his arm from her face, but it was pointless. She'd never realized how much dark power was still coiled in the old drunk.

"So maybe," Ray growled as he used his free hand to rip the covers from Annie in one clean jerk, exposing her now adult body barely covered in bra and panties, his glazed eyes flickering dully in the hallway light. "Maybe you need to take your mother's place, huh?" He looked down the length of her from neck to ankles. "Start taking over God-given duties of a grown woman now to match your mouth."

Tears, silent, as she was too terrified to willfully move, poured from Annie's eyes and over Ray Daniels' hand, her whole body starting to involuntarily tremor. All Annie wished, if she'd been able to speak, was to plead, *I'm sorry, Daddy, I'm so sorry.*

But Amos, the little brother she had always stuck up for, her best friend, would continue to respect and obey their farther through the coming years, just as his Bible had commanded, betray her for him. Or at least, that was the way Annie remembered it all.

News of Louisiana Elector's Shooting Breaks

*(Various Locations Around Country: Sunday, 4:18 a.m. PST /
7:14 a.m. EST)*

All stations across the country broadcast a video feed of police cruisers, flashing blue and red lights in the dawn murk, angled in front of a New Orleans' brick alley. Paramedics carried a body draped in a tarp toward an ambulance, only a lifeless black hand hanging from beneath the blue covering.

* * *

"Murder," the white liberal newscaster exclaimed into the camera only hours after Little Gumbo was shot, far before many facts had been confirmed about his death. "Don't we need to question if Lawrence Gatreaux's shooting is just another corrupt attempt to stop progress?"

It was Sunday and many people across the nation were not even awake, but it was potentially the last day before the election ended and so the most had to be made of any ratings opportunity. The liberal newscaster shifted his head back so he could look down through his glasses in that way his director said made him look more intellectual, and cleared his throat. "Isn't it suspicious that Gatreaux's death could keep the state's electoral count from going to the Democratic Party.

Facts are surely indicating the BLACK community leader was considering flipping his vote." The liberal newscaster breathed deeply. "Naturally, I do not want to enflame racial tensions under any circumstances, but do not intelligent minds have to wonder if this is not a Republican conspiracy? An outright murder perhaps?"

Damn, the liberal broadcaster thought, *that chick with the tattoos will have to like me now.*

* * *

"Murder!" The conservative newscaster's face twisted angrily into the camera. "An innocent Republican, business-owning, born-again Christian elector is shot in the jurisdiction of a Democratic chief of police on the eve of a vote the Democrats were going to lose?" The conservative newscaster shook her head in disbelief. "Is it not enough that so-called progressives have been flooding our media with porn, destroying our churches, and degrading our family values for years, but now we're supposed to just accept this assassination only a day before Hampton Stone's inevitable win?" She pounded her fist. "I say, no! Enough is enough! The Freeman/Daniels camp can't be allowed to get away with this, they cannot erode all of our standards to where murder is acceptable!"

She got paid extra for fist pounds.

* * *

@whoreads: Damn, somebody shot an elector in the Bayou, shit's getting real!

@professorofplants: Republicans is who! I've tried to use logic, but fuck it, all it ever comes down to is cops killing black men, so whites can keep the power.

@jessejameskickass: white power? Look at every sports star, musician and politician now, don't want to get shot, stop breaking laws! You want a war, you're gonna get one.

@mohammedfatah: You kidding me?!!? Perfect frame up by GOP bastards. Gastro gonna flip, they shoot em, make it look like Dems so Stone can lock up all Arabs. Maybe Jihad IS the answer?

@socialjusticewarrior: Trigger warnings! Trigger warnings, you bigots, homophobes, and religious radicals! I hate all you assholes! …Good point about Stone and Arabs, though.

@mrsCee798: Wait, so who shot him? Dems? Or Repubs? Was he a criminal maybe?

@whoreads: Who cares, Reboot is gonna reboot some shit! Ha. Turn the lights out on stupid rallies and marches.

@archiesuperhero: Tis lizards, fools, alien lizards.

* * *

Lawton Smith stomped back and forth before the rusty doors of his main silo in the crunchy dawn snow. He'd just gotten done trying to warn people on the Internet of the Illuminati yet again, to no avail. The time for yakking was done though, and he was now dressed head to toe in camo with an old Browning automatic rifle slung over his shoulder and a bear knife strapped to his thigh. Extra ammo was strung across his barrel chest. Buck, Slicker and forty-five other camo-clad militia members of the *Patriots of the Rising Dawn* stood in diligent attention for their leader's every utterance. The elector's shooting was one of the signs Mr. Jefferson had told him would happen.

"When night falls across this great land," Lawton bellowed, voice reaching the tops of the pines. "So too will their evil empire. I have seen the signs, and believe me when I say the reckoning for the Illuminati is nigh! Dawn will not break again without the purging of this country begun."

"And once things are purged, all good-like," Slicker asked, "you be our king, right Colonel? Usher in a new society, sir?"

Lawton's dark eyes darted over to Slicker. Lawton's stare always made Slicker's smile melt, the younger man swallowing nervously. "No," Lawton finally answered, wagging a wide finger. "Do not misunderstand. I am but a temporary vessel for the work, I am but tasked with eliminating the evil Illuminati of lizard creatures from this once pure land. There will be one greater than I to rise up and establish the just order, to lead the new America. Their name will begin with the letter A."

"But you're our leader, Pa," thirty-something year old Buck whined.

"I am but a wolf howling in the wind, child, heralding the dawn." Lawton leaned his head back and looked up at the fading stars in the dust-blue morning sky. He sniffed the air. "The chosen one is on the horizon, and they will reestablish this great nation from sea to shining sea." Lawton's gaze came back down, a rare smile full of snaggleteeth stretched across his black-bearded face. "But right now, put the dirty bomb in the truck, boys. It begins tonight. We're heading to Denver."

* * *

A tweet, attributed to *Reboot.org* read: *Today, at 4 pm, the revolution begins.*

* * *

"Given this morning's news regarding the Louisiana state elector," Buddy Dukes stated across the rancher's fence in Texas to eleven reporters. "I'd like to call for a peaceful, Republican-led march on Washington this afternoon." He nodded to the rancher who stood next to him in his red Republican T-shirt. Buddy Dukes removed his own cowboy hat, placing it on the fence post in the same way that was done yesterday. "It's time to show the Democratic administration that there won't be any tomfoolery regarding this election's rightful end, nor any delay in allowing the Louisiana State Republicans to immediately appoint a replacement elector before tomorrow's vote." Buddy Dukes slipped out of his plaid suit-coat, and pulled out his own matching Republican red T-shirt from the back pocket of his plaid trousers, wrangling it over his head for the cameras.

Buddy heard his cell phone ringing in his pants pocket as he struggled the somewhat tight shirt down over his dress clothes. Once the shirt was on, more or less, the Congressman yanked out the ringing cell phone to see General Harper was calling him. Buddy Dukes silenced the phone and shoved it back in his pocket. General Harper was always so angry, screaming about things Buddy Dukes didn't completely understand whenever Stone made him talk to him, that Buddy would wait and call him back later. Buddy didn't want to get all stressed out while he was in front of the cameras after all, as looking good and relaxed on camera was pretty much the most important thing in American politics. "Hoot for Dukes," the Congressman stated to the reporters with a grin and a double thumbs-up. "Let's walk right up to the White House and show Fuentes' that American patriots can't be pushed around any longer. Time to win this war, once and for all." Buddy wiggled his black eyebrows at the reporters. "Hoot for Dukes," he asked, "y'all like that? Catchy enough to sell some steaks too, huh?"

* * *

Text from Shay to Amos: *Can't make it Tampa, heading to New Orleans for exclusive interview with elector shooting cop. Crazy! Will text once I get your info, or when I can catch a flight to MacDill. Prob tomorrow.*

"Who?" Annie stammered as Henry watched from the end of the bed. "Gatmo?" She shot straight up from the rumpled blankets and pillows like a cannon had fired, light from the hallway flashing over her. She ripped her eyeshades off, blonde hair tangling. A disheveled Henry and Mayor Sam Buckhall had just burst into the darkened room, the door crashing against a heavy oak dresser.

The mayor had stepped on the paw of one of Kim-Su's cats, which screeched and scampered out, a lamp crashing to the wood floor somewhere behind them. Despite the chaotic adrenaline pumping through his trembling body Henry now watched Annie's every reaction, looking for the truth. "Sometime between two and four a.m., ma'am," Henry repeated. "A Republican Louisiana elector, Lawrence Gatreaux, was shot dead." Henry wondered if Annie had him shot. "You need to wake up, Senator."

Despite barely being sunrise, Annie's always-jolly husband Kim-Su had answered the front door downstairs for Henry. Annie's home was an old Victorian mansion restored to all its glistening dark wood glory, and Kim-Su was a towering, Chinese former-basketball-star, who stood before the two panicked men in a white apron the size of a small tent. Kim-Su also had on a lopsided chef's hat so large that it could have a small dog in it. Kim-Su was typically oblivious to the political stressors that dictated his wife's life, and Henry knew it was perfectly acceptable, and even essential at times, to ignore him. They had barged past Kim-Su, Henry taking the shining oak stairs two at a time with a massive cup of coffee in one hand and his iPad in the other. Kim-Su lumbered behind them for a bit with his bad basketball knees creaking nearly as much as their steps, happily explaining how he was cooking a huge birthday breakfast for himself. "It waffles, Henry Corwich. You and friend like waffles?"

Henry didn't even bother to knock at Annie's bedroom door at the top of the stairs, two conflicting thoughts spinning through his mind. *I've got to get Annie in front of this.* And ... *Did Annie have the elector killed?*

"Huh?" Annie now stammered again from her bed, the mayor cursing at the clattering lamp, Annie apparently in that bewildering Neverland between sleep and wakeful understanding. "Harmony?"

"No, ma'am, Harmony's fine. Gatreaux was an elector." Even with her sleep-puffy face twisted in confusion and her long hair gnarled, even considering she might be a murderer, the most dominant emotions inside Henry were still devotion and love. "There's already morning news of Buddy Dukes calling for a possible Republican-led march on Washington if the Democratic Secretary of State of Louisiana overrules."

"Good God." Annie's eyes lit with wakeful recognition at the two, her face saying she did not like what she saw. "What the fuck?" Her puffy eyes widened in shock and she kicked the bed sheets off and leapt to her feet, shooting a hand to the nearby dresser to keep from falling over in her groggy state. "How did you assholes get in here?" Annie glanced back and forth between Henry and Mayor Buckhall, her expression as if she had just caught aliens invading her room. "Who the hell is Lenny Gutmo?"

"Lawrence Gatreaux," Henry corrected.

"And I need you to speak to the EAL with me, ma'am," the mayor wrestled up pieces of the broken lamp. "The Environmental Avengers League has already gotten two hundred people to link arms on the Golden Gate because of the Republicans murdering people, bringing traffic into the city to a stop. Protesting paper bags, or maybe… supporting paper bags? I can never remember which is best now, paper or plastic, but—"

"The avenger's league?" Annie panted in confusion, shielding her eyes in the bright light and trying to focus. "Those are superheroes, right? They murdered someone?" Annie grabbed the coffee out of Henry's hand, popped off the lid and started gulping. "Gatmo," she gasped between gulps, "he our elector or theirs?"

Are you a murderer, Henry wondered. She wore a loose gray T-shirt that hugged the curves of her breasts, and baggy boxer shorts that somehow looked sexy as hell with her long, sleek legs sticking out of them. Henry realized anew it would forever be impossible for him to see the truth of her, he cared too much, but he had to try. Two of Kim-Su's fat cats waddled in meowing. "Gatreaux," Henry corrected again, scrutinizing every twitch and tone, looking for some sign as to whether she could be faking not knowing. "Louisiana. A Republican elector." Henry's brain swirled with all the conversations he and Annie had, especially with her asking specific questions about

Louisiana. The deceitfulness and desperation he had noticed in her decisions of late. Of course, those damned pills too. *Please don't have done this, Annie. Please don't.* If Louisiana was a coincidence, it was a big one.

With heavy breaths through wet lips she pushed the half-drunk coffee cup onto the dresser, nearly knocking her pill bottle of Zennies over grasping with sleepy fingers. Annie had bullied Henry into going out to retrieve more Zennies for her yesterday, and looking at her now he hoped he'd made the right choice with what he'd secretly done. She shook some pink pills into her palm, popping three, one dropping from her hand next to her bare feet to clatter-roll the floor to the dresser's base.

"Ma'am," Henry added, "this is potentially extremely serious, maybe not the time for pills. News and the web are already flooded with suggestions of Gatreaux flipping to us. People already implicating Democrats in his shooting."

"So if he was going to flip to us why the fuck would WE have him shot? Seems like the Republicans would have shot—wait a sec. How'd he fucking get shot?"

"Apparently New Orleans PD, madam." Henry watched as one of Kim-Su's obese cats waddled toward the pink pill on the floor, the mayor cursing behind as parts of the lamp crashed to the floor again. "No one is positive he was going to flip but that's apparently what some people he was out party-ing with the night before told a television camera."

"So who appoints a replacement for him?" Annie pressed one palm above her right eye like a migraine was beginning.

"The Louisiana state Republicans?" Henry shrugged, unsure. "Buddy Dukes has already called for a preemptive march on Washington based on it's their prerogative to appoint Gatreaux's replacement." Henry looked her in the eye, wanting to connect with her, to find a solution that would save both their careers and reassure him that she was innocent in all this, but all he saw was the same mysterious beauty in her blue eyes that had captivated and confused him for over a decade. "Senator, I have to ask—"

"It's not even seven a.m. for fuck's sake, and that moron Dukes is already in front of this?" Annie angrily gulped more coffee, slapping the cup back down. "So can we stop their Republicans from appointing a replacement or not?" Annie ripped off her T-shirt, no bra.

"Good lord," the mayor gasped, and more parts of the lamp clattered back to the floor.

"It's a female body, Mayor, grow up." Annie tossed the empty cup at a wastebasket and ripped open one of the dresser drawers with only pink-heart boxers on.

Henry stared at her plump breasts hanging with nipples the color of coral, her sleek curves, her glossy skin and lean perfection with a sheen of sweat clinging to her flat stomach and he wondered what he even would do if she had been the one to have the elector killed.

"So what's the standard process?" She rummaged through her drawer, long yellow hair covering the edge of the breast Henry's eyes were glued to. "Are they right? The state legislature chooses a replacement elector, or the Governor?"

"Um..." Henry realized he was staring and spun to face the mayor and the open door. "Seems like the state Republicans should at first glance, ma'am, but there's probably a debate there." Seeing Henry face him, the mayor broke his sight from the half-nude senator and spun to the door as well, stepping on the lamp's light bulb with a pop in the process.

"Never had an elector killed a day before the vote. Republican state legislature says it's their elector, so their choice, but if there was real evidence he was going to flip, then maybe…?"

"Options, Henry, options," Annie barked as drawers slid open and slammed shut. "This could be our shot. Louisiana Secretary of State oversees state elections right? That's Sheryl Paulson. Democrat. What if she were worried about the potential foul play? Didn't we help her campaign two years back? You have her number?"

"Ma'am, given the potential conspiracy, we really shouldn't act unilaterally on this. The president has Beatrice Howe on a plane en route to us right now, and Vice President Freeman requested no speeches or phone calls or action of any kind until she arrives. The West Wing wants us in a coordinated game plan."

"There's never a damn conspiracy, things are too complex for that. Everybody just always overreacts and looks for goblins in the shadows. Cops have body cams?"

"Not on them." Henry replied as a stray pink Zennie rolled past his feet, a meowing fat cat waddling after it, licking. "Gatreaux had a history of drug and alcohol abuse, ma'am, was apparently a deadbeat dad to at least four kids, which might work for us?" Henry wasn't sure, but thought he now heard Kim-Su's steps coming down the hallway and prayed Annie was putting on her clothes. "But if we want to do the right thing, an inquiry will take days at best—"

"No time to figure out the truth, the vote's tomorrow," Annie countered behind. "The important thing is to determine the morally correct lie. How in the hell was someone like him an elector anyway?"

If she wasn't involved, she's doing a great job of acting ignorant.

"Little oversight over who is picked, ma'am, all done on a local level. Most likely plenty of people worse than Gatreaux as electors out there, hardly anyone ever bothers to know who they are."

"And the goddamn Supreme Court will tie if the issue goes to them." Annie sighed. "This will be a fucking free-for-all.

"How every doing?" Towering Kim-Su appeared in the open doorway with his chef's garb on holding a can of whipped cream. He smiled warmly down at Henry and Mayor Buckhall, then over their heads to his naked wife. "Waffles?"

Please have your clothes back on, Annie, Henry thought staring up at Kim-Su. *Please have on clothes.*

"Black or white?" Annie demanded. "The color is critical."

"Babe-girl," Kim-Su's broken-English accent was friendly, but confused. "Waffles tan, but I put chocolate chips—"

"The elector, not the damn waffles, Kim," Annie snapped at her husband. "Was Gatreaux white or black, Henry?"

"Gatreaux was black, ma'am." Henry tried to return a smile up to the lanky man. "But also a recent born-again-Christian… allegedly. There's so many potential angles to play, I think the smartest, most ethical thing we can do is maybe to back off of it. Come out with a strong statement deferring to others to decide what happened, and who gets to appoint."

"No, there's got to be a way we can choose," Annie groaned, ignoring Henry's suggestion. "This is our chance for an outright win. We can't punt it away. We just need to find maneuvering room in interpreting the rules."

"There's state rules, federal election rules, and…" Henry answered as Kim-Su bewilderingly pushed him the can of whipped cream with a big grin. "It's…uh," Henry took the can, "just going to be an argument, with no time to argue though, ma'am."

"We can win back Louisiana with this. Win it all." Annie sounded lost in thought. "So when's the wicked witch of the West Wing arriving? I'm sure this only helps her conspiracy paranoia, will make Fuentes afraid to act."

"There are actually a lot of lunatics out there, ma'am," the mayor offered. "It might be good to play this one cautious, if you don't mind my chiming in?"

"And maybe you should try having a little faith in humanity, Mayor. Stop being such a pussy while you're at it." Annie opened her thong drawer to pull out her flask of Beam. "We need to seize this opportunity."

"Babe-girl." Kim-Su smiled, a huge forefinger pointed over the mayor's head to the corner of the room where the obese cat now lay flat and still next to the partially gnawed pink Zennie. "Look at Fat Albert. He playing dead. So cute, huh?"

News of Louisiana Elector's Shooting
Continues to Spread

(Various Locations Around Country, 7:49 a.m. PST / 10:49 p.m. EST)

Morning Headlines:

Pan-Continental Trade Protests Erupt in Burlington, Vermont... Heroin Suspected

Seattle "We Are Ungovernable" Rioters Throw Molotov Cocktails

What if Election Can't End?

* * *

Post on the official Facebook page of Louisiana Secretary of State: *Due to the uncertainty surrounding elector Lawrence Gatreaux's death, Secretary Paulson, overseer of Louisiana elections, will temporarily halt any state legislature appointment of a replacement until all facts of the case can be brought to light.*

* * *

Tweet from Governor Stone: *Heard the cops who shot the elector were Democrats. Just saying.*

* * *

Official statement from the Governor of Louisiana moments later: *As of yesterday, the Louisiana popular vote for president was determined to be won by the Republicans, with no further recounts planned. Therefore, according to state election rules, it is the right of the Republican portion of the Louisiana State Legislature to appoint a replacement for their deceased member. The governor's office requests the Louisiana Secretary of State, and all other entities, refrain from interfering with the proper functioning of the election process. A thorough internal investigation into the police shooting of Elector Gatreaux's death will be conducted over the coming days, and the governor's office requests Louisiana citizens remain calm and in their homes except for essential travel.*

* * *

Financial News Ticker: *All US markets falling sharply in concern over election's end.*

* * *

@wallstreetwizard: The economy is on the verge of collapsing, and I've got these Occupy Wall Street idiots in front of my office protesting shit they don't even understand

@hotpancake: Screw you, I'm Occupy Wall Street, and we don't need your corrupt ponzi schemes. You're the problem.

@wallstreetwizard: As in? What have I done exactly?

@hotpancake: GMO foods, man! And white slavery! And pesticides and NSA big-brother, asshole 1% guy!

@wallstreetwizard: Um… okay.

@professorofplants: With the Supreme Court deadlocked, only Fuentes can oversee an impartial reappointment of a new elector. All Dems within easy travel of DC must go there this afternoon to make sure Republican march doesn't pressure White House!

@jessejameskickass: Fuentes?!? Fuentes is a Muslim radical, helping the perv and the communist! There's nothing impartial about that, nigger!

@mrsCee798: Be positive, fuckers!

@whoreads: The important thing is to fight! Don't let THEM steal it, or the country is lost! THEY hate you!

* * *

Email to 3.4 million *American Civil Liberties Union* members: *In response to this afternoon's Republican-led march on Washington, we are calling on all those who care about protecting the rights of minorities to get out in your local communities and protest. Let your voices be heard. Democracy for all must prevail!*

* * *

News Ticker: *Due to the projected difficulties in US Judiciary being able to oversee a definitive answer to any electoral issues before tomorrow's vote, Independent Colorado Senator Ahmed Kaleel has announced the immediate formation of a temporary Joint Congressional Committee for Election Oversight. It will be comprised of twenty-one "independent thinking" members of both the House and Senate. It will conduct an expedited investigation into the electoral process and offer timely bipartisan recommendations for a fair and honest end to the election.*

* * *

Breaking News: *Tense Standoff Forming with Black Protestors at New Orleans Police Station.*

* * *

"Mostly peaceful here, Jack," a reporter yelled into a different news camera located in Birmingham, Alabama, as soon as coverage came to his location. "As you can see, this is a largely African-American crowd who seem to be peacefully vocalizing their frustration with police in general." The reporter was standing on a small library's concrete steps trying to be heard over the dozens upon dozens of Democratic protestors, mostly black, chanting, *hands up, don't shoot,* behind him. "Although lots of people are worried what might happen now that the group calling themselves *Oath Keepers* have started to show up."

The reporter pointed to the adjacent parking lot, where four pickup trucks were unloading men and women, all Caucasian, dressed in camo fatigues and carrying various firearms. One of those camo-wearing men went by *@jessejameskickass* on social media, and he brought his sniper rifle.

"The *Oath Keepers* are saying they are exercising their constitutional Second Amendment right to make sure all lawful Americans can check out books safely," the reporter explained.

* * *

@mohammedfatah had already seen the meme with Rosa's picture that *@socialjusticewarrior* had started. The picture of the beaten young Muslim woman was becoming an icon for many Muslim Americans. Seeing such graphic abuse of a Muslim woman by a conservative white man was making many realize it was time for them to get out in the streets as well, make their voices heard. There was only so much stereotyping, paranoia, and fear-mongering that they could take directed against Muslim Americans.

During his many lonely hours *@mohammedfatah* liked to dabble in chemistry in his garage lab, just for fun. With the advent of newer and newer technology, it was amazing what compounds could be created in someone's garage now. For instance, he knew he could turn the yellowish powder he'd created from an inert compound into a large amount of water-soluble *Flakka 3.0* with only the addition of some table salt, sulfur, and two hours more cooking. Upon reading even more inflammatory comments about Muslims online he decided, fuck it, he was screwed anyway, so he might as well dump *Flakka 3.0* in the Detroit water supply. If you were doomed to pay for the crime regardless, you might as well commit it. He wasn't even sure anymore if that would make Allah angry with him, or get him a nicer spot in heaven with more virgins. There was just too much information these days, too much incessant chatter, and *@mohammedfatah* was sick of trying to understand.

Approximately 24 Hours Until Electoral Vote

(New Orleans, Louisiana: Sunday, 9:17 a.m. PST / 12:17 p.m. EST)

As they jostled through air pockets on the way to her New Orleans interview with the shooting cop, mocha-skinned Shay's thoughts drifted back to Amos in high school, the cowlick of light-brown hair, the wide smile. She brushed strands of her own long black hair out of her sight, and reached for the tonic water on the seatback's tray. Part of her wondered if there was any chance that all could be forgiven, if they could start over again. *I still love him,* she admitted to herself, but she felt an immediate pang of dread entwined with the flush of euphoria. She set the plastic cup back down on the tray, and her emerald eyes drifted over the cabin wondering what her life might have been like.

Amos had a good reason to never forgive her. She had slept with his older sister, Annie. Amos had always apparently thought Annie had purposefully seduced Shay, but Shay had been young, curious and terrified that he was going to leave for the Army and never come back. Somehow she never thought one drunken night could change her entire future. *Stupid,* she thought about herself for the millionth time. *It was just stupid.*

No matter how much you'd fucked up though, life forced you to keep choosing.

* * *

While waiting for her luggage in the New Orleans airport, Shay didn't find the normal half-sloshed bead-wearing tourists, but a tense simmer in the airport's chilled air. Everyone smiled, but strained and overtly polite, as if the entire state were suddenly in a very important interview and faking ease. Shay's editor had connections to the New Orleans Chief of Police, and had convinced them to let Shay get an exclusive with the shooting officer of the elector on the premise of needing to get their side of the story out as quickly as possible.

Shay knew the truth of Lawrence Gatreaux's death would have a ripple effect into the election's end and across the country for years, whatever angle she ended up writing in her article. There were multiple possibilities of how it could turn out though. Officer Sonny Benson could simply be the next in a long line of racist white men abusing authority against the disenfranchised, racism pure and simple. But it could also be a Republican plot to influence the election. Or a Democratic one. Or maybe the claims coming out of New Orleans, as well as other cities, of the private prison industry's money increasingly causing people to get unjustifiably locked up and shot from aggressive, false arrests, had legs? Wasn't it always about money? But then again, maybe this shooting something completely different and unexpected—like a good cop using reasonable force against a bad guy, regardless of anyone's skin color? Whatever the truth was, of an elector's shooting just before the end of the election, it would have consequences. Large ones.

The taxi driver, an elderly Afghani man with a turban and

a bright red beard rolled his eyes when she requested the downtown police station. She pulled out a fifty-dollar bill though, and he drove away from the airport shaking his head like the whole world was going crazy. On the drive, Shay used her tablet to scour the Internet about anything regarding the police or Lawrence Gatreaux. She immediately noticed a headline quoting General Mace Harper as stating the elector shooting seemed "suspicious" this morning at a public military function though, and it turned her mind back to Amos' questions.

Shay pulled up plenty more things Harper, but none that weren't already complete public knowledge for the most part—die-hard Republican, reputation for both extreme bravery and being a hard-ass if not a bit of lunacy. He was tactically brilliant, a misogynist, a homophobe and bigot, and every president of the past three administrations, Republican and Democrat, had at some point singled him out as the "backbone" of the greatest military on earth. The rumor was that he also ran the CIA's clandestine "wet work" team, *The Activity*, but whether true or not, she was sure she would find no corroborating information on it. Hell, whether or not a Black Ops group called *The Activity* even existed was rumor for the most part.

Lieutenant Stoughton was a ghost for any information Shay could get access to. His being active Special Forces though, no deep public information on him wasn't that surprising. She was able to find some old high school photos of him in Wyoming, where he had a hilarious perm and apparently drank homebrew at rodeos, but after he joined the military at 18 it all went pretty silent. Zilch. Then against her better judgment, Shay found herself typing in the phrase "1776" into her laptop.

"1776" came back with so much information regarding American history that to find something truly material would have been harder than locating a flashlight on the sun. It was only by remembering bits and phrases of what Amos had mentioned during their conversation, and crosschecking the Nicaraguan official Deputy Lupe, that Shay found something that made her stomach cold, raised goose bumps on her forearms and neck.

Deputy Lupe had apparently been in DC as part of the *Pan-Continental Trade Agreement* talks only three weeks prior, where he had met with several congressional leaders and lobbyists from the military, prison, oil, pharmaceutical and food industries, as well as members of the Fuentes administration. Deputy Lupe showed up in several photos from the hundreds attending the event, but one picture in particular started Shay's heart beating quick as the taxi pulled to a slow stop on the other side of the street from a massive mob before the police station. It was a picture of Lupe shaking hands with Senator Annie Daniels in front of the Capitol steps. The picture, in and of itself, didn't mean anything. Unless, of course, you didn't believe in coincidences.

"See," the cabbie glanced incredulously in the rearview mirror at Shay, as if he now expected her to change her mind about trying to get through the mob to the police station. "See." He raised his palm toward the angry crowd.

A police line of riot gear-wearing officers was around the building's perimeter, several hundred people jammed between them and barricades before the street. Angry chants filled the air at an injustice everyone could sense, but no one really understood. Another black man had been shot at the hands of police, and this one somehow mattered even more than all the rest, as the election could hinge on it. Bricks and rocks were spinning through the air to bounce off the policemen's shields.

Once she managed to push and shove her way through the crowd and into the police station though, things would get even more disturbing. Inside, the sweaty shooting office Sonny Benson would shake his head in confusion, casually mentioning the anonymous tip they'd received that Gatreaux had drugs in his restaurant, and then the strange last words he gasped while dying.

"1776," the cop said Gatreaux had sighed from his red soaked chest. "1776."

* * *

Text from Shay to Amos: *Any idea if Stoughton worked for the Activity? You know, spec ops for CIA? The top secret of top secret.*

Shay Chases Ghosts

(Tampa, FL: Sunday, 9:24 a.m. PST / 12:24 a.m. EST)

With only a day to go before the electoral vote, all the news stations and the Internet were going nuts over the shooting in Louisiana, and Jacari needed to get away from it. On base, Amos' team used the old gym, and in the middle of the day that's where Jacari went for solitude, to think. During the last Republican administration influx of cash MacDill had built a massive, state-of-the-art new gym. It glowed with red, white and blue lights. It rocked music, multiple weight machines, electro-muscular stimulation, saunas, ice baths, biofeedback computers, protein shakes, and more soldiers hitting on each other than working out. The old gym had none of that indulgent crap. It was a tiny graveyard of mismatched dumbbells and free weights, ripped red carpet, and reeked of decades-old sweat and rust under three flickering fluorescent bulbs. The old gym was where Amos' team could get down to business, but Jacari was confident none of them would be there, not after the recent awful shit with Thump. Jacari just needed quiet, to process and think, but to still be moving and let the burn inside him out.

Jacari worked his hands and arms in the sand buckets Amos had set up months back. He hoped pain would rip the image of Thump's half-destroyed head out of his mind. The major had said that if something was good enough for Shaolin Monks, it was good enough for them. The idea with the sand buckets was to control your breathing and heart rate as you repeatedly drove your lower arm, fingers wide open, into the coarse sand, then squeezed them into a fist and twisted as if you were grabbing someone's uniform or throat, before ripping your arm back out. It didn't sound like much, until you had done dozens and dozens of them without stopping and every fiber of your forearms and tiny muscles in your hands burned and cramped, the rough sand scraping off your skin. The gym was so small that the two large buckets of sand were actually set up in what used to be the bathroom, before Rodriguez had broken the toilet.

What had happened in that Nicaragua hacienda? Stork was good, very good. *How could it be that he had fucked up so bad that Thump was now dead?* Jacari punched down into each of the buckets repeatedly, daggers of pain shooting up his arms. *Major's got to be taking Thump's death hard. Those two were like brothers.* The sting of the sand merged with the inhales of his breath and the beats of his heart. Amos was the best guy Jacari had ever known, and not just because he was his CO; Amos was just solid. Amos was the type of guy everyone would follow naturally because he loved and respected them, would never ask anyone to do anything he wouldn't do first. The worst knock Jacari had ever heard about *Famous Amos* prior to joining the team was that some had once feared he was too nice. That with his devout faith, his rock-solid morals and concern for everyone, some had originally worried he wouldn't be able to do what was necessary in the field. But then there had been a couple citations and awards for bravery and the

"Korpesh thing" had happened of course, which solidified that Amos Daniels was not just nice, but had the necessary *beast* hunkered down inside him too. Amos had not only saved a captured American journalist's life in the Korpesh Valley, but had killed four armed Afghani terrorists in the process with his bare hands.

In and out, Jacari's fists kept plunging into the sand, his breath like the churn of a train's engine. Sweat dripped off Jacari's forehead, dark plunks in the sand, then the churn of his fists wiping them out. Jacari thrust his arms quicker and quicker, the pain seeming to melt into an almost comfortable warmth with his breath in and out, the *swoosh swoosh* continuing as his breath smoothly, cleanly churned. The faster he drove his arms into the sand, the more his thinking calmed, cleared, and slowly there were no more thoughts of Thump. Instead, his mind became a gentle fascination with the predictable rhythm of pain beating through him, as if he was only a microscopic cell in the life of some much more massive creature. A blissful eternal now, without calculation of rights and wrongs. *Show forgiveness, speak for justice and avoid the ignorant.* It was a quote from the Holy Quran his parents had taught him. To think of the Quran, his parent's love, and the gentle and healing lessons he used to listen to as a boy helped him feel centered and calm. *Family.* That was another thing about their team he realized; it never mattered that he was Muslim, or black, or anything—they were family. And for the first time since Nicaragua, Jacari's breath began to deepen, his heart began to feel light. *We're family. We're gonna be alright.*

Jacari heard the old metal door to the main room creak open and a flood of sunlight splashed the darkened weight room behind him. It didn't reach all the way into the small room where Jacari worked the buckets though. Boot steps echoed off the metal plating, and through the partially closed bathroom door Jacari saw Stork. Jacari froze, went completely quiet. To just observe for a moment. Maybe he just wanted to prove to himself there was nothing to worry about with Stork.

Stork glanced around the small room, his eyes surveying to see if anyone else was in gym, and he then yanked the creaking door shut behind him.

OK, so he wants to be alone too. No big deal. For a moment, Jacari thought Stork's eyes had somehow found him through the crack in the door, but then Stork seemed to relax a bit, leaning back against one of the mirrors on the wall. Jacari wrestled with whether he should step out into the main room and say hello or keep watching.

Stork pulled a phone from his pocket and dialed with a grin, a little too relaxed. It wasn't his normal phone either. There was a little red symbol on the back of the phone. Jacari couldn't see exactly what it was from his distance, the fluorescent bulbs forever flickering on and off, but it looked like it might be a small red rabbit on the black phone. Weird. But then Jacari actually shook his head, realized he was thinking crazy. Stork was one of the better guys he'd ever known. Stork could never have done anything to purposely hurt one of the team. All the times Stork had his back leapt to Jacari's mind. It was wrong for him to be spying on his brother, so Jacari took a step toward the door.

Amos burst in the gym, frothing mad. The major came in like a storm. The metal door banged, strobes of harsh sunlight flashing through the small dark room. Amos' face was twisted in rage like Jacari had only ever seen a couple times before. Stork's immediately flashed fear.

Amos stormed to within inches of Stork and the black phone tumbled from Stork's hands to the floor. "Are you working another angle?" Amos leaned close, spit flying onto Stork's face.

"Amos," Stork stammered, palms up. "What—"

"Don't bullshit me!" Amos jabbed a finger into Stork's face. "The laptop. What was on it?"

"Boss," Stork said. "You need to relax—"

Whap! Amos slapped Stork hard across the face. "I swear if you don't tell me the fucking truth..." Amos grabbed Stork's collar with his left hand, his right curling into a fist. "The truth!"

Then, weirdly, Stork's face became calm, more controlled, a hint of a smile on his lips, even as Jacari saw him moving his feet for a countermove. "Major," Stork said with a wicked gleam in his eye, "you can't even imagine the TRUTH."

"Thump was our brother!"

Jacari had seen Amos fight many times, but typically in controlled settings, where Amos was leading Krav Maga techniques for close-quarters lethal combat. Jacari had never seen him actually fight with rage. Stork was no chump either, having been trained in hand-to-hand combat for almost his entire adult life, but Amos began beating his ass. Stork's nose busted bloody from one right hand, then Amos also cracked the other fist to his throat. Amos was a fraction faster than Stork, a fraction stronger, a fraction more accurate. The gym was small, and all around them were cluttered bench presses, squat racks, slabs of free weights, and weight racks with dumbbells cluttering the floor. After a barrage of punches and elbows and knees where exchanged, Amos had Stork's head clutched with his right hand by the back of his hair, Amos' left hand grasping an iron weight rack and ramming Stork's boney face into it again and again. Things in Stork's face popped and blood sprayed with every crack. It was fast and brutal, and Jacari was about to burst from the room to stop Amos before he killed him, but then Stork somehow shot a sharp elbow up under Amos' chin. Amos staggered back, stunned. Stork suddenly had a ten-pound weight and swung it hard, grazing Amos' face. Amos' left heal hit a dumbbell on the floor and he tumbled backward, careening over a bench and crashing into a stack of twenty-five pound free weights with a grunt.

"You motherfucking ignorant fuck!" Stork bellowed, towering over Amos with a huge forty-five pound iron weight brought up over his bloody face. Jacari could see in Stork's crazed eyes that he was going to do it, he was going to bring that forty-five pounds of iron smashing down onto Amos' head and neck, squash the major's skull like rotted fruit. "You holier-than-thou prick," Stork snarled as blood spilled from his shattered nose, bubbles of blood popping as his breath wheezed in and out of his mouth. "You can't understand the truth!"

Jacari pressed the muzzle of his 9mm against the back of Stork's head.

"Brother against brother?" Jacari whispered. "Nah, we ain't like that. I'll shoot both you fucks, put a bullet in my own head, if this is what it's come to."

Stork and Amos' eyes both widened, Stork with the weight in his hands.

"Now," Jacari continued, gun still pressed to Stork's head, "I'm going to step back, okay, Ty? Then you're going to set the weight down softly on the floor, alright?" Jacari took a deep breath. "And then you, Major, are going to stop whatever the fuck you're doing, okay? We gonna talk this out like brothers. Everybody with me on this?" Amos' and Stork's eyes went from Jacari back into the other's, each glaring like whatever they were battling over might be worth a trip to the grave.

Jacari took another deep breath and thought that if they didn't relent within the count of five his next move was to blow Stork's kneecap off. But then the metal door banged open again, sunlight flashing over the darkened room as General Harper stomped through in full Dress Blues.

"What the fuck you faggots doing?" Harper's tone of disdain was only matched by his scowl of disapproving incomprehension at the scene.

Jacari holstered his weapon and snapped up straight. Stork clunked the weight down to the side and straightened himself. Amos clamored to his feet and threw his shoulders back, saluted.

Harper snarled, "I need a team to the Ops room, Major. You're wheels up in ninety minutes."

"Mission, sir?" Amos asked, all of them staring straight ahead, blood splattered over their faces. "Where—"

"At ease, goddammit." The general scowled. "There's a massive Republican march on Washington, convening in protest over the goddamn liberal pansies shooting the elector and now the fucking Democrats are rallying thousands to DC." The slits of Harper's disapproving eyes seemed to survey the scene before him now a little more thoroughly as he spoke— the haphazard weights, the rumpled uniforms, the cuts and blood. "The White House requested backup security, and you numbnuts are it." He glanced around the room in disgust. "Why you snake-eating cunts always insist on running your drills in such weird places? This gym sucks." He squinted down at a ruptured medicine ball on the floor. "Expecting to fight a terrorist at a spin class or something?"

"Can't run too many disarming drills, sir," Amos answered. "No matter where the location."

"Fucking idiots." Harper snorted as he spun toward the door. "Bullets can't kill ya, only pussies can. Get your asses to the White House."

> *"If freedom of speech is taken away, we*
> *will be led like sheep to the slaughter."*
> —George Washington

(Washington, D.C.: Sunday, 9:54 a.m. PST / 12:54 p.m. EST)

"The nuggets are much exceptional," Yanic Goran said to the private-prison industry lobbyist while dipping another Slappy Nugget into his Slappy Sauce. Goran tried to keep his hand from trembling as he ate his lunch. "Only ninety-nine cent for six-pack." As he chewed, he used his other liver-spotted hand to politely cover his mouth, trying to act as calm as possible, trying to act like he was a master of all situations despite the elector shooting news, despite the increasing images around the country of hostile people on both the right and left, despite the flood of angry people entering DC. "Anyone try the Slappy crossword yet?" he asked the group with a nod toward the paper placemats. It was essential to his business model that he always appear calm, if not cavalier, in his projection that everything would be fine.

Besides the lanky private-prison industry lobbyist who stood next to the laminated table-booth, there was a private-military contractor, a lobbyist from the foreign oil conglomerate, and representatives for the pharmaceutical industry, the *National Rifle Association*, a Wall Street hedge fund, the movie industry, a military weapons manufacturer, the attorney for a current ambassador to China, and an aide to General Harper, all sitting or standing around the aging, super-lobbyist in the garishly red and yellow fast-food restaurant in Washington, DC. They were all there to hire Yanic Goran, completely legally, to assist their employers. They intently observed his every tremble and chew.

"Can we please discuss business?" the Arabic man across from Yanic said. The Arabic man was squeezed into the booth with two other individuals. "We need," the Arabic man continued, "to secure a meeting with the next administration. You can guarantee that, no? How much?"

Ever since Yanic Goran formed his dark money Super-Pac, *The Spirit of 1776*, he'd been almost in demand as much as the West Wing itself. It was the opportune Supreme Court rulings in 2010 and 2014 that skyrocketed Yanic Goran's power to dizzying heights. The 2010 rulings of *Citizens United v. Federal Election Commission* and *Speechnow.org v. Federal Election Committee*, followed by *McCutcheon v. Federal Election Committee* in 2014, had rocked the landscape of political donations like a massive earthquake, although most Americans knew nothing about the rulings. Removal of restrictions to political donations hit at exactly the right time for Yanic Goran to take advantage of his massive web of political and monetary connections, and exponentially increase his political power.

Prior to the 2010 rulings, political candidates had been limited from receiving more than $5,000 from any single citizen, and could not receive any donations from corporations, unions, or special interest groups. For the bulk of the 20th century this had made it very difficult for any wealthy entity, whether individual or special interest group, to directly influence an election at the expense of individual American citizens. The 2010 rulings though, allowed for the formation of special political action committees known as "Super PACs," which would not be limited on receiving any amount of donation from any individual, and could even receive any amount of donation from businesses or special interest groups. It immediately opened the floodgates of billions of dollars toward influencing the outcome of elections with Yanic Goran already perfectly positioned to be a gatekeeper for a bulk of those funds. In late 2010 it only took him $300 and forty-five minutes to register *Spirit of 1776*. Within thirty days, Yanic Goran had solicited the largest arsenal of campaign funds ever compiled in the country. In fact, all the mega-rich around the world, including hostile foreign powers, wanted to donate to Yanic Goran's Super PAC in order to secure his good graces so he could serve as their influence into government. *Spirit of 1776,* and its massive treasure chest, was used at Yanic Goran's sole discretion.

"I do not eat filth," the Arabic man sneered, flicking his tray as Yanic continued to chew.

"Suit yourself," the man with a Boston accent next to the Arabic man said, and reached for the Arabic man's abandoned Slappy Burger. "This stuff was like gold when I was a kid." The man with the Boston accent, a lobbyist for the $150 billion dollar private military contracting industry, was built like a circus strongman. He had a shaved bald head and wore a tight short-sleeved collared shirt that had *Griffin Contracting* embroidered on its front. The private military industry was made up of retired US military who took big payments to do anything the US government didn't want on the books. He was pressed so tight between the Arabic man and the elderly woman in the sequined gown that he accidentally knocked both with his elbows while reaching for the food.

"I'm not even sure what I'm doing here," the elderly woman in the sequined dress, a new representative for the movie industry, sighed. "I was told you could help secure my clients' meeting with the winner, regardless of who it is? We need to discuss revamping the movie ratings system." She glanced at everyone waiting. "I don't understand, nor see the purpose, of a group function. I don't have anything to do with oil rights in the Sudan."

"And I have only eleven minutes," Mr. Goran answered her between chews with a glance at his diamond-encrusted gold watch. "I leave in eleven minutes for meeting with more important people." Yanic pulled a pickle slice off his Slappy Snapper and set it to the side while letting the weight of his words hang in the air for a moment. "So... anyone hoping for your clients to become my clients, I suggest you complain less and more offer."

"Excuse me, Mr. Goran." The attorney for the ambassador to China leaned toward the back of Yanic's head from the other booth. The attorney wore a green jogging suit. "I simply need to know if it looks likely that my client will be offered the book advance or not? That's all."

Yanic Goran chuckled over his shoulder. "Well, that entirely dependent on election winner, no? Publisher not pay millions in advance for tell-all book if administration gone. Winner of election determine winner and loser of many, eh?"

"I guess I'm confused since I'm not normally a lobbyist," the elderly woman continued. "I was supposed to be headed to a wedding, see, but our Governmental Affairs Manager was stuck on the West Coast so they asked me to fill in. Are you going to be able to help us get the ratings changed or not? It equates to billions of dollars for Hollywood."

"I assure you, madam," Yanic Goran replied, "I provide simple solutions to complex problems, at MOST affordable price. Of interest, would Hollywood be willing to make some propaganda films for next administration, disguise them as blockbusters maybe?"

"But is this even okay?" she pressed, glaring around at all the other lobbyists. "Legal? Seems like we shouldn't be so blatantly exchanging money and favors, right?"

"Legal?" Yanic exclaimed, dropping a half-eaten french fry to the tray. "Of course is legal, madam! This is free speech, your right to petition government. This your most cherished and important right of freedom as protected by First Amendment to Constitution of United States in action." Yanic Goran's wrinkled old face looked legitimately shocked. "The highest court in the land ruled time and again, money free speech, free speech is money, they the same thing."

"Money is free speech?" The women in the sequined dress looked genuinely puzzled. "But everyone has speech, not everyone has money?"

"Democracy," Yanic Goran smiled at the elderly woman, "goes where the money flows, madam." Yanic Goran reached for a Slappy Sugar Twist. "Lobbying is democracy in its purest form, and I am liberty's..." Yanic Goran searched the air for the word. "Grease."

The Griffin Contractor popped the last bite of the Slappy Burger into his mouth, an eyebrow cocked at Yanic. "We're prepared to offer eight figures for a first-week sit-down with a new Republican administration." He used the back of his hairy hand to wipe some Slappy Burger mustard off his lips, then poked a finger toward Yanic Goran. "But the best we can do if Freeman and company keep the reigns is sub five. We've been barking up their tree too many times to pay top dollar for the same old song and dance, ya know."

Mr. Goran nodded, picking up a pencil next to his Slappy Burger tray and pulled a Slappy Burger napkin out from his pocket. He unfolded it and began to write. Yanic's napkin, besides for having a spot of yellow Slappy Sauce on it, had two hand-scrawled columns running down either side. One column had "*Rep*" written at its top, the other had "*Dem.*" Several lines of dollar amounts were written beneath the two headings. Yanic Goran quickly wrote *$10m?* beneath the Republican column, and added a *$5m?* beneath the Democratic side, with a notation it was an offer from the private military contractor.

"We then pay 25 million," the Arabic man sighed with a sideward glance at the private military contractor. "If you can secure our interests in the Gulf with next administration. But we need the first meeting, we do not care who wins."

"Excellent." Yanic Goran smiled warmly at the Arabic man. "That makes it much easier."

"Sir," General Harper's military aide politely interrupted from the other booth. He was dressed in Marine khakis, and looked extremely young and extremely serious. "Sorry to interrupt, Mr. Goran, sir, I just need to report back to the general on whether or not you think he will have the analyst job lined up. In case the Republicans loose. He thinks he may get sacked by a Freeman administration. If you can just give me an answer, I can get out of your hair."

Yanic Goran glanced back at General Harper's aide in annoyance, raised a finger.

Goran scratched a *$25m* below both the Democratic and Republican columns from the oil lobbyist, then hunched tighter over the napkin so no one could see and, with his tongue sticking out in concentration, quickly tallied the current totals for both columns.

Goran spun back to the booth with the military aide. "Tell General Harper I am in contact with all major news stations and think-tanks, but things do not look good for him being as he once said the N-word seven years back. Unfortunately the tape is out there, and after all, language matters. He should hope the Republicans remain in office."

Yanic Goran estimated, with current totals from all his meetings over the past week, he could immediately bring in around another $100 million from a Republican win, and closer to $65 million for a Democratic. Of course, there was still the real meeting, the most important meeting of all, this afternoon.

"$2.5 then," the elderly woman blurted with a shake of her head. "$2.5 million is what Hollywood will pay for an early meeting with the next president. If it's a Democrat, that is. We'll probably pass on Stone, as he'll probably let the religious right ban anything not from Disney." She snatched up her purse and stood. "And I'm still not sure about this whole lobbying system, seems off."

"Early, as in…what?" Yanic Goran prodded. "First six months or first week?"

The elderly woman searched through her purse for her car keys. "I'm not sure. Does it matter?"

"I only ask, because Tobacco, NRA, and Big Pharma," Yanic Goran nodded toward a sharply dressed woman and two fat men sitting patiently on the interior Slappy Burger plastic playground set. "They currently bidding three million for first-week meetings." Yanic shrugged apologetically to the Hollywood lobbyist. "Maybe you wish to let your clients know a little more money could be helpful?"

"Whatever." The woman sighed and yanked out her keys, turning from the table to sling her purse over her shoulder. "If we don't get in, I don't care, I'm going back to writing scripts." She walked toward the exit, chuckling. "DC is as sleazy as Hollywood... just uglier people."

Yanic wrote her additional compensation offer under the appropriate Democratic win column on his napkin, as he mumbled, "Freedom is not free, madam."

* * *

His immaculate kitchen was all chromes and polished blonde wood. Within his very nice penthouse condominium in Georgetown, Mr. Jefferson used a slightly rusty carrot peeler to scrape sections of flesh from his chest while looking out over the icy Potomac River. Before the crimson blood started to seep, he would notice how the nearly translucent curls of his pigment-free skin resembled the thin sheens of winter ice hugging the brown banks of the river below. The pain was to tame the guna of rajas roiling inside him, so he could concentrate on the final part of the task. Now, with the elector's shooting, a new timeline had opened and he must stay clear in mind to perform the final act.

Kama bubbles like lava from the guna of rajas, roiling so warm in all those born in Kali Yuga. He pressed the edge of the peeler against his left nipple. *The price of taking incarnation in this human form at this ripened time. The Kama leads all astray, causes the splits and fissures. Kama births the lies in those without discipline.* He breathed deeply once, looking back out the window at a single black bird hopping hungrily on the edge of the icy riverbank. *The ignorant look outward to quell the hot Kama boiling inside them, rather than tame their own rajas. Like a hand grasping at its own shadow.* He ripped his right hand down and across and his nipple cut free, dropping to the Travertine tile floor without a sound. Mr. Jefferson winced in pain as the bright red blood began to flow and the pain began to burn, but he did not make any sound except for a slightly deeper inhale.

Then, "Wooo… Lordy," he couldn't help but gasp, reaching for a folded white towel on chrome counter. "Damn. Burns."

He pressed the towel to his bleeding chest and tried to concentrate. *Kama births the lies, and the lies destroy all. For what is country, or family, or God, except trust in one another… lies destroy the trust.*

"Son of a bitch that stings." With his free hand he leaned across the counter to pick up the leather holster holding his service weapon, then used his pinky to also scoop up his ID badge.

I must help them in their evolution, Mr. Jefferson thought, gritting his teeth as he walked toward his bedroom with a glance at the digital clock on the wall. *And hopefully, I can stop this damned bleeding before I'm late for my shift.*

* * *

In Dayton, Ohio, in the baking hot kitchen of Milton's Diner, Rosa Sanchez watched the news of the Republicans getting away with murdering the elector on her Smartphone. It was so hot in the kitchen she was sweating, and Rosa's entire face still throbbed in pain from the attack in the park on Friday, bandage on her nose. She hoped they found evidence of the Republicans shooting the Louisiana guy, but instead only saw more evidence of right-wing corruption in the media. Somebody had even started claiming she was Muslim on the Internet, and she didn't know what in the hell that was about.

"Best not let Milton catch you." The cook nodded his eyes toward the phone. The cook was an older Mexican man with an accent much heavier than Rosa's, and was slicing shriveled lemons for the dinner crowd. "You no papers. He no like breaks."

"Whatever." Rosa didn't lift her eyes from her phone, reflexively touching the homemade bandage over her massive purple nose. "I'd work Milton's fat ass into a stroke."

"Goddammit, girl," Milton suddenly barked as the kitchen door swung open before three hundred pounds of white, sweaty blubber in a tight, yellowing T-shirt. "What I tell you? You got a lull, best be out back scrubbing the garbage cans."

"This is the first time I've stopped moving in six hours, Milton. And I'm not paid to scrub garbage cans." Overwhelming emotions of rage and despair battled inside Rosa. "You know I never leave a table—"

"I pay you," Milton smiled through brown teeth, clutching a meaty palm to her ass, "to move." That wicked gleam came into his eyes. "You got to earn your money some way, sugar, either scrubbing out back, or in my office scrubbing my—"

"Get off me." Rosa slapped his hand from her ass, tears welling in her eyes. "You even saying that is fucking illegal!"

The cook disappeared into the walk-in freezer, and Rosa's heart clenched with fear of things Milton might do.

"Illegal?" Milton chuckled, leaning forward closer to her face, coffee breath panting over her. "Bet ya I find something illegal in your immigration papers, huh? Oh, that's right, you don't have any. Ain't your boy gonna be hungry with you in jail? Deported maybe."

"Leave me alone." Rosa spun toward the backdoor, wiping at tears around her broken nose as she stomped into the parking lot.

Rosa knew life was rigged. The whole fucking thing was rigged against her no matter how hard she tried. Tears started pouring down her cheeks as she thought how if Freeman and Daniels didn't get into power and change things, she didn't know what she'd do. She'd rather scrub the filth out of every garbage can in the world than get one inch closer to the filth of that disgusting white man though.

Amos Preps for Mission

(Washington, D.C.: Sunday, 12:00 p.m. PST / 3:00 p.m. EST)

T *he snake deserved to die.*
Annie sat in a high-backed, red leather chair behind a dark oak desk in her home study. It was after yet another night of only three hours sleep, blonde hair in a loose bun on top of her head. She was trying to concentrate, as well as keep her arms crossed over the inappropriate graphic on her T-shirt while she spoke with the president and vice president. She was more tired than ever, and had been popping more and more Zennies throughout the morning to try to keep her thoughts clear while she had been waiting for Beatrice Howe to arrive. In the chaos of the morning she had confusedly clothed herself in a joke T-shirt that said, *I Shaved My Balls for This?*

Annie's study was large. The wood shutters kept the foggy San Francisco day outside, and the door to the upstairs hall was shut. Only light from the overhead chandelier glossed the wood furniture and an organic red apple on her desk. She had fitfully dreamt of rabbits and snakes before Henry woke her. Henry now sat to her left, Beatrice Howe to her right. Both of them were in small rolling office chairs they'd brought in from Kim-Su's sneaker room down the hall. Buzz-cut Castor was on duty just outside the door. All three looked intensely into her computer monitor.

"Great work, Senator Daniels." President Fuentes was buttoned-up tight in a fresh charcoal three-piece suit, dark jowls hanging slightly over the stiff white collar to his shirt. Freeman still had the sleeves of the gray shirt he'd been wearing for over a day rolled up to his elbows, his yellow tie partially undone. She could tell from the diamond windowpane behind President Fuentes and Vice President Freeman that they were sitting side-by-side in the small Presidential Annex connected to the Oval Office. It was the president's personal office, more utilitarian than the Oval Office.

"Thank you, sir." Annie blushed from the president's praise, but shrugged a bit in confusion, her arms still crossed to cover her T-shirt. "But I haven't done anything since yesterday?"

"Exactly," the president sneered, and Annie's blush of pride morphed into a bitter heat at the president's sarcasm. "Now," he continued, "when is the joint speech between you and Stone agreed to happen?" The president cracked his knuckles, rubbed a brown palm over his wool white hair. "Beatrice should oversee drafting the statement. It's important more than ever that it strikes the perfect bipartisan tone." He glared sternly through his round glasses. "And Annie, we need it out there by dinnertime on the East Coast in order to make sure that whatever replacement elector is appointed tonight in Louisiana is publicly accepted. Can you confirm with Stone, or do you need Marcus or I to reach out?"

"No," Annie replied glancing at the apple, the breakfast she had yet to eat. "Not neccessary."

"Excellent." The president exhaled and leaned back in

his chair with a relieved smile at Freeman. "And Miss Howe, you've got carte blanche editorial power on—"

"No," Annie clarified, her blue eyes narrowing into the camera even as her left leg began to shimmer nervously beneath the desk. "I mean I'm not making any joint statement with Stone, sir. I've actually got a new idea, based on information since Miss Howe arrived." Annie needed this to all be over tomorrow. She couldn't take anymore, couldn't just keep popping Zennies to make it through. Her brain felt fried and she was having difficulty keeping things in check. She needed this to be done, so she concentrate on the only thing maybe more important than this election, her daughter's well-being. There was no longer any time for weakness.

Beatrice Howe had arrived an hour earlier, the frail black woman not seeming the haughty, bossy extension of President Fuentes' power Annie had been expecting, but shaken and nervous, maybe feeling in over her head. She looked into Annie's eyes for support. In crisis though, Annie knew there was always opportunity, and Annie had politely asked Henry to leave while gently guiding Howe to her kitchen table. Annie had even found some Oreos and made tea.

"I actually think the conspiracy I was afraid of had Gatreaux shot," Howe had eventually blurted. "I didn't want to say anything to the president before, because I just wasn't sure, but... there was *RedRabbit* communication at the Louisiana elector's location only a day before. What if... " Howe dropped her face into her brown hands. "What if, Madam Senator, there's actually a plot to steal the election? I had hoped I was wrong."

"There, there," Annie had said into Howe's tear-rimmed eyes, wanting to be shocked too like a normal person. "Don't worry." Annie actually pulled Howe to her chest for a hug, Howe's hair reeking of cheap perfume. "I think I know what to do."

And now Annie stated to the president, "You should move troops into New Orleans."

"Jesus," Henry gasped from her side, Annie feeling the burn of his gaze.

"What?" the president stammered. "Federal troops into an American state?" He shook his head in shock, glared at Marcus, then back at Annie. "You can't be serious?"

And internally, Annie was not completely sure if she was serious or not. But it was the most direct way she had come up with to make sure the election was not lost, while having the bonus of making sure there was not another riot that hurt an innocent kid like Joey Thompson. It was extreme, but everything else left too many loose ends, too many things that could break against them and for the Republicans, or into chaos. That *Joint Congressional Committee* just formed for Election Oversight was a nearly even split of Republican and Democratic senators and congressmen, but led by the staunchly independent Colorado Senator Kaleel. Who knew what they would find and publicly recommend? What if they proposed a delay to the electoral vote and nationwide recounts? She couldn't keep going at this indefinitely. Her daughter needed her, and Stone had been gaining steam. Wouldn't a show of executive power be the safest way to close out these final hours for everyone, to make sure there was a calm, definite conclusion?

"Ms. Howe," Annie clarified to the president, "has found what she believes are *RedRabbit* communication signatures only a little over twenty-four hours ago at Lawrence Gatreaux's restaurant. She thinks, and I am in agreement, that his death was probably orchestrated by Republicans."

"Those sons of bitches," Marcus Freeman exclaimed. "I told you, Mr. Pres—"

"Now hold on a second." The president glared back and forth between Annie and Freeman. "Even if there was *RedRabbit* communication at his location, how does that materially tie him to a Republican-led conspiracy?"

"Who else would it be, sir? Occam's Razor. It's got to be political-based if there was *RedRabbit* communication from there only twenty-four hours prior to his murder. Isn't that far too bizarre to be coincidental? So that makes it them or us, and WE didn't have him killed, sir, especially when there is plenty of anecdotal information he was flipping to us." Of course, Annie knew there were other possible solutions, but… "The Louisiana Republican state legislature assumes they're going to be able to appoint someone more loyal with no questions asked, so it being Republicans is the most straightforward solution."

"She's got a point, sir," Freeman said. "Everything is lining up for it being them."

"Really, Marcus?" President Fuentes glowered incredulously at Freeman. "None of that is concrete evidence of a crime. All conjecture, guessing."

"Of course there's nothing to hold up in court, sir, yet." Annie dug her nails into the skin of her shaking thigh. "But with the vote tomorrow, we've got to make decisions now. If we delay it would only help them fraudulently appoint a new elector and succeed in stealing the election. Frankly, I'm worried if we hesitate much at all the Republican governor of Louisiana is going to issue an Execute Order to allow the Republicans to pick the replacement. And if I went ahead and made some sort of bipartisan speech with Stone it is simply playing into their hands."

"Presidents don't invade their own states, Annie." The president sighed, pinched the bridge of his wide nose with two fingers. "I just want this to be over, you two. Peacefully, over."

"And the best way to do that is to quarantine New Orleans until we've won the Electoral College vote by one." Annie breathed deeply, hugged herself tighter. "And I'm obviously not talking about violence, I'm talking about PEACEKEEP-ERS. Send the Army into New Orleans before the Louisiana Governor overrules the Secretary of State or rioting will surely increase, sir. Use an Executive Order to quarantine strategic parts of the state, with no shots fired of course, to ensure the peace and calm. Then YOU state the Electoral Vote needs to occur tomorrow as scheduled, to keep things on track. If you think about it, it's actually the most responsible thing, sir, especially knowing any electoral concerns can't go to an eight-man Supreme Court which will only tie."

"Christ, Annabel." Freeman smiled. "I thought I was the crafty one. Federal troops moving into New Orleans to keep the peace, and an unfortunate side effect of a statewide curfew for the next twenty-four hours would mean the impossibility of Republican state legislature to convene. There would be no way they could officially appoint a new elector. We'd win the vote 269 to 268." There was a twinkle in Freeman's eyes. "That's brilliant, Annie, absolutely brilliant. No tie, no House, no more riots."

"But Kaleel's Congressional Committee," Henry argued, his eyes panicked at Annie's suggestion. "Couldn't they go against letting the electoral vote occur tomorrow?"

"No constitutional authority," Freeman answered with

a grin. "The congressional committee really can only make a recommendation."

"This would be stealing it," President Fuentes exclaimed. "Maybe legally stealing it, but—"

"With all due respect, sir, I don't think 'legally stealing' is a thing," Annie countered. "It would just be a statewide lockdown until peace and calm can be assured. Just for one day."

"On the electoral vote day? Ordering federal troops into an American city would be unprecedented." The president shook his head furiously, glasses slipping down his nose. "We are not there yet, you two, the Republican Governor has not overruled the Secretary of State, and there's been nothing local government can't handle. I won't do it."

"We're less than a day away, sir." Annie placed both her hands on her desk and straightened to convey as much sensibility as possible. "This will show leadership to a confused country—"

"Does your T-shirt say something about testicles," President Fuentes asked, leaning toward the camera in dismay, pushing his glasses up on his nose. "What in God's name is wrong with you?"

Annie threw her arms across her chest again.

"I'm sick of it, Daniels, sick of your shoot-from-the-hip extremism." The president waved a dismissive hand toward her through the monitor. "This is a Republic, we're not allowed to interfere with a state's electoral process." His voice rose in frustration. "You will get off this goddamn call right now and immediately phone Governor Stone to make that joint speech as you promised me. Now!"

And for a moment Annie wondered if she were making the right decision, if at some point she should stop doubling-down, just give up, and do what they all told her, trust that everything would turn out okay. But she could feel the snakes crawling beneath her skin, about to hiss in the darkest corners of her mind, the stakes too high for mere trust. "Well when I think of us making choices that cause us to lose this election, sir," her voice sure, even as she felt little muscles within her legs twitch and crawl like bugs, a subtle facial tick began to quiver beneath her left eye, "inevitably my thoughts go back to how much more acceptable *Cyber-Care* would be to the country if everyone simply knew the truth of the *Uncle's Eyes* program." She used all her internal resolve to confidently hold the president's steel gaze while giving her less-than-subtle threat to expose the details of the secretive surveillance program. "You secretly rounding up innocent people through *Long Knives* is far worse than what I'm suggesting, sir."

No one made a sound for several moments, and she knew she had now crossed an irrevocable line. President Fuentes was not a man to make enemies with. Marcus Freeman glanced back and forth between Annie and the president as if he was fearfully watching a tennis match, and Annie waited for a tidal wrath to flood from Fuentes, but instead, his calm almost chilled her more.

After a moment, the president simply pulled up his suit sleeve to glance at his watch, and calmly stated, "We're ending this call for an hour or two. I will personally reach out to Governor Stone to see what possible alternatives may be for achieving the bipartisan speech for this evening." The president reached up a hand to shut off the communication, the last words Annie heard being, "Rethink your position, Daniels, you're punching above your weight class."

As the screen went black, Annie saw Henry was staring

at her like she had gone insane. "What's wrong with you?" he stammered. "You're willing to use force just to win?"

"I would never," Annie declared, truly shocked that Henry was misconstruing her recommendation to the president. "I'm not saying to use force, I'm saying to prevent potential violence before it happens by moving troops in."

"You've got the crow's feet again," Henry declared. "You're lying. Can't you ever stop fighting? Just have some faith?"

"No, because faith is exactly what is destroying the world." Annie's eyes burned with determination to end this fight once and for all, however necessary. "Results are what matters, results that actually help people, not how we get there."

Henry leapt to his feet, glared down at her with his cheeks flush above the beard. "I need to know, Annie, right now, did you have the elector shot?"

"What? No!" Annie couldn't fathom what was happening to Henry, why her most trusted aide and most loyal friend seemed suddenly like he was turning against her just when she needed him most. "All my life I've stood for safety and peace, for real liberty and equality."

"No, not the political response," Henry snarled, his eyes wide. "Not the bullshit. Tell me, right now, Annie, what principle do you hold higher than winning. What ideal would you lose for, before breaking."

Hiss. Hissssss. She could hear the snakes hissing again. How was it that he suddenly acted like he didn't know her, was forgetting how hard she had to fight as a woman to get here, like she were somehow wrong for playing by their rules? How was her most trusted friend now turning against her? "You think I, in this sea of opportunistic political vipers," she growled, "am the one without any principles?"

"Give me your word, Annie, give me your word right now that if it comes to it, before anyone else gets killed, you will quit. Promise me that you will put the sanctity of the Constitution, the preservation of the Union, of American life, ahead of any personal gain if it comes to that."

"And if I promise, you'll shut the fuck up and do what I say?"

Henry swallowed, took a deep breath. "Yes. Just promise you'll quit before letting any more violence happen and I won't question you again."

"Fine." She snatched the apple off her desk, and took a bite. "I promise, no violence. And now you anonymously leak the tape on Stone. Or get the fuck off my team."

Henry Leaks Tape Online

(Washington, D.C.: Sunday, 12:51 p.m. PST / 3:51 p.m. EST)

The Democratic mayor of the District of Columbia wanted to make sure to avoid any insinuations of partisanship this close to the election's end, so made sure to clear all the roadways for the influx of Republican cars, trucks and buses into the city for Buddy Dukes' march on Washington. The mayor of San Francisco always got good national press for doing things like this, so the mayor of DC figured a show of graciousness would help his national profile. He even had the police hurriedly set up extra parking areas, help barricade off a long walking path down Pennsylvania Avenue to the White House fence, and encouraged hot dogs vendors to set up early.

As a cold but sunny morning had worn on, dozens filtering onto Pennsylvania Avenue had become hundreds, then thousands, then too many to count. Some had bright red shirts already on as they got out of their beat-up trucks, others put them on as they lumbered off buses that provided free transportation by the RNC from neighboring states. The huge mass of people grew into a semi-organized mob that inched their way down that same pavement that newly-elected presidents walked, the stately white dome of the Capitol in the background. From news helicopters circling above it looked as if a slow current of blood was moving toward the White House.

On the side streets leading away from the barricaded Pennsylvania Avenue, Democratic volunteers financially backed by the *American Civil Liberties Union* scurried up and down the sidewalks, feverishly handing out bright blue T-shirts to anyone who would agree to wear them. They were determined to not let the Republican march overtake all of the press in these final hours.

* * *

The conservative news anchor dropped into her seat to start the afternoon block. "Breaking news." She straightened the American flag pin on her lapel, patting her hair. "Republican Louisiana Governor John Talbot has just signed an Executive Order overruling Democratic Louisiana Secretary of State Paulson on the elector appointment. Governor Talbot has granted full authority for the Republican-majority Louisiana State Legislature to convene in New Orleans as soon as possible to appoint a new elector." She cleared her throat. "Thank goodness there are still brave, sensible patriots like Governor Talbot in this nation. From his leadership we can look forward to having a just and timely end to this election."

* * *

"But how do I find truth in all this madness?" In Boulder, Colorado, Harmony saw long spears of late afternoon pink light splitting mountain peaks in the distance like a painting of heaven. An occasional cold burst of wind kicked over her long blonde hair from the open garage door. Some tiny muscle just below her sternum near her heart quivered in fear.

"All the world, all of time," Dr. Mokeba had told Harmony

moments ago, "depends on your sacrifice. We are each a precious warrior in the battle between light and darkness."

She was sitting on a straw mat in the 'ceremony room' of the clinic, wide double doors to the backyard open on the snow-dusted mountain range in the distance, an oil stain on the garage floor. A warm wood fire pit burned just outside the open garage door, and there were faded posters of African vistas on the walls. The warmth felt good, reassuring on the skin of her arm, and the low drum beats of Bwiti tribal music did stir some courage deep inside her. But she was still scared, as in her hands she clutched a brown, hollowed-out gourd with a yellowish liquid in it that Dr. Mokeba called *Soma*.

Or *Death Drink*, as Jon-jon the assistant had called it before Mokeba finger-waved him quiet. Harmony kept reminding herself that she didn't believe in ghosts, jinn, or whatever else Jon-jon had been whispering would interact with her in the spirit world. He said they occasionally bled through into this world too and you could tell who they were because they were marked. She couldn't tell if Jon-jon was trying to scare her or be helpful. Dr. Mokeba had emphasized many times though that it was not important to fixate on the human terms of what you would encounter in the spirit world, and it could be unhelpful if your expectations morphed into fear. Trust was everything. Faith over fear.

"But am I really going to die?" Harmony asked Mokeba for at least the twentieth time.

"The old Harmony will die, those ego attachments to this world which make you sick," the doctor said. "And a new Harmony will be reborn healthy... probably."

"Probably I'll be healthy, or probably I'll not really die?"

"Oh." Mokeba seemed to remember something as he

raised a hand. "Hold on, I must get the adrenaline syringe." He darted from the garage into the main part of the house.

Jon-jon, who wore big rubber boots on the white snow, was mashing some sort of roots in a blue plastic bucket just outside the open garage door. He looked at Harmony with a sad shake of his head.

Looking down at the yellowish *Soma* Harmony felt like she was holding the power of a black hole in her hands. Her mind immediately flashed back to the scene in that old movie *The Matrix*, when that goofy guy was staring down at two pills and he had to choose between taking the red one or the blue… the consequences being to alter his mind forever to new, and potentially terrifying realities, or to go back to being permanently stuck in his mediocre, but safer, delusion of reality that he had always known. That was suddenly Harmony's choice too, and she could feel the blood-sweat pressing against the interior of her skin, her anxiousness like a dam about to burst. She tried to reassure herself she had already done the DMT and that had turned out fine, but this was another thing altogether. Ancient, extreme, irrevocable. Pinpricks of red blood began beading on the bottoms of her palms, a reminder that, either way, death was coming.

Mokeba reappeared. "The only thing we have to fear, my dear, is fear itself."

"That's FDR," Harmony tried to find her courage somewhere down in her twisting stomach. "But I don't think FDR ever scarfed down some hallucinogenic *death drink*."

Mokeba chuckled. "Yet maybe if he had, World War II wouldn't have happened." Mokeba thought. "Or, at least if Hitler had?"

"Will I see God?" she had asked.

"Yes," he stated unequivocally. "You will absolutely see God, my dear. Whatever part you are ready to see, whatever word you use for it. And it will either burn disease and darkness from you, child, or it will burn you away from this world it is perfecting to start again with your parts."

Harmony now looked down at the bowl again and tears welled up to her eyes. A drop of red blood plunked from her forehead into the yellow liquid, curdling like a dying snake. Harmony wondered why the hot, weird guy from the coffee shop had never called her. All she really wanted before she died was one real kiss. The recorded drum beats filled the air, and Mokeba began wafting a smoldering leaf, its smell thick and sweet.

"I'm not ready. I'm not ready to die."

Mokeba looked down at her. He placed the smoldering leaf into a ceramic bowl behind him with a sigh.

"Child." His voice was soft and tender. "I think you need to say goodbye. Truth is calling."

* * *

In Ohio, Governor Hampton Stone's thin blonde hair danced over his orange scalp as he lumbered down the stairs they'd wheeled up to his campaign plane. He was internally debating what to berate Buddy Dukes with first as the metal steps squeaked and popped with every footfall. They had landed at a small municipal airport just outside of Dayton in order to take a break from the press, and the whole stair contraption seemed to vibrate under Stone's grip on the flimsy metal railing. Stone wondered if they had welded the stair steps together just that afternoon.

Besides his normal lower back pain, and Dukes making that boneheaded declaration of needing a march on

Washington, Stone felt good. He was confident at having heard the news the Republican Louisiana Governor would make sure the right elector would be appointed, and as long as Buddy was handling the issue with General Harper correctly, his wife would soon be picking out new curtains for the Oval Office.

Congressman Dukes waited for Stone at the base of the stairs, their limo parked only a few yards away on the tarmac. The Ohio sky directly above was clear, cold and sunny, but off to the east Stone noticed dark clouds. He wondered if Buddy had bothered to check the weather report before scheduling their outdoor victory rally, presumptive, in Bixley Park for this evening. The rally was purposely chosen for the same spot as *Atheist Annie's* riot in an orchestrated gesture of good triumphing over evil.

Buddy wore his trademark plaid suit and a cowboy hat, his goofy face looking a bit concerned. Maybe Buddy had seen the distant blizzard clouds himself? Or maybe, Stone considered, the knucklehead had just forgotten what end of his hat was up. "Can you not buy a normal suit?" Stone asked as he planted both feet on the tarmac, sweating profusely. "One that isn't plaid?"

Buddy didn't say anything. His black brows furrowed, and he thrust his phone out to Stone.

"What?" Stone looked down at the phone. "What's this?"

Buddy lifted the phone a couple inches closer to Stone's eyes. Stone snatched the phone from Buddy's hand. He had to move the phone in and out, tilt his head back a bit until his eyes and glasses could find just the right distance to read the small print. Then Stone's stomach dropped.

"That fucking whore," Stone whispered. The article was from

a marginally reputable online news magazine, but no matter the source, Stone knew it would flood the airwaves by nightfall. "That fucking…" Stone growled, his entire body trembling with rage. "Fucking…" He wound his right hand back and hurled Buddy's phone high above the tarmac. "Fucking cunt!"

Stone clenched both hands into fists and gritted his teeth, his whole body shaking with anger as Buddy's phone spun through the air. It went twenty yards then whacked against the tarmac to shatter into hundreds of tiny plastic and glass pieces.

The news story read:

> *It has been confirmed an audiotape recording exists of Governor Hampton Stone, former pastor and Republican candidate for president, stating in part, the following: "Sure, God's bullshit, but I know He's good for getting rich, and for getting rednecks to vote for you." The full audio of the recording provided by an anonymous source is now available on our website. Several House Republicans have indicated they will no longer be supporting Governor Stone's candidacy if the audio is authenticated.*

* * *

In Birmingham, Alabama, *@jessejameskickass* peered from the back of a white pickup truck at the protestors on the library steps with suspicion, his scoped rifle laying across his camo pants. The largely black protestors still had their hands up and were softly chanting *hands up, don't shoot* for the couple of local television cameras nearby. Between chewing on a toothpick and occasionally adjusting his grip on his rifle, *@jessejameskickass* would check his phone to see the news. Seattle appeared to be having protests, a big march on Washington was starting up, and New Orleans looked like it was turning into a war zone. On top of everything, the Democrats had obviously just leaked a fraudulent, doctored tape of Governor Stone, trying to claim he didn't believe in God. *@jessejameskickass* knew there was something nefarious afoot in the country, and it probably had to do with Muslims having that elector shot.

He took his toothpick out and raised the brim of his bedazzled trucker's hat. In back of the protestors, slinking around in the shadows and offering them bottles of water occasionally whispering things in their ears was a real suspicious looking dude. The guy had a short-trimmed black beard, light brown skin, and one of them weird tiny little white hats on top of his dark head just like pictures he'd seen of ISIS assholes. *@jessejameskickass* was pretty sure the dude was Muslim, and somebody had to protect the homeland.

* * *

News Headline:

New Orleans Devolving into Multi-Cultural Violence

* * *

At a DC sandwich shop two blocks off Pennsylvania Ave, a proud member of both the *American Civil Liberties Union* as well as the *Black Panthers* had just checked her phone and saw increasing reports of violence against people of color at protests across the county. She had been handing out Democratic blue T-shirts to as many liberals as she could find, but needed to now motivate about two dozen of them in the shop to go join the larger group that was already organizing in front of the White House to meet the Republican march. Her blood was pumping faster and faster every time she checked her phone, and before she even realized it she had paraphrased a line from *@professorofplants'* video of the prior day to her group. "Is it not time, my brothers and sisters, to stand up for ourselves? Arm ourselves and fight if we must?"

* * *

Exactly at 4:00 p.m. Eastern Standard Time, thirty-two websites attributed to *Reboot.org* went live. A corresponding email blasted out to 171 million of Americans, inviting them to go to one of the *Reboot.org* websites to "find the truth." They had somehow hacked into the *Uncle Eye's* master files.

Once on any of the websites, a person could type in any other person's name. That was all it took to access all information about any individual. All pictures, videos, emails, texts, phone records, medical records, banking information, GPS locations traveled to with days and times, all websites visited, and all online searches conducted for approximately the past five years. It was all immediately available on everyone, to anyone, for free.

Many would claim much of the information was fabricated, including doctored videos of people doing obscene things and artificially generated emails and texts implicating people in conversations that they never had, committing crimes, having affairs, or just talking behind their best friend's back. Regardless of the information's veracity, no one could stop it from being seen, and everyone had someone they wanted to check on. Most assumed that everything not about them was accurate.

"We hold these truths..."
—Declaration of Independence

(Washington, D.C.: Sunday, 1:11 p.m. PST / 4:11 p.m. EST)

So much sweat was seeping through Yanic Goran's shirt by the time he dropped into his limo's backseat that it was actually making his wool suit coat damp. He breathed hard and his chest ached. The march on Washington was apparently turning into a tsunami with tens of thousands of Republicans already flooding the city and busloads of Democrats starting to respond in kind. Fires and looting were reported in New Orleans, with at least a dozen other cities around the country supposedly now facing serious rioting. And with the *Reboot. org* data breach and public dump, who knew what the next shoe to drop would be? The only positive was that there was so much data clogging the *Reboot.org* sites that it would take weeks for anyone to sift through it all, some of the websites already crashing due to volume of people trying to snoop into others' private data. Goran had already seen some reports that there was evidence in the data dump of serious voter fraud in dozens of different states and Diebold voting machines hacked, but like everyone else, he was more worried about his personal information than anything else. And then, of course, there was the video of Senator Daniels and Governor Stone in the basement he'd secretly taken and uploaded to the cloud. Lord knows that was supposed to be his black-mail ace-in-the-hole, but now it could already be public?

He willed the old hand clutching his soaked shirt to release from his chest, and leaned it against the monitor mounted to the partition's wall. It was important, most important of all, that he compose himself for this meeting. He glanced around to make sure the soundproof windows were clamped tight, the soundproof glass to the front driver was up, and then jabbed a trembling finger into the power button on the *RedRabbit* video system. As it flickered to life, Goran ripped off his coat, having to grunt and groan and twist in the back seat to get the damn thing off, then flung it down in the foot well to the side. He undid his tie and tried to inhale deeply again, hoping his chest pain would subside as he waited for these most powerful people in the world, inevitably now angry, to appear before him. Yanic Goran knew if things could not get resolved quickly, a possible heart attack would be the least of his worries.

"Forty-one seconds late, Yanic." President Fuentes scowled from the screen, his blue tie synched tight, his white mustache curling in annoyance.

"I beg your pardon, Mr. President." Goran wondered if they could hear the slight shake in his voice. "I had some—"

"Get on with it. We don't have time for excuses, 1776 needs a plan." The president's tone said he was completely fed-up.

"Governor, you there?" Vice-President Marcus Freeman asked, sitting pensively next to the President on screen in a gray shirt and loose yellow tie, both apparently in the President's private annex. "Hampton?"

"Here," Governor Hampton Stone's face finally *pinged* to life on the screen before Goran. The screen split with equal divisions for both spray-tanned Stone and the president. "Just landed in Dayton, where I found out your awful, awful, BITCH of a running mate has just slandered me, Marcus. What in the hell is going on here, something happening I don't know about?"

"And your imbecile of a running mate," Freeman countered, "just got thirty thousand people to start marching on Washington, Hampton. This isn't a perfect scenario for anyone."

"He may be an idiot, but he's not a psychopath," Hampton snapped back. "Daniels doesn't know about our bargain, does she? About *1776*?"

"Of course, not," the president barked. "She's a loose cannon, an ideologue believing her own crazy socialistic bullshit. She doesn't know anymore than Buddy Dukes."

"First things first, Mr. President," Goran politely interjected. "Do you know if *Reboot* actually hacked the *Uncle's Eyes* servers, or are they getting the data from somewhere else?"

"We're not sure," the president answered. "We're looking into it, but for all we know they could be just making some of it up. CIA is telling me some of it is so specific and accurate though, they had to have breached something."

"I'm here as well, Douglas," a whispery voice, male-ish, added with a second *ping*.

The screen before Yanic Goran cut into three parallel sections, and Goran shuddered at the last attendee of *1776*. Mr. Anton Clay Bilderberg was a frail man with glasses so large and thick they nearly looked like goggles, the hint of almost reptilian-like bone structure protruding his nose and jaw. He wore an ink-black toupee, and was so pale and flaky it was as if he lived on the moon, his eyes a faint jaundiced yellow. "Pleased to see everyone driving ratings up," Bilderberg wheeze-chuckled. Bilderberg's laugh sounded more like someone softly groaning from a hernia than anything joyful. "Excellent work, gentlemen. Extra plums in the Christmas stockings for all of you."

"Glad you're enjoying this, Mr. Bilderberg," the president said. "Some of us have concerns beyond money though. There is already a sea of angry Republicans and Democrats trying to confront each other in front of this very building. It's time *1776* made some hard choices. Quickly."

"And with all due respect, Douglas, your little fiefdom is but only one concern of mine." Bilderberg licked his chapped lips. "A global economy, as they say."

Goran knew that besides for being physically bizarre, Mr. Bilderberg was also the richest man in the world. Anton Bilderberg was so rich no one could even prove he existed. It was whispered within the world's most elite halls that his family had been beyond nations, beyond databases, since thirteen generations before this latest bizarre version was born. For centuries the Bilderbergs had supposedly been amassing incredible wealth and connections, and Anton was now simply continuing the family tradition of shepherding their family power into exponentially greater wealth and connections throughout America and the world. Among numerous other interests around the globe the Bilderberg empire currently controlled 38% of the US pharmaceutical markets, 41% of US oil and energy interests, 44% of American food manufacturing, 57% of the US private prison system, 61% of world weapons manufacturing, all of Monsanto, and arguably the most important of all, 79% of all US media outlets. Of course, his controlling power was divided through hundreds of shell corporations and individuals of different names around the globe, so that his web of control could never be traced directly back to him as an individual. When any of the strings of the web were pulled though, Bilderberg was supposedly the spider at the center. Mr. Bilderberg was the only man that Yanic Goran had ever felt a creepy foreboding about, like he knew much more about the game than Goran himself, and doom always simmered in Bilderberg's fishy eyes.

"So." Bilderberg licked his lips again. "How do you intend to protect my interests, good King?"

"Well, that's the trillion dollar question, isn't it?" Fuentes cast his eyes down in thought, Goran always noticing with amazement how even the egomaniacal Fuentes seemed to weirdly fall into a subservient line with Bilderberg. "Your *Pan-Continental* trade deal is still of primary importance, Mr. Bilderberg, and I assure you I will get it passed. But with regard to the election and the riots?" Then a bit of disdain crept back into the president's voice. "Yanic, what the hell is going on? How is this so out of control with only hours to go before the end? Rigging the election was *1776*'s job."

Goran brushed some sweat from his brow. "I've certainly been working overtime in my network, sir, paying off local affiliates, pressuring higher-ups, rigging the voting machines. Everything had been going toward a definite Stone win as agreed, with the House locked up on his side once it gets there, except... the elector getting shot, sir, and... and Daniels." The problem was that Yanic Goran didn't know what the hell was going on. "I didn't foresee her passionate speech's rapid implications or...or the Reboot breach. Today's technology is making things increasingly difficult to control."

Yanic Goran had overseen the ground operations of rigging every presidential election for decades, but now an elector had suddenly been shot hours before the conclusion and the whole train seemed in danger of derailing off the tracks. The "*1776* sensible bargain" had all begun decades ago when Goran had first started lobbying in DC. One night after a fundraiser Yanic Goran had surprisingly found himself in a small cigar room located in the basement of an exclusive DC hotel with both the Republican and Democratic candidates for president on either side of him. That election had, like this one, no incumbent running, and it just so happened that both political candidates had been, although publicly on staunchly opposing sides of the political spectrum, true friends since their Ivy League collegiate days. It was then, somewhat as an interesting philosophical point, Yanic Goran had proposed the idea of whether the three of them, if appropriately tight-lipped, could actually decide who won the election right there before the public even voted.

Goran had truly brought it up as only an interesting thought experiment, but as the single malt had continued to flow the three realized it was not only possible, but fairly straightforward. If they had enough money to control both sides of the media, and therefore the public's perception, what could stop them? The popular vote didn't even really count, it was the electors, which could be easily rigged. They just needed the media to help them make it all legit and answer any questions. That was where the Bilderberg family came in. The Bilderbergs had been a prominent donor to every candidate of each side of the political spectrum since the inception of the country, never concerned with who won as long as their business interests were protected regardless. The Bilderbergs would give a lot of money if *1776* could assure each administration's compliance with their worldwide business interests.

In that cigar room then, it had been decided with only a handshake and a smirk that each party would more or less take turns winning the elections from there on out, the losers financially compensated by the Bilderbergs through *1776*. Since that original negotiation decades ago, every presidential election since had been successfully brokered by Goran's *1776* fund. Those very few in the know, smaller than the number of men who had walked on the moon, referred to it with a sly wink only as *1776* or *a sensible bargain*.

"If I may ask, Mr. President," Yanic cautiously inquired, "why was the elector killed?"

"I didn't have him killed. I wish this whole damned election were over." President Fuentes barked. "The *Pan-Continental* trade deal is what's important, that's the only way Mr. Bilderberg keeps economics moving smoothly in the world. I'm the last one who would have the elector shot. The surest way to keep world peace is if everyone's too fat, overworked and entertained to fight or question anything."

"Are you certain about that?" Stone challenged the president with a twisted scowl, a strand of his wispy blonde hair seeming to rise off his head in heated anger. "This is supposed to be my election, Fuentes." The poisonous snap in Hampton Stone's tone indicated he was furious. "Agreements were made. No one is suddenly changing their mind, are they? Who shot the damned elector, if not you?"

"Hampton," the president's dark face became stern. "I will be addressed as Mr. President by you, and advise you to remember you're not in this chair yet." Yanic Goran's heart skipped a beat. If this small group fell apart with infighting though, Goran was getting most terrified of what could happen next. Amazingly, these five might be the only thing actually keeping the world together.

"Unforeseen contingencies have occurred, gentlemen, that is all." Goran tried to sound optimistic. "Most unfortunate contingencies, but nothing we can't solve long as we stick togeth—"

"Contingencies, you weasely shit?" the president snapped at him. "This isn't a fucking school play you're directing, Yanic. You are only allowed to continue the position you have because of your ability to foresee and prevent contingencies. The whole country is going ape-shit, and one way or another we need this election to end on time tomorrow, and in a way that looks acceptable to everyone."

Goran stared back. Something about being sworn in seemed to make the arrogant SOBs forget that it was Goran's Super-Pac of *1776* that had essentially assured their presidential victory. Goran fought his bitterness though, and strategically whined, "Please, gentlemen, if we do not have trust, what do we have?"

"Yes, yes," Bilderberg giggled, a frail reptilian-like hand holding on his jet-black toupee. "Honesty is imperative."

"Are you just going to laugh, you freak?" Stone growled. "You could be guiding a slightly calmer tone through the media, trying to calm tensions rather than always escalating things, you know."

"Tsk, tsk, tsk, pastor con man," Mr. Bilderberg replied. "You, of all people, know that inflammatory language through the news and media is the best way to keep control, to keep the sheep divided against one another and believing in your silly two-party system. *'You had better be for this 100%, or you are against it.'* *'You better either be with the good guys, or you're with the bad.'* Etcetera, etcetera." Bilderberg adjusted his wig with a wheeze. "If we don't keep them fighting each other with their little dualistic simpleton ideas, they might start to actually think about things and that could be… problematic, eh?"

"I don't give a shit about that weirdo's pocketbook, Fuentes." Stone's voice rose even further. "I want accountability. I want assurances that y'all haven't suddenly decided to switch to Marcus in the closing hours become of some damned liberal ideals or something." Stone's orange cheeks puffed for a moment, his eyes glaring wide. "Agreements were made. Do I have to go public?"

"I'm getting goddamn sick of people who can't be trusted to keep a secret." President Fuentes ripped off his glasses and growled at Stone. "Remember, Hampton, there are still scenarios where *The Activity* cuts your head off and sews it to your palms for your wife to find. Don't make me see you as a national security risk."

This is bad, Goran thought. *Very bad.*

Bilderberg clapped his hands in amusement. "And to think, I almost went polar bear hunting instead of attending this." His thin white eyebrows wiggled beneath the lopsided black toupee. "It's almost like you all buy into your own two-party propaganda. You all should start wearing blue and red shirts so I can keep score."

"Please," Goran pleaded, "let's not bicker, gentlemen, all is not lost. We simply need to regroup, to determine the next move from here, given the Louisiana Governor might be taking things into his own hands. If he appoints, the electoral vote will still tie, and the House can give the win to the governor as agreed."

"Unless Daniels now succeeds with turning some of those true-believer idiots against me," Stone spat. "At least the Governor of Louisiana has some balls, but this has got to end before Daniels' tape makes any more House Republicans drop me. I wouldn't be surprised if that rabid bitch was the one who had the elector shot. Are you sure you don't know anything about this, Marcus? Not having second thoughts about losing are you?"

"You're accusing me of murder, you fraudulent sack of shit?" Marcus Freeman incredulously snapped. "And how do we know YOU didn't have him killed, Hampton?"

"I'm considering moving federal troops into Louisiana." President Fuentes sighed. "Since there are so many open questions, the Supreme Court essentially going to be useless with a hung result, I'm considering writing an Executive Order to halt the electoral vote and let the *Joint Congressional Committee* decide what happens next. I have word they'll probably try to push the electoral vote back for several weeks. Everything could be back up for grabs."

"What?" Stone exclaimed. "Are you out of your mind? Let the Louisiana Governor and Republican legislature appoint and I win!" Stone's head shook, and for a moment his tiny mouth floundered with no words coming out. "Why in God's name would you send troops in and try to give power to some wildcard senator? That's not even constitutional. I can't win this late without Louisiana, without it going to the House. Screw the committee."

"I said considering it," Fuentes snapped back, pinching his nose and wrinkling his brow in pain. "This is all getting out of control." He rolled his eyes upward before glaring back into the camera. "Eleven more cities rioting since the governor's announcement, sixteen more dead Americans as of thirty minutes ago, and for all we know there might actually still be some outsider plot to influence the election's outcome that had the elector shot."

"A conspiracy," Stone stammered. "What are you talking about? You're now claiming a third party shot the elector? Who? Why?"

"We don't know." The president threw up his hands. "Beatrice Howe thinks she found some sort of conspiracy, but she might just be picking up on our own *1776* communication anomalies in the *RedRabbit* system. Or... the elector shooting might simply be justified police action." The president shook his head in genuine disgust. "I don't know though, and we don't have time to figure it out."

"Might I suggest," Goran smiled, "the joint speech between Governor Stone and the vice president, Senator Daniels and Buddy Dukes, still occur. If they all spoke together, asking the country to accept whatever decision happens tomorrow, it would possibly calm things down so that troops were not needed in Louisiana. The Congressional Committee's recommendation could therefore be ignored if necessary, then the tied vote would still get to the House where—"

"I will never," Stone exclaimed, spit flying out of his fleshy mouth and his small hands gesturing in the air, "never speak in public with that... that... treacherous, lying slut! Not after what she's done. That jezebel tricked me." Stone gritted his teeth. "This is crap. I've done my part, agreements were made!"

"Get a grip, Hampton," Freeman snapped. "You've got to realize this is bigger than either of our individual careers."

"Then don't be a little faggot and just concede," Stone purred back at Freeman. "If you're so concerned with the well-being of the country, why not make a concession speech this evening, Marcus? For the good of the country and all."

Freeman's reddening face flickered between nervousness and rage. "You know I can't do that. It's agreed to be mine next time. I can't damage that chance by being perceived as a quitter to the country."

"That's what I thought." Stone smiled.

"And so how do we know you didn't screw up again, Hampton?" Freeman added, "You already leaked information to a third party once. Was your laptop even destroyed?"

"Of course," Stone gasped, suddenly defensive. "Buddy confirmed with General Harper just yesterday, the Nicaraguan mission was a success. The laptop was destroyed before anyone else saw the contents. Nothing about *1776* got out."

"Congressman Dukes?" The president's tone and face now flooded with incomprehension. "You told that moron Buddy Dukes about *1776?*"

"No, no, of course not! You think I'm actually going to tell him that I had terms of an illegal agreement to broker the election between the four of us typed out on my laptop?" Stone shook his head in disappointment at himself. "I know it was boneheaded to make the notes, but I like seeing things written down." Stone clenched a fist in frustration. "I didn't expect that Lupe idiot to pick up the wrong laptop before he left the trade meeting. I'm just not good with electronics; wish we'd just go back to pen and paper."

"And what then did you tell your running mate, Hampton," the president prodded. "We agreed YOU would contact General Harper for the off-the-books mission so I could avoid having to answer questions about it through the DOD. Your North Carolina ties to Ft. Bragg were supposed to be able to get this done more quietly, not bring in additional people. What were Dukes' conversations with the general?"

Stone glanced down. "I'm not sure. I just wanted a layer of deniability as well, you know? Harper can be a bit of a nut like we all know, so I didn't want to talk to him directly in case something got botched with the mission, so I had Buddy make the calls, that's all." Stone shrugged. "I told him that you lying liberals had fabricated a bunch of negative documents about me on the laptop. Who cares? I didn't mention *1776* and he got Harper to destroy the laptop."

"Jesus." Freeman sighed. "And you have the gall to complain about Daniels?"

This is all getting out of control. Goran focused on keeping his slightly sweaty face looking relaxed, even as his hand crept up to his squeezing chest. *Everyone's turning on each other. It's all falling apart.*

The president stated, "The only reason I ever agreed to *1776* was because I could see some value in it providing security for a peaceful transition of power between parties, and—"

"Not because it was your turn to win," Bilderberg giggled.

"Don't press your luck, Anton," President Fuentes finally snapped at Bilderberg. "I could have you—"

"What?" Bilderberg asked, his own tone suddenly serious. "What exactly could you do, Mr. President? Destroy me? And your own economy with me? I'm not as easily intimidated as some fat preacher-man from North Carolina, Douglas." Bilderberg leaned toward the camera and sneered so that sharp, tiny, yellowing teeth showed, his voice wicked. "I'm too big to goddamn fail, Mr. President."

"I just don't want more violence," President Fuentes cowered. "That's all. If I move troops into Louisiana it should calm rioting, and pushing everything to the *Joint Congressional Committee* will more easily appear that there is an honest and transparent end, the world will accept it as a nonpartisan. Things will calm down."

"This is crap," Stone mumbled. "I can't trust any of you. You're just trying to steer things to Freeman and Daniels. You all are trying to go back on your word, just trying to give it to Marcus."

"There, there, Pastor Stone," Bilderberg said in a wheezy chuckle, "just trust in your demonic lizard overloads and we will look out for you." Bilderberg flickered his thin tongue again at the camera. "Once I reveal my true nature, I will put you in a very comfortable zoo, with all those humans I deem entertaining."

"Good Lord," President Fuentes shook his head in exasperation, "let's end this for now. I'm going to put more thought into what to do, and Yanic, please go to the Supreme Court justices one by one, explore any options for buying one of them to break a tie, if they have to get involved. Let's talk again in two hours."

As Fuentes clicked the communication dead, Yanic found himself almost hoping Bilderberg were actually an alien. It might make things a little more straightforward.

* * *

Leaping out of his limo, hand clutching chest, Yanic Goran took a deep inhale of the cold DC air. He collapsed back against the car door, his lungs flooding with fresh air and the tightness is his chest evaporating. He looked up at the bright sun. As the rays warmed his old face, he remembered for the first time in years that there was simple beauty and joy in just being alive. *However,* his mind immediately argued, *I'm also entangled in a net fifty-some years in the making.* A snare that would not come undone unless he went back to Supreme Court justices he barely had any working relationships with and somehow convinced one of them, within hours, to become part of a plot to give the election to Governor Stone. *Or maybe no matter what happened, the country will break apart?* The rich and the government had purposely made things more and more legally complex through the decades, so they could be the only ones who had the resources and ability to navigate the system and thereby keep their power. But maybe they had gone too far and could no longer understand it themselves? *Pride does goeth before the fall.*

Goran pushed himself off of the car with a feeble arm and told himself that this was his last battle, his last effort to make an honest living in this corrupt world. If he could just pull it off one last time, he would enjoy the cool sunshine in peace for the rest of his days. The only problem was he had seen nothing but honor and incorruptibility in the eyes of most of the Supreme Court justices at the last party he threw, and brewing catastrophe with the *1776* group. The American election process might unravel for the first time in nearly 250 years, almost like some larger force were mysteriously at work, leading them all toward a precipice.

Goran dropped back into the limo and picked up the phone to the driver. Instead of telling him to head back to the Supreme Court, Goran told him to drive him to the private military contractor's compound, posthaste.

Screw those lunatics, Yanic Goran thought. *They can fend for themselves.*

On the outskirts of Detroit a Juggalo festival much smaller than the main "Gathering of the Juggalos" each year in Minnesota, was in progress. It was compromised mainly of the more hardcore, gang-minded clown people. The entire wooded campground was thickly entwined in scents of rustic weed and noxious excrement. Snow clumped in the shadowed bases of sparse trees as several thousand chaotic clowns had been partying for three days straight beneath the broken-toothed skyline of a perpetually half-abandoned and still limping Detroit. People in mud-streaked clown face paint in various stages of undress tumbled, danced and slept beneath much garbage and a cool late morning sun as never-ending metallic beats from one of many stages thumped up into the sky. The music never stopped and the booze never dried up while lots of people with shaved heads, tattoos and piercings got "down with the clown." People had cartoons of little hatchet-wielding men etched on their skin. There was a barn with weary strippers, goats, moonshine and a vomit drinking contest. A dwarf happily hung from hooks piercing the skin on his back, and occasionally a big wrecking ball smashed pretty much anything people brought to be smashed. People were constantly getting sprayed with Faygo soda, and a booth was proudly offering $5 "vaginal fumigation."

Without anyone so much as noticing, or caring, *@mohammedfatah* poured about a quarter of his *Flakka 3.0* liquid into a giant kiddie pool filled with rum punch set up in the middle of the campground. He then sputtered his scooter onward to the unguarded water reservoir that serviced the entire city of Detroit.

W*hap, whap, whap.* The chopper's blades made it too loud for easy talking. Amos noticed a pink, low sun outside the chopper, seeming to rest atop the DC skyline. He pressed his thumb to the cut above his right cheekbone, the wound so fresh that even the wind whipping in from the chopper's door stung. The gash was from the ten pound free weight Stork had swung at him, and the only reason why it hadn't broke Amos' cheekbone was because Amos had smashed backward into another pile of heavy iron. The buzzing in his head came from both ears now, and he realized he might have a concussion, his thoughts slow and foggy, light halos from the incoming dusk around the heads of the other eleven warriors in the hull with him. They hadn't even had time to go by a medic to get their myriad of cuts and bruises dressed before *wheels up.*

Amos gripped the 10-gauge tactical shotgun he'd brought and glared across at Stork, wondering if he could explain it if his field knife happened to fly out during turbulence to stick into his lieutenant's long neck. Stork glared back, and Amos was pretty sure Stork was thinking the same thing about him. Amos noticed Jacari was watching them both, hunched forward on the bench and trying to chew his gum casually. It looked like his whole body was tensed to spring onto either of them if the fight erupted again.

At most it would be only twenty-four hours of glorified security guard detail at the White House until the election was over and then Amos and Stork could get back to settling their personal score. From what little Amos could see out his angle of the door, the White House wasn't on the horizon yet. The massive crowd of red shirts walking down Pennsylvania Avenue below definitely were though. And for a moment, the sheer vastness of the people down in the street cut through Amos' burning rage, brought him back to the mission.

Annie's craziness is still screwing shit up, just now on a colossal scale.

They were a mile still from the White House and it looked like a red, white and blue Mardi Gras below. A sea of protest signs and banners moved slowly up Pennsylvania Avenue toward the White House. Instead of beads and breasts though, flags and Uncle Sam hats. Amos wished he'd been able to talk to Shay more, get a better grip on what all the political shit meant. Some protestors appeared to be chanting things, others looked bored and sweaty, and some were just jumping around screaming like they thought they were at a concert. From their lack of forward momentum though, Amos surmised that the crowd must already be backed up from the White House to this point.

Forget protecting all those self-interested politicians, who's going to protect these poor people from themselves? If something unfortunate happened like a fire, or a gun going off, the whole crowd could potentially stampede and cause worse injuries than the Dayton Riot. *Too many people,* Amos had the odd revelation, *and things always break down. Betrayal, distrust, chaos. Maybe we were never meant to be around so many other people.*

Amos had his full team of eleven men with him, minus Sergeant Houzma, whom he'd left behind to continue the BRAHMASTRA tests. Amos knew it was definite overkill, the Secret Service was fully capable of handling their own business and they had a plethora of skilled counterterrorism experts on their squads for any worse case scenario, but Harper demanded a full crew for some reason. The crowd of Republicans below, although massive, looked largely middle-aged or college students, more likely to get bored and tired and overrun a Starbucks than intentionally engage in any violence in front of the White House. The Secret Service was never really one for relishing "help" from outside agencies, and so would probably relegate Amos and his team to taking the president's dog for a walk on the south lawn or something. At best, Amos' team would maybe just hang near the fence on the outer perimeter of the White House lawn as a presence to deter any espressoed-up college kid from trying to jump it or throw a rock. Honestly, the people below mostly looked like a version of an angry PTA on steroids, and Amos was again hit by how this was beneath them. Millions of dollars spent on training them for the most covert warfare in the world, and now they would spend the next day having angry Republican grandma's shouting at them? *Maybe everything is just going to shit*, Amos bitterly thought.

"You're right, Major, Thump was ordered taken out." Stork was suddenly sitting close to Amos. "I was recruited to the show, The Activity," Stork said. Amos could barely hear him over the whacking of the chopper noise. "I'm in the CIA,

Amos." Hot repulsion surged up again inside Amos at Stork's sudden proximity, but confusion at his admission too, even if Shay had thought it was possible. "That's why Thump had to go. Orders."

"Bullshit," Amos growled. "Thump wasn't a traitor."

"The CIA recruited me after Berlin." Stork's face was sincere. "Ever since I've been working with them to root out potential national security threats from within the system."

"Bull. Shit." Amos' cloudy brain spun trying to determine if this could even possibly be the truth now that Stork was admitting it. Neurons popped and fired as Amos tried to connect the dots, tried to deduce if it was even marginally possible that Stork was part of the most selective and secretive Special Ops division in the world. As Green Berets, they were trained on how to project sincerity when having to lie under duress, so how the hell could even know if Stork was lying or not? And whether or not he was, did it make a single shit of a difference to Thump having died? "Fuck you."

Stork's eyes were unblinking, unflinching. "For the past two years, my mission has been locating and eliminating double agents."

"Thump wasn't a double agent," Amos growled. Even as he internally debated the veracity, he wanted to burn holes into Stork's beady, bloodshot eyes, chew them with his teeth. "You're just trying to cover something up, something bad and wrong, and I'm going to find out what the fuck dirty shit you were into."

"Harper can verify it, Amos," Stork stated. "He runs The Activity for the CIA. Think about it. The graybeards have been worried for a long time about the potential for Muslim radicals, or even Chinese or Iranian sympathizers, double agents of all kinds working their way up the military, Major. Even into Spec Ops. I'm one of the safeguards against that."

"You're trying to tell me that Thump was an Islamic radical?" Amos whispered incredulously. "Working for ISIS or some shit? Fuck you." One of Amos' hands unconsciously slipped to his knife handle, images of plunging the blade into Stork's skinny, freckled, lying neck and pushing him out the chopper door still flashing in his brain. "I say, fuck you."

"No, we've found evidence of a DEMOCRATIC faction trying to steal the election, Amos, not Muslims, not Iranians or Chinese this time, but a group of liberal radicals from within the government, all the way up to the current administration, and Thump was part of it. The laptop had fabricated information on it, doctored notes that the liberals were going to use to doom Stone's win so they could continue gutting the military."

"What..." Amos' words floundered on his tongue, his brain trying to grapple with any remote possibility that what Stork was saying was true. "But Thump loved his country."

"There's not one country anymore, Amos. He loved THEIR country, not ours. The general got NSA information regarding an even broader Democratic plot to steal the election, one of their operatives trying to incite radicals against Republicans, maybe even had the Republican elector shot."

"No way." Amos' hate was giving way to incredulous confusion. Of all things to hear, this was not what Amos expected. The sheer possibility, the weirdness of everything he was being told, seemed almost too farfetched to completely dismiss. "A Democratic plot..." Amos' head throbbed with pain, an actual half-smile breaking onto his lips. "Bullshit. You're just taking what I said earlier and using it, spinning it trying to get yourself room to maneuver." Stork almost had him for a minute.

He leaned back, turning his gaze from Stork in exhaustion, and rubbed a couple of gentle fingers to the side of his head, actually chuckling at the absurdity of Stork's tall tale. "Just go back to your station, Lieutenant. Keep your mouth shut and concentrate on your job. We'll deal with our personal issues after the mission."

Stork shook his head. "You better get your mind right, Major, realize which side you're fighting for." He moved back down the bench.

Amos was amazed at all the endless lies and confusing bullshit of this world. He forced his gaze out toward the horizon and now saw the White House. Even through the heat of his anger, he felt a chill. That iconic building up ahead was what he'd dedicated his life to protect, and the White House's image could always cast patriotic flutters through his stomach. It spun Amos right back to the only time he had been here before, when his father had taken him as a boy.

Ray Daniels had taught young Amos about all the ideals the White House symbolized. He told him about the noble hearts, souls, and bodies sacrificed to forge this nation of freedom, this nation "of the people and for the people," this greatest country the world had ever known. It had been the trip here with his father, seeing Ray Daniels stand tall in uniform and salute the American flag flying proudly over that building with a tear in his eye, that had made Amos realize who he wanted to be. It was then, holding his heroic father's hand and looking at that building that transcended time and place, and mattered more to the perfection and glory of the world than any single individual man could, that Amos knew he wanted to continue his dad's legacy of fighting for it. Looking on the White House that day, Amos had felt his first rush of adult pride, and known he would spend his life for God and country.

Eventually, everyone is going to die, his father had explained, *so all that matters, Amos, are the ideals you live with while you are here.* Amos brushed at the edge of his eye. *Beliefs matter.*

He forced his mind back to the task, checking to make sure his personal cell phone was powered down. On a higher level Op he wouldn't have brought it, but on this glorified security detail, and the quickness with which it had all transpired, he still had it in his pocket. As he pulled the phone out though he saw a text from his wife: *are you going to like the photo today?*

Amos erased it with a bewildered shake of his head. But there was also a blinking voicemail from Shay, and his heart leapt a bit in expectation. Maybe, just maybe, Shay was the future, the way his whole life got filled with light again. The way he finally found that good, whole family that he and his father had always wanted, something simple and beautiful to believe in and fight for. Even with his finger in one ear, he could barely make out Shay's anxious voice. *"Amos, we need to talk. I know this sounds nuts, but there might be a Democratic contingency trying to steal the election. There's some connection between 1776, the Nicaraguan, the elector shooting and the Fuentes administration. Crazy, but we need to talk, in person. Call me back. And delete this message. And call me back."*

As Amos pressed the button to power down his phone his stomach seemed to drop all the way through the floor of the chopper into the angry crowd below. *Stork's telling the truth?*

He looked back at Stork. Stork smiled. *A Democratic plot?*

No. No, no, no. Can't be real. Amos' breath started to shallow, his heartbeat started to quicken. Little did Amos know, in a matter of seconds the shock he was now feeling would nostalgically be remembered as *the simple days.*

"Major Daniels." One of the pilots turned back to him with wide eyes. "General Harper on the com, sir."

* * *

"It's getting to be a war zone down there, Jack," a reporter said, now in a helicopter circling over New Orleans. Below him multiple fires could be seen coming from buildings, teargas plumes wafting into the air, and hundreds of people running through the streets, sometimes fighting, sometimes throwing bricks through windows, some shooting guns. "It started as a protest against the police over the Gatreaux shooting, it has quickly morphed into a Democrat versus Republican stand-off over whether or not the Republican legislature should be allowed to appoint his replacement. And now, well..." The reporter pointed the camera at a large downtown warehouse, flames leaping from its black-rimmed windows, part of its roof collapsing inward. "Now it's just turning into anarchy. Lots of people using the chaos to loot and steal. We've heard a rumor that *Reboot.org* has instigators here, potentially inciting the crowds, but of course, with all the doxed personal information flooding the airwaves, it's hard to know exactly what's true. Hopefully the violence here doesn't even spread to other cities as night falls."

* * *

Moments later, Amos' size-twelve boot, stained in mud and blood, was stomping down from the chopper onto the snow-dusted lawn of the White House, his mind spinning faster than the helicopter's blades overhead. Two Secret Service agents in black suits walked toward them as Major Daniels still tried to process what General Harper had just ordered him to do. Amos gripped his 10-gauge tactical shotgun in both hands and tried to breathe easy.

"Take the White House," General Harper had barked to him over the headphones moments earlier.

"What?" Amos had stammered.

"Take control of the goddamn White House, son, and don't you dare say WHAT again," Harper said. "The White House is in the hands of opposing force, secure it by any means necessary."

"But…" a stunned Amos had said so softly he could barely hear himself over the rumble of the helicopter, "but sir, it's the White House… of the United States of America, sir."

Amos swore he could feel the heat of Harper's glare radiating through the headphones. "Substantial, material evidence has come to light, boy. The current administration is acting in an illegal capacity to fraudulently steal this election and had the elector in Louisiana shot. They have become terrorists, son. Enemies of the state."

"Isn't that an issue for law enforcement, sir, not—"

"We are not prosecuting them, son, we are stopping them from stealing the election. Law enforcement can do whatever the fuck they want after, but I do not intend to let America's election be stolen while I can stop it. Use the least amount of force necessary to achieve the objective, but lock America's house down, boy. Detain the president and vice president until this can be resolved. That's an order. Do you understand me?"

"Sir." *Insane. Fucking insane.* Amos' thoughts were so

confused he couldn't even figure out what he really wanted to say. "But sir, it's President Fuentes and—"

"Amos," Harper growled, the general's rage barely tethered. "Your oath, son?"

"Yes." Amos sighed, remembered the conversation they had in Harper's office. "I swore to protect the Constitution, sir."

The blades thumped as the chopper had lowered toward the White House lawn.

"From whom?"

"All enemies, sir."

Whap, whap, whap.

"From all enemies foreign, AND DOMESTIC, goddammit!" The general's voice surged so deep and loud Amos had to pull the crackling headphone away from his ear. "Now, I am giving you a direct order to protect the Constitution of the United States from domestic terrorists, Major. You will either execute that order or you will be brought up on charges of treason, and make me shift command to Lieutenant Stoughton. Do I make myself goddamn crystal fucking clear, Major Daniels?"

"Yes, sir." Amos' body reflexively straightened, his voice finding more strength in agreeing to do his duty, no matter if it felt 100% sane or not. "Absolutely clear, sir." He was a soldier, and it was his oath.

"Excellent," Harper hissed. "Get back to me once you've got a com established, Major."

And now, with a possible concussion, Amos led his team out of the chopper, his mind churning on how to take over the most secure building in the world. Eleven of America's best warriors in camo and dark body armor, and weapons in arms, walked behind Amos toward the two dark-suited Secret

Service personnel. Behind the approaching Secret Service, the rear of the White House stretched before them. More Secret Service snipers were on the roof, Marines with German Shepherds patrolling the grounds. For a moment, even though he walked with shoulders back and eyes firmly ahead, Amos felt like he was going to throw up. Sickly hot sweat beaded beneath his collar. It was too much, all too much, and he felt like the world was shifting beneath his feet, like there was no stable ground to stand on or correct thoughts to think, like everything was becoming untethered, and as if the Earth itself might be careening out of its orbit in an aimless wobble toward oblivion.

"Good afternoon, Major." One of the Secret Service agents held out a large, pale hand. "Thanks for coming." He appeared albino. "Although if you don't mind me asking, who was it within the administration that requested your assistance?" Sunglasses covered his eyes and his hair was short and white. The agent's face was alabaster pale skin, very flat, with a bizarre purple-brown squiggling birthmark down one cheek. He gave off a single-minded intensity, like an attack dog, and the agent's tone didn't indicate the slightest intimidation from Amos or his men's presence. "We were radioed by MacDill a few minutes ago that you were coming, but honestly I'm a bit confused as to why."

"Don't know." Amos shrugged as the boot steps from his team crunched up behind him with the squeak and rustle of body armor as he tried to formulate a game plan. "Just told to report to you guys." From so many years Amos' brain automatically defaulted into clandestine operations mode, both trying to appear straightforward and honest, while actually giving away no information and probing for weaknesses in ·

the opposing force. "We were just told to assist with security."
Amos smiled.

Insane. Amos thought. *This is all insane.*

The albino agent glanced at the other, both their expressions giving away a bit of bemused concern, but nothing more specific. "It's been fairly hectic in the West Wing the past few days, Major, as I'm sure you can imagine. We'll look into who initiated the request on our end, and in the meantime let's give you a quick look around, then probably post you and your men at the front gate." The albino agent swung his arm wide toward the White House behind him in a welcoming gesture even though there was no trace of friendly on his birthmarked face, his jaw set firm. "Seems like you might make a good visual deterrent for any rowdy protestors in the street. And it will also keep you out of our way, so you don't fuck anything up."

* * *

Lawton Smith was ecstatic as his militia caravan raced down I-80 toward Denver.

Lawton stood tall in one jeep, cold wind raking over his silver-streaked hair. "It's time, children," he called toward the glorious star-studded sky. "Time for truth to raze the rotten from the earth, to separate the wheat from the chaff!"

His voice was so loud and passionate it could be heard by Buck and Slicker over the howling wind and the rumble of the cars. Buck drove the first jeep in the twenty-five-car caravan, Slicker sitting to his side, and they looked at each other with grins at the excitement of it all.

Lawton let his head drift back so he only saw the sparkling stars above and shouted, "Our destiny, to purge the reptilian

Illuminati from our lands!" Then let a long wolf-call out into the blustery air.

* * *

Online News Update: *Due to increasing security concerns within Washington, DC, Senator Ahmad Kaleel, acting Chairman of the Joint Congressional Election Oversight Committee, is relocating the committee meeting to Denver, Colorado. Almost two dozen of the most senior leaders from the House and Senate are boarding planes to reconvene in downtown Denver in order to discuss recommendations for a peaceful, transparent, bipartisan resolution to the election. Attorney General Blake and FBI Director Chuu will be attending the closed-door meeting as well to offer current updates to the elector's shooting. Senator Kaleel has stated that his committee members might not get much rest, but they will be prepared to offer solutions to the country late this evening, or tomorrow morning at the latest.*

* * *

It was December in Ohio, twenty-two degrees outside, but Hampton Stone was hot, still pissed from the *1776* meeting.

Hampton purposely wasn't watching the news, trying to wait calmly until the president called to reassure him the election was settled. The darn white suit he had spent ninety minutes with some effeminate man poking and prodding him to supposedly get it to fit right now felt like it was strangling every part of his body. Maybe it was his thyroid, or maybe he was just sick of this whole damned election, but even with frost icing the corners of the limo's windows and the hot air already turned off, if Hampton Stone couldn't find a restaurant that wasn't blasting heat soon, and maybe get an ice cold sweet tea to go with a regular old American cheeseburger, he was going to flip out. He leaned past Buddy and pounded on the glass partition between him and the driver.

"Cheeseburgers," Hampton Stone shouted. "Find 'em." He thumped the glass another time.

"General Harper called again, Hampton," Buddy said with that annoying quiver to his voice. "I was busy talking to my southeast steak distributor, but do you want me to call him back and see what he wants?"

"Are you serious?" Hampton scowled. Further implicate themselves in a potential plot as Beatrice Howe scoured communication streams for clues? "I honestly keep thinking you're going to start waving your hands around some morning and say 'Ah-ha, I got ya Hampton!'" Stone shook his head. "Bad enough you got Fuentes freaked out with that damn march on Washington. I already explained we can't talk to anybody until I hear from the White House. It's called hunkering down, Buddy. Being smart."

Buddy looked around the back of the limo at nothing, nervously smoothing down his shiny cheap plaid pants. "He said it was important."

"Jesus." Hampton glowered at him. "My laptop was destroyed, right? That was already confirmed?"

Buddy nodded.

"And you haven't told anybody else about it, right?"

Buddy Dukes made a silent motion like he was using a key to lock his lips tight and then throwing the imaginary key away over his shoulder.

Stone breathed out and seemed to relax some. "We're staying silent until Fuentes calls. It's just a few hours."

Buddy silently wiggled his black eyebrows at Hampton and smiled.

"Fuck." Hampton sighed with a weary shake of his head, and a silent admission to himself he actually was a bigot. "You are a goddamn retard." Hampton lunged forward, his massive weight squeezing the thin Buddy Dukes downward into the crack between the door and the seat, his fist excitedly banging on the glass partition again. "There," Hampton barked. "Milton's Diner, up on the corner. We're stopping there!"

Rosa was one of the waitresses on duty.

* * *

As Amos approached the White House beside the two Secret Service agents his men followed behind. Amos silently lifted his hand behind his back to his men, his thumb and pinky held out from a fist. He was able to cast a quick glance back and tell by the teams' unified look of utter bewilderment that the message had been received. The silent hand signal was their covert sign for "prepare to assault," although Amos hadn't even really determined what he was going to do.

His men followed behind like normal, their eyes widening in confusion even as their hands casually slinked to their weapons. Jacari's face had a look like *what the fuck*, but Amos knew his men would follow him no matter what. Second-guessing was deadly in their line of work. The only person who didn't seem to have the look of confusion in their eyes was Stork, who nodded confidently back at Amos. Where Stork's allegiance truly lie, that was another question.

Completely insane. Amos' gauzy brain whirled trying to figure out if it was treason to follow orders, or to not. *There's got to be another way.* General Harper was ordering Amos to lead an assault on the White House, which was treason, unless... what Harper, Stork and Shay were saying about the Democratic administration trying to steal the election was true. And even if it was true, some might still consider it treason. But it would certainly be the morally right thing to do if the Democrats were guilty and Amos could stop some corruption of democracy, right? If what Harper was saying was misguided or inaccurate though, Amos would certainly be making the worst mistake of his life. Same as if he didn't follow orders and it turned out an American election was completely hijacked like some third world country and he got a court-martial in the process. *I don't know who to believe, but second-guessing orders gets people killed, killed Thump. Follow orders, Daniels. Have faith.*

"Do not speak to the administration unless spoken to first," the albino agent with the snake birthmark dictated. The agent had a bit of arrogance to him, or was it just cold calculation? "I will be your only point of contact, Major. You can address me as Agent Simms."

There were more German Shepherds than Amos had expected. At least six he could see on the perimeter of the grounds, and at least a dozen Secret Service officers on the roof at various other locations, and those were just the ones he could see. There were probably more counterterrorism specialists bunkered up somewhere on the grounds. Amos considered he would have to count on immediate opposing force of probably about three to one to realistically take control of the West Wing, and that didn't account for the uniformed Marine guards who stood at attention to either side of the open doors they entered.

We're the best, Amos told himself. *We can do this, we're the best.* But then again, *this is insane.*

"That hall leads to the East Wing." The albino agent pointed in one direction down a skinny, blue-carpeted hall. "The West Wing is where most of the protected assets are going to be located today."

Amos' team had to proceed single file down the hall behind the major as he continued following the albino agent, their weapons and body armor sticking out far enough from their sides to not allow anyone else to comfortably walk next to them, all their squeaks and rustling, coughing and grumbling, a distinct breeze of potential violence to this calm, refined structure. Amos held his shotgun tight, it heavy and comforting, its muzzle able to bring down a charging bull.

"Again," the albino agent warned, "silence while passing the Oval Office unless directly spoken to. Above all, keep in mind that anything you happen to overhear within these walls is considered the highest level of national security."

They marched down the final hall before the Oval Office and Amos recognized the vice president's voice speaking up ahead. "But sir, you've got to send Marines into Louisiana, Mr. President, you must." They had just rounded the last corner before the Oval Office, passing an office called the Presidential Annex, where Vice President Freeman stood with its door ajar. The vice president was looking back into the office where the president sat in front of a computer, and was saying, "I think you've got to take control of at least New Orleans and Baton Rouge tonight."

The vice president flashed twitchy surprise at the group of Green Berets moving toward him down the hall, but upon seeing the albino Secret Service agent in front, seemed to lose a bit of his anxiousness. Marcus Freeman was more beady, more suspicious looking away from television cameras Amos noticed. Or maybe, Amos considered, that was just because he was trying to steal an election?

"Never thought I would be considering taking over an American city with American troops," President Fuentes was saying to someone over the monitor with a tired shake of his head. "Maybe it's the only way though." And like a lightning bolt through his mind, Amos knew what his choice would have to be.

"But if you use a pretext of civil unrest and ensuring public safety, sir," Freeman said to him, "even most Republicans will buy it."

Hesitation got people killed, and Amos' free hand lunged to his weapon, like a good soldier.

Amos Pursues the Objective

(San Francisco, CA: Sunday, 2:17 p.m. PST / 5:17 p.m. EST)

*S*hould I call Stone? Am I actually on the wrong side? Henry momentarily wondered, wracked with guilt over releasing the tape on the Republican presidential candidate, and questioning more than ever what the other sounds, the sighs and grunts were, he had heard on it. *But I've got to give her a chance to keep her word. She promised she would quit before things went too far. And what am I thinking, Stone's no better.*

Watching Annie, everything within Henry was conflicted. Sitting off to the side of her dark oak desk, he pretended to review news stories and emails, the ever-changing poll numbers and social media trends as night approached on the East Coast. Chaos was increasing around the country.

There was some possible mass leak of almost everyone and every company's protected information which only made knowing which news stories and social media statements to believe harder to know. Many were claiming the doxed information from *Reboot.org* was largely fabricated, but if that was the case, were the news stories about riots in various locations false too? Looking at Annie out of the corner of his eye, Henry knew he at least had to determine the truth of her. Was she behind the elector's death? In a million years, he'd never expected Annie to stoop to forcing him to leak the doctored audio of Stone, of her choices and strong-armed, deceitful tactics with the president, of her idea of moving troops into New Orleans. *What I decide to do, my choice in regards to her,* Henry realized with a sinking stomach, *could determine the fate of the country.*

She and Howe were sitting in side-by-side chairs in front of Annie's computer monitor, Henry was banished to the side by Annie as the two spoke again with the president and vice president. The screen, though, had suddenly cut to black.

It sounded like Annie and the vice president had almost convinced President Fuentes to order the United States Army into Louisiana, a potentially incendiary move in these already tense closing hours to the election, when luckily, like from an unseen guiding force, Annie's connection to the White House had gone dead before Henry heard the president give in. Maybe Henry would have time to convince her of another course, of maybe putting her trust in the Congressional Committees' recommendation.

I've got to do something to help her keep her promise about not causing any harm.

"What the?" Annie now tapped her torn red nails to the edge of the blank monitor with a glance at Beatrice Howe. "It just died." *Tap. Tap. Shake.* "Technology, huh?"

"We should check that there's nothing wrong at the West Wing, madam." Howe's expression was tight and nervous, as it had been ever since she arrived. To Henry, Howe seemed honestly worried, presumably trying her best to navigate these murky waters they were sinking into, while Annie just seemed to be getting more determined, erratic and bold in her effort to win.

"Lights are still on in here." Annie glanced up at the overhead chandelier. "Computer still on. It would have to be the monitor."

Did you have Gatreaux shot? Henry wondered again. *Is this just all going according to your plan?*

"Or on the White House's end." Howe pulled her phone out of her leather purse and began clicking.

But Annie placed two fingers on Howe's brown hand in a gentle request for her to stop dialing. "If you don't mind, Beatrice, can we take two seconds before we call back in? I'm sure everything is fine, but I need to talk to you for a second. Make sure we're making the right decisions."

Henry's ears and eyes perked up. He waited for Annie to ask him to leave the room, but she did not. Henry just needed something, some definitive statement or action from Annie where he could decide if she had been behind the elector's killing. Decide if he should be working for her, or against her.

Not every choice could be justified by a supposedly good end. Truth. That was why Henrietta had changed herself to Henry. That was why a girl had gone through all the cuttings and the mutilations, that hacking off of flesh in some areas, and the amalgamating of it into shape and symbol in others, in order to become what could hopefully be accepted by all their judging eyes as a boy. Truth. The ingesting, the injecting, the ceaseless monitoring and manipulating despite the ridicule and shame, despite being thought of as a freak, a Frankenstein creation; it was all for truth. Henry had endured the hell of his life just to get one step closer to the true TRUTH of his own being, the sense of knowing who you were beyond circumstance, beyond the happenstance influences of time and place, to know beyond all shadow of a doubt and throughout every cell of your existence, THIS IS I. For without it, you would never be able to truly love anything in this world, and all you ever did was a lie. Henry was ready to give his life for truth, but was she?

What are you? he wondered, watching Annie.

"I need more information, Beatrice. What exactly do you know?" Annie smiled. "Earlier, I might have pushed the envelope a little with my accusations that the Republicans were behind the shooting. I'm taking some pretty large risks here, trying to do what's right with the president, for the country, and I've got to know whatever you've got through *Uncle's Eyes.* Even if it's not concrete."

Are you trying to figure out if Howe is on to you?

Howe sighed, seemed to not want to say. "That's just it, madam, I think you're assessment was correct. Your suggestion for troop movement into Louisiana maybe not even extreme enough."

"You really think there could be a Republican plot?" Annie asked. "If Gatreaux was actually purposely killed, who specifically? Some disgruntled Republican fanatic? What do you really fear, Beatrice? Talk to me."

Howe kept looking into Annie's eyes, and finally breathed in deep, as if she had to trust someone, unburden herself with her suspicions, no matter how crazy. "I've long worried about the Republicans leading a military coup, madam, especially with yours and the vice president's hard stance on closing bases, shrinking military funding. There's a tremendous amount of money, and extremely powerful people, entrenched in the military-industrial complex. Staunch conservatives."

"Coup?" Annie scoffed, and to Henry she seemed honestly

amused. "Our own actual United States military turning on us? For money? Miss Howe, please, this isn't Lebanon."

"With technology is would be easy enough to doctor information to make us look like the villains." Howe's face became dejected, embarrassed. "I believe..." Howe paused, as if now she couldn't be sure of her own conclusions. "Governor Stone's running mate, Congressman Dukes, has placed several recent phone calls to General Harper at MacDill Air Force Base. Harper's within the *RedRabbit* system, so I couldn't access what they were actually saying, but because Dukes isn't yet I could at least see the calls were made to him. Many calls within the past few days surrounding the elector's death. Coupled with the *RedRabbit* calls around Lawrence Gatreaux's location, well..."

"Harper? And what do you think this Republican general wants? To become president or something?"

"Or Stone, maybe? He could be working on his behalf." Howe shrugged. "I'm not sure who's at the center of the web. Maybe they just want anyone but Democrats, but it could be a growing contingency, madam, a vast number of traitors even."

"A military coup." Annie repeated, her face shocked. Or at least, Henry considered, she was doing a damn good job of faking concern if she was actually the one pulling the strings of a conspiracy. "The entire military turning against the administration..." She put long fingers to her pale throat. "That would certainly mean my suggestions to the president weren't extreme enough."

"I don't know, madam." Howe threw up her hands. "I'm not sure, but if some conspiracy were actually happening along party lines, who knows where it would stop. It could be a contingency of Republicans across numerous groups and institutions—military, government, CIA? Maybe the NSA data I've been using isn't even accurate. Once I started thinking about it, if the threat is from within the government, there's no way to be sure how deep or wide it goes or whose information to trust." Howe shook her head. "If accurate, there would be no way of knowing who's on whose side, so the more quickly President Fuentes can establish hard control of the situation and the country, at least until the election is settled tomorrow, the harder it would be for any traitors to make a move. Extreme, yes, but maybe the most reasonable action based on the potentialities."

"Or," Henry blurted, "what if it's nothing? What if Lawrence Gatreaux's shooting is actually just another black man shot by bigoted cops?" It just all seemed like it was getting so crazy, like no one was thinking clearly, and with the *Reboot. org* doxing it was even harder to tell what was real. "What if it's our own fear and paranoia of the other side that will cause us to exacerbate this situation beyond all control?" Annie's cold gaze moved to him, but he continued. "What if the right move, Annie, is you and the veep to publicly giving support to the *Congressional Committee's* recommendation. Whatever they end up being. Not worrying about your own goals, but actually acting for the greater good."

"Senator Kaleel is a devout Muslim," Annie growled. "When the chips get down you want a feminist and a gay man to cede our candidacy to Sharia law? What do you think a Republican controlled Senate that has successfully blocked Fuentes' Supreme Court nominee will recommend? What if they are the coup?"

"That's absurd," Henry stated. "Senator Kaleel is known for his integrity. There are nearly two dozen other leaders from both Houses and parties on the committee as well. You're just lashing out."

"Would you be lecturing a man about potential missteps, Henry?" Annie snapped. "Can I even trust you at this point?"

Only two options, he thought, glaring back into her icy eyes. *The pills fried her goddamn brain, or she's the conspiracy.*

"For the record," Annie turned back to Howe with her tone losing its bite, "I don't believe we have enough evidence to jump to conclusions about anything as extreme as a Republican-led military coup, Miss Howe. Let's not let worst case scenarios cloud our judgment. However, as the potential risk is extreme, despite Henry's seeming newfound desire to hand the election to Stone, I believe we should probably bring up your concerns more blatantly for the president to explore." Annie nodded at Howe's phone in instruction for her to continue her call to the West Wing. "My guess is the connection is probably working again."

As Howe lifted her phone back to her ear, steps suddenly pounded up the stairs outside the office, and all three spun toward the door.

The office door crashed open to reveal a panting Kim-Su. "You hear?" Kim-Su's eyes were wild. "Internet they say. You hear?"

Howe's phone could be heard ringing and ringing, but no answer.

"Shots fired at White House," Kim-Su said. "Someone attack White House."

* * *

@mrsCee798: Gunshots and flashes occurring within White House grounds! Muslims? KKK? Aliens? Someone's attacking us!!!

@professorofplants Serious? People of color got to rise up and fight against the bigots once and for all!

@jessejameskickass Bring it! Some good old Jesus-boys going to fuck your dark asses up! Long live white America!

@wallstreetwizard Military helicopter seen landing and taking off. Markets already freaking out. Hippies attacking cops on Wall Street.

@hotpancake Helicopter? Oh snap, supposedly cloned Wooly Mammoth loose in Boston too.

@axegrinder13: There's no real news stories on this people, relax! Was firecrackers! But… there might be an Ebola breakout in Houston.

* * *

"On social media, Jack, I'm hearing rumors that *Flakka 3.0* has been put in the Detroit water supply." On a dirty downtown Detroit street a reporter held up his hands to the camera. "I really have no idea what's going on here, Jack, its just craziness." Behind him there was a crash somewhere far down the street, metal hitting metal. Several people who had earlier been at the Juggalo Festival, their faces still painted like clowns, sprinted up and down the streets of the business district. They evaded police, sprayed graffiti on walls, and threw bricks and garbage cans through storefront windows. Someone tried to eat a grandmother.

"The police have supposedly started cracking down, but I'm also hearing reports of some police leaving their posts, either refusing to arrest people or, although I'm not sure if this true, joining in with the looting."

Several hoodie-wearing youths and one lanky kid with a green clown's wig ran past him on the street, the group veering to a stop next to a sidewalk bench. The group grunted and groaned and eventually ripped up the heavy bench. As the reporter watched, they lumbered toward a pristine piece of shop window glass, managing to awkwardly throw it a couple feet into the glass. *Smash!* Whoops and high-fives.

"It just seems like they're just lashing out." The reporter shrugged. "Honestly, Jack, it all seems a little nuts." Shards of glass clattered sparkling to the sidewalk behind the reporter. "Hopefully all this will quiet down after the electoral vote tomorrow... if there is a tomorrow."

* * *

News Headlines:

Black Lives Matters Protestors Confronting March on Washington Republicans

Minnesota Muslims Take to Streets in Protest

Can we Clone Wooly Mammoths?

"We have staked the whole future of our new nation... on each to govern ourselves."
—*James Madison*

(Washington, DC: Sunday, 2:44 p.m. PST / 5:44 p.m. EST)

The finality, the absurd horror of the now infinitely bad repercussions of what he had just done, howled through Amos' head like a hurricane hitting shore. Papers were strewn over the Oval Office floor, the president's large chair was toppled to its side, and a 200-year-old ceramic bust of Thomas Jefferson had shattered near the main door. Gunpowder scent charred the air. There had only been two shots fired, both by Green Beret Sergeant Axl Chicory.

As soon as Amos had overheard President Fuentes decide to move federal troops into Louisiana he had known everything General Harper, Stork, and Shay said must be true. The Democrats were truly trying to steal the election. Federal troops taking over a state? Must be guilty. Amos had been trained for fourteen years to act with courage and decisiveness, and if he and his team had continued following the Secret Service agents to other parts of the White House the opportunity would have been gone, so he made the call. For the good of the country.

Amos cracked the butt of his shotgun into the albino Secret Service agent's head and barked, *"OSKIE, OSKIE!"*

Without hesitation, his entire team reacted to Amos' verbal override, throwing themselves into hot-assault right on the entrances to the Oval Office and Presidential Annex. The albino agent crashed backward through the Annex door to the hallway, knocking the vice president backward as he collapsed to the floor, unconscious. Amos heard grunts and thuds behind him and saw the flash of dark movement as Stork and Jacari took down the other agent.

Amos spun his weapon to his shoulder, training it on the president and vice president. He stepped over the unconscious agent's body into the Annex as Marcus Freeman, eyes wide in shock, backpedalled toward the door connecting the Annex to the Oval Office. The president had leapt from the desk chair, his face ripped with anger and disgust.

"Hands up, sirs," Amos said, moving the aim of his weapon back and forth between the president and vice president, his face a chiseled mess of a mangled ear and cuts and bruises from the fight with Stork. "Put your hands up right now." The thin vice president raised his hands, but also took another backward step toward the Oval Office door.

Bam! A gunshot cracked loud behind him, from within the Oval Office. Then another. *Bam!*

Out of the corner of his eye Amos could see five of his Green Berets bursting through the door into the Oval Office, a third Secret Service agent rolling on the ground holding his shoulder. One of Amos' men cracked a fist to that agent's face, while three Green Berets moved with urgency to the windows and doors of the Oval Office. They posted up at all access points to the room. Amos knew the other six of his team would be hunkered down behind him to secure both directions of the hallway and Secretary's Alcove. Their backs would already be to the Oval Office and Annex with muzzles pointing out toward the opposing force sure to come. Everyone had moved with ruthless efficiency, trusting in the brothers on their team and in Amos' call.

"What's the meaning of this?" President Fuentes growled, his hands in the air but not the slightest hint of fear in his voice. "What is the goddamn meaning of this?"

Amos was respectful but firm. "Sir, I apologize. You will get answers in due course, but now I'm going to have to request you and the vice president move into the Oval Office." Amos jabbed the muzzle of his shotgun toward the open Oval Office door. "Please, sir?"

"How dare you," the president bellowed. "How fucking dare you hold a gun on the president of the United States."

"Sir, please, the Oval Office."

"Do you even understand what you're doing?" The president didn't move, his brown eyes glaring through the small circular glasses. "Who are you, ISIS, or just some damned maniac?" He seemed to become more angry, more righteous as his big hands drifted downward. "Do you understand what you've just done?"

Amos took a short step, right hand slipping off his weapon and curling into a fist, then crushed it into the vice president's nose. Blood sprayed as Marcus Freeman's nose shattered, the vice president crashing backward with a grunt to the floor. Amos coldly stated to the president, "I'm not going to ask again, sir." President Fuentes' eyes went wide, his hands returning higher. "I need you to immediately move into the Oval Office, Mr. President."

The president glowered as he marched around the Annex desk and through the doorway into the Oval Office, stepping over Freeman, rocking on the floor clutching his face. "You've just committed treason, soldier." Amos followed behind with his weapon pointed at the president's back. "If you even are actually a US soldier," the president growled, "you'll hang for this."

In the Oval Office, the president stopped between the front of his massive desk and the sofas, slowly turned in a 360 surveying the scene. Four Green Berets now hunkered at all entrances to the Oval Office with weapons poised as they surveyed the perimeter for retaliation. A total of three Secret Service agents were zip tied on the floor, their mouths duct taped, one grimacing with a shoulder wound, the albino one still unconscious. The sofas were ajar, and Sergeant Chicory's stray bullet had cracked a tiny spiderweb in the tall tempered glass of the window closest to the American flag. "I'll make sure you hang for this," the president growled. "If, that is, you don't die in the next few minutes."

Amos answered with a glance at the zip-tied agents. "No offense, but I think we can handle the Secret Service, sir."

"And the FBI? And DC Swat? Homeland Security and all four branches of the United States Military? Can you handle essentially every federal employee who can carry a gun, you goddamn lunatic? Once news breaks of what you've done, you can't hold off everyone."

"No one has to die, sir," Amos said. "But I'm going to need your help with that."

To the side, Jacari was roughly helping the vice president back to his feet, pressing a small green towel into Freeman's hand and then guiding it up to apply pressure to his busted, gushing nose. As the vice president teetered on his feet, Amos pointed Jacari toward the windows.

Without a word, Jacari then moved to each of the four tall windows, pulling the long gold drapes shut over them. The vice president moaned where he stood, his gray shirt and yellow tie splattered with crimson stains, cloth held over busted nose.

"I'm not helping you," President Fuentes snapped. "You're out of your mind." He dropped his hands to his sides. "I demand you tell me who the hell are you."

"Major Amos Daniels, sir, United States Army." Things relatively under control, Amos let his shotgun drop to his side. "And if you refuse to assist me, you've got to understand the probability of several deaths is extremely high." Amos was confident his team had locked down the immediate portion of the West Wing radiating from the Oval Office, but was already starting to feel like the last holdouts at the Alamo. With only his eleven men, Amos had been able to set up a perimeter that essentially encompassed the Oval Office, the Secretary's Alcove, the Presidential Annex, and the nearest portion of the hallway leading away from the Secretary's Alcove before it took a sharp turn leading to the other offices and rooms of the West Wing. His men watched all the doors and windows and the hallways, but as every second ticked by, Amos knew overwhelming retaliation was imminent. "I need your help to do what's right for the country, and to end this election justly."

Ironically, the Oval Office being one of the most secure structures on Earth meant that once you were the one inside it actually made a decent place to hunker down. The glass and walls to the Oval Office were virtually indestructible, so it would be like they were holding off intruders to the world's most impenetrable cave. In Special Forces though, they had a saying: *a cave is a grave.* Even though it was a good position to defend, there was nowhere to go, nowhere to escape. They were trapped, and every moment odds were mounting against them. Despite their firepower and training, Amos knew their situation was inherently untenable. The only real ace Amos and his men held to not being quickly dead or in handcuffs was that they were holding the two leaders of the free world, Fuentes and Freeman, at gunpoint. Amos needed to find a real solution to all of this quick, the right one for everybody.

"Major Daniels, do you understand the ramifications to the country, the world, by your actions?" The president's ebony face was incredulous, his white brows furrowed. "No matter what you think you're achieving with this, the results will be catastrophic; a pebble dropped into a lake rippling into tsunamis. Put down your weapon immediately, stop this. That's what's just for the country."

Amos looked out the un-curtained glass door leading to the Rose Garden. He could see the glints and shadows of what must be the Secret Service's counterterrorism team already taking up positions in the dusk around the exterior of the Oval Office. His ears picked up the grunts and shuffle of boots down the main hallway leading from the Oval Office too, surely more Secret Service setting up positions around the corner in the hallway. By Amos' professional guess, there would be at least two dozen Secret Service agents already getting into positioned at every angle of the Oval Office and its attached rooms, with an army on the way. "Sir, I believe we can resolve this peacefully, but I—"

"Major, this very moment I'm in the middle of talks with Iran over their nuclear bomb." The president crossed his arms over his suit vest. "I'm defusing a hostage situation in North Korea, trying to convince China not cut trade ties with Taiwan, and attempting to convince Russia to turn over international criminals. All while trying to finalize the biggest international trade deal in history and at the same time as bringing the country's tightest election to a happy close for all. What good, in God's name, do you possibly think you're accomplishing for the election, or anything, by this insane action?"

"I was ordered to secure the White House, sir, to make sure the election isn't stolen."

"Ordered? By whom?" the president exclaimed. "As Commander-in-Chief of the military I sure as hell didn't order you to bust in here, attack my security, break my vice president's nose. I'm fairly certain, Major, you're actually taking part in a military coup."

"I heard you ordering federal troops into Louisiana, sir, attempting to tip the win to your side."

"Peacekeepers, Major," the president incredulously declared. "I was CONSIDERING sending peacekeepers, so no more innocent Americans would get injured until either the Congressional Committee or Supreme Court can help resolve things fairly, but I hadn't given any order yet. What you've done is far more egregious than simply talking about trying to keep New Orleans calm, you're apparently helping implement a military usurping of the American presidency."

No. Amos, despite his best efforts, let fresh worry flash through his brain. *No, no, no.*

"Have you considered that, Major? That you're following the wrong people? That you've maybe been tricked into leading a military coup? Who ordered you?"

Amos took a deep breath. His bruised brain now swirled with panic. Things were happening so fast, what if there was more to this than he knew? *Keep calm. Stay on point.* "Mr. president, I'm going to need your cooperation, if this is to end well."

"End well. Ha," Freeman now grumbled. "You're plunging the country into chaos, you idiot." The vice president, his face now twisted red and hard in violation, silently paced in tight circles between the sofas with the blood-soaked rag to his nose. "This isn't going to end well unless you drop your weapon, right now, you damned traitor."

"Where you want the coms station, boss?" Stork asked Amos. Amos pointed Stork toward the Annex door, even as his mind continued whirling with fresh doubt. Military coup? What if Shay's making a mistake? What if Harper and Stork are the coup?

"Chaos is correct, Major," President Fuentes added. "What you're doing will send this country and the election into anarchy, not help it get resolved, if that's what you truly care about. You're holding the president and vice president of the free world hostage for God's sake, you're being lied to by someone."

Amos tried to not doubt, told himself to not betray any confusion. "That's why it's in both of our interests for you to help me defuse this situation as much as you can, Mr. President. Tell everyone to back off." He needed time to figure out what was right. Time to confirm the truth. "Put out a public statement that nothing has occurred here, that there was just some sort of gas explosion in the kitchen or something, quickly contained, everything under control."

Marcus Freeman chuckled through his bloody cloth.

President Fuentes sighed. "This is the White House, Major. Do you realize that I am not even allowed to act as president under this kind of duress. The Secret Service will be executing the chain-of-command protocol as we speak, swearing in the Speaker of the House as acting president until this crisis is resolved, and immediately working to neutralize YOUR threat."

"Well then help me formulate the best plan, sir," Amos blurted. "How do we keep things calm?"

"President Fuentes!" The sudden shout came from an unseen Secret Service agent somewhere around the corner at the end of the hall. "Are you alive, Mr. President? Are you okay?"

The president glared at Amos.

"You can at least buy us time, Mr. President," Amos said under his breath. "Time for me to get this worked out before complete anarchy happens. Help me get this right, sir."

The president sneered back. "This already is complete anarchy."

"Mr. President," the agent called again. "Proof of life, sir. If you are conscious, please respond."

Amos looked into the president's dark face, motioning his hand toward the open door in indication that the president should respond to the agent, the Major's brown eyes pleading.

"Jesus," the president finally snarled, his tone suggesting the magnitude of bad choices in all directions was sinking in. "I'm only trying to do what is right, soldier, don't mistake this as me agreeing with anything you're doing." The president took a deep breath, then yelled back toward the open Oval Office door. "Stand down!" The president stepped into line of sight of the hallway so that he could be seen by the Secret Service agent peering around the corner on the other end of the hallway. "I'm fine, and giving you a direct order, stand down. I repeat, do not breach." The president stepped back from the hallway's line of sight, adding to Amos with a disgusted shake of his head, "They won't listen to me. They're trained to ignore me saying exactly that. In exactly this type of situation. They're going to come when they think it's time to come, and no one can stop them."

"We just need time, sir," Amos whispered. "Can you also put out some sort of statement, something to convince the public as much as we can that nothing out of the ordinary has happened. That everything is fine."

"Absurd," Freeman snapped. "How can we trust you?"

The president's face was disgusted, but also conveyed that he at least agreed with some of the logic in keeping the general public calm. "I'll need to call Gerald Coops, press secretary."

Amos nodded, and the president stepped to his desk, reached for his desk phone. "Keep in mind, Major, even if the Secret Service doesn't burst in and kill us all, and even if I can keep the country and the world from melting down over what you've done, in the end you're still going to be prosecuted."

Stork appeared behind Amos in the Annex doorway. "Com's hot, Major. General waiting."

Who to trust, Amos' frantic thoughts kept spinning, *who to trust?*

* * *

Milton's Diner looked like one of those family-owned restaurants Stone loved, both personally and professionally. It dripped authentic Americana, from signed black and white photos of Elvis and Joe DiMaggio, both probably fake, to very real brown stains on the brick walls after generations of grease smoke wafting from the kitchen. The functional carpet might have been another color decades ago, but now was a shade between gray and sickly green, depending on where things had spilled. Nothing really matched in the restaurant's décor, and in that way it all perfectly worked for Governor Stone, screaming "family-owned business of hardworking Americans," and so he allowed one of the news cameramen setting up at the park to film him and the others as they ordered their food.

Stone pointed Buddy to the empty seat across the table from him. "Why don't you sit over there, partner, let our esteemed guests sprinkle in here amongst us." Anything to get a few feet of breathing space from the moron. Stone had a couple of Wall Street hedge fund managers showing up. Buddy Dukes grinned and nodded, always seemingly unaware of Stone's abject detest of him.

"Henry Corwich keeps ringing my phone, by the way, Hampton," Buddy whispered as three well-suited men approached the table.

"Daniels' she-male." Stone snorted in disgust. "What's it want?"

"Not sure, been ignoring the calls, same as from Harper. Just like you said."

"Good. Not sure there's anything more to discuss with anybody except Fuentes, and can at least have some time to just to enjoy a good hamburger until he calls." Stone was scheduled to start his rally speech in a little over an hour, but wasn't going to start until the president called and reassured him everything was still on track for his win. And if the president didn't call, well, then he'd have to consider making an entirely different speech. Expose 1776, but just make sure it was the Fuentes administration that took the fall. "Soon find out if we're gonna have to play hardball or not."

While the news guy circled around the room, a single camera mounted on his shoulder, Rosa slapped down silverware at the table. The three guests, two hedge fund guys and the lead spokesperson for the NRA, were serious-looking. The NRA was scheduled to reaffirm their endorsement of Stone at the rally. "Gonna be ready to light those liberals up tonight, Governor?" the NRA spokesman asked with a grin as he sat.

"That Daniels twat sure seems to have it out for you with that fake audiotape. Fight fire with fire, I say."

Rosa did not make eye contact. She did not want to breathe next to them, did not want to infect herself with their racist, woman beating, corrupt, filth. She had not wanted to work this table, but Milton had forced her. Serve this vile filth, blow a fat white guy, or be fired and deported; those had been tonight's only options if she wanted her son to eat.

"I most certainly will, Joe," Stone answered, using a tiny forefinger to keep his aging eyes trained on the small text of the menu, peering through the bottom of his glasses as he continued to spout rising indignation at the country's moral decay. "I most certainly will. Common decency, that's what's missing from this country now. These new-age types like Daniels, they're just missing a common decent core, missing goodness and morality."

Rosa heard every word, watching as Stone's fat jowls danced over his three-thousand-dollar suit. She guessed the gold watch he wore would alone pay for her son's healthcare needs until he was eighteen. How many dreams of Latinos, women, blacks, gays, and anyone else who didn't fit into Hampton Stone's club of entitlement had been crushed under his stupid, expensive shoes?

"They've all just lost their way," the NRA spokesperson agreed with Stone, daintily unfolding a napkin into his lap. "Just crazy people who don't even understand the perils of communism and porn stars. Wanting to take away everyone's Second Amendment right, and destroy families."

"Evil or stupid, take your pick. Exodus 32 said the Lord instructed the faithful to *strap a sword to his side and go back and forth amongst the camp from end to end, each killing their* brother, their friend, their neighbor if they'd lost their way," Stone mumbled as Rosa topped off his water glass. "If we get this election stolen from us it might be time to fight, or this whole country will be overrun by morning with dirty, lazy Mexicans." And Rosa took his words to heart.

* * *

"You'll only need to hold the fort for twelve hours," General Harper told Amos. The conversation was over the Spec Ops laptop Stork set up on the Annex desk. "Maybe twenty-four hours at the most before I can mobilize troops into DC proper. Good job, son."

"Troops, sir?" Amos leaned toward the camera lens in new shock, stretching and flexing his hand that had broken the vice president's nose. "I don't think moving additional troops is a good idea." Amos sat in the same chair President Fuentes had been in less than thirty minutes earlier. "Don't move troops into DC, sir. Just don't."

"I believe," Harper growled, "that you've already got your hands full without worrying about giving unsolicited advice up the chain of command."

"General, with all due respect, this is already an incredibly volatile situation. I don't see how you personally leading a battalion into DC is going to deescalate anything. Why not—"

"I do not intend to deescalate anything, boy, we aren't the State Department." Harper sneered. "I intend to win!"

"Win?" Amos shook his head at the monitor. "How? Why don't we contact the Justice Department, let them take this over now that—"

"The Justice Department that serves at the pleasure of the president? Who exactly are you going to trust to resolve this fairly, Major? Once the election is over in an honest capacity we can allow them to start all their slippery legal mumbo-jumbo bullshit to wrangle out of any culpability, but not before."

Amos suddenly realized that he didn't know who you would contact if the president himself were potentially committing a crime. Or a four-star general. "But finding the truth is what's import, sir, of the elector's death and getting everyone involved in deciding a fair—"

"The vote's tomorrow, Major." Harper's eyes twisted like he was talking to a fool. "You confirmed yourself that they were about to quarantine New Orleans to steal this election, correct? They're guilty. What more do you want?"

"But what if that is a misunderstanding, sir? What if the president was trying to actually find a fair solution?"

"Little late for second-guessing who the good guys are, son." Harper shook his head in bewildered disgust. "Boy, now that you and I are in the position we're in, let's not just hand them the knife to cut our throats, eh? There's a win-win for the country, and lose-lose." Harper's eyes were sharp, determined. "If Freeman is sworn in, the first thing he'll do is start closing bases and the next thing we know the damned towel-headed barbarians will be running through the gate. Letting Freeman win is as good as letting WWIII start. There's a reason I've got these goddamn stars on my shoulders and you do not. Your orders are to hold that fucking hill until I get there with reinforcements. And that is the only way you, me, your team, and a bunch of other people who love this country don't go to jail, and we get an honest end to this election, with Hampton Stone rightfully in office. Do I make myself clear?"

"Yes, sir, but—" Before Amos could complete his sentence, Harper shut his side of the call down. Amos stared at the blank monitor for a breath. And then another. He set an elbow down on the desk to briefly rest his achy, concussed, forehead in his hand.

Insane, this all insane.

How the fuck was he inside the West Wing of the White House, holding guns on the president and vice president of the United States with all the rest of the guns in the world bearing down on him soon? Was he doing the right thing, or was he helping a crazed American general take over the White House?

Life had seemed simple once. Amos remembered going to sleep at night listening to his parents laugh together in the living room and had felt that he was forever safe, that every day would be filled with joy. He never really understood what had happened between them all, why his family had started to crumble, except that he knew people had suddenly started to break their vows, to change. So, Amos had taken it upon himself to never be the one to break his vows from then on, to tell the truth, because he knew the destruction it could cause. *For the love of God, why does it all keep going to shit?*

And that's when he realized who his only savior was… if he could trust her this time.

"Jones," Amos barked at the closed door. "Jacari!" There had to be a way out of this, out of all of it, for everyone. A way to make sure no one got hurt, no one was arrested for treason, and the country had an election result everyone could agree upon. A way the truth still won.

Jacari opened the door, stepped in. "Major?"

"Track down my sister." Annie, whom he had barely spoken to in years, was possibly the only one in the world who could help him get this crisis resolved before potentially horrible, irreversible things started happening. She had the connections, had the power, and she, maybe, even had the truth. "Get her on the com, she might be the only solution to all this."

Seven Years Earlier

F or reasons Amos could never fathom, Annie had seduced Shay, the love of his life, just prior to his leaving for the army, and it had destroyed his relationship and future. Or at least that was the way Amos remembered it.

Brother and sister did not speak for years, and the next time they saw each other was as their father was dying. Ray Daniels, gaunt as a sun-rotted fruit, lay in the VA hospital bed attached to so many chords and tubes it looked like he were some student's bad science project. The sheets had yellow stains on them, and the air bit of chlorine. The slowness of monitor's beeps only highlighted the weakness of the patriarch of the Daniels' family's raspy, occasional, breaths, his eyes watery as a dead fish, gazing blankly up toward the ceiling. It was as if someone had skinned a younger Ray Daniels, glued sporadic tufts of grey hair and liver spots to it, and then draped that skin over a small skeleton trying to convince people there was a living, breathing, thinking man still in there.

"There's nothing left to decide, Amos," Annie said holding the clipboard.

Amos stood ramrod straight by their dad's bed in his full army uniform, his newly won Green Beret at a precise angel on his head and his hand gently resting over their father's wrinkled one. Annie stood near the door, smartly dressed in a woman's suit worthy of her newly won California Congressional seat.

"I've already decided," she added. "It's for the best."

"You can't," Amos did not turn back to face her. In his free hand, the thin sliver chain of their mother's crucifix draped from his closed fist beside his thigh. "You can't, Annabel."

"He's already brain dead, Amos, pulling the plug is a formality."

For a moment there was only the slow beeping of the machines. "He could still pull through," Amos said. "Can't you just try to have a little faith for once? Why can't you ever just believe in something good, instead of... instead of always trying to tear things apart. Maybe if you tried to pray—"

"Amos," Annie eventually sighed, "you've got to grow up, stop living in a fantasy world."

"Me?" Amos laughed. "Me living in a fantasy world? You don't mean grow up, you mean GIVE UP. You can just unilaterally decide to kill our dad."

"You were away, Stubbs. The DOD said you would be unreachable for at least sixty days. I was given sole authority."

"Don't call me that," Amos still didn't turn around, instead squeezing his father's hand tighter. "You've always hated him. Never given him a chance."

For several moments there were just the occasional monitor beeps, the shuffles of nurse's footsteps in the hall, the incongruent giggles of a random conversation.

"He's not a good man, Amos, he's done awful things."

"Don't start that shit again, Annie. Don't use your delusions to justify it."

"Delusions," Annie exclaimed. "You want to defend that monster, after what he did? Keep being an apologist for whatever another member of your good 'ole boy network wants to do, no matter how vile? There's no chance for him, Amos, even if he deserved one, which—"

"And that's it, Annie, isn't it? You don't think our father 'deserves' to live, do you? You've been wishing he were dead since we were kids."

"Yes, Amos," Annie growled, straightening, returning her brother's hard stare. "You're right. I've wished Ray Daniels dead ever since he beat and drove our mother away, ever since that night when I was only fifteen and he—"

"Oh please, Annie," Amos's voice rose louder than hers. "You tell that story like he raped you. Like he touched you." Amos shook his head in disbelief. "He'd had too much to drink and grabbed you by the jaw to shut your incessant antagonizing up, he didn't sexually assault you."

Annie's face scrunched in bitter offense, but for a atypical moment no words came out of her moving mouth. "You can't justify the way he was, Amos. He might as well have raped me, I saw it was in his eyes. I saw what he wanted to do!"

"Insane," Amos glared at her over his shoulder. "You claim I'm living in a fantasy world because I believe in God, yet you can condemn people by what you are so sure your intuition tells you about them. Never facts, just your interpretation of them. Our dad is as good as a child molester because of what you THINK he thought one night."

"Is everything okay," the attending doctor asked with a lean into the room.

Annie didn't even look at him, her eyes still drilling into the back of her brother's dark uniform. She instead raised a single forefinger toward the doctor's voice, already becoming comfortable with the public power she wielded.

"Sorry, Congresswoman," the doctor said before withdrawing from the room. "Let me know if you need anything."

Amos moved his hand to his father's forehead, brushed a long strand of gray hair from his father's glassy eyes.

Annie sighed. "Look…," she finally whispered. "I am truly sorry for some of the choices I've made, the thing with Shay, but… we were young, and you were abandoning her, and we were both drinking, needed comfort, and…," Annie took a step forward, and Amos tensed at the sound. "And that's what I mean, Stubbs, you've got some romanticized belief of what life is and it just isn't. It's messy and it's ugly and besides that was just one night of sex, big deal. If you truly had loved her, you would have forgiven—"

"Messy and ugly," Amos growled toward the ceiling, "because of people like you. Because of people like you who don't believe in anything greater than themselves." Amos' face flushed red with rage. "You're not good."

"That's not fair, Stubbs, I'm trying to make real differences in the real world, not pretend to live to some honor code that only supports what a bunch of old white males like him think the world should be—"

"Don't call me that, you goddamn whore. We aren't brother and sister anymore, don't call me that."

And now Annie's entire face turned crimson in silent fury as well. She took another step toward her younger brother's back. "Grow the fuck up, Stubbs." She lifted up the clipboard and used the pen to loudly scratch her name to the form authorizing the hospital to stop medical treatment on their father, clapped the pen to it. "He's never been any hero," she stated turning toward the door, "he killed innocent people over there, and the world is better off with him dead. Better watch out that you don't become the same thing."

And as his older sister's high heels echoed off the hallway floor, a single tear rolled off Amos' check and down onto the edge of his dad's hand that he held. He stayed silent for a long time, just breathing.

"I know, dad," Amos finally whispered. "I know you were just trying to do what you thought was right." And his father's hand weakly, maybe, squeezed back. Or at least, that was the way Amos remembered it.

* * *

It was a month and a half later when Amos would be deployed in the Korpesh Valley of Afghanistan that the events would occur to evolve his military reputation into someone to fear. A dark spot on Amos heart had formed years ago in the exact wound where Shay had broken it, and with his father dying that blackness had started to creep wider like a bloodstain. Amos thought of the rage inside him as something he needed to keep tethered. A fuming, snarling beast that wanted revenge on this world, and he must never allow it off its chain.

The first Muslim Afghani Amos had killed had been in his fifties, his long beard dyed bright red, ridiculously bright against his white robes. The man had arrogantly grinned, in stark contrast to the look of pleading horror twisted over the kidnapped female reporter's face. The terrified reporter was on her back on the rocky ground, her shirt torn, blood dripping from a broken lip, her eyes riveted up on the Afghani elder's knife as he stepped toward her, laughing. That's when Amos had felt a single-purpose of rage-fueled clarity scorch through his soul, the ravenous beast inside him begging to be let off its chain—some things could not be tolerated.

"Give to them according to the evil of their deeds." *(Psalms 28:4)* sung through his head as Amos twisted from the guard's hands. Tolerance for others' beliefs was what had allowed these men to justify their twisted ideology. Tolerance for wrong-thinking was what had toppled the Twin Towers, had killed thousands of his uniformed brothers. Tolerance for all their lies about God was exactly what had allowed evil to flourish since the dawn of time, and Amos would tolerate no more.

As the smiling Afghani elder had leaned toward the woman, his wretched wrinkled fingers stretching toward her torn shirt, a certainty had gripped Amos' mind; a certainty he was going to decimate them all and there was nothing they could do about it. Both Amos' thumbs went two knuckles deep through the old Afghani's eyeballs before the guards could even comprehend the American soldier was free. And the guards… they had died even worse, as a liberating surge of purposeful destruction gloriously howled through Amos' heart, the justice-seeking beast inside him finally allowed to eat.

Amos had been unable to scrub all the blood from beneath his nails for days.

New Orleans Burns

*T*his can't be happening, Annie thought. *There can't be a Republican coup, it's got to be a coincidence.* Over the past hour they had tried to reach the president directly, then the vice president, then the White House operator. All came up empty. *I didn't have the elector killed. Is the whole world going nuts, or am I?* A vein on each side of her temples throbbed, and she thought she heard the slither of the snake beneath her desk. *Hissss.*

They kept changing between news reports and social media looking for any clarifying information. Individuals in the March on Washington crowd were posting claims they'd heard gunshots from the White House, but it might have just been people trolling for reactions, possibly trying to push the already very tense scene on Pennsylvania Ave into violence. *Reboot.org* instigators were rumored to be in the crowd and *Blank Panthers* were in multiple altercations with right-wingers calling themselves *Oath Keepers.* New Orleans and Detroit were supposedly already in such states of anarchy people were starting to make comparisons to the Hurricane Katrina meltdown, but in all the noise it was difficult to know what information to trust. Someone had done an excellent Photoshop of a Wooly Mammoth stampeding through the streets of Boston for instance, and others were claiming that someone had been dumping *Flakka 3.0* in the water supplies of several major cities making people go crazy enough to dress themselves like clowns or be cannibals. Bullshit was everywhere, so mercifully no legitimate news source had picked up the White House story yet in an abundance of caution. The only potential corroborating information Henry had found, after she made him directly call the DC Mayor, was that a helicopter had possibly landed and taken back off about an hour ago. The Secret Service had then moved the increasingly tense crowd a bit farther back from the White House gate. That didn't necessarily mean anything suspicious though. Helicopters brought dignitaries in to the White House at times and the Secret Service often adjusted crowd control just to keep any potential bad guys guessing. Illuminati-alien conspiracy nuts were going bonkers though, claiming they had seen a spaceship, not a helicopter. *A coup can't be real.* Annie tried to calm herself even though her whole body felt so tense it could crack. *The White House is fine. This will all be fine.*

Hissss.

"Try Coops again." Annie pointed Howe to her cell phone. "Get the Press Secretary." Annie bit into her thumb nail as she paced before her desk, ignored the soft slithering sound beneath her desk as it was obviously just something going a bit sketchy with her hearing from the stress or the pills. *Just breathe, stay calm.* She glanced around the room, her eyes resting on the Zennie bottle on the windowsill, then felt her shoulders soften. *Don't give in to panic.* Precise, pink peace was still waiting in the Zennies, like her rabbit's eyes had once been. *Hissss....*

"Hypothetically, madam." Howe's fingers trembled as she dialed her phone. "If the military and government truly were to split along party lines, Democrat and Republican, how would we determine who is part of it? Republicans are half the government, half the country."

"You're asking me?" Annie snapped, not wanting to take more pills in front of them, peering through the cracks of light from the wood-shuttered window instead and hugging her arms around her red cashmere sweater. "How should I know?" For a moment she caught herself wondering, *what if I had just forgiven my dad about the rabbit? Was that where everything went wrong, where choices started rippling through time into disasters?*

"There's good and bad people in each party," Henry sanctimoniously said. "We can't assume anyone who's ever voted Republican is in on it, Annie."

Asshole. Henry was becoming more and more combative, disloyal, even questioning if she was involved in the elector's death! Maybe Annie was just fated to have everyone betray her? *Snakes. Snakes everywhere.* The question was, what to do about it?

Henry kept talking, "In all honesty, the solution to a diametric political battle within the country should probably be to find a nonpartisan solution, not exacerbate it."

"But we don't know what's happening, so how do we know what will cause harm?" Annie snatched up the Zennie bottle as Henry's expression soured further. "We don't know the truth, so blindly trusting in someone else is stupid when we don't know if they are in fact trustworthy."

Howe held the phone to her ear, her voice shaking. "What if the coup triggers a civil war?"

Annie's eyes widened at the scope of ramifications, of the open-ended craziness of what they were discussing. She shook two, then three, pills into her palm with a scowl at Henry. "Until we get proof, Beatrice, actual concrete FACTS there is something going on at the White House, we can't assume there's any definite plot, conspiracy or coup. Everyone remain fucking calm." Annie threw the Zennies in her mouth and then snatched up Henry's glass of water to swallow them. Henry glared in judgment as she took the pills.

Annie slammed the empty glass down next to him, flipped him off. "Remain calm, dick."

"Mr. Coops," Howe finally gasped into her phone once she got an answer. "It's Beatrice Howe. I haven't been able to reach the president for over an hour, can you—"

Annie watched Howe's eyes worry, the president's National Security Advisor straightening in her chair. "Yes. Okay." After a moment, "You're saying—I see." Howe's gaze went to Annie, her face becoming even more grave. "Okay, thank you, Mr. Coops. Please proceed." Howe ended the call and her hands drifted into her lap, her expression stiff.

"Well?" Annie feared the answer.

"Gerald Coops said he's been INSTRUCTED to release a public statement saying there were no shots fired at the White House. That any sounds will be publicly explained as coming from one of President Fuentes' daughters playing with firecrackers."

"The president's daughters are in New Jersey," Annie whispered, her throat tightening.

"Yes, ma'am." Howe nodded. "They are, and Mr. Coops sounded very concerned."

"Shit." Annie reached over the desk for Howe's pack of cigarettes. "Check social media again, Henry."

Hissss…

"Annie, I've already scoured Facebook, Twitter, YouTube.

The problem is that with the doxed stuff, more information is not necessarily good information."

"Well fucking check again!" Annie glared down at Henry. "If I say check, fucking check. Don't argue."

"Madam," Howe said. "Somebody on Twitter says they are in front of the White House, swears they saw US military personnel shooting at Secret Service through the Oval Office window."

"Jesus." Annie tried to light the cigarette, but her hands were trembling too much. "This can't be real."

"And now it looks like one of the news channels has picked it up." Howe pointed at the muted television on the wall with the remote, turning up the volume.

A talking head from one of the stations was in front of the White House fence, one hand covering an ear to hear over the noise of the protest march, her other holding a microphone. "It's a little bit confusing as to what, if anything, is going on at the White House, Jack," the reporter shouted. "We don't know if there is a situation or not." The reporter pointed back toward the White House. The camera angled across the grounds to the Oval Office, then zoomed in on the Oval Office windows with curtains closed to outside view. "As you can see from this angle, we really can't see anything out of the ordinary, but according to a few protestors at this section of fence, they claim to have heard gunshots." The camera went back to the reporter looking at the noisy, chanting crowd, mostly red shirts, but several blue. "Of course, there's been at least three small violent altercations between Republican and Democratic groups broken up by the police in the past hour or so, and the noise volume here makes it a little problematic to trust what anyone heard."

"It can't be," Henry whispered, nervousness seeming to get the best of him now too. "It just can't be, Annie, it's only a power outage or something. That's all, we can't overact."

"I know." Annie finally lit the cigarette, inhaling. "Of course it's a power outage. But..." She wiped at the sweet on her forehead with the back of her hand. "Contingency plan. If something's happening at the White House, who's in charge now? What do we do?" Annie sucked down the cigarette in two long inhales, threw the butt on her hardwood floor and stomped it into ash, ripped another from the pack. "We need to get some actual facts. Is there anyone we completely trust in the military we can check with—" Annie's eyes popped wide. "Amos!" It dawned on her that her brother might be able to help. Despite their ongoing feud, he was the most honorable man she'd ever known, and completely apolitical. "Henry, get my brother on the phone, on a secure line. Maybe he can find out if the military knows of any threats."

Before Henry could even begin to move though, they heard new stomps up the hardwood steps outside. Several boots, voices of stern urgency behind them. When the door burst open this time, instead of Annie's husband it was a fully uniformed female admiral, so wide and square in her proportions that the insignia on her shoulders couldn't be seen in the door frame. The admiral clutched a white cap to her chest, the woman's steel eyes landing on Annie like a bird of prey. "Admiral Kerns," the broad-shouldered woman announced to the room. "Chairman of the Joint Chiefs of Staff." The admiral's free hand snapped in salute at Annie. "Reporting for duty, madam."

Annie shook her head, stuck the fresh unlit cigarette in her mouth and tried to inhale. "There's some sort of mistake."

"In completing my duties under the Presidential

Succession Act of 1947, madam, you ARE the acting president of the United States until the current crisis is put down."

"What? No…" Annie stammered. "No, no, no. This is a mistake." Annie waved her hands in refusal. "I get the vice president might be involved in whatever misunderstanding is temporarily happening, but that means the Speaker—"

"Speaker of the House Donald Newton is in surgery, madam, and you are Senate President Pro Tempore. That puts you next on the succession list in the advent of something happening to the president and vice president of the United States. The Chief Justice is on the way to swear you in, but in the meantime, I have taken wartime authority to transfer power to you. I serve at the pleasure of President Daniels to assist you in analyzing and coordinating an appropriate response to the current threat."

"Wartime?" Annie sank back onto the edge of her desk, the cigarette dropping from her mouth to the floor, the insane jolt of it all hitting her anew now that someone stated it as fact. "There's just a power outage or something, Admiral, once this ridiculous confusion gets cleared up—"

"Madam President, please be advised as your first national security briefing, the West Wing is currently under enemy control. A faction of domestic terrorists, possibly Republican-led from within the United States military, has commandeered the White House. The terrorists are holding the president and vice-president hostage."

"Republican terrorists?" Annie felt lightheaded. "Hostages?"

"A coup, Madam President. I'd advise immediate counterassault." Admiral Kerns took another heavy step across the hardwood floor. "In order to assist the Secret Service's CAT team in defusing the situation I can have SEAL Team Six wheels up in eleven minutes, breaching White House grounds within the hour. A quick assault would be best given the country's tensions, Madam President, before any potential news story leaks and causes additional public panic."

"Jesus, hold up." Annie tried to control her breathing. "And don't call me Madam President."

"Time, Mad— Ms. Daniels, is critical in these situations. The longer delay, the higher the risk."

"These situations? These situations? There has never been a 'these situations' before!" Annie spun to Henry. "Get Amos on the phone. I've got to talk to someone sane about this. Find my brother, Henry!"

"Madam President," Kerns said, a look of disapproval twisting over her flat, acne-covered face. "You should be advised your brother is one of the terrorists."

And Annie felt another block tumble from the foundation of her reality.

Hisssssss...

* * *

At 6:45 p.m. the Department of Homeland Security raised the terrorist threat level to "imminent threat" throughout the US. *If you see something, say something.*

Night Falls And Goblins Slink From Shadows

*(Various Locations Around Country: Sunday, 4:05 p.m. PST /
7:05 p.m. EST)*

As Yanic Goran's limo sped to the private military contractor's offices on the outskirts of Manassas, Virginia, he realized he had never been more worried. He wondered if even that video he'd secretly taken from the top of the basement stairs between Senator Daniels and Governor Stone was safe in the cloud, or if it too had also been hacked by *Reboot.org*. It all seemed out of control, as if the strings of the multiverse were unspooling before his eyes.

Goran compulsively scrolled past headlines on his tablet:
Louisiana Governor Declares State of Emergency

Possible ISIS Shooting at Christian Church

Crazed Clowns in Detroit?

Occupy Wall Street Rally Turns Violent

*Confederate Flag Maker Set on Fire, Black Panthers
Suspected*

Christians Firebomb Atlanta Abortion Clinic

No One Knows Where 'Off' Button is For Internet

Conservatives Smash Gay Club

Black Teen Shot by Off-Duty Cleveland Cop

Kardashians/Jenners Commit Mass Suicide For "Hope"

Possible Poisoning of Seattle Water Treatment Plant

Rioting in 16 Cities Spreading

Goran powered his tablet off without reading any articles. Who knew what was real now? He looked out the window at night descending over America.

Goran could no longer see the fields of snow he knew they were passing. Somewhere out there in the black was the Manassas Battlefield, where the bloody Battle of Bull Run was fought over a 150 years before. Goran thought about how those earlier Americans had once killed their own brothers and sisters, butchered friends and family over differing ideals and, in the end, been butchered themselves. Goran felt sick to his stomach and wondered what would happen as darkness continued to creep westward across the country. All he'd ever wanted was the American dream.

Goran rapped on the partition window, told the driver to speed up. The wolf was at the door; it was time to get guns.

* * *

Despite a gargantuan ax hanging over their heads, brother and sister each looked into their monitor and remembered their oldest friend. Those childhood days when pure trust had always smiled back in each of their eyes, back before Shay and their father had crept confusion into their lives, back when everything still made sense. Each was now a small ray of hope to the other, to return to some life of sanity and peace before all had sunk away into a deep abyss. A lifeline to saving their own necks, as well as the country's.

"Stubbs," Annie whispered, "how are you?"

Amos was in his camo and body armor, his face bruising blue across one cheek up to the mangled ear from his fight with Stork, the cross Annie had once given him as kids hanging exposed at the base of his neck. Annie's long yellow hair hung disheveled over the shoulder of her red sweater, her blue eyes strained with worry.

"You know." Amos glanced around the presidential Annex. "Keeping busy."

Nervous smiles.

"Jesus, Amos," Annie said sadly. "What's going on? What are you doing?"

"I need your help." Amos' face was sincere, stern. "I need your help to end this the right way. For the country. For everyone."

"Absolutely." Annie said. "I'll do whatever I can to get your sentence reduced, I'll speak to the president, any judges or prosecutors I can. We'll make sure they know you're a decent person."

"No." Amos shook his head. "I'm not talking about surrendering, Annie. I need your help to end this the right way."

"What on earth—"

"Are you alone?"

Annie shrugged, brushed a long blonde strand from her eyes, and glanced to the side. "Yes, I'm alone, but you've got to quit this, to let the president and vice president go. Immediately."

"Annie, there's a Democratic conspiracy to hijack this election."

Annie's jaw dropped in surprise. "A DEMOCRATIC conspiracy? Amos, I don't know who—"

"I need to know." Amos glared into the camera. "Tell me honestly, Annabel, do you know anything about a Democratic plot to steal the election? About the elector being shot? Tell me you're not part of it, Annie."

"Absolutely not!" She shook her head, crow's feet crinkling next to her eyes. "And there's no Democratic plot, Amos. But there sure as hell appears to be a Republican one."

"I'm not part of a coup, Annie, that's not what this is, at least not from me. I'm just trying to protect the country."

"Amos, this is madness, you're holding the president and vice president hostage. If someone is ordering you to do this they are lying to you, Amos. It's they who are trying to steal the election. Think about it."

Amos leaned back from the monitor. He looked up at the ceiling and sighed, and for a brief moment his face betrayed worry that what she said could be true. "Can I trust you, Annie?"

"Amos, just give yourself up. Before you or the president, or the VP or anyone else, gets killed. Do the right thing, before the entire country has a meltdown."

"I can't do that." Amos shook his head. "There's evidence of someone from your side having the elector shot. The president was talking about moving troops into Louisiana, Annie. If you're not a part of it, then you've got to help me. Can I trust you?"

"I promise you the Democrats are NOT trying to steal the election, Amos, whatever you think you heard."

"Can we trust each other this time? Are you alone?"

"Yes!" Except for the tiny crow's feet etching with time, her blue eyes looked exactly the same as that afternoon twenty-five years before when they had promised to always look out for each other.

His fingers went to the cross, touched over the tiny pink stones glinting beneath the light. "General Harper is preparing to move troops out of MacDill into DC," Amos confided. "He wants Stone sworn in as president. He thinks Stone is the rightful winner, and that you guys are breaking the constitution to steal it from him. If you and I don't figure out a way to solve this, Harper will be marching the United States Army on the White House."

"Jesus." Annie put a hand to her forehead like a bolt of pain went through her eye, blonde strands swaying in front of her face. "This really is a goddamn military coup." She pleaded, "Amos, you've got to see you're a pawn of General Harper, that this isn't right. Just let the president and vice president go and turn yourself in."

Amos' wet eyes fluttered toward the ceiling again. "It's not that simple, Annie, the truth matters. I've got to make sure this ends correctly. Please, Annie, can I trust you? Will you help me?"

"Yes, Amos, you can trust me." She tried to smile bigger, the corners of her eyes crinkling more. "How?"

"Will you reach out to Stone? Maybe if you can get him to publicly broker a truce with you it could stop anyone on either side from being able to complete their plan. Claim you're speaking for Freeman and agree to delay the Electoral College vote for a month or something, until somebody can determine the correct solution for the elector issue."

Annie nodded, swallowing tears. "Good idea. Hadn't thought of that."

"And you've got to do it quick, Annie, you've got to get in contact with him and get something on video that can be released publicly, okay? As soon as possible, before Harper can move."

"Okay." Annie nodded again.

"But, Annie," Amos talked fast, "you've got to remember to make sure there is some sort of firm agreement between you and Stone for both parties to find the truth of who shot the elector and prosecute them. Something we can broadcast. It's got to be released on all the news stations, so that everyone can see it, alright? Once everyone sees it they'll calm down, and Harper won't dare move troops if he thinks Freeman and Stone are in agreement, he'd just be dooming himself then."

"Okay," Annie said. "Yes."

"Good." Amos smiled, breathing easier. "And soon as the video is on the news I'll let the president and vice president go, then turn myself in to be judged accordingly."

"Excellent, Amos. I'll have your back then too."

"Can you think of anything else though? Is there anything I'm overlooking?"

"Only... what is Harper going to do in the meantime?" Her eyes were wet. "I mean, I'm going to get Stone to video the truce with me as quick as we can, but is there any danger of Harper escalating things? I'll need a bit of time to convince Stone, of course."

"Don't worry, I'll convince General Harper that Stone has already agreed to delay the election results, that a truce has already been worked out between you and him and Freeman, that the statement is imminent. Hopefully he won't risk starting to move the troops. Honestly though, I'm not sure how much contact Stone and Harper have, so you've got to act quickly. Can you get back to me with Stone's agreement within the hour?"

"Yes, an hour, Amos, I'll be back in touch." She nodded, flashing her eyes to the side again. "But please just take care of Harper, make sure he believes it's already been agreed to, we can't have him marching on DC. Innocent lives would be lost."

Amos smiled. "Thank you. I always knew I could trust you."

The connection went dead. As soon as the screen was black her smile dropped, and she looked across her desk at Admiral Kerns who had been listening to every word. Annie had betrayed her family again. She once again tried to tell herself it was for the greater good. To put things right, but she heard the snake.

* * *

When Annie was eight, she had made friends with a white rabbit with gentle pink eyes. Annie and her dad were still best friends then. Annie had been coaxing the white rabbit out of the woods for weeks, hoping to surprise her dad with their new pet.

Every day after school, Annie would race home to show the rabbit that it could trust her to take celery sticks from her hand, and each day the rabbit would hop to her a bit quicker. Annie had already written a *Squirrel Constitution* to protect the animals living near their mobile home park by that time, and knew she was a friend of all God's gentle creatures just like the youth pastor told them in Sunday school. She knew she would never hurt another living soul as long as she lived.

Annie was sure her father would love the rabbit as much as she did. It was after almost an entire autumn of her kindness that the rabbit started lopping out of the woods when it heard Annie walking in the tall grass. It would hop quickly to her and let her rub its velvet ears and chomp celery as its long whiskers tickled her fingers.

One afternoon she'd been petting it in the low October sunlight when her father suddenly appeared behind her. Ray Daniels snatched the rabbit up by the scruff of its neck. Annie didn't know that Ray Daniels had not only recently been laid off from his job for no fault of his own, but was also terrified his wife was cheating on him, and because of his ongoing PTSD from doing his best to serve his country Annie's father now felt like everything was coming unspooled inside, like he no longer knew what to believe in. Although he loved his family, he didn't even know where their next meal was going to come from, and the rabbit could be cooked and eaten for at least one meal. Honestly, it seemed better to Ray for him to direct the rage brewing inside him toward a rodent rather than a member of his family. He was still trying hard then, desperately, frighteningly hard to be the best man he could be.

"No, daddy!" Annie would always remember the horrible high-pitch shrieks as her rabbit thrashed and kicked, his pink eyes ripped wide in fear and betrayal. *"You'll hurt him!"* Annie instinctively leapt for her dad's arm, thinking it was all some misunderstanding that her loving dad would scare her pet, handle him so roughly.

But Annie's dad was too tall and too fast, and Annie could not reach the horrified bunny no matter how high she jumped. Ray snapped the rabbit's neck with one ferocious spin of its furry white body as he gripped its long velvety ears. *"Sorry, Annabel, but we've got to eat too."*

The rabbit hung there dead, her love turned to death with no warning. Her faith in the world being a loving place snapped like its tiny bones. That was the day something changed in Annie toward her father, a brand new realization that even those you most trusted could at any time betray you, that anything could happen and that good things might not last. Tears began to pour from her eyes.

"Now, now," Ray said tenderly, too confused in his own mind to understand how his actions were affecting her, just thinking that in the big scheme of things it was a freaking rabbit and they would eat part of it, tossing the inedible parts to his pet snake. *"It's just life, little girl."* Her dad smiled as he held the dead bunny by the ears. *"Don't worry, Annie, he's in rabbit heaven now."*

Later that night, as her parents fought of things she didn't understand, tear-streaked Annie slinked out into the yard to be alone. She tried to remind herself that her father had always been good to her and the hate she felt toward him must be misplaced. Tried to believe in rabbit heaven and that all things worked out for the best.

That was when she found the bunny's white head in the mouth of that damned black snake her father kept in a box behind the shed. He'd kept it there for weeks, and that night she watched as the black snake coldly, soullessly twisted over the once warm fur of her friend. Annie watched in renewed horror as black death swallowed those trusting pink eyes Annie had loved, so beautiful and alive just hours ago.

It was rage that finally dried Annie's tears, and before she realized it she had a rusty hoe from the shed, bashing and slicing her father's evil snake to writhing, bloody chunks. In that moment, Annie decided what the world really was: broken. A world where trust was not real, and you had to be smarter, angrier, colder to have any chance of protecting what you loved, of creating something better than this flawed reality. Nothing was watching out for them. Only she, and she alone, could save the world.

One timeline had shut and another opened.

She snapped out of her fury within minutes of slicing the snake apart and was horrified at what she had done. Flooded with guilt and confusion, she took the snake parts and flung them far out in the woods so that her father would never find them, then vowed to never physically hurt another creature as long as she lived. But she also vowed to find the people guilty for this broken world, and beat them.

She started addressing her father as "Ray" instead of "daddy" the very next day, and things continued tumbling forward through time in a never-ending cascade of cause and effect.

*(San Francisco, CA and Washington D.C: Sunday, 4:18 p.m.
PST / 7:18 p.m. EST)*

Annie noticed Admiral Kerns had a slightly protruding forehead, like a gorilla, red pimples on the pale skin. Kerns had her navy cap clutched tightly to her side and her dark hair wedged in a tight bun, and had been listening intently to every word Amos said.

"Madam President," Kerns now stated, "you've heard what the traitor disclosed about Harper. The clock is ticking." Ever since she had arrived, Kerns had not sat, bent at the waist, or even let lose a sigh, only offered suggestions of attack, and observed Annie's every movement like an intense German Shepherd awaiting the order to rip someone's throat out.

Both Henry and Howe were in the room as well, sitting in the two smaller office chairs Annie had set up on the opposite side of her desk. Outside the closed office door, Annie knew there was already a staff of about a dozen navy intelligence personnel the admiral wanted to bring in to set up a mobile command center, like a remote Situation Room. Annie was reluctantly the acting commander-in-chief, and had just set her little brother up in a way that would most likely crush his entire life.

For the greater good.

"Fuck." Annie collapsed back in her chair and put a palm to her forehead. At least maybe there was a way she could make sure he lived. Obviously something would have to be done, decisions made, but it was all happening so quick. The thought of betraying her brother again made her insides twist, and she clutched her stomach with shaky arms. She hadn't wanted to win this way. *Hissss.* The snakes slithered through her mind. *Hissss.* Too many things, too much information. Too many potentialities and she would not, could not, afford to fuck up now. They were the good guys, and they had to win. But she couldn't order violence against anyone if there was any other possible way, and she just would not order an attack against her own brother.

"There's possibly a contingency plan, madam," Howe offered. "*Operation Long Knives.* I could modify it."

Kerns' already flat, beastly face soured a bit more at Howe's input. The hard woman said, "If you don't make a decision, Madam Pres—"

"Don't call me that, Admiral," Annie snapped. "For God's sake we have a president, and it's not me. I'm only acting while he can't." Annie stood, began pacing back and forth behind her desk, suddenly realizing part of the reasons presidents had desks in the Oval Office was to give them something to hide behind. "This is all happening too fast, much too fast. We aren't attacking my little brother. I'm just not."

"Ms. Daniels," Kerns said, "I understand this is a difficult situation for you, finding out that Major Daniels is a terrorist, but we still must counterassault or risk—"

"Terrorist? You say that like its fact."

"He has taken the White House by force, Ms. Daniels. I believe that's the definition of a—"

"He is a good man, Admiral."

Kerns' face was hard as concrete, and Annie was quickly starting to hate her. "Regardless of your personal confusion regarding Major Daniels' intent, the facts are that he has just confirmed General Mace Harper is actively preparing to seize Washington, DC, and install a de facto government of his choosing. This is a military coup. You MUST act to put it down, or you will be betraying your country. Those are the facts."

Hissss.

"I'm not going to overreact on this, Admiral. I'm not killing my brother." Annie walked toward the side table with the liquor bottles and glasses thinking Jim Beam would have do until she could sneak another pill. She had already taken too many in front of people, been too reckless.

"There's still the option of keeping your word," Henry stated. "Of doing what you agreed to with both the president, and now Amos, by reaching out to Stone. Or you could let the *Congressional Committee* know about General Harper maybe, rally everyone to stop him. For once you could just trust in other people, Annie, have faith in something bigger than—"

"There are Republicans on the committee, Corwich." Annie didn't understand what was going on with Henry. Now, of all times, she didn't need her oldest advisor undermining her and figuring out ways to lose. "We're the good guys, not them."

"Are we?" Henry snarled.

"And that still does nothing definitive to actively stop General Harper, Mr. Corwich," Kerns added. The Admiral took a slightly larger breath though, and looked back to Annie as Annie used a trembling hand to drop ice into a glass. "Delay will only embolden the rogue general, madam. Unlike civilian decisions, there is no "everybody wins" scenario in war. This is completely a zero-sum game and if you are not actively working to destroy the enemy, the enemy uses that time to destroy you." Kern's emotions seemed calm, but her goddamn gorilla eyes still burrowed into Annie. "I recommend you give me authority for surgical strikes on Harper's radicalized troops at MacDill, Ms. Daniels, and to order the SEAL counterterrorism liberation of the White House. Just give me the go, I'll do the rest."

"Fuck." Annie snatched up the bottle of Jim Beam to slosh two fingers worth into a glass. "I will not order Americans to die!"

"Do President Fuentes and Vice President Freeman deserve to die, madam?" Kerns took a step toward Annie, her boots thudding the floor. "Once you give the order there will still be forty-five minutes of prep before I can get birds scrambled from Pensacola toward Tampa and the SEAL team wheels up to the White House. We can't afford further delays. Give me the go."

Annie glanced between Howe and Henry. "I can't do it, Admiral. I was arguing for the president to move troops earlier but that was as peacekeepers, not an assault where people will get hurt." Annie had somehow always assumed a smart person could always find a way, but this had no good options. "I will not condemn my brother to death." Annie downed the bourbon in one gulp. "I just won't."

"*Long Knives*," Howe offered again, her eyes down to the notepad in her lap as if she were somewhat embarrassed by the idea. "*Long Knives* could be modified to target the most probable members of a Republican coup."

"Using *Long Knives* to round up Republicans?" Annie asked. "How?"

"I adjust the parameters *Uncle's Eyes* searches the master files with. It can analyze all the data in everyone's emails, texts and phone calls to see who would be most likely be a staunch Republican, and most dangerous, then you sign the Executive Order. We can round them up en masse, peacefully detain all deemed 'unfriendlies' across the country in one fell swoop. Maybe make Harper think twice about further action."

"Republicans leaders..." Annie mumbled. "In that way at least no one would get hurt."

"Congressmen and Senators," Henry scoffed incredulously. "Military officers, federal workers and community leaders rounded up only for being Republican? You'd start a second civil war."

"Or prevent one," Howe countered. "It would only be for twenty-four hours, most likely. No harm would come to them."

"We can't leave the president and vice president in danger, Henry." Annie poured herself more bourbon. "We just couldn't let any press find out we were doing it." Annie dropped back on the edge of her desk, glass in hand,. "I can't let Stone and Harper steal this election. They are the enemy of the country, not us."

"Annie," Henry now implored, his cheeks and forehead were so red it looked like he might pass out or cry. "Please don't do this. I'm warning you, this will be a terrible mis—"

"What's the alternative, Corwich," Annie barked, but added, "we're not issuing *Long Knives*... yet." Annie turned from Henry's judging eyes, her mind lingering on Amos. It was hard to admit after all that had happened between them that, besides Harmony, Amos was still the purest, most sincere love Annie had ever felt. Her heart cramped with regret at the situation. She knew she had made some bad decisions in the past, but everything she'd worked for, the fate of the country itself, depended on what she did next. She should not let her personal feelings cloud her judgment. Only, what was the right call? And Harmony, her poor, sick baby. She hadn't even had time to check on her in all this madness, see if she had made it Denver okay to see her friends.

"Find Stone." Annie pointed at the cell phone Henry held in his hand, determined to find a way to end this well, and quickly. "Text him, email him, call Buddy Dukes if you have to. Hell, get on a plane and go knock on doors, Henry, just find him."

"To negotiate a mutual statement with him?" Henry asked hopefully, his hands fumbling with his coat collar. "An agreement to let the *Congressional Committee* decide things?"

"No, of course not," Annie snapped. "What if Stone's in with Harper? And if he's not aware of the coup, he's still not going to agree to a truce after we released that audio, I've already burned any reconciliation bridge with him." Annie shook her head. "No, we've got to go all-in on that play, threaten him again, tell him if he doesn't concede immediately we will have him arrested as part of a plot to overthrow the government. Tell him the FBI is already notified and we're just giving him the option to do the right thing."

"Madam, the clock is ticking," Kerns growled with eyes that said Annie was making rookie mistakes. "The surest way to resolve this is strikes on the two terrorist locations, not with diplomacy, or tricks."

"But I am acting president." Annie glared at the different species of woman in the eye, and used every internal tactic she could think of to keep her voice as steady as possible, sound like she actually felt confident. "I'm going to try for an hour, two at most, to end this with no one getting hurt."

Admiral Kern's broad face wrinkled in apparent disgust at the weak woman before her.

"However, Admiral, I do authorize you to begin preparations. Move forward with preparing for the airstrike on Mac-Dill and the SEALS to liberate the White House so that, if and when facts dictate I must give you the go, we are not forty-five minutes out from both strikes, but under five."

Admiral Kerns straightened as Annie continued.

"Hopefully, we do not ever need to use that option, as Henry will try to pressure Stone to concede." Annie downed a slug of bourbon. "Beatrice, I'll want you to send FBI agents to MacDill, maybe under the guise of questioning Harper about some classified intelligence or something, I don't know, anything to slow him down. If we can take out one of the two prongs, either Stone or Harper, then the coup can't work and Amos will then see that he won't have any reason to hold the president any longer." Annie glanced around the room. "Everyone understand? This is our Plan A for the next sixty minutes. Got it?"

Kerns and Howe both nodded, Kerns somewhat reluctantly. Henry just glared.

* * *

News Ticker: *Joint Congressional Committee on Election*

Oversight expected to make announcement of bipartisan recommendations before 11 p.m.

* * *

Waiting for the military transport plane she'd negotiated a ride on from New Orleans back to MacDill AFB in Tampa, Shay tried to convince herself things would get back to normal soon. Downtown New Orleans was quickly turning into a war zone, and commercial flights were rumored of soon being halted. All streams of information online were going nuts with false stories from the *Reboot.org* data breach, and Shay needed the truth. She was hoping Amos would call her back, but knew he could be working in one of the secure zones on MacDill and not able to get her message yet.

She searched through the video footage from Little Gumbo's restaurant on her laptop. The recording had actually been from a teenager across the street who had propped a pair of his video glasses up on the windowsill as part of a school project. The police hadn't found him, but Shay had with a quick stop at the restaurant. The teenager freely offered to her that he had an unedited week-long span of video that happened to point right across the street at the restaurant's entrance.

As she fast-forwarded the video, all the expected random people over the last seven days hurried down the New Orleans sidewalk. Clunky, Charlie Chaplain-like movements. Fat tourists in T-shirts and flip-flops, shirtless kids trying to look tough with low-hanging pants, delivery people hustling, bead-wearing college kids stumbling. Daylight gave way to streetlamps, streetlamps gave way to daylight, again and again.

As the flickering images lulled into a pattern, Shay's mind wandered back to that core question she would never be able to unravel. *Republicans and Democrats.* What was really causing all the hate when most of the country identifying with one of the two parties didn't even understand or care about what the majority of the political positions actually were? *Big government versus small? Freedom versus responsibility? I'm born this way versus I choose? Skin color, tax brackets, or income inequality? Privacy versus safety? God or science, or just liking the color blue or red more?*

She saw him easy enough. An albino man, extremely pale skin and short white hair, standing in a suit beneath a lamppost. It was late Friday evening according to the video timestamp. He talked into a cell phone then walked into the restaurant. Something about him seemed out of place, very out of place for that neighborhood. Like most cameras these days, the high definition video footage was easy enough to zoom in, and it only took a couple of minutes with their company's facial recognition software to match the man's unique features to an identity. Upon finding the match, so much adrenaline started to pump through Shay's body that her hands trembled as she typed the email to Amos.

"*Was at Gatreaux's restaurant night before shooting*, her email read. Shay attached both the still photo showing the albino man standing before the restaurant, as well as another photo of obviously the same man as part of Vice President Freeman's Secret Service detail. "*Boarding flight to MacDill now. Please call me as soon as you can.* She stopped for a minute, breathed deeply, and then thought about how short life was, how few chances people ever really got, and how everything was actually a leap of faith. She added, "*Love, Shay.*"

* * *

The problems with Democracy, Vice President Marcus Freeman thought as he casually circled closer to Agent Simms, *are the idiots*. Marcus Freeman wasn't actually a liberal. Marcus Freeman wasn't a conservative. Hell, Marcus Freeman wasn't even gay, but had started sleeping with men just to get millennials cheering for him as an underdog. Marcus Freeman was for Marcus Freeman, and had long ago divorced himself from any idea of truth in order to give himself absolute permission to do or say anything in order to fulfill his goals. That was true freedom, the absolute power to do anything. *Exactly why the founding fathers created the Electoral College, because they knew the average American was too dumb to have their vote count. Someone has to rule them.*

The Vice President still paced with the rag held to his face, knowing everyone in the Oval Office had grown relaxed with the slight freedom of movement he and the president had been allowed, trying to casually move toward his secret operative. The president was sitting on one sofa, head back and eyes closed, as if he were trying to find a momentary calm. The major was holed up in the Annex, and the black officer in charge was perfectly distracted, arguing in hushed tones near the Rose Garden door with the Green Beret that looked like a bird. *Dumb brutes*, Freeman thought.

Now that Agent Simms was reviving, if the vice president kept his voice down maybe he could get to the bottom of what went wrong with his plan to subvert *1776* and tip the election to him. Agent Simms met the vice president's gaze with a quiet smirk and a twinkle in his pink eyes, a trickle of blood seeping over his alabaster pale face from the gash in his forehead.

What the fuck are you smiling at, you weirdo? Freeman thought. *You've fucked everything up.*

Freeman scooped up one of the small pillows off the sofa,

careful not to cause the president to open his eyes, then moved toward the desk, thinking he could still maneuver this all to his advantage, if he could just figure out the point things had started to go off the rails. *They actually expected me to wait in the wings for another eight years? The technological power is here, so someone will have to control it. Fuck them and their 1776 sensible bargain. I'll be damned if this doesn't get back on track.*

Freeman casually glanced around the room to make sure no one was paying attention, then knelt next to the bleeding albino agent. Agent Simms hands were zipped tied behind his back and he was on the floor propped up against the desk, as yet still without his mouth duct tapped.

"What the hell is happening?" Freeman growled. "Why are these men here? And what happened to our elector?" The vice president pulled the albino's bleeding head off the side of the desk, and wedged the pillow behind it, his plan to look like he was only mercifully tending a wound if anyone noticed him. "What about the plan?"

The plan had been to strategically place several electors around the country, in various swing states that the vice president could then coerce however was necessary, through bribes or threats, into switching their votes as needed to win in the final hours. Agent Simms, his principle Secret Service Agent for the past eight years, was the only one he'd trusted with the truth, the one who'd been his boots on the ground.

Marcus Freeman had long seen the ability coming for someone to achieve total power over the country, maybe even the world, so he had decided it had better be him. Hijacking the Democratic party was the means. Freeman had once felt sorry—actually disdain, for all those like Henry Corwich, who apparently really was born the way he was, and Annie

Daniels, who actually believed in all the ridiculous utopian ideas of equality she droned on and on about—as he publicly mimicked their love-saturated phrases and ideals. The problem with Annie Daniels was that she never wanted to go far enough, was always a weak-willed woman ready to give in to peace when only the sword would do. That was why he'd never entrusted her with the truth of his plan. Democracy had always only been an experiment in history anyway, even Plato knowing that the ideal government was a philosopher king.

And once he was in office, Freeman would become that king, for the good of the country. The first step would be to use Daniels' *Cyber-Care* chip, if he could get it passed, to slowly wean the average America off free speech and thought. With the preexisting *Uncle's Eyes* data it would be the easiest way to herd and track the superficial American sheep, cull the ones who were outspoken against the government or any ideals he deemed inappropriate at that time. After seeing the *Long Knives* protocol enacted he realized it would even be possible without the chip as long as the appropriate marketing was behind him, which through the fraudulent media and stupidly mislead social media systems, it would be. Once free speech and thought were curtailed, outlawing guns would be a walk in the park, getting neighbor to turn in neighbor. Then he could move on to consolidating all the power, slowly blackmailing all opposition power into loyalty to him alone, no stupid right or left ideals, just jailing or executing anyone as traitors to America who went against him. Freeman occasionally laughed at all the right-wing lunatics, whose rantings made his plans even easier to implement once all of society had written them off as lunatics. Once the main opposition was strategically castrated by any means that worked, he would get the Constitution changed to eliminate any restriction on presidential terms so he could stay in power indefinitely. As long as he kept a tight lip on what was allowed to be said on social media and gave the masses just enough entertainment and food to keep them from the point of complete desperation, the pharmaceuticals he pumped into the water supplies would take care of the rest. Within a generation there would not be anyone left who remembered when he wasn't essentially king, or at least no one who would have the courage to speak about it. And with the advances in technology and healthcare, he was sure it would soon be possible that he could stay alive indefinitely with the resources he would have. He would make sure America stayed strong, but just on his terms. All of it, however, every part of the beautiful, perfect world that could be, must first put things back on track by finding out why in the fuck it was coming undone.

"The world is inherently unpredictable," Agent Simms said with a tired grin.

"Did you get your brains knocked in?" The vice president scowled. "I need answers." He used the rag for his nose to begin softly dabbing at the blood streaming down Simms' face. "What happened to the elector, Gatreaux."

"It's America." The albino shrugged and chuckled. "Black men get shot by the police all the time."

You think this is funny? The vice president stopped dabbing Simm's head wound, his face hardening into wrath at the belligerent fucker's cavalier attitude to his entire life's work crumbling. "Are you working for someone else? Some other motive?"

The albino only rolled his eyes and giggled.

"Who? Why?" Freeman gasped in shock as a pulse of fresh

blood pumped from the gash at the edge of the man's white hairline. "I trusted you."

"Trust?" The albino grinned wider. "Karma is all we can trust."

"Are you fucking brain damaged?" The vice president couldn't stand looking at the stupid smirk on the albino's face any longer, and had no idea what he was babbling about, but someone had gotten to him, was purposely screwing up his plans.

"Fuck you." Freeman jabbed his thumbnail into the wound in the untrustworthy albino agent's head.

The agent's scream brought Jacari Jones running. "Mr. Vice President," Jones said. "Control yourself, sir." Jones yoked his arms beneath the vice president's and gently pulled him up and away from the Secret Service Agent. "Stork. This one's awake now, get some duct tape on him."

"We won't dissolve the Union, and you shan't"
—Abraham Lincoln

(San Francisco, CA and Washington D.C: Sunday, 5:16 p.m.
PST / 8:16 p.m. EST)

While the rest of the country became increasingly unhinged, Jacari paced the Oval Office with his own concerns, weapon held tight. As the outside world had lost its light Jacari felt more and more dark inside. The whole situation seemed off, and he hoped Allah was watching out for them. He trusted Amos to the end of the earth, trusted him with his life, but wondered if they were finally in over their heads. Amos had gone into the Presidential Annex and shut the door, so Jacari was left overseeing the team.

It was silent, the phones having suddenly stopped ringing. So quiet that Jacari noticed the Oval Office floor creaked a bit with his footsteps between the sofas. The sturdy president sat in his chair behind the desk, glowering but currently not arguing, at least. Amos had insisted the president and vice president remain unrestrained as long as they complied with his requests, and now that Jacari had stopped the vice president's weird freak-out on his own Secret Service Agent, the vice president had resumed his tight pacing. Marcus Freeman was off in the farthest portion of the room next to the glass door to the Rose Garden, still clutching the bloody rag in his hand but now with the bleeding of his broken nose mostly stopped. A purple bloodstain was crusted on his upper lip, and the nose itself was bruised blue and starting to swell.

Four others on the team knelt in positions by some of the windows and doors, fingers on weapons. They peered out slits in the curtains, around corners, eyes and ears constantly on a swivel for any incoming noise. The three Secret Service agents were still sitting on the far side of the floor, their hands zip tied behind their backs and tape over their mouths, except for the newly resuscitated albino guy. Stork held torn duct tape in his fingers, but hadn't yet put it over the albino guy's mouth for some reason, hunched down next to him probably trying to get tactical information regarding their counterterrorism protocols. Every time Jacari saw Stork though, he thought back to the gym and wondered if his and Amos' shit was cool now, or if there was yet another explosion waiting to happen.

For a while, phones had been ringing crazily through the West Wing; on the president's desk, and farther down the hall in some of the offices they didn't have control of. No one answered them, as the entire building had probably been evacuated. Those endless incoming calls were but one of the many reasons why Jacari, and Amos too, both knew there was no way this would fly under the radar long, even if the president had told the Secret Service to stand down and the Press Secretary had tried to cloak events to the outside world. This was the epicenter of world democracy, and even if the rest of the country were going crazy people noticed when the White House wasn't participating. Jacari had cursed the phones as they continued to ring and ring and ring, but now that they had suddenly stopped he felt even worse.

Things were too quiet. Something would have to happen soon, a counterassault of some kind. As night had fallen over the Rose Garden, Jacari peered around the drawn gold curtains a couple times and caught the quick streaks of pinprick light from black-clad agents sprinting here and there, constantly repositioning and adding additional troops. Jacari was reminded of that last scene in the old *Butch Cassidy and the Sundance Kid* movie, where Paul Newman and Robert Redford were shot-up and hemmed in to a tiny cantina by the entire Bolivian Army. The two gunslingers had cracked jokes and remained defiant and courageous to the end, only they didn't realize there were hundreds of soldiers outside, waiting to blast them down as they tried to escape. Bravery in the face of doomed odds. Jacari had always loved that movie, but now realized he couldn't think of a damn joke to save his life. Their team was going to die. Or, if they were lucky, just get stripped of rank and spend the rest of their lives in Leavenworth. *Why didn't I become a realtor?*

Earlier, Amos had called Jacari and Stork into the Annex to brief them on General Harper's objective. Amos had told Jacari to reestablish contact with Houzma at MacDill, to tell him to prep the BRAHMASTRA in case a Plan B was needed. Jacari's jaw had almost hit the floor. "Major, we don't know BRAHMASTRA will work, and even if it does… Amos, we don't want it to work, not on American soil."

Amos had looked back at him and said, "Let's hope it stays a Plan B."

Come on, Amos, Jacari thought again as his eyes now drifted up to the high white ceiling above. *Come up with that Plan A.*

Jacari thought he could hear creaking from the ceiling.

They were surely just above them. He tried to breathe easy, in and out through his nose, and gripped his weapon a little harder for reassurance. In most ops they had time to get schematics, to figure out what the opposing force would most likely do and rehearse the different possible scenarios of engagement. With this though, hell, they knew no specifics at all. They knew the Oval Office windows were bulletproof, but not what was above or below them, or even what the layout of the rest of the West Wing was. The Secret Service and about a dozen other armed agencies could already be amassing dozens, hundreds, of people to breach them from four or five different access points. There was no way to know who all was out there, and there was no way to know what their move was going to be.

Come, on, Amos, Jacari prayed. *Make it good, brother, make it good.* He looked over, noticed Stork was still talking with the damn albino agent. Hadn't yet put the tape over his mouth.

* * *

The Governor of Louisiana issued the following statement on social media and most major news channels: *As of 10:00 p.m., Louisiana National Guard is instructed to use live rounds on any citizens within Baton Rouge and New Orleans who are violating curfew. The governor would also like to state, in definitive terms, the online documents from Reboot.org claiming he is part of a child pornography ring are utterly and completely fabricated. The governor urges everyone to calm, and to stay indoors.*

* * *

Amos had gone into the Presidential Annex for a few minutes to clear his foggy mind, to slow down and think. He potentially held the fate of the election in his hands, and he didn't know who or what to believe in. He had seen no concrete proof, and arguments were battling back in forth in his mind. He just wanted the truth, a world that made sense. That was all he'd ever wanted.

Amos remembered he had his cell phone on him and pulled it out of his jacket. He pressed the button so that it would power up, but then replaced it in his pocket, eyes going to the monitor on the desk. In the artificial blue darkness of the small room, door closed and blinds drawn, he watched the monitor playing breaking news in front of the White House fence outside.

A crowd of at least a dozen angry red shirts and a dozen yelling blue shirts were separated by several riot-gear wearing police. The reporter reiterated they didn't know the facts of what was happening, but it appeared from another camera angle that DC Metro Police seemed to be pushing the massive, mostly Republican, March on Washington crowd back down the street some. Water cannons were being used and the camera showed dozens of uniformed police officers, many cop cars and a few SWAT assault vehicles. The reporter mentioned that there had been online reports of some sort of break-in at the White House, but this had been unconfirmed and the movements by the DC police were most likely because of Homeland Security raising the terror threat level, he said. Probably a radical Islamic threat, the reporter offered. Whatever the reason, the protestors did not like it, and several scuffles with the police had already broken out, as well as between different factions of conservatives and liberals.

Over the past hour Amos had noticed a rapidly increasing confusion to the news. Not only did there seem to be legitimately chaotic events cropping up in multiple locations across the country, but there also seemed to be increasingly false reports happening on social media and online news outlets, confusing traditional media as well as some law enforcement and rescue agencies as to what was legitimately happening. There had supposedly been some massive data dump of personal information, but he didn't know by who or what. It could just be a result of tensions across the country becoming a collective hysteria feeding on itself like a forest fire, or it could have been some sort of strategic disinformation campaign by an outside enemy. Maybe Russian or China? It was a common PSYOPs strategy in Special Forces—if you could get the enemy so confused as to what was going on within their own ranks and communication, it was much easier to invade.

He clicked off the monitor, and the tiny room dropped into pitch-black. Liars and confusion seemed all around him. Who was the guilty party regarding the elector's death? Amos wasn't even sure about some of his own team now. He trusted Jacari with his life, but could he fully trust Stork? Stork corroborated Harper's stance on things, but even in the best case, Stork had already admitted he'd been working on the their team with an ulterior motive for years. Was anyone else here working a different angle?

Liars. Damned liars everywhere. He leaned his head forward and rested it against his fist, hoping his sister would be the Annie of old, the one he could trust like when they were kids. He touched the crucifix. Not knowing what else to do, Amos stood from the chair then and kneeled down onto his knees to pray. He didn't know if God would hear him or help, or even if he was sure there was a God or not, but he had to try. He pulled the crucifix free from beneath his body armor and covered it with both hands next to his heart, closed his eyes and bowed his head.

"Lord, I need your assistance," Amos whispered. "I know I have doubted at times, not believed like I should, but please Lord, guide me, and my sister." Amos traced his fingers around the cool metal edges of the crucifix, trying to remember when his belief in God had come as natural to him as knowing the sun would rise each morning, tried to fully let down his guard, stop doubting and speak from his heart. "I'm not sure who to trust, who to believe in, so am putting my faith in you... through Annie." Amos paused. "I just want a good end to all of this whereby no one gets hurt and we all get to go home." Amos eyes were squeezed tight, and in the deep blackness he started feeling himself close to God, his faith renewing as if he could sense a presence listening. "Please help Annie to do the right thing, the truth to be revealed and just people succeed."

"But wouldn't a JUST God," the vice president remarked, "want us all to succeed?"

Amos leapt to his feet, his knife ripped off his thigh and to the vice president's throat. The vice president had apparently opened the Annex door while Amos' eyes had been shut, listened to Amos' most private words, and Amos lunged, crushing the blade to Freeman's skinny throat with fire burning in his eyes, violated rage scorching through his blood.

"I'll kill you," Amos growled, his mind suddenly back in the Korpesh Valley, flashing with clear images of the Afghani captors. "I'll fucking kill you all!" Marcus Freeman, petrified, leaned his broken-nose face backward as Amos pressed the knife blade deeper against the vice president's soft neck. *Can't*

I just talk to God, can't I just try to believe? Amos panted, fuming with gritted teeth and wild eyes as a wrath flooded through his body like a burst dam and he wanted to rip and tear and burn the entire corrupt world asunder. *Fuck it, fuck it all.* Lies were everywhere in this modern world, because everyone just accepted it. Amos' jaw ground, the blade ready to slice flesh and vein of the vice president's throat with just a twist of his wrist. *Wipe evil from the earth.*

"Major," the vice president whispered once his head could go back no more. "A loving God, if He exists, wouldn't want violence against ANY of his children, would He?"

Stop. It's the vice president, you maniac, part of Amos' traumatized brain screamed, *STOP!*

"Fuck," Amos pushed himself off the vice president and stumbled into the small desk. Amos thrust a hand to his hurting head, staggering. "You, you…" Vicious thoughts still raged through his hazy mind, flashing images from Afghanistan and an overwhelming rage at everything insincere in this world. "You just almost got yourself killed, sir. You shouldn't sneak up on people." Amos thumped into a seat on the small desk edge, his eyes wide, pupils dilated from the concussion.

"And with all due respect, Major." Freeman touched two fingers to the red scratch Amos' knife had left across his Adam's apple. "You probably shouldn't be holding people hostage." The vice president took another step into the Annex, closed the door. He was already completely composed again as if nothing had happened, a cool smile quickly returning. "You'll have to forgive me if I don't respect your 'privacy'… in the office you stole from us."

"Not stole, sir." Amos pushed himself into a stand, trying to concentrate. "Just trying to do what's right."

"I assure you I have made no efforts to illegally influence this election, Major." The vice president was calm. "And I can certainly attest to seeing no such indications from the president or Senator Daniels." The vice president held the major's gaze, and Amos tried to see truth or lies in his eyes. "I'm not sure where you are getting your information from, but it seems like you're being misled. If your concern really is justice?"

"I have faith in God that the truth will win out, sir, if I do the right thing."

"Just trying to follow God's will, huh?" Freeman tapped a finger against the air like he was remembering something. "Just trying to fight evil? I believe that's an ISIS refrain as well… when they're beheading people."

"I'm not beheading anyone." Amos' temples throbbed, his mind confused. "But evil would win if this election is stolen."

"And evil, Major, let me guess, it looks like me?"

"Sir?"

"A queer, Major. A hedonist by Biblical standards. A pervert." The vice president crossed his arms over his tie with a grin.

"No, sir, I'm fighting for truth, not a side."

"Right. Right," Freeman chuckled. "You know what your God did to punish me when I embraced who I truly was, Major? Nothing. Absolutely nothing. Because He doesn't exist, Major, that's truth." Freeman leaned back against the door like they were two old friends catching up. "No avenging angle came down from heaven to smite me for being gay, because genetics determined me, no God."

"I try not to judge, sir. Everyone has freewill, I'm just trying—"

"Aha." The vice president raised a forefinger. "But maybe

that is where the root of your delusion starts, the genesis of all the poor, tragic decisions that have haunted you through your life to this very precarious moment, Major—this moment which might doom yourself and your country to chaos."

"My delusion?"

"God and freewill, the delusions at the heart of all your poor choices. If He really existed then why would He let you make these poor choices, let the love of your life betray you?" The vice president shook his head sadly as if he were speaking to a confused child. "How would a real God have kept you from ever getting the love of a good family, and let your friend and your father, your responsibilities, die? Only answer: He doesn't exist."

Amos recoiled, the vice president's words hitting him like a fist to the heart. It registered with Amos that the vice president had obviously spoken to Annie about his most private and personal information, but it didn't alter its impact. His life was a shambles, and he was in an awful position. It was probable that Harper was insane, this whole situation was insane, and everything in his life had gone wrong. No love. No real family. Friends dead. Now possibly treason. What if God did not exist? What if there really was nothing listening to his prayers? What if Annie had always been right, and everything he had tried to believe was just a lie? *What if God is a lie?*

The vice president's voice was stern, certain. "Science has proven that we are all genetically programmed at birth, Major. So if we are, how could we possibly have freewill to CHOOSE good over evil? What would the point of God be? We are only who we are, Major, no choice in the matter at all, like any animal on this planet. Don't damn yourself and America over false ideas, embrace reality."

Amos was so tired. Tired of fighting to be strong, to be perfect, fighting to believe in greater things, and it never working. He just wanted for things to be easy for once, to be simple. To have a truth he could understand. *God is a lie,* he finally let himself think as real.

"You are being tricked into leading a military coup against the government, Amos, but I can correct this whole situation for you." The vice president leaned even closer. "Stop struggling to be a brave man, Amos. Stop trying to make the world live up to some standard it never will and that it doesn't even want. Stop fighting to overcome those parts of you that you have been told are wrong. As soon as I am president, I will get you completely pardoned, and whatever else you need so you can start over, you have my word." The vice-president put a soft hand on Amos' shoulder, looked into his eyes. "Stop being afraid to admit that God doesn't exist, Amos. Love yourself and put your faith in something real… in me. Lay down your weapon and this will all finally make sense."

There was something in the vice president's words that were such a relief. All Amos had wanted for years was to take a break, be allowed to be weak and scared and not be judged for it, to be materialistic and greedy and sinful and lazy as the next guy. To not try, for once. Down inside Amos the words *God isn't real, God isn't real* churned sadly in his chest, as the fingers around his knife began to loosen.

Buzz. Amos' hip began to vibrate. The phone in his pocket. He shook his fuzzy head and stepped to the side, the vice president's hand slipping from his shoulder as he pulled out his phone to see Shay's text coming through.

"Amos," the vice president continued, not knowing what he was seeing, "I'll get all the charges dropped and I'll make sure Harper takes all the blame. Just tell your men to stand down."

Amos looked at the photos on his phone, and his despair bled into anger. The first picture was of that albino Secret Service agent in front of Lawrence Gatreaux's restaurant. The next showed that same agent standing next to the vice president, obviously head of Freeman's Secret Service detail. There was also a picture of Annie shaking Deputy Lupe's hand. Amos now knew beyond a shadow of a doubt that the vice president must have been the one to have the elector shot, his sister's involvement the only question left.

Liars, fucking liars everywhere, Amos thought.

* * *

"I don't understand how everything depends on me taking this."

"Fear is a message, a calling for you to overcome," Mokeba said, but stopped smiling as he saw that Harmony was still very scared, maybe getting more so the longer she looked down at the yellow liquid. "It is always your choice, dear girl, you need not take it, but just remember fear is always the lie."

Harmony had just finished writing a quick message to Amos on her phone, but had yet to hit send. Mokeba had told her that in the ancient times people would give messages to their loved ones, unburden themselves with their last thoughts and wishes prior to journeying to the spirit world in case they did not come back. He had suggested writing something to her mother. Harmony had thought about it, but then imagined her mother too embroiled in the campaign to even be able to read it. She decided to write her Uncle Amos.

Uncle Amos, I hope we get to see each other soon, but I just wanted to let you know how much you inspire me. I know my mom can be difficult, and you and she don't see eye to eye on things, but if you can, please just remember what you told me that last Christmas we saw each other... about forgiveness. I've never forgotten what you said, 'God judges no man until the end of his days, so why would we ever think we should do it beforehand?' You're so wise and kind and brave, Uncle Amos. I hope to grow up to be just like you. Your loving niece, Harmony.

"And there's no coming back?" Harmony asked Mokeba for maybe the third time since she had hit send on the message. "I take this and my mind is gone for good, right?"

"Correct, but can we ever truly come back to anything, as all forever changes?" Mokeba smiled again softly. "The mind of the old Harmony will be gone forever. A new Harmony returning, most likely, from the spirit world."

"And people have really died from this stuff before?"

"Several times, my dear." Mokeba nodded somberly. "But that is still nothing to fear. It is all just a splinter of infinity which you are already fated to experience."

"Not really sure what that means." Harmony sighed as she looked down at the liquid in the gourd again. She thought how impending death didn't really make you more courageous, only more desperate to find love. "Well," Harmony said with a smile she didn't completely feel, "here's to what's next."

Harmony lifted the gourd up with both hands and drank.

Harmony Enters the Spirit World

(San Francisco, CA and Washington D.C: Sunday, 5:44 p.m. PST / 8:44 p.m. EST)

H*issss. Hissss.*
Annie was waiting for news, staring across her office desk to the bathroom door, knowing if she didn't get some Zennies soon something was going to snap inside her. At least a dozen people bustled between her and the relative sanctuary of a locked bathroom and a handful of pink pills. Henry and Howe were still there, but also several new suits she didn't know. Kerns barked orders to at least six uniformed military as they installed a mobile situation room. The noise was incessant, phones ringing, people chattering, the whir of drills as new television screens were attached to every spare section of her office wall, the old television continuing to blast ever-increasing horrors from around the country. Between the mass doxing and the increasing riots, the United States appeared to be on the verge of a meltdown.

Think, Annie, think. She crossed her arms to keep anyone from seeing them tremble, swiveling her chair to the angle that faced only her oak bookcase. There were probably another twenty people coming and going from the house, sporadically rushing into the office and shouting information, or sometimes accidental misinformation, at Annie or Kerns. *I just need some goddamn pills.*

One of the reports said international financial futures were plunging based on indication that the US presidential election would not be resolved tomorrow, and that there might be an armed standoff at the White House. There was possibly also an ISIS-inspired shooting in a Chicago neighborhood, a bomb scare at the Kansas State Capitol building, and a possible release of anthrax in Cleveland. Many local law enforcement agencies were apparently becoming overwhelmed with the ever-spreading urban rioting across the country, and a town in Delaware might have experienced a mass prison riot after all of the police in the city abandoned their posts for unspecified reasons. For good measure, Portland PD might have driven several armored vehicles through a crowd of Buddhist protestors in some unfathomable screw-up. Someone estimated the total number of dead Americans during the last six hours at over 1,000, with the numbers of injured in the tens of thousands nationwide, completely overwhelming hospitals and emergency services in many locations.

Because of a blatant public absence by the president over the past couple of hours, several governors were now declaring martial law and sending out their National Guards. The chaos and lack of direction was causing many normally calm citizens to disobey authorities and make runs on food, guns, ATMs, and even fight back against authority. There were also reports that *Reboot.org* was orchestrating "flash looting" in spots, whereby random teens got messages through social media to ransack a particular store at a particular time in such large numbers that no law enforcement could do anything to stop them. The only advantage to the overwhelming Biblical-sized flood of insanity was that no one knew whether to believe if there was some armed standoff actually going on at the White House or not.

Or maybe none of that was real at all.

Annie bit her nail, trying not look at anyone, afraid she might lose it. She'd been desperately hoping that they'd be able to either immobilize Harper with the FBI or get Stone to concede, but those two options seemed to be turning into nothing. Annie wasn't sure what to do, but she was considering more and more contacting the *Joint Congressional Committee*, who were locked away in a Denver hotel conference room, asking for their assistance in bringing order and calm back to the country. For that track though, she would need to throw herself on the mercy of whatever their decision was, even if they decided on massive recounts and a delay to the electoral vote. Of course, the other option could be issuing *Long Knives* and having a chunk of all those committee members temporarily locked up along with a good portion of Congress.

"Anything?" Annie barked at Henry, who was pacing next to her desk, his cell phone plastered to his ear.

"No one will put me through to Stone," Henry said. "Can't even get Buddy Dukes or any of his aides on the phone. Like they're purposely avoiding us."

Howe worked on the desktop computer and two cell phones. "Sentries at MacDill refused to let the FBI Agents through the gate, madam." Because Stone had been nonresponsive to all attempts at communication, Kerns and Howe had both taken it as a definite sign he was aware of, and condoning, the White House coup.

The pills are all I can count on. Annie stood, looked across her desk to the bathroom. A momentarily clear path from people. If she could just make it to the bathroom she could take some Zennies. She stepped around the side of her desk and, with an exhale, headed toward the relative sanctuary of the bathroom.

But goddamn Admiral Kerns stomped in front of her. "I need your go order, madam." With General Harper refusing to even let the FBI agents on the base, Kerns was barking more and more frequently in Annie's ear for permission to forcibly put down the threat. "The country is falling apart, madam, you must have the courage to act."

Annie ground her jaw tight. She looked away from the cinder block of a woman toward the bathroom door. *Can I not just go to the fucking bathroom for a minute?*

"Madam," Beatrice Howe now interrupted from behind. "The Admiral might be right. By trying to send the FBI, General Harper will have already been tipped off we're aware of him. It will only serve to hasten his movement of troops."

"Annie," Henry argued, "you shouldn't make things worse. You shouldn't escalate things further."

"I'm thinking," Annie said, while in reality she was doing anything but, she was panicking. "I'm carefully weighing all options." She stepped back, trying to subtly escape the proximity of the massive admiral before her, all the competing voices in her ears, and immediately bumped back up against her desk. *Hissss. Hissss.*

"The SEALs are repositioned to a staging area ten minutes out from the White House, madam. They're on the tarmac with rotors running. Jets are also on standby in Pensacola ready to strike MacDill. I can have the lid back on this situation in under forty minutes, if you just give the go order."

"Don't, Annie," Henry growled.

"It would," Howe agreed with Kerns, "be easier to tackle the domestic issues if we at least knew the coup was put down and the president safe. Once the president is free, him making a public statement will go a long way toward calming things. Stabilize power."

"Annie—"

"Jesus." Annie put both palms to her ears and spun away from the admiral toward her desk. She closed her eyes, but immediately the smoking corpse of her brother flashed across her mind. She wasn't a killer, wasn't one of them. She wasn't her father. She fought for life, not taking it. "Fuck!"

"This is the beginnings of a revolution," Kerns stated. "It is no time for weakness, madam." Annie felt one of the woman's beefy hands actually thump to her shoulder in an awkward gesture of connection. "We know Harper will take DC unless we stop him. Someone must die, you can only choose if it is innocent people or the terrorists."

"Jesus-fuck." Annie knocked the admiral's patronizing hand from her shoulder, then slammed both her palms on the desk. Her head hung, her long blonde hair falling to either side to cover what she knew must have been panic washing across her face. "Everyone shut the fuck up." The overstuffed room of people kept clamoring, things buzzing, whirring with multiple conversations. "PLEASE SHUT THE FUCK UP!"

Everyone stopped talking. Only the phones kept ringing and the television murmured as Annie straightened, breathed deeply, turned back toward the room. All eyes were on her. She took two steps to the window, peering through the shutters at the passing headlights of cars below on Gough Street and hoped, waited, for some sort of clarity to strike. An answer.

On the sidewalk, two young people laughed and walked

as if the country weren't unraveling. It relaxed Annie a bit, but also immediately reminded her that there were a lot of normal, sane, calm spots in the country which she could still completely fuck up if she made the wrong call. There truly could be a far-right conspiracy within the government or military to take control of the country, or it could just be one rogue general and Annie would be dumping gasoline on a flame if she went too far. One thing Kerns had correct though, any failure to act would surely be to a broader conspiracy's advantage, and whatever Annie did would only be exacerbating a catastrophe unless she went hard enough to win. There was no margin for error, and no looking back. She had to be quick, decisive, and most of all, right.

"Annie," Henry said, his hand over the microphone of his cell phone. "One of our people in Denver is saying the *Joint Congressional Committee* is nearing a decision. Looking at all of the information— the current vote totals, Louisiana, federal election laws, all facts from the Attorney General— the Committee is supposedly leaning toward advising the House just needs to go ahead and vote on who wins tonight."

And there it is, Annie thought. *The Republicans end up stealing it no matter what.*

"So here's what we're going to do." Annie hoped her voice was not shaking as she looked at Beatrice Howe, tried to fight nausea swelling inside her. "I see no way how we can risk leaving unknown members of a larger conspiracy still in operation to galvanize efforts against us. Miss Howe, I authorize you to initiate the *Long Knives* protocol and quarantine any and all government or military officials who the NSA matrix labels as potentially 'Republican sympathizers' in the FEMA camps. Even any on the *Joint Committee*, if they fit the bill."

"What are you doing?" Henry's face sank in what she could only describe as shock and disgust. "Don't do this, Annie, remember your promise."

"Certainly, Madam President," Howe answered. "The list is already generated; I can have the order issued across the country within nine minutes."

Kerns growled, "But the White House, madam? General Harper's troops at MacDill, they are mobilizing as we speak."

Annie's shoulder knocked against the admiral's wide arm as she marched toward the bathroom. "You have your orders, now execute them."

Hissss.

* * *

Since all of her friends knew how politically passionate she was, Rosa's phone kept vibrating with texts about the violent and shady shit Republicans were doing around the country. Rosa was so angry as she served food and drinks to Governor Stone she accidentally bit her tongue. Rosa snatched up Congressman Dukes' mustard-streaked plate and stomped toward the kitchen wishing that fat-ass Stone would get up and go to his damn rally, get out of her sight and hearing forever. She passed Milton, who grabbed his crotch and winked at her with a grin. By the time Rosa thumped through the swinging doors to the kitchen and dropped the dirty plate in the sink, she didn't know if she needed to cry or scream. She couldn't take anymore, not one more damn thing.

"Girl," one of the other waitresses exclaimed. She was leaning against the kitchen sink and looking down at her phone. "You never believe this girl, but it says online that the Republicans, they stormed the White House. Holding

President Fuentes hostage and shit. They're even having to arrest a bunch of them in Washington."

And that was it. Rosa looked down in the kitchen sink and grabbed the dirty butcher's knife. She was sick of getting screwed.

* * *

In her office bathroom, Annie leaned forward with her eyes on her cell phone, her hands on the marbled-granite sink. She had turned off the bathroom light after locking the door, and now only the blue glow from her phone lit the mirror and her frazzled, shadowed image in it. Like she was looking at her own ghost. She was counting down the minutes.

She was counting down the nine-minute period before her orders to Howe would be unstoppable and irreparable ramifications would occur as hundreds of Republicans in positions of leadership were rounded up around the country. She knew she wasn't going to backtrack on the execution of *Long Knives*, but she wanted to be aware of the exact moment she possibly saved, or destroyed, the country. It had been agreed upon that until President Fuentes could be released, they would leak to the press there was a potential Islamic plot against the US government. Kerns had suggested it would be easier for the military and various agencies to fulfill their duties if they thought the troops under Harper at MacDill for instance, or those eleven congressional members of Muslim Senator Kaleel's Election Oversight *Joint Congressional Committee*, now named to be detained under *Long Knives*, were actually Islamic insurgents masquerading as US citizens and soldiers. Howe would begin leaking the cover story to a few media outlets for believability.

Luckily, besides those congress members meeting in Denver, all other members of both houses had been called in for emergency night sessions to deal with the possibility of an unresolved electoral vote the following day. The bulk of American government in only one of two locations made it much easier to corral the most partisan factions of the Republican leadership. For the lower-level threats, Howe had already done the due diligence so the order was ready to go out immediately to the cell phones of those determined by *Uncle's Eyes* to be the staunchest Democratic loyalists within the Justice Department, FBI, CIA, DOD, Homeland Security and all military branches. The order contained a specific list of those names determined by *Uncle's Eyes* to be in the upper fifteen percent bracket of extreme right-wing sympathizers and simply identified them as "*potential Islamists*" with requests for their brief detention. Coworkers would turn against coworkers, friends against friends, and local police would pick up thousands across the nation.

After she secured the president's release, Annie would claim it to all have been an "error, from an overabundance of national security". Annie and Howe knew it would not be flawless, that many Republican sympathizers would not be arrested and many non-conspirators detained, but they hoped by taking out the highest ranking Republicans in both the government and military they would catch whoever the real culprits were, as well as put brakes on the spread of any anti-government fervor. To her credit, Howe had already gotten the CIA to shut down any potential cameras or news people near the Capitol in the District of Columbia, so there would be no leaked video footage of the Republicans being ushered out in handcuffs. Hopefully Henry would be wrong, and instead of her choice propelling the country over a cliff, it would help her not have to order the deaths of Americans.

Annie took the bottle of Zennies out of her pocket. She

shook four pills out next to her phone and turned on the water, loud, to cover the off chance anyone might be able to hear over the office din what she was about to do. She needed peace, clarity, supreme knowledge, immediately. Truth. The pills no longer shimmered pink in the darkness, but looked almost blood red. She used her phone to crush the four pills into four tiny piles of chemical dust. She leaned down over them with one nostril pressed closed and snorted.

She leaned back as a rush of warmth exploded in her head and down through her body. With two more deep snorts to each nostril, making sure the powder was in her system as quickly as possible, she thrust her hands back onto the sink and glared into the mirror at herself. *You're going to get through this. You're smart, you've made the right calls.* She held her own eyes in the dark mirror and tried to see confidence. *And once the dust settles, Amos will make the sensible choice, set the Oval Office free. It's going to work out. Just believe in your—*

She gasped, lurched back and smashed against the opposite wall.

Hissssssssssssssss.

The dying rabbit's blinking pink eye, dark shadows on the mirror curling into a black snake and swallowing all. Annie's heart thumped wildly, her legs buckled, and she thrust a hand out to the towel rack affixed to the wall to hold herself up, trying not to scream, her wide eyes glued to the bizarre images in the mirror which was no longer her own reflection.

Hissssssssssssssssssssssssssssssss.

The snake's hiss louder than ever before, Annie felt in the blue half-light as if she were tumbling through outer space, a massive black snake slithering, twitching, tightening its coils around the entire Earth before her. The hiss turned into an insidious whisper in her head. *All burns to ash, Harmony dies, America burns. Because you can't believe.* As she watched in horror, the snake opened its mouth and inside of the gaping, fanged-maw tens of thousands of people were in a downtown city. *Choose.* With the flash of an explosion in the mirror, the people were melting, screaming and shrieking, skin melting off the young and old. *Bow down to your Lord or perish.* Like the flapping scenes from an old broken film reel, again and again in the mirror she saw those agonizing faces wrenched in surreal screams like an expressionist painting as every American liquefied, their flesh and bones melting beneath a tornado of roaring light. *Choose.* Annie shot a hand over her gaping mouth to hold in her scream. She clinched her eyes and threw the other hand to one ear trying to stop the voice.

A metal trash can clattered over the wood floor, and suddenly, as quickly as it had started, Annie realized that the surreal screaming in her head had stopped. She must have kicked the garbage can. She opened her eyes and the scene was gone, only her own startled image glaring back at her in the blue half-light.

She shook her head, blinked her eyes again, and panted for breath, concentrating to not scream out in fear. She looked at the mirror again—nothing except her own face. It had been so real though, so detailed, so horrific, as if she were watching a firsthand video of an atom bomb explosion, and the voice, that horrible, terrifying voice that seemed to somehow have been outside of her. Yet it, too, was gone.

Her legs wobbled, her heart thumped. *What the fuck was that? God? Breathe…breath…breathe.* For a full minute she stared wide-eyed at the mirror, mouth open, breath coming in shallow gasps and one hand clutching her chest. She stared and stared, waiting for the image to return, but only saw her own terrified face. Had anyone else heard? Was she going insane? *No, get it together. Breathe. Don't go crazy. It's the pills. Just the pills.*

She grabbed the bottle. It had to be a hallucination from snorting the medicine, too much built up in her system, too much shooting across her blood-brain barrier without going the normal digestive route. *You idiot.* Or maybe some sort of panic attack brought on by the stress? All of the above, that was it. The bottle said the Zennie's could cause hallucinations, she remembered that. *Keep it together.* She wasn't going crazy, she hadn't had a vision, the voice had just been her own brain. It hadn't been God. *Breathe. Too many people's lives are at risk, Daniels. Relax. Breathe.* She just shouldn't have snorted the goddamn pills, she had to stop taking so many of the goddamn pills. Annie flipped on the light and breathed deeper.

With the lights on things looked more normal, she felt better, more real. *Just rest in here for a moment and you'll be fine.* Someone knocked at the door. *Dammit.*

"Yes," she said as confidently as she could, splashing cold water on her face. "What?" She took a deep breath and patted her face dry with a towel.

Two more knocks.

"Yes?" she demanded. She glanced at her phone and saw that she'd been in the bathroom for almost twelve minutes now. "What the fuck is it?"

"Annie," Henry said through the door. "Amos demands to speak with you."

* * *

Before the call came across from Amos, Henry's heart had sunk in despair over the doxed information he had found online.

The suspicion over whether Annie had been involved with the elector's death kept gnawing at him, and once she'd ordered Howe to implement *Long Knives* and round up her political opposition it had seemed like the only answer must be that she was guilty. In desperation, Henry had hoped he might find something in the *Reboot.org* doxing websites that would clear Annie of all wrongdoing in his mind, restore his trust in her. The doxed video he discovered however made him sick to his stomach, and confirmed Henry's worst fears that there wasn't a truly moral cell in her body.

He had watched the short video four times in shock, making sure to turn his laptop so no one else could see, even as Amos yelled at Annie to his side. Kerns and Howe were already out executing their orders, Annie having dismissed everyone else from the room except Henry.

Henry wondered if Annie was placed on this Earth to kill the faith of others, and if she really had any idea of the implications of her success in doing so.

"Did you lie to me," Major Daniels now bellowed over the monitor at Annie as Henry looked from the video on his laptop to see Amos' face twisted hard in anger at Annie on the monitor. "Did you lie? Again!"

"What are you talking about, Amos?"

Major Daniels thrust his cell phone up to the camera. Henry could see it clearly showed a photo of one of the vice president's Secret Service detail, the unique-looking albino. The agent was standing beneath a restaurant sign that read *Little Gumbo's*. There was a date and time stamp on the photo from the night before Gatreaux's death, the implications obvious. "So tell me the fucking truth for once, Annabel," Amos growled, "are you a part of this?"

"No," Annie said, her anger giving way to shock. "No, I swear. Of course I didn't." She glanced to Henry for support, but after what he'd just seen online, how could he rule out any depth that she might go to?

Amos said, "The vice president must have had the elector killed, Annabel. Your running mate did it, and you're telling me you're not a part of it?"

"That can't be, Amos," she said. "That just can't be. You've got to keep in mind that picture might not be the whole story, these days photos can be doctored so easily. The vice president might not—"

"Do not fuck with me." Amos leapt up and flung his phone at the wall, it shattering into pieces of metal, glass and plastic. "I'm sick of it. I keep trying to do the right thing and all anyone ever does is lie. You lie, they lie, everybody fucking lies, and I'm sick of it." Amos ripped out the crucifix with the small pink stones from beneath his collar and held it to the camera. "Do you swear you're not part of it, Annabel? Swear to God, Annie, swear to God right now you're not part of this, and that you will do whatever it takes to end it. Look at the cross, Annabel, and swear to God."

"I am not part of any conspiracy, Amos," Annie said.

Henry wondered if she would say it. He watched her as intently as she stared at the crucifix, Amos demanding she account for herself on an eternal scale of truth, and Henry wondering what her answer would be, wondering if all of Amos' beliefs hinged on what she did as well.

"Swear to God." Amos' voice became hoarse, and he suddenly sounded almost like he was pleading as much as demanding. "Swear you're not a part of it, Annie, and that you will immediately do whatever is necessary to stop all this. I've got to believe in something."

"I swear, Amos. I swear to God." Her eyes flitted over to Henry, then back to her brother.

"Then end it," Amos declared. "Just end it, Annie. There's no time for the joint statement now, and after Freeman doing this he needs to go to jail if there is any justice left. End it right now, like you just swore."

"What do you mean?"

"I mean quit." Amos glared into the camera. "Immediately send a message to Stone and the press that you're conceding, release a concession tape for you and Freeman. It's the only right thing." Amos' eyes were red, his voice strained. "Keep the promise you just made." He swallowed. "Please. Just keep your word for once. Let me believe in you."

Annie looked back into the monitor for a moment, her lips moving, but not saying anything. "Okay," she finally whispered. "Yes, you're right. Okay. I'll quit." But Henry saw the crow's feet crinkled around her eyes.

"If you concede, Harper will stand down." Major Daniels nodded, seemed to breath slightly deeper. "I have two of my men interrogating Freeman and the agent right now, and I will speak with the president. Once we've crossed-checked their stories, I'll turn over whoever seems culpable to the authorities and we will assist you in holding Harper accountable too. I'll turn myself in to be judged as well. We're all going to do what's right, regardless of the personal consequences. Okay?"

"Yes," Annie nodded, and Henry could tell she was still lying. "I'll prepare the Democratic concession statement as quickly as I can, thirty minutes tops. I will talk to Stone right now and have the statement released very soon, just tell Harper it's coming. We can't have him do something stupid and make things worse and get people killed. We've sworn to God, and let's keep it."

Disgust saturated Henry's soul as he watched, wondering how he ever could have thought he loved her. The video tape he'd found proved there were no depths she wouldn't go to. All of what she claimed to stand for, from helping the downtrodden to protecting the marginalized was not done for the truth, but power. Henry knew he had to stop her.

Apparently there must have been an unnoticed security camera in the church basement where Annie and Governor Stone had met. Henry could only assume the video had somehow been part of the system tied into the NSA's data collection and facial recognition filtering system, what *Reboot.org* had apparently hacked. It had shown, in the half-light, Annie Daniels on her knees with Pastor Stone's head leaned back in ecstasy, letting herself be abused in the basement of a church just so she could trick him, create a lie to win.

As the call with Annie and Amos ended, Henry said, "Quit." The most sincere word he could remember speaking in years. "Keep your promise to me, to him, to the country. Just quit."

"I told you, Henry, I waited and waited for a sign from God, but none ever came. Not a single unexplainable thing happened. A vow to nothing is… nothing, this is the reality we find ourselves in."

"Just quit. For the good of the country, for the sake of truth, quit. You can't beat hate by becoming it."

"Right now, I am America's only truth." Her blue eyes turned toward him, hard. "Find Kerns and tell her to order the airstrike on General Harper. Let her know that we've got less than thirty minutes to decimate all the rebels at MacDill so my brother will be forced to surrender."

Eleven Minutes Later

(Various Locations Around Country: Sunday, 6:27 p.m. PST / 9:27 p.m. EST)

As a squadron of F-18s in Pensacola prepared for an assault on rogue troops at MacDill Air Force Base in Tampa, Florida, and Beatrice Howe's *Operation Long Knives* order trickled down from the Department of Homeland Security into various state and local law enforcement agencies, Lawton Smith peered intently through his binoculars toward the Colorado State Capitol Building a few blocks north. Lawton was squeezed into the passenger seat of the small hatchback with the tinted windows they'd brought along for surveillance purposes while Slicker fidgeted behind the wheel. Yellow streetlamps illuminated drifting snow, and the flashing red and blues from a dozen parked patrol cars bounced over white-dusted streets.

"There's so many, Colonel," Slicker worried. "Did you expect so many police?" Lawton did not even realize that two dozen of the most powerful congressional leaders were currently meeting with the Attorney General and Director of the FBI only a half-mile away at the Ritz Carlton.

The plan was to detonate the dirty bomb on the steps of the capitol building and irradiate everything and everyone in a three-mile radius. Lawton and his boys would be spread out at the major exit points around the city and take potshots at the authorities as they attempted to respond. Lawton thought he could kill around 150,000, once all was said and done, with the radiation setting in. If he played his cards right, he'd still have his militia back in the woods to fight another day. All those within the radiation zone were already slaves to the Illuminati, so it was actually merciful.

"They seem on red alert."

"Worry not." Lawton adjusted the focus of his binoculars. "The universe doth conspire with the good to smite the wicked, whether mountains must tumble or oceans burn."

At that exact moment Howe's *Long Knives* order was working its way down through the DHS and FEMA. Only minutes earlier, CIA and FEMA agents burst into the congressional sessions in Washington, DC, to begin slapping handcuffs on the 106 Republican members of the House and thirteen Republican members of the Senate. The Republicans, of course, screamed in outrage. Many of the Democratic members protested as well and demanded answers, but were only told "national security." The Republicans were herded into the FEMA vans and driven off to undisclosed locations before the press could get anything on camera, though many tweets and posts on social media added to the chaotic information flooding the Internet.

In Colorado, the Executive Order reached the Denver police chief via the Department of Homeland Security in a stern request regarding "a national state of emergency." The chief of police didn't understand the bizarre demand from DHS, especially after the FBI had just requested him to send units to the Ritz Carlton for additional security to the *Joint*

Congressional Committee meeting on Election Oversight. Prior to implementing anything, detaining members of congress, or providing them protection, the confused chief decided he needed to check with the mayor at a minimum, and possibly the governor. The chief decided to temporarily recall all patrol units to the station in order to brief everyone in person once he knew the night's course of action. Within moments, all twelve police cars parked before the capitol building turned off their flashing lights and raced down the street.

"My word," Slicker gasped, "this is truly meant to be, Colonel. Like a guiding hand is assisting us."

Lawton proclaimed, "As the enlightened *MrsCee798* once said, one must think with positivity to achieve greatness."

* * *

Staring at the antique grandfather clock, Annie still hoped *Long Knives* was going to work and the airstrike against Harper would be enough that she could then avoid sending troops to liberate the White House and potentially endangering her brother. The Zennie-induced hallucination she'd experienced in the bathroom had left her even more rattled. It had seemed so real, like she saw Satan devouring the world and heard God demanding she repent to prevent it.

Annie wished things were actually that simple, wished she could bend a knee and apologize to some all-powerful entity and have things go back to peace and calm. Unfortunately, reality was much more complex. That's what Amos had never gotten—it wasn't simple, it was complex. All her life she'd been trying to protect the innocent in America, and almost all her life she'd known what real evil looked like—her father. What Amos could never understand was that the wickedness she'd seen deep down in his eyes that night was just as bad if had done the deed. So what if he hadn't raped her? She'd seen his potential, known what he was capable of, and therefore it was the same as if he'd actually done it. In an honest world, weren't you guilty as soon as you had the urge? Now, in order to protect America, there were no other choices except to crush the rebellion and all those who were potentially sympathetic to it, all who had the urge. The gold pendulum of the clock kept swinging, slowly, methodically as Annie sat in her office chair, the murmur of voices and ringing phones all around her.

Admiral Kerns and Howe had already returned from initiating their respective orders. When Henry held his iPad to Annie's face though, the news network's feed of what had just occurred at somewhere called Milton's Diner made Annie suddenly realize how little any of that mattered. The video of the tragic event looped, again and again, with Henry's face burning with utter disdain at Annie like she could have seen this horrific development coming. Admiral Kerns, standing on the other edge of the desk from where Annie sat, now leaned down to peer at the iPad screen Henry held thrust out to Annie so defiantly.

Kerns' mouth dropped open.

Annie felt sick to her stomach, knowing one timeline had closed and another had opened, and there was no going back to the way things had been only a moment before. Thought once again how seeming to be alive was simply the illusory result of many biological processes, like a chemical combustion causing fire, and when those random biological chemicals in each person were snuffed out that life simply ceased to exist, no meaning to it at all. Like that sweet rabbit's pink eyes had simply extinguished when her father had snapped its neck.

"Madam," Kerns whispered as the video continued to

loop. "Given this… development, you realize it is far too dangerous to leave the White House in the terrorist's hands. There's now no other option but to send the SEALs. It is time to put down the threat with extreme prejudice."

Annie's eye stayed fixed on the video, the same scene playing over and over again. She did not want to answer Kerns, did not want to condemn her own brother to die, even though she knew the Admiral spoke the truth. There was no way she could hold off sending the SEALS to save the president, no way she could risk retaliation after this though. Milton's Diner was the final straw.

"Go," Annie whispered, a single tear rolling down her cheek. "Send the SEALS to kill my brother, Admiral. Just save the real president."

* * *

Before General Harper came on the com, Amos' desperate hopes churned like a river flooding its banks. *Annie will come through, Annie will come through. God will help Annie come through.*

Once Annie conceded for herself and Freeman, Amos would let the president go before General Harper could begin moving troops, leave it up to the FBI to investigate the elector's shooting and the vice president's involvement. He'd then hopefully be allowed to head back to MacDill, where Shay's open arms would be waiting. He and Shay would forgive each other for everything, he would resign his command, then they would go somewhere away from the arguing of this world and start over. They would raise their kids, be simple and happy, and he could keep his faith that good things happen to good people. But it was all coming down to this, to Annie.

Stay on point, Amos told himself as Harper's image

appeared before him. *God and Annie will come through, and this will be over soon, stay on point.*

"Has Freeman confessed?" Harper growled after Amos had finished bringing him up to date on the plan with Annie. "What about Fuentes, is he involved in this?"

"As we speak, sir, I've got Jacari interrogating the vice president, and Lieutenant Stoughton interrogating the Secret Service agent. With what each of them finds out separately I'm going to question the president myself, sir. We'll get to the bottom of who was involved in the conspiracy, at least enough to know who to hand over to the authorities."

The general glowered, seeming to size Amos up, but said nothing.

"I wanted to update you without delay, sir, so you could see it was better to hold off any troop movement. We're about done here, and Senator Daniels will be conceding the Democratic ticket any moment."

Harper started to shake his head with a chuckle. "You think your sister is really conceding, boy?"

"Yes." Amos stood firm. She wouldn't betray him again, she couldn't. *God is real,* he tried to convince himself. *God is real, God is real.* "I assure you, sir, she is contacting Stone as we speak and conceding. She will even be crafting a video message to be released across the country within moments, so there will be no need to move troops toward DC. Once she concedes I will turn over whoever seems most culpable to the authorities, along with the pictures."

"Excellent." General Harper sneered. "I'm relieved you're on the case, Miss Marple. But do you realize we'll most likely be goddamn dead by that time, boy?"

"But Senator Daniels is going to concede, sir, this is all working."

"BULLSHIT, BOY!" Harper bellowed like gaskets were popping in his soul, his face beet red and spit flying. "That lying whore sister of yours tricked you again. If not, why is there a squadron of fighters racing toward me from Forrest Sherman Field at this very moment?"

Amos shook his head in confusion. "That's not possible, sir, she wouldn't do that."

"Turn on the goddamn news to any channel, boy, and then you decide which side you're actually fighting for, because the war's already begun and you need to stop pulling your punches. Your sister is on the other side, and you need to do what needs to be done to protect this goddamn country for its real citizens."

General Harper shot a hand to his monitor and shut the call to black.

The news? Amos ripped open the desk drawers of the table, flinging two to the ground before he found the remote control and had the small television on the wall lighting up. He was still wondering how he was going to find whatever news report Harper was so concerned about when all of his questions were answered. Shockingly, horrifically, blatantly answered.

No, this can't be. The video showed a butcher knife slicing into Stone's barrel chest with a spray of dark blood at a place called Milton's Diner. It was ripped out and plunged back in through his white shirt, again and again, before a shrieking girl was tackled by secret service. Every station across the country was showing it in slow motion, the screaming brown-skinned waitress with a Democratic-blue streak in her hair plunging it down to its hilt into the evangelical Republican governor's chest. The video was not framed well, shaking, and the audio was shrieking with the sounds of things crashing to the ground, but from the ferocity and location of the knife strikes, the depth of the blade's penetration, Amos knew Stone was dead even if the anguished look ripped across that poor man of God's face didn't tell the tale.

"She lied to me," Amos mumbled, his faith in the goodness of the world finally really dying. "That evil fucking bitch lied to me again."

God is a fucking lie.

* * *

News Headlines:

Stone assassinated by Muslim?

White House Under Siege?

Congressional Republicans Arrested.

Numerous Cities Declaring Martial Law

Four Republican Governors Close State Borders

* * *

In Birmingham, Alabama, *@jessejameskickass* saw the video of Stone being assassinated by a Muslim operative and had enough. He raised up his sniper rifle, trained the scope on the Muslim man on the library steps with the protestors, and fired.

* * *

In Chicago, a group of young Muslim men, afraid of additional attacks against them, took *@professorofplants'* words to heart and opened fire on a group of *Black Panthers* who were walking toward them with guns.

* * *

On Pennsylvania Ave, hundreds of blue-shirt-wearing Americans swinging bats and bricks and knives surged into a crowd of red-shirt-wearing Americans. The red-shirt-wearing Americans fought back, stomping on the bones of anyone wearing a blue shirt.

* * *

Online statement from Texas Governor Madge Mullins: *The great state of Texas formally secedes from the Union until clear Federal authority can be restored.* And a subsequent statement followed thirty-four seconds later: *Don't mess with us.*

* * *

The private military contractor was puzzled. He had not expected to see this strange Yanic Goran character again so soon. Hell, he'd barely been able to brush the taste of those god-awful Slappy Burgers from lunch out of his mouth. Here in the contractor's main office, in all of its polished chrome and metallic lines, Yanic Goran looked smaller, frailer. Worried.

"I can see why someone of your ilk might need security, Mr. Goran." The contractor wore a short-sleeve shirt that showed a fading green Marine Corps globe and anchor tattoo on one round bicep. He crossed his beefy arms over his chest, leaned back in his leather chair, determined to not make things easy for this creepy Goran character.

"My ilk?" The oily man arched his eyebrows. "You insinuate something?"

"Yes." The contractor slid open a metallic desk drawer in search of his Cuban cigar box. "Unlikeable. Shiftless, arrogant and greedy. Someone ruthlessly concerned only with their own well-being to such an extent that they exude a vile, weak vibe." The contractor removed the cedar box with a smile and set it on the desk, his tone more relaxed and congenial than the words themselves. He flipped the box open and took a deep whiff of the forest musk from the seven cigars inside. "Someone who is so fearful that they are actually quite dangerous, like a pathetic dying snake that has nothing left to lose. That sort of ilk."

"Ah." Goran nodded with a half-smile. "Cigar?" Goran pointed at the open box.

"Yes," the contractor replied, putting the expensive cigar into his mouth. "They are." Then clapped the lid to the box shut without offering one to Goran. He placed the box back in its drawer. "So normally, Mr. Goran, people seeking bodyguards go to one of the smaller, more... domesticated security firms. Most of our contractors are former spec ops, or intelligence personnel." The contractor rolled the cigar in his mouth as he lit the other end, puffing. "Hell, maybe you should go to the nearest mall and offer some of those shopping-cart fatsos a bigger Slappy Burger budget?"

Yanic Goran sighed. "You are not taking my request seriously? Maybe believing I have wasted your time, no?" A boom thundered outside and Goran leapt in his chair, spun toward the window. The explosion's shock shuddered a bit through the heavy walls and glass. Goran clutched his chest, breathing deeply.

"A bunker buster." The contractor smirked. He continued puffing the cigar to life over the flame. "We specifically built this fifty-million-dollar building state-of-the-art, with highest grade glass to completely muffle all tactical noises from the training grounds below. After two weeks of sitting up here in the goddamn insulated quiet though, I realized I missed the sound of combat and paid another mil out of my own pocket to rip those first windows out and put something else in that at least let a little bit, a hint, of the fireworks from downstairs through." He smiled and leaned back.

"Excellent choice," Goran said. "May I ask, what are they training for? On the way in, it looked like there were hundreds of men and much equipment."

"Anything." The contractor shrugged. "Everything." He jabbed the cigar toward the window. Outside, the red smoke streams of two, then three, RPGs arched up into the windows' range several hundred yards out. "There should be a whistle with those, but the damn glass is still too good."

"Specifically, please," Goran demanded. "That particular training exercise below, I noticed there were several things that looked like oil-tanker trucks. What exactly are they training for?"

"Well…" Against his will, the contractor unconsciously acquiesced a bit to the sudden sternness in Yanic's being. "Have a lot of security work going with various oil companies, with some of the oil states themselves. It's an urban warfare oil refinery scenario down there this week, counterterrorism mock up. Lots of people don't get the sheer bulk of what us private companies do now. If you put us all together, the whole industry, we've got more personnel working worldwide than the actual military." The contractor stood, headed to the window and pointed out the various buildings in the training ground below. "Got about two hundred operators mocking defense of a few dozen radicals assaulting a shipment and—"

"Only two hundred?"

"Yeah." He looked back at the other man, unsure where

Yanic Goran was going with his question. "Two hundred and twenty, I believe."

"And how many operators did you say you employ overall?"

The contractor shrugged. "Officially, here and abroad, about fifteen thousand, for me. Unofficially, people we can't have on the books, over twenty-five. Lot more if I negotiated some assistance from other groups, but never had cause to do that."

"Interesting." Goran sighed, a definite look of disappointment on his face. "I had mistakenly thought you were the man to see about hiring security, but maybe you do not have the resources after all. Is one of your competitors more robust?"

"Not have the ability?" The contractor laughed incredulously. "With all due respect, Mr. Goran, even someone of your wealth can rarely justify having a security team of more than twelve men, and that's assuming you've got big grounds, lots of movement, and require twenty-four hour protection. What would you even do with a dozen men?"

"Twelve?" Goran chuckled with a shake of his head. "Twelve? I do not need twelve men, sir. The world is rapidly changing."

The contractor's eyes widened, smoke puffing from around the cigar. "The fuck then? How many you talking?"

Yanic Goran looked with those old, flickering snake-eyes. "I was thinking more of 50,000... to start."

"Fifty—" The contractor hacked smoke out of his lungs that he had to wave a hand at in order to still see Goran. "You want to hire 50,000 trained mercenaries?"

"I would need men actively trained in assault, not just defense. Vehicles and ammunition too. Maybe lease this building as a bunker from which to operate securely."

For a moment, the contractor stared blankly at Yanic Goran, his mind catching up with understanding that the man was talking about hiring a personal army. The military contractor hustled back to his desk. "Of course. I know the heads of the other big four firms." He leaned down to quickly open the cigar drawer again. "Between all of us there's easily 50,000 personnel that could be coordinated. Probably much more. Relocate them to wherever you need."

"Excellent," Goran replied. "I worry this new world will be slightly more unstable and, of course, one can never be too safe."

The contractor grinned cautiously, offering the cigar box out to Goran. "That type of coordination and manpower, of course, would... um, not be cheap."

"Would gold bullion avoid any sort of annoying paperwork?"

* * *

Back in the Presidential Annex, Amos realized in bewilderment that his older sister had killed Stone, was arresting Republicans, and sending an attack on American troops at MacDill. Annie WAS the plot.

Lies. Everything, everyone, fucking lies.

Later, Amos wouldn't really remember stumbling into the Oval Office, his bruised brain fuzzed with stress and rage. He would remember, however, the vice president's chuckle. In the Oval Office, they had the television showing the clip of Stone's death again and again, the former pastor's red face twisted in agony as he was assassinated in brutal fashion before the country, the entire world. From behind his desk, President Fuentes' face showed genuine shock and pain. Marcus Freeman's was another sight altogether though. Freeman was sitting on the edge of the desk, smiling. Arrogant and smiling as the universe seemed to conspire to help his selfish dreams come to life, help him complete his insidious plan. "Looks like your coup lost its figurehead, maybe your God wants me to win," Freeman scoffed. "There is a war coming, Amos, between ignorance and enlightenment, and when my term begins I intend to win it."

Amos raised his shotgun, not knowing what he intended to do, only that he had to shut up Freeman's arrogant fucking face. "You aren't going to get away with it," Amos bellowed as he cracked the butt of his shotgun into Freeman's already broken nose, the man toppling backward off the desk in a screech of pain. Amos took two steps around the desk, ripped up on the vice president's tie, and shoved the 10-gauge barrel against his forehead. "Maybe I'm your avenging angle, you slimy fuck."

Jacari grabbed Amos, yanked him backward. "What the hell you doing, man? The vice president doesn't know anything about the conspiracy! He didn't do it, man!" Stork leapt to Amos' other shoulder.

It took both him and Jacari to push Amos up against the wall, keep him away from the vice president. Stork whispered, "It's true Amos. I confirmed it with Agent Simms. He says the tape's been doctored by Islamists. Simms is part of The Activity too, we can trust him."

"Trust him?" Amos, his face strained in rage, then saw over Stork's shoulder that the albino Secret Service agent had his hands untied, the tape off his mouth and was standing between the sofas watching the chaotic scene with a soft smirk. Additional members of Amos' team hunched at the windows and doorways glancing back in worry, everyone watching things spiraling increasingly out of control.

"I don't even know if I can trust YOU." Amos shoved

Stork off and pointed his shotgun at the agent. "What the fuck's he doing unrestrained?"

"I told you," Stork rasped. "He's with us, Amos, he's part of The Activity. I can vouch for him."

"Bullshit," Amos declared. "I'm not taking your word or his." He pointed Stork toward the agent. "Tie him back up. You're all fucking liars." Amos swung his weapon from Stork to the president. "I want to know the goddamn truth! What the fuck is going on? Who's guilty?"

"Amos, man," Jacari whispered, "take it easy, bro, breathe deep. You shoot one of them and nothing ever goes back to normal... ever."

"President Fuentes." Amos trained his muzzle on the president's head, gritting his teeth, his eyes rimming wet in frustration. "Tell me the truth, sir, what the fuck is going on? Who killed the elector, who's the bad guy?"

President Fuentes raised his palms into the air from where he sat, shrugged his shoulders. "Son, I promise you, I don't know."

"I want to do what's right, sir, but I'm tired of bullshit. I'm getting so tired of everybody lying, of bad people doing as they want. I'm starting to think more and more that what's right involves this gun and me just deciding who to kill. The whole situation, the whole country... something's off."

"Major," the president said calmly holding Amos' gaze, "please remember there are no purely good or evil men, but a line of good and evil cuts through the heart of every person." He sighed softly. "I assure you, I understand your frustration, and you must believe I want the same thing as you, this election ending with no one else getting hurt." The president glanced at Freeman in disapproval. "Regardless of who that power is transferred to, the country's peace is my priority. If you let me go, I promise you, Major Daniels, you have my word I will not let Marcus Freeman and Annie Daniels take control. I will use an Executive Order to authorize a new election, bar both of them from running, and have the election held with all new candidates. You and I can still find justice to this."

"What?" Freeman exclaimed from where he sat on the floor clutching his smashed face. "You can't do that! That's not right."

"You promise, sir? If I let you go, you promise to call for a new election and investigate the vice president, my sister, and..." Amos jabbed the shotgun back at the pale agent with a *fuck you* look, "this fuck?"

"I promise you, son," the president said. Fuentes pulled a small crucifix chain out from beneath his shirt. "I swear to God." And at those words, Amos' gun started to drift downward to his side. Looking into Fuentes' eyes, Amos nodded in agreement even as he admitted, "I'm no longer sure what I believe, sir."

"I will not lie to you, son."

"Will you address the nation then, sir?" Amos asked. "Try to calm things."

The president nodded. And for a moment, with the president's help, Amos could again see a light at the end of the tunnel. A way, the only way, this could possibly still end up right.

That's when the bullet went through Stork's skull. It cracked down through the ceiling and Stork's head burst like a melon, blood and brains spraying over Amos' cheek, Stork's body cracking to the floor like a felled tree.

One of Amos' guys yelled, "*Incoming, incoming!*"

Pings of more bullets ripped through the ceiling. Chopper blades could be heard overhead and the hallway leading from the Oval Office burst alive with shouts, thundering automatic weapon fire. It was the explosion from the floor near the Presidential Annex that knocked Amos back with orange fire and wood, concrete chips flying. His already bruised head was thudded like a sledgehammer as his body crashed to the wall and then to the floor, the hazy dark blurs of Navy SEALs springing up through the hole.

Rolling on the floor, Amos' arm searing with fire and his eyes stinging with smoke, he saw the albino agent rip a glinting knife from a calf sheath and lunge toward the president.

America Erupts

(Location Unknown, Time Unavailable)

Mokeba had said the ancient texts described Soma as a waking dream, a walk with the dead and unborn. Harmony had to admit even though she was terrified she was also excited. Excited to finally know the TRUTH. The liquid had burned like acid down Harmony's throat, wrenching her stomach in knots, even as she realized she hadn't hit send on her message of forgiveness to her Uncle Amos. Almost immediately her head swelled with heat, blood sweated into her eyes, and she began to wretch. The medicine, or poison, seemed to burn its way into her every cell, into her very soul. Her insides boiled with intense warmth and her vision blurred. The last thing she experienced as normal reality was twisting in pain on the cool concrete of the garage floor. It seemed that every muscle cramped as her vision faded to gauze, her ears roaring with the sound of a thousand buzzing hornets. Suddenly she no longer knew if her heart still beat, if her lungs still breathed. She was sure she was dying.

But then she noticed the cold of the concrete more prominently, refreshing, her heat melting into the cool of the floor. Then all sensation left and she was profoundly comfortable. There had been the feeling of dissolving then, everything within her sight a blur of soothing gray as the weight of her physical body slipped from around her like shedding wet clothes to leave her more naked and alive, lighter, than she had ever known. The buzzing in her ears and the hazy shapes before her eyes faded into nothing, just like the weight of her flesh, and then there was only blackness. Beautiful, rich blackness, as deep and complete as the mouth of a black hole. She no longer knew time, but was engulfed in utter, brilliant, eternal blackness, and felt as if all before it had been the dream. Wherever she was, whatever she was, was now more real than anything, she was utterly free.

Floating, no weight. No sound, or up, no down; we are complete. Returned.

Light up ahead. A pinprick far in the black.

Glorious white spot of light, memories of excitement, love, life. The light expands into a shining beam, and a tunnel of clear warmth embraces, soothes. Luminous intensity vibrates, solidifies.

I'm alone on top of a high mountain peak in the endless black, my body not flesh, but shimmering crystal light like dew clinging to the memory of Harmony. I can see a vast plane of all things, a churning molten kaleidoscope of colors shifting, blistering, bursting into all possibilities beneath me, an endless roil.

Above the vast plane a glow of light seeps out of the darkness into crystal clouds, and with it a million voices hum a most glorious song in a language I do not know, but once did. The swirling tapestry of colors and shapes below morphs into a living map of the United States. From the golden coasts of the Pacific, to the man-made towers of the Atlantic, to the craggy Northern skylines and the wet Southern bogs and bayous, I can see it all. I can see any individual life that ever was or ever will be within those borders: love, anger, guilt, sadness, fear, forgiveness, hope; and I crave to experience each and every one of them, to be with them, one of them.

But then, from their interactions I see tiny dark slivers twists and rise like snakes, friction of their attempting to find love. The rising black tendrils draw into one another above the humans' heads like smoke. Fear.

Those wisps combine into a single horrible hovering mass of pure black over the country like a bank of dark fog. As it grows in mass it whips dark tendrils back down like black lightening into the humans below, infecting their hearts and minds like a cancer. They turn on each other, blood spilling and bones breaking, the wailing of the innocent and the gnashing of teeth.

The black smoke snakes toward me and congeals next to me. It is all the darkness of mankind, and on the mountaintop beside me, it becomes the pale man from the coffee shop.

"My love," he says, "do you not wish for us to reach paradise?"

"But why must you cause them pain?" I ask, even as my heart leaps at recognition of his flawless white skin and hypnotic pink eyes.

He responds, "The dark exists so the one can break into the many, for without the many there can be no love." He reaches out his hand and gently takes mine. He leans forward, and what I had waited a lifetime for happens as his lips push to mine. The electricity of a thousand joys and sorrows sparks through me. I am complete, I am perfect, I am finally not alone. He sweeps his hand toward the plane below. "We break ourselves into splinters with the darkness again and again, my love, until little by little, bit by bit, we no longer fear the illusion of death, but live in immortal bliss, forever our chosen parts, but always together."

"But what must we do to end the pain, my love," I ask,

gazing out over the roiling tapestry again and trying to understand our beautiful march toward perfection through all ours births and deaths, emotions and dreams, disappointments and joys. I smile, seeing their lives as a massive, wonderful game of amazing highs and lows where in the end the pain would never last, and they would all eventually be reborn into an eternal bliss once complete. Holding his hand I understand, know that we are on the verge of reaching that paradise where we would all forever be happy, and the darkness truly gone forever, if we just understand what we are now to do. "What is truth?"

"Om pishlay toth," *he counters wickedly.* "I am the fire, the anvil upon which all is beaten pure until the truth is reached." *the pale man drops my hand and swells into the giant black cloud again, more massive than before, churning like a giant black snake over the country below and I am overcome with horror at what he will do.* "And you cannot save them, until you stop me."

As if the endless dark cloud had broken open in a storm, tendrils from the black mass whip down more violently than ever over the earthly plane like thousands of ebony angels riding black horses of death. America floods with turmoil, breathing, burning and blackening the entire country; all awash in blood. I see fields of wheat crackle with flame for Kansas miles, Mount Rushmore faces crumble beneath the thunder of cannons, Boston skyscrapers twist into piles of red-hot steal, and the Golden Gate Bridge plunge beneath lapping cold bay waves as the second civil war begins. I try to scream, but words do not come.

On the Western side of the country I see a giant liberal army in uniforms of blue, and on the Eastern, a conservative army in red. Their violent clashes of tanks and planes rip up and down the Rocky Mountains and across the Grand Canyon. Two-thirds of the country is plunged into darkness without lights or safe water with brother taking up pistol against brother, and neighbor slaying neighbor. Small warring tribes form of whites, black, Latino, Asian, Muslims, Jews, men, women; all trying to survive in the madness of the dark cities. Or trying to escape through the diseased, radiated and lawless wilds where worse things thrive. I see a crazed militia leader, a bear of a man take tyrannical control of the snowy north. And a shifty, old suit with a pile of gold raise a mighty army of mercenaries to carve out his own tiny kingdom. Many separate warring kingdoms construct walls where states once were. Christian Crusaders thunder on horseback across all lands attempting to persecute nonbelievers, and some areas smolder in glowing ash from radiated blasts. All is insanity and death, anarchy and blood, from sea to shining sea.

And I know I must follow the pale man starting this war down into the madness, if I am to catch him again, and learn the eternal truth that can bring peace.

* * *

Trending on all forms of social media: *Dirty Bomb Explodes in Downtown Denver?*

M*otherfucking weak-ass, backstabbing, lying pervert, cock-sucking liberals want a goddamn war?* Mace Harper thought. *I'll give them a goddamn fucking war.*

Beneath the floodlights his boots clacked down the sidewalk and onto the concrete of the massive MacDill flight deck. Three tanks, four Humvees, eight jeeps, fifteen military transport trucks and all four hundred troops of the 13th Mountain Artillery Division waited in formation. Mace Harper hadn't backed down from a fight since the sixth grade, and he sure wasn't going to now. Not from a communist slut, a pansy, and a darkie. "Right up their fucking dicks," Harper screamed without slowing his march. "Prepare for incoming, boys, this ain't no fucking drill!"

It took less than two seconds for the command to be echoed throughout the captains and lieutenants to their subordinates. Everyone leaped into action even as their wide eyes gave clear indication they didn't know what the fuck was going on. With General Harper there was always a sense of not understanding the purpose of the orders he was giving, only that you'd better follow them or else.

"Cut the floodlights!"

Harper marched up to the lieutenant with a bullhorn on the edge of the tarmac. The lieutenant couldn't have been more than twenty-six, and Harper snatched the bullhorn from his hands. "Defensive positions, motherfuckers." Harper's voice wailed across the blacktop, a screech of feedback trailing his words. "We've got an enemy squadron torching toward Mac-Dill, intending to horse-fuck us right off this goddamn rock!" Harper took two strong steps up the bumper of a Humvee and into its back next to a mounted anti-aircraft gun. "Do not misunderstand," Harper screamed through the bullhorn. "Lots of you are going to die." With his free hand he ripped out his saber, it glinting with a ring of metal on metal, and held the bullhorn tighter to his mouth with the other. "But I do not give a fuck about your deaths, nor do you." Harper squinted toward the horizon and thought he could make out specks of distant light in the night sky. "Our glorious country depends on your actions, so gird your goddamn vaginas and do what you're trained to do and knock these traitorous motherfucking birds from the sky. Now move, move, move!"

* * *

Green Berets versus SEALs was a mythic faceoff that had occupied the drunken conversations of more than a few of the military's most elite warriors through the decades, but no one ever imagined a possible scenario where it could happen. Now, in the reality of the moment, American warrior versus American warrior, Amos regretted good men dying, even as he killed them.

The hole the SEALs blew in the floor was close to the Presidential Annex, an explosion of smoky orange flame, wood, concrete chips and singeing heat. It was obviously strategically placed as far away from the captives as possible, although they did severely wound one Secret Service agent in the process. He got a sharp piece of wood harpooned in his groin, muffled wails coming from his taped-shut mouth as he squirmed on the floor. Chaos erupted as the first wave of SEALs breached the floor into the Oval Office, while the Secret Service counterassault team attempted to storm the front. Amos had been in gunfights and hand-to-hand fights before, but nothing like this. It was old-school close quarters combat, his remaining eleven men against probably twenty opposition force coming from the front and the floor.

Amos reeled from the blast, trying to find his shotgun through the smoke. His lungs sucked for air as if through a crimped straw, no oxygen coming, and he could barely see. From the rapid fire of three of his men who faced the Rose Garden entrance, Amos was certain more SEALs were trying to breach from that direction too. His ears rang and he twisted on the floor for footing as he glimpsed the albino agent darting with a drawn blade toward President Fuentes. Fuentes was the only hope left for putting this right, possibly the last good man in a pit of vipers, and Amos had to save the president.

Amos' felt the cool metal of his shotgun's barrel and leapt off the floor, trying to make it to the albino agent amidst the churn of bodies. The flash of a blonde beard and a knife blade in Amos' smoky sight, he pulled the trigger at point blank range for a gruesome explosion of bone, blood and flesh, and the blonde beard was gone. Amos' right arm sprung upward to block the edge of a metal baton swinging at his skull, pain shooting through his forearm. Amos spun, cracked the butt of his shotgun straight ahead into the black face of another SEAL and then threw two quick jabs with his left at another, exploding the guy's nose and sending him two steps backward.

Amos leveled his weapon and blew a six-inch red hole through his stomach.

A pair of arms wrenched around Amos' neck from behind and Amos' shotgun fell from his hands. He twisted his hips and shoulders, sending his assailant flying over one of the sofas. Even as that blue-black clad form was tumbling, Amos' left hand was ripping out his sidearm and squeezing twice, putting one in the face, one in the chest of a counterassault agent racing toward him. The man spun backward from the gun blast, eye and ear disappearing into gristle. Amos spun to the left and fired two more shots into a squat guy leaping at him through the smoke. The thick guy crumpled to the floor moaning and Amos spun again, looking for the albino.

Bullets flew. Machine gun fire from the hallway ripped into walls, wood chips flying. One of the secret service agents, heroically loyal to his cause even in the midst of his restrained position, lunged himself in front of the prostrated vice president as bullets thudded his body. That's when Amos spotted President Fuentes behind his chair and the albino agent stumbling around the desk toward him with his knife still clutched. Amos leapt, cracking into the albino's ribs with his shoulder, both of them crashing to the top of the president's desk and rolling off the side.

There were knees flying, knives flashing, and gunshots blasting in that surreally small space, smoke and flame all around, but Amos focused on the albino man before him. He did not know why, but this man was bent on President Fuentes' death, and even in all of the madness Amos knew he must protect the president of the United States. Amos got his feet under him first and grabbed the albino just as the assassin pushed himself up. Amos wrapped his arms around the other man's neck in a rear naked choke, hoping to suffocate him into unconsciousness, but the albino agent was strong. The albino twisted and lunged forward, Amos hurling feet-over-ass into the unbreakable glass of a window, smashing it hard enough to cause cracks but thumping him hard back to the floor with his wind bludgeoned from him. The albino spun looking for his fallen knife.

Amos crawled back to his feet with his own knife drawn. The albino agent found his knife through the smoke and scooped it up, spun back toward the president. The president still hunched behind his desk, his hands gripping the large chair as a shield, his eyes searching frantically for an escape as the albino stepped forward. Amos' elbow cracked into the albino's temple and the agent tumbled over the corner of the desk and to the floor again, dazed. As Amos lunged for the stunned man, a knife tore through Amos' left shoulder, severing meat from bone and making him drop his own weapon.

Amos grunted, pain scorching up his arm as he turned to see a female SEAL, long, red braided hair and a tattoo of skulls down her neck, preparing to strike again. She thrust the knife toward Amos' ribs, but he caught her wrist with his injured arm and leveled a hard right fist straight into her jaw, smashing her backward to the wall. Even though he hit with all he had, she did not go unconscious, only dropped to a knee and looked up with a grimace. Amos spun from her just in time to see the albino agent already on his feet again with knife in hand, lurching around the desk toward the panicked President Fuentes. There was no time for Amos to reach down and retrieve his own weapon, so he dove at the man. It was his already-injured arm that the albino agent's knife plunged into up to the hilt and stuck, Amos tumbling into the president, all three crashing to the ground. A barrage of bullets ripped over their heads.

On the floor, the albino cracked an elbow into Amos' jaw, knocking his arms loose. The albino's face was twisted in rage and determination, and he scrambled onto all fours to grab a sidearm from the hand of a dead Green Beret. The albino spun on one knee to finish off Amos and the president, but Jacari flew in from the side and crashed the albino into the wall, both then wrestling for the gun.

Bodies were smashing and dying all around them, and the president was hyperventilating, his arms and legs thrashing as he tried to get to his feet. There was a blast and Jacari's stomach opened up, spilling his blood over the carpet as he sank down the wall clutching at the albino agent's weapon. The female SEAL's boot suddenly cracked into the albino's face, knocking him backward, and the two began to fight as Jacari began to die. Amos scrambled toward Jacari, while the president leapt up and darted through the Rose Garden door, directly into the heaviest of the gunfire.

* * *

"Come on, you pinko motherfuckers," Harper growled at the horizon, still standing on the back of the Humvee, now with his gnarled hands around the metal grips of the anti-aircraft gun, his steel-gray eyes grimacing ahead. His men were in defensive positions behind the armored vehicles and around the edges of hangars three and four. "Let's see if you got the balls."

"Binoculars, sir?" the Captain asked.

"I'm not a cripple, boy." Harper scowled, not moving his naked eyes from the horizon. Tiny specks of light along the horizon grew bigger, and the faintest rumble of jets shook the air as the attack squad raced toward them.

"I cannot die," Harper bellowed into the night sky. "I cannot fucking die!"

* * *

If the president lives, there's still hope. Amos pushed off the floor, forced to leave his dying comrade for the one last shot at holding the country together. Fuentes had just darted through the open doors and into the night. All was still smoke and struggle as Amos burst around the edge of the desk and out the doors after him, bullets whistling past his cheek as he raced into the black. Gunfire roared around him.

"Stop," Amos yelled at whoever was shooting, at everyone, as he sprinted over the grass. "It's Fuentes!" They were all Americans, they would have to stop. "It's the president, hold your fire!" A bullet ripped through Amos' thigh and his leg went out from under him. He tumbled across the grass, the president a streaking shape in the black up ahead.

Amos was too filled with adrenaline now to feel the pain and tried to push back into a run, but got another blast to his leg and tumbled once more.

"It's the president, don't shoot!" Amos rolled up onto one knee with a grunt of pain and stretched his arm toward the dark suit racing several yards before him. "Stop!"

"Hold," a female voice barked from somewhere behind Amos. "Hold your fire, there's been a mistake!"

But Amos, his hand still outstretched, watched helplessly as little red holes exploded from the back of the president's dark suit like tiny fireworks, his body dancing, lifeless from the crackling gunfire. And behind them, in the dark and confusion, the albino agent slipped away into the night.

Carnage.

The jets, as any rational person would have expected, sliced through Harper's battalion like lasers through bread. Admiral Kerns' squadron ripped through the men and vehicles with gunfire and missile strikes blanketing the tarmac in wave after wave. From their initial haphazard battery of antiaircraft fire Harper's men managed to wing one of the jets by sheer luck and sent it spinning into the MacDill Central Command building at Mach 1, the F-18 bursting into a ball of blue flame and flying shrapnel, the building turning into an inferno. But after that first pass, the squadron of jets took huge arcing turns out of gunfire range, and then hurtled back over the battalion, again and again and again, far too quick for anyone to actually aim a weapon or come close to hitting one. Each pass left a wider gash of wailing, burning men and body parts. Buildings all across the air force base were bursting into flames, exploding with impacts.

Harper, his jaw clenched like a bulldog on a leg bone, held the anti-aircraft gun with a single hand, his other having already been ripped from his arm by a chunk of burning tank hurtling past him. One foot was propped on the dead captain's head as the general, soaked in his own blood and that of others, blasted the anti-aircraft gun into the sky. With over ninety percent of his men and equipment reduced to molten rumble, Harper was still certain he was going to win. As the squadron took their long lazy arc over the Tampa horizon again, and the faint whine of their engines reverberated the sky like a swarm of megalithic wasps, Harper's only real concern was how to better wipe the blood from his left eye with only one hand now.

The jets began their streak back toward him, specks quickly growing into hawks and Harper gripped the weapon's handle again harder, eyesight be damned. "Here or in the next life, you stupid fucks," he whispered to the nearing jets, "I'll get you."

Russia, China, Iran, North Korea and ISIS Learn of America's Problems

(San Francisco, CA, 7:31 p.m. PST / 10:31 p.m. EST)

For Annie, it was like waiting for a doctor to tell you if you had cancer, seconds passing like hours, minutes passing like lifetimes. Except it was far worse than that, as it involved the life or death of the entire country she had meant to lead into better days. While waiting for news of whether or not the White House mission had been a success, if her brother and others were alive, the rest of the world had become aware of America's meltdown and the dozen newly installed phones had never stopped ringing; officials from multiple state and federal agencies, reporters, the World Bank, United Nations, European Union, Russia, OPEC, China and seemingly everyone else in the world receiving word that Annie Daniels was possibly de facto president, and trying to find the truth of what was going on.

All Annie wanted was for this to be over, the president to be safe, and to get her sick daughter in her arms and never let go. Only Admiral Kerns, Henry, Howe and she were now in her office, Annie staring with unblinking eyes at a full glass of Jim Beam, unable to even take a sip. She actually now wished she'd quit, just let them take over the country.

Kerns, however, was confident, almost happy. Within the last fifteen minutes news had been received back that Harper had been killed, the traitors at MacDill decimated. Almost all of MacDill had been destroyed, but Kerns had stated that collateral damage was unavoidable and the important thing was that the White House objective was achieved. Under Howe's *Long Knives* implementation of the *Uncle's Eyes* matrix, barbed-wire FEMA camps around the country continued to fill up with *'persons of interest'* in the fabricated Islamic plot, the dangers seeming to somehow spread the more they tried to stamp it out.

Word was breaking that the Republican Governors of Michigan, Alabama, Mississippi and Utah were following Texas' lead and had declared their states seceded from the Union until definitive corroboration of who was in charge of the federal government could be ascertained. Annie again wished her earlier horrific hallucination in the mirror had been a vision from God, that life could be so simple. She would gladly suffer lifetimes of punishment just to avoid this moment, to avoid what she had seen in that mirror and haunted her as a real possibility now, the utter destruction of America. "Amos?" Annie whispered for the fourth time to the admiral, her eyes shifting from the whiskey, glinting brown in the light, to the white bottle of Zennies, back to the whiskey. "I need something… facts, Admiral."

"Commander Jackson is the best of the best, madam," Kerns replied. "I predict she'll be calling in with the all-clear from the White House any moment."

Annie's vacant gaze went to Henry. She could see he hated her even worse than before, and it seemed like he was almost taking angry pleasure in announcing the endless barrage of awful updates streaming across multiple media formats during the past hour. "Thirty-one cities across the country now estimated to be in complete anarchy," he declared. "Law enforcement and National Guards have given up, letting the rioters do what they want." He added, "A sixth Republican governor has temporarily seceded from federal authority until President Fuentes emerges and order can be restored. That puts Montana on the list."

Annie dropped her forehead into her palm, a tear escaping down her cheek and onto her hand. She brushed it away before anyone could see. Howe was at least practical, somehow regaining her composure as the country was melting down around them, all her nervousness evaporating and almost becoming a coldly logical machine in her decision-making.

"I'd suggest you make a statement soon, madam," Howe said. "Confirm yourself as acting president and announce that all traitors will be dealt with severely. Demand a public oath of loyalty from all governors, agency heads, and military leaders. Put anyone who doesn't agree under arrest. It is incredibly important the public sees singular leadership."

"President Fuentes and the vice president." Annie's voice was hoarse, her fingers tapping against the glass. "Once they are free, they will be back in power and can make whatever statement they wish. It would confuse things if I jump the gun." What Annie didn't say was that while picturing her own brother's death, the death that she had ordered and the horrific destruction of the country her frazzled mind had projected onto the bathroom mirror, Annie had finally realized she really had made all the wrong calls. All the wrong calls in this event, and throughout her entire life. Everything inside her felt whipped and decayed and stupid. And she suddenly realized she had always been an awful person, no matter how she tried to justify her choices. As soon as she knew the president and vice president were safe, Annie vowed she would resign from everything and spend every day from here on out taking care of Harmony, trying to be a better mother and wife, a better person. She realized she couldn't slay all the world's monsters, without becoming the monster.

"But what if something happens to them, madam?" Howe asked the question Annie hadn't dared to voice. "What if, madam, the president and vice president don't make it?"

"That's not going to happen," Annie cautiously countered. "Is it Admiral Kerns?"

"Absolutely not, Madam President." Kerns chuckled. "No way one Green Beret team can withstand the entire Secret Service and SEAL Team Six."

Howe pestered, "But what's the contingency plan, Admiral?"

"Annie," Henry interrupted, a sudden tenderness and worry in his tone that surprised her, so different from his recent tinge of disgust that it made her look up and over. "Annie…"

"What? What now?"

"Reports of a dirty bomb in downtown Denver."

"Jesus." Annie shot to a stand. "Harmony, my baby—"

"We can't know for sure if it's true," Henry cautioned, raising his palms. His brown eyes held that deep look of concern for her like they used to. "And even if it is, she should be out of the most dangerous zone, Annie. Dirty bombs aren't like traditional nuclear warheads. Unless you are within a couple of miles, the radiation won't get you. Harmony was in Boulder, not central Denver."

The heavy glass tumbler clunked from Annie's hand to the floor as the horrible vision from the bathroom mirror flashed even stronger through her mind, the voice demanding she repent echoing again and again. The glass tumbler continued to spin and roll with hollow reverberations until Howe leapt to it and snatched it up.

"We've got to save her, Henry, we've got to get to her right now! How could I have been so stupid? Jesus."

"I'll coordinate getting someone to her immediately," Henry said. "I'm sure the story is most likely not even true. Remember, there's so many fake—"

"Madam President," Kerns announced, her United States Navy laptop flashing red on the desk. "Commander Jackson calling in."

"Thank God." Annie's mind was still reeling with the horror of Harmony possibly being in danger. She put a hand to the desk corner to steady herself. "Put her through and let's get this over so I can go get my daughter."

"As I said," Admiral Kerns sounded a bit cocky, opening the laptop and squatting onto one of the small roller chairs, "Commander Jackson is the best of the best. We never really had anything to worry about, madam, and now this is all wrapped up I'm sure we'll be able to get your daughter just fine."

Annie exhaled, scooted her chair as far as she could away from Kerns while still being able to see the laptop screen, and dropped into it. Focusing on the laptop, Annie saw another brutal woman staring back at her, but this one leaner, more svelte and savage than Kerns. The woman, Commander Jackson, had skull tattoos down her neck, long red hair in a braid, and red splatters of blood on her face.

"Daniels." Commander Jackson sneered to the camera with more than a twinge of disrespect in her tone, and Annie's stomach immediately began to sink. "Kerns."

"Commander Jackson." Annie tried to summon the cautious optimism of her political nature. "Please… tell us the good news."

"You told us that these were terrorists," the blood streaked woman scowled.

"Status of the mission, Commander," Admiral Kerns barked. "Remember your place."

"You didn't tell us these were American soldiers." Commander Jackson's lip curled into a snarl. "American Green Berets, Admiral. You said they were Muslim terrorists. You lied."

"Commander, stay on point," Kerns snapped. "Status of the mission."

"Status?" Commander Jackson asked incredulously. "The status is the president of the United States is fucking dead."

"Oh." Annie heard herself gasp, felt her fingers go to her own throat, everything seeming a bit unreal.

"I, however, am still alive, dear sister."

And hearing his voice, Annie's stomach dropped all the way into the bowels of the earth.

On the other end, Amos turned the camera to his face, sitting immediately next to the SEAL commander. Then what become incredibly real and clear to Annie was that premonition of the horror to come. Her muscles felt weak and she could feel death in her bones, like the ache of a brewing storm. In his eyes, Annie saw the glimmer of Ray's hate staring at her, and hell coming with it.

"Amos." Annie tried to smile. Her upper lip shook and her voice trembled. "I'm so glad to see you."

"Yes?" Amos stood, titling the camera upward to follow him. His eyes were dark slits without the slightest kindness, his eyes somehow darker, more fearless and vengeful than ever before. She couldn't conceptualize exactly what awful things would soon occur, but she knew that they had crossed a demarcation line that was about to plunge their lives, their country, and their world into ruin. Her little brother was alive, and in his cold, wrathful face all faith in goodness was gone. Bad, bad things were about to happen. "I am glad to see you too, Annabel. Glad to know there is still a chance for me to repay you for your lifetime of loyalty and love."

"Amos, this has all been a colossal misunderstanding," Annie pleaded. "I didn't want you to get hurt, I never wanted anyone to get hurt, only to do the right thing. You know that. If you and I just work together, we can still—"

"YOU SWORE TO GOD," Amos bellowed, and Annie leapt backward from the monitor.

Amos' face had twisted red and his fist clenched, veins bulging from his face and neck. "You swore to God never to betray me, but it was all lies even from when we were kids!"

"I didn't wan—"

"You sent them to kill us! You sent them to help you steal the presidency of the United States, and you, YOU, killed the president, and hundreds of decent American soldiers!" Amos looked insane. "And you killed Shay! You killed anything I ever fucking loved just so you could be right! Get everything you wanted."

Annie gasped. "What are you talking about?"

"She was at MacDill," Amos growled. "I thought there

was some slight hope of making up for the past and starting over, but you had to make sure I never could, didn't you?"

"Oh God, Amos, I'm sorry," Annie said. "I didn't know. You've got to believe me, I didn't know. I didn't—"

"You always destroy it, you cunt," Amos said with a sneer. "All of it. You destroy it all, and now you've won." He chuckled. "Your kind have finally won, finally gotten your way."

"Won?" Tears pressed against the back of her eyes, and a knot in her throat as terror gripped her soul. "What do you mean won? We can make this right, Amos."

"No, Annie." Amos leaned toward the camera, his words cold and flat. "No we can't. Because you've WON, your kind, the nonbelievers, you beat me." He moved a hand down beside him, off camera. "All my life I tried to believe in something bigger, tried to hold myself accountable to a higher standard and be a better man, but your kind wanted to beat it out of me, force me to give up on believing in better things." Then he smiled, with his eyes looking even more crazed, and Annie felt so sick in apprehension she gripped an arm to her stomach. "All I ever wanted was to just be good. To be happy. But no. Your kind couldn't have that. Your kind had to teach me I was wrong, had to break me from believing there was any greater meaning to our lives. I tried to fight it, but you all never gave up on trying to prove we're just processes, animals, genetically programmed data with no meaning, nothing greater to our brief lives than getting everything we want at the expense of others, the best people being the ones who can lie the best."

"Please, Amos," Annie begged, tears rolling down her cheek now, not understanding. "Please, stop."

"So you won, Annie. You and Freeman and the rest

won—convinced me God is a lie. We are all just random biological blips and twitches in a meaningless universe."

"I don't understand, Amos. Please let me speak to Vice President Freeman. He and I can still make an announcement."

"But you know what else is part of being just a soulless animal, dear sister? You know what's wired within my genetic programming once I stop trying to live by the rules of a myth?" Amos grinned crazily as he lifted up the head of Marcus Freeman by its hair, blood dripping from its severed spine. "Killing."

Annie bolted up from her chair and a hand shot to her mouth. She stared at the decapitated head and her lungs froze.

"I've got nothing left to live for, no standards left," Amos whispered, winding his arm back. "And I'm coming for, you fucking bitch."

Amos flung Freeman's bloody head into the camera. The connection went to static.

Annie lunged to the side, one hand holding herself up against the desk as she heaved everything out. She hacked and wretched, a thin strand of vomit hitting the floor as her stomach twisted in pain. Annie could hear nothing in the room except for a whistling in her ears.

She collapsed on her knees by the desk, pain from the wood floor shooting through her kneecaps. There was no one left, only her. Stupid, idiotic, faithless her. The acting president. Annie clasped a hand to her throat, the other up to the edge of her desk, and looked up at the ceiling. Why couldn't that vision in the mirror have been from a real God, instead of a trick of bad pharmaceuticals in her brain? Why couldn't she have ever had some event in life, some moment, just one, that was beyond justification that somehow made her believe in something bigger than herself? Or at least made her realize she didn't know everything, that there were possibilities beyond her comprehension. That made her humble?

"Madam President."

"Send everything you've got to the White House, Admiral Kerns," Annie said barely above a whisper, wiping her mouth. "Level it to the ground if necessary, but kill my brother."

"Bomb the White House, madam?" Kerns asked. "But—"

"Don't suddenly become a pussy now that you've helped me create this fucking disaster. We can rebuild a house, but I need my brother dead, immediately, Admiral, or I promise you something worse than anything you've been trained for is coming for us." Annie reached for the bottle of bourbon. "And, Admiral Kerns?"

"Yes, Madam President?"

"Begin preparations for the Army, Navy, Air Force and Marines to overtake any of those states claiming they are no longer under federal authority. We cannot let the rest of the world believe America is breaking apart." Annie wiped at her mouth again and smoothed her blouse. "There is a revolution and our only option now is to wipe it out. We cannot let America fall."

She looked out her window into a night sky that held unknowable horrors… and wondered if Abraham Lincoln had ever considered killing himself.

* * *

Standing in the Presidential Annex doorway, Commander Jackson looked across the destroyed Oval Office. Many dead bodies, mostly Secret Service from when the SEAL team and Green Berets had joined forces once Commander Jackson realized they had been misled, lay tangled across the Oval Office.

It smelled of burnt flesh and hot iron. Looking back into the Annex over Amos' shoulder, she saw Freeman's decapitated head on the rubble of the broken monitor. Plaster from the grenade-decimated wall was strewn across the small Annex office and the desk was charred from fire. Commander Jackson had seen worse. "Major, I know this has been difficult for you."

Amos still stood in the same spot in the annex as when he had thrown Freeman's head at the monitor, but now with his own head slightly bowed, a crucifix on a chain pulled from his chest. The major clutched it so tightly a trickle of blood ran down its edge, and he seemed lost in thought, questioning. Commander Jackson wasn't worried about his having decapitated the vice president, but she was concerned by some of the things he'd said. The major's pupils were dilated, eyes wide but staring at nothing; he probably was a bit concussed.

"Sir," Jackson continued, pulling the band from her red hair to let it shower over her shoulders, "in my heart of hearts I know you're chosen by God to fight evil. We all face doubts, and challenges, sir, but I've believed your sister was the antichrist ever since she first originated the *Cyber-Care* chip plan. It is all black and white, Major. Scripture, mark of the beast, no doubt about it. We use our blood and breath to eliminate evil, or we waste our time here on Earth and allow it to flourish, no better than them. Inaction is not an option." She waited for a moment, then whispered to the man she had heard the rumors of, had admired for so long, Famous Amos Daniels, the fearless Special Forces legend. "Even if you are having doubts about believing in God, sir, He still believes in you."

Amos looked at her. His eyes had lost some of the fury,

but she could still see he was a warrior for God. He simply needed support.

"You're doing the right thing, sir. I knew it from the moment I recognized you as you tried to save President Fuentes' life. And my reward, like yours, will be in heaven. I'm ready to follow you to the gates of hell and back, Major, if need be. And my men will follow me."

Amos nodded. His eyes took on a glint of more certainty. "Okay."

"And more will join us, sir. God will provide, you'll see."

"Okay," he rasped.

"Immediate concerns though, Major. The heathens and your sister will be coming at us with everything they've got. Quickly. It will take time for us to rally a rebellion force."

"There's a Plan B, Commander," Amos said softly. "As long as Lieutenant Houzma was in the underground BRAHMASTRA bunker in Tampa when the airstrikes came." He glanced around the destroyed room, toward the destroyed Oval Office and at the numerous destroyed bodies.

"I'm sure God will forgive us for what we must do. For all this."

Amos wearily slipped his crucifix into his pants pocket, looked with a bit of confusion at Freeman's head. "Exactly why it's becoming harder to believe in Him."

"I am a sect unto myself, as far as I know."
—Thomas Jefferson

(Over Virginia Airspace, 8:11 p.m. PST / 11:11 p.m. EST)

About thirty minutes after the conversation with Amos ended, Annie, Kerns, and Howe stood before two screens in her office. Henry typed on his laptop in a chair off to the side of the desk, not having spoken in some time. More people than ever milled in and out, Secret Service Agent Castor at the door diligently watching the flow. One of the screens was a radar showing blips representing the squadron from Langley Air Force Base racing the short distance to the White House, the other was an onboard camera in the captain's cockpit looking out over the night horizon.

Kerns had a smug grin. "Well, in about five minutes, they—"

"Don't, Admiral."

The admiral looked a bit offended at Annie. "I was just going to say tha—"

"That we'll blow them off the map in five minutes and all our problems will be solved." Annie crossed her arms, her eyes glued to the two screens even as she shook her head. "Let's not break open the champagne yet." The lit skyline of DC became visible through the captain's cockpit glass. "Let's wait for celebrations until we actually win something this time."

The admiral glowered. "With all due respect, ma'am, I think I'm a bit more familiar with combat than you, although there have been some hiccups…" The admiral's words slowed to a pause and she leaned into the same position as Annie, hunched toward the screen, their eyes peering close to the camera facing the DC skyline. Kern's voice took on a hint of worry. "What in the…"

Annie noticed the odd glow growing on one side of the captain's monitor. It looked like aurora borealis in the distance, like colored Northern Lights swirling, but that only lasted a second, then there was a gigantic flash, but no noise. The light raced across the camera's view, engulfing everything on camera like a blue-green wave.

And then the camera went to static.

"Admiral?" Annie asked.

"Shit," the Admiral whispered.

All the computer equipment in Annie's office suddenly died, the chandelier lights and corner lamps flickering, then the room dropped into complete darkness. "What the hell's going on Admiral?" Annie asked. "What the hell was that? Are the planes on target?"

Kerns answered from the dark. "I'm not sure."

"EMP," Howe stated somewhere to the left. "I don't want to cause panic, but I believe that was an EMP. An electromagnetic pulse."

"What?"

"No," Kerns said. "No, no, no. SOCOM hasn't completed the technology yet."

"Check your phone, Admiral," Howe suggested. "Is it working?"

Kerns could be heard rustling in her pocket in the dark. "Son of a bitch."

"It fucks up electronics?" Annie asked Howe. "Across the country?"

"Anything with a microchip or transistor, madam. If the EMP is big enough."

"Okay." Annie exhaled. "So when does it all come back on? When does it pass?"

Henry spoke, his voice a told-you-so sneer. "Well, if another country is willing to assist us, probably ten years or so."

"What the fuck?"

"EMPs don't just turn electronics off, they fry them. Anything it hits with a microchip, which is most everything these days, is dead."

"The jets? The strike against the White House? What happens?"

"If Ms. Howe's guess is correct, madam," Kerns said, "the rebels are still alive. Unless the jets crashed into the White House as they fell from the sky."

Annie took two steps to her window. She peeled down one of the wooden slats of the blinds and for the first time in her entire life looked out on a San Francisco skyline with no lights. Nothing. Zilch. She might as well have been staring into a black hole. She wondered how long until the zombies arrived.

Dawn Breaks Across New America

(Various Locations, 4:52 p.m. PST / 7:52 p.m. EST)

As the sun rose, fires burned in many cities.

Over sixty-seven percent of the country had been struck by the electromagnetic pulse, permanently knocking out power grids, cars, computers and cell phones in a single instant. Radiation clouds wafted with the breeze from a Denver filled with dying. Nationwide, planes and drones had fallen from the sky to crash into buildings, trains derailed, and looting and riots spread with abandon. ATMs went dead, grocery shelves were stripped bare, and water treatment plants and gas stations stopped pumping. Much of the federal government was dead or under arrest, without the majority of people understanding what had happened or why, and who to turn to for help. People were banding together in small, violent tribes, simply trying to survive. From the perspective of those in the quickly growing DC tribe, Major Amos Daniels was a man worthy of following in a frightening time.

The sun was rising over the buildings of Washington, DC, but some in the crowd still carried torches for the deep darkness in a city without electricity. Many in the crowd had been part of the March on Washington to the White House, had heard the gun battle that erupted and then watched as the jets crashed from the skies. They had watched Governor Stone killed, and the attack on MacDill before the electronics had stopped. They knew that their old lives had ended as quickly and simply as the lights, but hoped that before them was a man who could lead. A man of principle.

Amos stood tall upon the Capitol steps wearing camouflaged fatigues, Green Beret on his head. His face and clothes were splattered with cuts and blood. Behind and to the sides of him stood at least twenty other military personnel spread out between the government's white columns, some in green fatigues, some head to toe in black body armor. A determined-looking black man with bloody bandages over his stomach stood next to Amos, as well as a ferocious female warrior with red hair roped in braids. The red-haired woman held an American flag on a pole in one hand, a Bible clutched against her chest with the other.

"We are at war," Major Daniels bellowed down the white steps leading to Pennsylvania Avenue. "A war against evil, a war against those who would destroy America." Amos had a red sash draped over his chest with the words *Make America Great Again* sewn into it. "We did not wish to go to war with our sisters, our fathers and brothers, but the liberals were seduced by the devil and good men must fight or we are no better than they. We must protect God's earth and children from those who would corrupt it, those who would allow the devil to infest our land and lives." The dawn sun crept its way up the Capitol steps, warming Amos' chiseled face of determination.

"Their lies and immorality have torn this once great country apart, destroyed America's promise." The dawn light continued spreading over the major, standing tall and fearless, and over the white columns and his warriors standing between them.

"The Democrats have taken the holy and declared it

profane. They promote the devil's works and wish to purge God's faithful from the land." Amos took the Bible from Commander Jackson's hand and raised it up high. "But I promise you one thing." And in his other hand he raised up his shotgun. "Together, we will stop them."

The crowd cheered.

"Patriots and Christians, good Americans, it is time to rise, and to fight. Together, we will make America great again!" The crowd cheered louder. What those in the crowd could not see was how dark and hard had Amos' heart become. How love had been scorched into wrath. How he was lying about knowing anything of God's will. How he did not know the truth of anything more than they did, but he was prepared to kill anything and everything so that this world could finally make sense, so his pain could be answered. "We shall cleanse this land with rivers of hedonist blood, and together we will restore God's favor upon us!"

Yes, the crowd shouted, *yes!*

* * *

Castor didn't know how Henry had gotten his gun. The EMP from the BRAHMASTRA had dissipated enough by the time it raced across the western part of the United States that San Francisco was actually only partially fried, some lights blinking on and off through the night. No one in Annie's office had slept though, and Castor was mentally frazzled. During one of the power dips, Henry had apparently pulled Castor's gun from his holster, and now with the lights briefly back on a wild-eyed Henry stood only ten feet away from Annie, the gun pointing at her head. The Secret Service agent was calculating if he could leap onto Henry in time, or if he would have to try throwing himself over Annie, in front of the bullet.

"You aren't a good person," Henry said to her.

Castor was off to the side of Henry and Annie by about six feet, Henry on the other end of Annie's desk from him unfortunately.

"There are things that good people just don't do." Henry's eyes flickered back and forth between Castor and Annie with a desperate look. "You're just a bad person. No matter how long I hoped, how much I've deluded myself, in the end… you're bad. You've destroyed this country. You could have quit. You could have put the Constitution above yourself. Or God. Or something."

"Pretty subjective, Henry. It was either us or them, I made the most intelligent call I could. Now put the damn gun down before pretending to be a man gets you hurt."

Castor was surprised, even with a gun in her face she still had the balls to sling shit. He considered trying to inch around the desk toward Henry, but that would then make a protective jump over Annie all the more difficult.

"See? You're not good." Henry whined. "You justify your beliefs with intelligence the same way idiot fundamentalists justify things with God, so they don't have to really question anything. Most things you claim as facts have nothing even to do with being known." Henry started shaking his head, a panicked smile on his bearded face. "You quote supposed scientists you've never met like Catholics quote the Pope, yet, it still all ends in shit. You never have actual facts, it's just your ego."

"Henry, you're hysterical," Annie said. "It was us versus them, that's all. Progress versus tyranny."

"This is progress?"

There's no way, Castor thought. *There's no way I can get around the desk to the gun before he gets a shot off.*

"More bullshit," Henry continued, his eyes darting over

to Castor again, but the gun never left Annie's face. "You don't believe in anything except yourself, the labels are just your justification. You act like you live by superior thought, but you really don't hold yourself accountable to the actual method of science." Henry laughed. "You don't live by any code, you think you ARE the code!"

"Fuck you," Annie snarled. "Someone has to be the code, Henry. It's called leadership."

"No." Henry shook his head, straightened his arm at her head. "That's what they all say." Henry's face and voice seeped with sadness. "Hitler, Mussolini, Chairman Mao and Saddam Hussein. Every fundamentalist preacher and bigoted extremist. Every revolutionary who becomes a tyrant, they all think they know the answer for everyone, because they don't truly live by any code above themselves."

"Living by dogma isn't enlightened, Henry."

I've got to get in front of her. Castor judged the distance over the corner of the desk between them and was certain he could make it and take the bullet, if he timed it right. *I can do it, I can make it.*

"A dogma of humility would be," Henry babbled. "You use words like enlightened and intelligence and progress but your mind is already closed. I tried to help you for so long, but you wouldn't fucking stop. I even switched out those goddamn pills with pink sugar pills in the hopes you'd calm down, but you wouldn't stop!"

"You what?" Annie said. Castor didn't know why, but for the first time with the gun pointed at her Annie's face truly looked shock. "You replaced the Zennies with sugar pills? When? When the hell did you do that?"

"On the plane to Ohio." His expression perplexed as to

why she cared so much. "Why does it matter? You're still missing the point."

"I've only been taking sugar for the last forty-eight hours?" An odd smile passed over her lips and Annie eyes seemed glazed with wonder. "The snakes and... and when I was in the bathroom it was only sugar?

"See, you're not even listening." Henry glanced at Castor, as if he almost wanted agreement from someone sane. "A fucking gun pointed at your head and you're still missing the fucking point, lost in your own self-absorbed bullshit!"

Castor let his weight sink into his thighs. Henry's frustration was building. He was about to do it, and Castor would have to jump.

"Henry." Annie's voice was suddenly light, happy. "You don't understand. I had a vision. An actual vision from..." Annie shrugged, smiled. "From God maybe? I saw things that came to pass, things that can't be explained." Annie clasped her hands over her heart and looked toward the ceiling with her gentle smile widening. "Henry, maybe we can still all be saved."

"No!" Henry, exasperated, shook his head like someone refusing to be tricked yet again. "You're a psychopathic liar and I should have said this back in college—fuck you." Henry's finger squeezed the trigger, and Castor sprang.

* * *

Mr. Bilderberg waited for the call in a downtown London penthouse, the late-morning sun completely hidden behind a cold veil of fog and haze. He listened to his old radio as it broadcast scratchy updates to the world about America's meltdown.

He had eaten eggs for brunch, fertile and organic, sunny-side up over toast. Mr. Bilderberg felt it was important to get protein, as fresh and chemically free as possible, to start off an important day. There would be many deals to be made, and new alliances to form. He sipped his black coffee and looked off his balcony into the drifting mist. The skyline was shrouded in a dimly lit haze of limitless potential, the morning chilly but vibrant. The *RedRabbit* cell phone buzzed next to his plate.

Mr. Bilderberg turned down the radio and picked up the phone, pleased that the *RedRabbit* system withstood the EMP blast. Being part of the *RedRabbit* system had been part of his requirement for continued funding of the Fuentes administration's off-the-books military endeavors in the Yuan Chin territory of China over the summer.

"Good morning, Mr. Jefferson," Bilderberg chirped. "Glad to find you're still alive."

"We hold these truths, Mr. Washington…"

"No more formalities, Mr. Jefferson. Your goal has been achieved."

"Yes, sir," Mr. Jefferson said. "And will there be anything else, sir?"

"I will be in touch, Mr. Jefferson, if your services are needed again. And your payment will be at the specified location."

"Yes, sir," Mr. Jefferson said.

Bilderberg sensed a pregnant pause from the other end. "Yes, Mr. Jefferson?"

"Question, sir?" Jefferson asked.

"Certainly."

"Why, sir? I've been doing the rituals. I've tried to understand what you've told me, but…"

Mr. Bilderberg smiled. He covered his mouth to keep from giggling. They always wanted to know why. It was like a curse of theirs, needing to know the answers to things they never could, so they could feel "right" and keep the fear of their own inherent mortality within an infinite universe at bay. That overwhelming need to know with absolutely certainty was really their Achilles heel, their arrogance, which Bilderberg always successfully used to make them devour each other and leave him holding everything. "When your garden grows large enough, Mr. Jefferson, things can only be made healthier by pruning dead branches."

"I suppose it also doesn't hurt," Mr. Jefferson prodded, "that you own all the weapons that both sides will purchase to kill each other?"

"And don't forget the medicine and alcohol." Bilderberg chuckled. "They will drink my alcohol to celebrate their victories and drown their defeats, purchase my bandages to tend their wounds." Bilderberg sighed contentedly. "Is it not an exciting time to be alive, Mr. Jefferson?"

There was another pause, and Bilderberg could hear Jefferson still breathing, wondering on the other end. Eventually, Mr. Jefferson asked, "One more question, sir?"

"Certainly. I have all the time in the world."

"Are you the devil, sir? Or... maybe God?"

And at this, Mr. Bilderberg rapped his knuckles on the table twice, a large smile ripping across his pale face as he looked up into the tiny dancing particles of mist and tried not to chortle with joy. Such a good question, for a quantum world.

"Or maybe an alien," Bilderberg replied with a chuckle. Maybe I am that over the horizon which your human mind is fated to never see, all that you can never truly know after all, despite your calculations and your blips and bleeps, despite your prayers." Bilderberg sighed, licked the phone once from end to end, then dropped it over the side of his balcony into the mist.

Just As Annie's City Hall Speech Ends

(Harmony's Bedroom, Friday, 9:35 a.m. PST / 12:35 p.m. EST)

Harmony gasped, snapping back from the DMT trip into the reality of her bedroom. It had seemed like more than a year had passed from her mother's speech, to the crumbling of the country into chaos, and a long, bloody, civil war.

Still in her red T-shirt and green boxers, she was actually still lying on the rumpled bed of sheets and books, the used pipe lying on the beige carpet with a thin stream of smoke curling from it. The bedside Donald Duck clock said only eleven minutes had passed. "Mom." Her breath was shallow, rasping, and there was sharp pain like she had never felt before in the center of her chest. Her hand leapt to her chest, and for a moment her heart did not beat. "Mom?"

The room lurched. Both hands lunged out to her sides, fingers wrenching into the sheets as her lungs sucked to breathe, but seemed stuck. The worst fear she'd ever known crashed over and through her like a wave. "Mommy," she gasped.

Am I dying?

But then mercy came and her lungs opened, her heart beat again, that icy drape washing off her.

Hot and clammy, she kicked the comforter off the end of the bed for more air. Gasped. She touched her forehead and felt the hot, sticky blood beading there. Her entire body was sizzling and she reflexively snatched up her phone to dial 911 as her heart beat faster and faster, but then stopped. She opened her mouth, almost yelled out to the Secret Service agent that should be in the hall, but then did not do that either.

She concentrated on breathing slowly, scrolling to her mother's name on her phone, her thumb poised over the icon to connect the call. Her heart slowed a bit and she understood.

Yes, I'm dying, but it's okay. Everyone does, she thought with less fear now, more wonder. *It's here.*

She had seen it all during her DMT trip, as she'd left the confines of linear time and space traveling to another dimension, to the possible future, or maybe just to the deepest cellar of her imagination. Maybe she'd just had an intense dream, but with death now sliding cold tentacles around her limbs, the permanent exit to this existence widening before her, she knew what she'd experienced had just as much validity, as much truth, as anything in this reality. She'd seen the entire country's destruction in a vivid apocalypse of a second civil war, and lived every moment of it as real.

Every second from her mother's speech this morning to a standoff between her mother and Uncle over the soul of America, and then the country falling into conflict. She had traveled across a decimated countryside for over a year to get home and, in the end, help that correct side to win. She had witnessed the anarchy of Americans plunged back into the Dark Ages as they lunged toward each other's throats over ideology, brother fighting brother, neighbor killing neighbor, she'd experienced every moment. Harmony had lived through wild militias taking control of vast swaths of darkened territory, private militaries of the wealthy enslaving the weak, disease and radiation and starvation in a post-electronic country even as some powerful maniacs still accessed technology on a level that made them near demigods. All while the US government fractured into vast red and blue armies of conservatives and liberals battling for ultimate control, and governors led Natural Guards against their neighboring states. It had seemed so true, so terrifying. She had eventually found the albino man, chased that rabbit of eternal truth down, in order to show the country the way back to peace. It had felt more real than a dream, as if in some alternate timeline of possibilities it had happened.

Om pishlay toth.

Now, she knew she must speak that truth again in hopes of the correct side winning now, before the inevitable war could begin. It was all fading fast like a dream though, like spilt water evaporating under a noon sun. And like anyone trying to bring back deep universal wisdom from an altered state of consciousness, somehow just trying to form her new knowledge into real words and sentences made the truth start to garble, confuse. She could still remember the core, the root, the lesson she was supposed to bring back to help the correct side win, if she acted quickly, before she left her body for good.

It's all so much bigger than we can imagine… than our fear will let us believe.

Hey pishlay ashta.

The only important thing was what she did with the time left.

***

Harmony had to take several breaks, once dropping down on one knee and wheezing, bloody sweat dripping down her face and onto the carpet for a full minute as all light shrunk to a pinhole in her black sight, before being able to regain enough strength just to mount the phone at the right angle on her night-stand to record herself. She weakly propped herself against the pillows, no makeup, but somehow looked stunningly beautiful and pure even with the red streaks down her nose and cheeks, her eyes full of loving kindness, the red line of blood continuously beading at her forehead like the wounds from a crown of thorns. Her long blonde hair hung gently over her shoulders and the straps of the purple-flowered dress her uncle had bought her made her look ready for a summer picnic. Her vision was fading in and out though, from hazy to clear, and her balance wobbled at times as if she were on a boat. Her breath wheezed more and more shallow, and although her emotions had calmed somewhat her heart beat sporadically like a dying clock. If she explained it right, she knew untold horrors would be prevented.

It was a live stream to the Internet through her blog. She didn't know actually what she would say, only that she had to try to convey the truth she'd learned from the pale man in her trip, the truth she'd found in her journey through a war-torn America before she left this life.

"We're all God." She swallowed hard, talking becoming difficult. "Not each one of us a god, but collectively I mean, together we all make up God." She shook her head with a weak smile. "I know this probably doesn't make sense, but... we're all splinters of our one original unified self. Like Martin Luther King said, 'we are tied together in the single garment of destiny, and I can never be what I ought to be until you are what you ought to be.'" She wheezed. "Separating our individual selves from the original source into many individuals is the only way we could experience love, companionship... not be alone, but know others. Separate, but together."

For years, people would debate if there had been an actual

supernatural glow emanating from her as she spoke. Others confidently agreed it was a just a weird effect from the camera and room lights. Regardless, the bright red blood kept beading on her forehead in a crown of thorns, and everyone noticed that her palms looked like they had the bleeding wounds from nails being driven through them. But, of course, she could have done that herself.

"The one thing I now know, is that no one of us knows anything, because how could they, each of us only ever being a sliver of the whole truth. But you've still got to choose." She tried to push herself up a little higher against the pillows, but had to stop speaking for a moment as the vertigo swirled. "You may think you know God DOES exist, but you don't, and even if you did, it's not your place to judge. Everyone needs the free will to make mistakes, travel their own path toward truth. And you may think you know God does NOT exist, but you don't KNOW that either. And even if you were right, then personal responsibility matters even more. With technology evolving exponentially, it won't be long before almost every individual has the ability to destroy us all, so if we don't have faith in a moral code beyond our personal interest, we're done. So it's just about your sincerity to that higher truth, only up to you and you alone." A streak of blood trickled down between her eyebrows, over the bridge of her nose, but she didn't bother to wipe at it. She sucked for air, her lungs seeming to dry inside her, shriveling even as she tried to speak. She did not want to cry on camera as her last part of existence, so she leaned her head back for a moment and tried to ease her breath, calm her floundering heart. "We all have free will, and it is the only path to finding any God, so you should never stop another's, just focus on your own." She began to get lightheaded, but it was comfortable in a way, like being on a gently rocking boat. "So… sincerity. Choose what you honestly want the world to eternally become."

She looked around the room, everything beginning to glow with silver light. She smiled. Her mouth opened and she starting sucking hard for air, her eyes wide and one hand leaping up to clutch her chest. For a moment, an awful wheeze slinked from her open lips, her head back and blood from her forehead now staining the white pillowcase she pushed against. She took a deep breath, her eyes coming back into focus at the camera.

"I'm dying, but… this never ends until we get it right." She smiled and lifted a hand, waving gentle fingers goodbye at the camera. "See you soon." She sank back against the pillows, her hands drifting to her sides and her eyes closing, her breath leaving.

The video of the vice presidential candidate's only daughter dying went viral around the world within minutes. For years people would debate if her illness had been completely explainable, or something holy-inspired. People would come up with theories of it being an election stunt. Others claimed Harmony wasn't sick at all, but had been deranged from drug use and harmed herself. Illegal DMT would be found on the scene.

Regardless, the video would smother coverage of Annie's *God is a Lie* speech and no riot would take place. The country would be in shocked sadness over a beautiful young girl, so intelligent and promising, suffering an untimely death. There would be no violence for the last three days leading up to the electoral vote. And one candidate, moved by Harmony's message, would concede.

For the good of the country.

The End

Want to know who won?

Coming soon from Primal Light Press,
the sequel to Blood Republic…

Wolves of Liberty

Wolves of Liberty will follow Harmony's harrowing journey through the alternate timeline of America's second civil war as she searches for an eternal truth to stop the madness. Like Game of Thrones in a post-apocalyptic United States, violent factions will battle for America's soul while Harmony hunts the pale man who can give answers, the country's peace or final destruction hinging upon her success.

From the west, de facto President Annie Daniels will lead remnants of the federal government against numerous usurpers: governors seceding from the union to declare their own sovereign lands, wandering tribes of outlaws and mercenaries in a country without electricity, and most deadly of all, her own rebel brother, Amos Daniels. From his captured headquarters in Washington DC, a black-hearted General Amos Daniels will rally the resistance against his sister's overwhelming power with a God-like wrath to stop her forced implantation of the Cyber-Care chip into all Americans. Meanwhile, deranged separatist Lawton Smith will lead a militia army out of the radiated ashes of Denver to purge the land of an enemy only he sees, while in the south, a duplicitous Yanic Goran will create his own army of hired mercenaries in an attempt to become America's ultimate ruler. And as the world's sole superpower suddenly goes offline, global anarchy will give the mysterious Mr. Bilderberg additional means to enact his master plan that might have more far-reaching effects than anyone can foresee.

Will Harmony be able to navigate across the blood-soaked countryside and find the mysterious pale man in time, or are America, and the world, already doomed? Until truth is found, the battle must continue...

Please visit www.primallightpress.com to join the Primal Light Press newsletter to stay informed of Wolves of Liberty and all other new release updates.

And if you enjoyed Blood Republic, please remember to leave an online review.

Thanks.

Primal Light Press
A Purveyor of Fine Fictions

Acknowledgments

The author would like to specifically thank those individuals who gave their time and effort to make this book the best it could be.

First and foremost, authors Jeff Hess and Sam Best whose tireless support and insight on this project, and many others, has been invaluable.

Also, advance readers Jen Alper, Brandon Caston, Ann Mullen, and Susan Turner for their superb feedback, and Elizabeth White for her excellent editing. And last but not least, the amazing graphic artist, Jim Stancampiano, for his original suggestion which inspired the cover art design.

Additionally, my older brothers, and all those friends and family, too many to name individually, who have provided support and encouragement. I know I've traveled down a path at times that has probably been difficult for you to understand, and I truly appreciate anybody who is still taking my calls at this point. It turns out I really was writing a book.

Bruce County Public Library
1243 Mackenzie Rd.
Port Elgin ON N0H 2C6

CPSIA information can be obtained
at www.ICGtesting.com
Printed in the USA
LVOW11s0211041116
511542LV00001B/204/P